Before the Storm

Before the Storm

Marian Perera

SAMHAIN
PUBLISHING

Samhain Publishing, Ltd.
577 Mulberry Street, Suite 1520
Macon, GA 31201
www.samhainpublishing.com

Before the Storm
Copyright © 2011 by Marian Perera
Print ISBN: 978-1-60928-009-3
Digital ISBN: 978-1-60504-972-4

Editing by Anne Scott
Cover by Kanaxa

First Samhain Publishing, Ltd. electronic publication: April 2010
First Samhain Publishing, Ltd. print publication: February 2011

Dedication

In loving memory of my mother, Shirani Perera 1949 – 2004
And for Jordan Helin, who read the first drafts

Acknowledgement

My thanks to Anne Scott, who is everything I hoped my editor would be, to Kanaxa for the wonderful cover design, and to everyone else at Samhain Publishing for their input and hard work.

And to Kathy France, for her kindness and generosity.

Part One:

The Wind From the West

Chapter One:
The Mare

Only one man ever entered her room without knocking.

Alexis Khayne slipped a black ribbon into her book to mark her place, then looked at the man who stood in her doorway. She felt her blood cool as it slid into the muscles of her face, keeping her features expressionless.

"Stephen." She did not stand up; the master of the castle had told her that such bowing and scraping was unnecessary between them. She hated him all the more for that.

"You're called for," Stephen Garnath said.

It was always the same words. Alex rose at once and went to her dressing table. She had already bathed but her face was unpainted, so she opened a pot of eye enhancer. Stephen pulled her wardrobe open and hooked the black sheer with a finger.

"Wear this." He tossed it to her, and Alex caught it. The full-length gown was fragile black abstract over translucent sheer. Wearing either of the fabrics was tantamount to being naked, and together they were not much better. She laid it aside and slipped out of her dress.

"Take everything off." Stephen watched her obey, but she was long since used to that, and she removed her underclothes with as little reaction as if he had commented on the weather. Naked, she stepped into the sheer.

It was difficult to fasten and lace tightly about the bodice. Years ago, Alex had asked if she could have a lady's maid. Stephen had pointed out that she wasn't a lady, which was true, but she also knew he didn't want her making friends. She pinned up her hair and painted her face, outlining her eyes in black. When she was done, she looked like a portrait in earth tones, and only her eyes were out of place. The enhancer made their green paler, like ice.

She wondered why he had chosen the black sheer. It was a beautiful gown, but it didn't make *her* seem beautiful. It sharpened her so she appeared intense and dark, with a cold feral look in her eyes. Instead of looking like the kind of woman a man wanted to ride, she looked like a panther hauled snarling out of the woods, then drugged and caged.

This will be an unusual night, she thought. *I wonder who it is. Sir Thomas Vallew? No, he's gone north on business. The Duke of Goldwood? Surely even Stephen wouldn't offer me to a man married barely a week. Oliver Lant? I wish it was Oliver. And I wish he hadn't said he liked me—didn't he realize Stephen would never let me near him after that?*

Of course he didn't. There was nothing wrong with Oliver's heart, but his mind didn't work in three directions at once. She studied her face for one last time, noting that it was still as expressionless as when Stephen had first entered, and rose.

"Very nice," Stephen cupped her breast and rolled his thumb over the nipple. Alex looked at him, waiting for an order. "Very nice. Let's go, the baron's ready."

The baron?

Alex didn't think that any of the barons of Dagre were close to the coronet city, Radiath, much less to Stephen Garnath, who dominated it. And what had this particular baron done to deserve the services of the most highly prized mare in the city? She pulled on a black cloak and followed Stephen out. When they stopped at the guest rooms, she risked a look at the man-at-arms who stood outside, but she didn't recognize the lightning-bolt sigil on his leather armor. Bowing, he let them into a public room where apple boughs burned in a fireplace. When he knocked at a door, the baron emerged, another man following him.

Alex barely took in the baron's nondescript face. The man behind him was far more unusual. She kept her features still with the ease of long practice, but she was startled at his appearance: a line of raised flesh ran along each side of his face, beginning just below the inner corner of the eye, dipping down in a curve and rising again to touch the top of each ear.

10

So he was from Iternum. No wonder Stephen wanted to please the baron. Even locked away, she had heard Stephen employed an Iternan sorcerer, so the baron had to be nearly as powerful. She fixed the beginning of a smile on her face as Stephen began the introductions, waiting to expand the smile.

"Robert," he said, "may I press upon you a small gift that I hope you'll enjoy? No doubt you recognize the Black Mare that Sir James Taeros praised at Goldwood's wedding feast."

"The description could fit none other," the baron said. Alex met his stare and kept her expression seductive, even as she thought how ridiculous he looked with two lines of red dyed into his beard. That might be the latest fashion, but it called attention to the plainness of his appearance; it was like attaching a peacock's feather to a hen's behind.

Stephen turned to her, smiling. "My dear, may I present Lord Robert Demeresna, baron of Dawnever?"

The blood fell from Alex's face and her features went slack; she pulled them back into order in the next moment, but she couldn't stop the sudden thudding of her heart. *Talk, damn it, talk*, she thought.

"It is my pleasure, Lord Robert." *They call him the Bloody Baron. They say his fields are filled with scarecrows made from crucified men. Curtsey.* She did so, her body following a practiced motion. *They say he once impaled an opponent, driving an iron spike through the man's pelvis.* That had earned him his name, and he had lived up to it.

She wondered if the streaks of red in his beard were blood. No, certainly not; blood would have dried to a rusty brown shade difficult to distinguish from his hair. *Get a grip on yourself. It will only be for a night, and then I can go back to my room and bathe. I can finish my book and try to forget.*

Smile.

She smiled, which felt like stretching a clay mask placed over her face. The baron did not. He looked from her to Stephen, and the suspicious gleam in his eyes never altered.

Stephen grinned, curling a lock of her hair around his finger. "I must admit, Robert, I'm going to miss her. She is very skillful, you know. But you deserve her, since loyalty such as yours is always rewarded. Perhaps she's a poor gift, but I can't promise gold or land until my accession. When that happens, my supporters will be richly rewarded, but until then, I can only give you what hospitality and service I possess."

The smile didn't fall off her face that time, it drained away. *I can't be hearing right. He can't have just given me to the Bloody Baron.*

The baron didn't seem to believe it either. "Lord Garnath, are you *giving* me this woman?"

"Why, yes. I beg your pardon for not making myself clearer. Take her, Robert, as a token of my gratitude!" Stephen frowned, and concern crept into his voice. "I hope I haven't offended you by such an offer? Your unmarried state and your...detachment, shall we say, from the Quorum Mandates led me to believe that you would not find her unpalatable."

Please find me unpalatable. Alex had wanted to escape, but not like that, not to be taken like a parcel to the far edge of the land, not to be a bed-slave to the Bloody Baron. *Stephen wouldn't have killed me, I'm too valuable. But this is a man who orders adulterous wives to be whipped naked in the streets—what is he going to do to a whore?*

Stephen continued smoothly. "Do tell me if I'm mistaken, Robert. Are you considering a formal union? Or have you embraced the Quorum's ideals to the point where my standards are not yours, so to speak?"

"No, Lord Garnath," Robert Demeresna said. "Of course you're not mistaken. I was taken aback and my manners deserted me. If you were offered the east of Eden as a gift, I dare say even you might be somewhat tongue-tied."

"Only for a moment," Stephen said, which made the baron laugh. The Iternan wore a bored look, and Alex thought he might have seen such a scene played out many times before. *Let me survive until we set out for his province. I'll be outside the city then, and I'll find a way to escape. Just let me live through this night.*

"Well, I'm glad my gift is suitable." Stephen released her hair. "You may keep her, and another filly will take her place in the stable."

"Lord Garnath," Alex began, struggling to keep her voice level and courteous, "may I return to my room to collect a few possessions that I would—"

"No." Both Stephen and the baron spoke at once. Stephen, the first to recover, stared at the baron, who said, "Forgive me if I presumed too much, but I would like to furnish the woman with whatever she might need, to suit my own tastes."

There was a pause, long enough for Alex to see that Stephen

didn't believe that answer either. "Of course," he said. "And certainly, my sweet, Lord Robert is more than capable of providing you with anything you need. Don't insult him by implying otherwise."

Alex knew what the Bloody Baron did to people who insulted him. "My apologies, my lord." She tried not to think of her few books, or the silver locket that had been her mother's.

"No need for that." Robert Demeresna inclined his head to Stephen, and his mouth stretched into a grin. "I thank you for such a valuable gift, Lord Garnath. Rest assured I'll put it to good use."

Alex's stomach turned to a chunk of ice. She welcomed the feeling, knowing the coldness would spread over her body so that she wouldn't feel anything he did to her.

Stephen chuckled. "Once you see that all your visits to Radiath are likely to yield fruit, Robert, perhaps you will do us the honor of a journey more often. This is the first time you've visited the city, isn't it?"

The baron raised his brows. "There are many miles between Dawnever and the rest of Dagre. But you may always expect my support, Lord Garnath, even if I prefer country life to the coronet city."

"I'm glad to hear that." There was a slight undercurrent in Stephen's tone, so subtle that if she had not known him intimately, Alex would have missed it. "And now I'll leave you to be acquainted."

The man-at-arms opened the door for Stephen, and Alex did not turn to watch him leave, despite wanting to run out after him. *Take the first step*, she thought. She was sweating under her cloak, and she hoped there would be no obvious stains as she began to slip it off.

Both the baron and his sorcerer tensed, staring at her; she froze in return, her hand on the clasp that held her cloak together at the throat. "My lord?" She kept her voice low so that it did not shake. "Is something wrong?"

"No, no." The baron gestured at the man-at-arms. "Gavin, stand guard outside."

Did he simply want privacy? No, the Iternan still remained, and Alex wondered if he was doing magic. She supposed bleakly that she would feel it soon enough if he was.

"Take your cloak off," Robert Demeresna said. "Mayerd...help her with it."

Alex unfastened the cloak and let it drop, wondering if the

13

sorcerer would flip it through the air with magic. Instead, he was at her side as the velvet slipped off her shoulders, and he caught it before it hit the floor.

He moves too fast and too silently for a man of learning, was her last thought before the air struck her skin, chilling it. She let her mind go blank and her body doll-like, waiting for further instructions. The baron seemed to prefer it that way.

He cleared his throat. "Take it off."

"Of course, my lord," Alex said. The Iternan backed away, running his hands over her cloak, patting the velvet in a caressing way that would have disgusted her if she had been able to feel anything at that point. She unfastened the black sheer and let it puddle at her feet.

"Step out of it," the baron said. "And your shoes."

There was something strange about his terse orders, and the unfamiliarity penetrated even her gelid calm. She obeyed, watching as the Iternan dropped the cloak on the hearth and picked up her shoes. He examined them before he set them beside the cloak and gave his attention to the black sheer, shaking it out, turning it this way and that. *He looks like he's going to try it on for size,* she thought and killed a spurt of half-hysterical laughter. She didn't know which man would be worse when angered.

"It's very skimpy," Mayerd said finally.

"I beg my lord's pardon." What in the world did he expect the Black Mare to wear—armor? She looked at her bare feet, noticed the sheen of sweat that gleamed on her breasts, and wished she wasn't standing so close to the fire.

The baron took a step closer and Alex glanced up, startled at his nearness. He was not very tall, but he was large, and her skin crawled as she noticed the width of his shoulders. This was a man strong enough to hurt her with his bare hands, and she supposed he would start soon. She concentrated on floating, allowing years of training to take over while her mind drifted.

"I see you wear no jewels."

"No, my lord." Valuables or money of her own would have been far too liberating.

"You don't need them." The baron's tone was quieter. "Take your hair down."

She raised her arms slowly, letting her breasts move with them, and kept her gaze fixed on the baron's face as she did so. His body was tense, as if waiting to pounce, but his expression was not so much lustful as wary. She didn't understand that, but what did it matter at this point? The pins fell and her hair cascaded down.

"Stand still," the Iternan said from behind her. Alex braced herself for pain. Instead, she felt his hands in her hair, running through its length, moving upwards to rub lightly against her scalp and behind her ears. She wondered whether to purr with feigned desire or pretend she didn't notice. Was this a trick, to see if she would respond to a servant's touch or if she would keep herself for the baron? But the man touching her hair was no servant. Despite her familiarity with men, she had never submitted to an Iternan sorcerer, and the first threads of terror began to penetrate her shell.

After what seemed like an hour, Mayerd stopped and moved away. Alex focused on keeping her breathing steady, the slight inviting smile still nailed to her face. She was mildly surprised to see that neither of the men was aroused. *Perhaps I should try to do something, take control of this—*

"All right." The baron jerked his chin at the fire. Before Alex could say or do anything, Mayerd bundled her clothes up in his arms and tossed them into the fireplace.

"What are you doing?" The words burst from her before she could stop herself, and she dropped to her knees beside the fireplace just as reflexively. It was already too late. Red spots appeared on the velvet, glowing like baleful eyes, growing larger as the cloth burned. The black abstract crisped and disappeared in smoke. Alex stared into the flames, realizing dimly that her body shook.

Maybe he burned them because I won't need clothes any more. Maybe I'll never leave this room either.

She clenched her teeth on a cry and drew in a long breath. When she rose, she felt the coolness seep back into her face, stilling her features, and she knew that now she looked merely amused at this new clothes-burning game. "I see you meant it, my lord, when you spoke of clothing me in your own tastes."

Robert Demeresna looked at the fire and then at Mayerd before turning away. "Get her a drink of dragora."

What was dragora? Alex wanted to reach for the wall to steady herself, but she locked her legs and watched as Mayerd filled a cup with a foaming green liquid that smelled of mulberries. He handed it to her, and when she forced her fingers to close around the cup, she felt a film of moisture on its earthenware surface.

"What is it?" she said.

"Something to make you sleep." The baron did not meet her eyes.

To sleep forever, Alex thought. Her arm stayed frozen, the drink halfway to her mouth. Death would not be so bad, but this might not kill fast. It could be a poison that left her writhing in agony on the floor.

But would he murder Stephen's gift to him, bare minutes after receiving it? Stephen might feel slighted at that. She looked down at the opaque surface of the liquid. Could it be an aphrodisiac? She was used to those, even with the internal damage they did, but if so, why had he said she would sleep? Were his tastes so perverted that the mares had to be drugged before he used them? She saw the minute shivers of the liquid and knew that her hand was trembling.

"Please drink it." The baron still wouldn't look at her.

I could refuse. And he could force it down my throat, or make his sorcerer do it.

She brought the cup to her mouth and took her first swallow; liquid ice penetrated her body and prickled her skin. If the drink had a taste, she never noticed. She drank again and again, careless of the hurt in her teeth or the tightness behind her temples. When she was done, Mayerd reached for the cup and she tossed it into the fireplace.

The flames leaped up, not green, but brilliantly white. Then they subsided, but in the moment of pure light, she saw the baron's startled gaze fixed on her, and he looked as though he was seeing her for the first time.

Or maybe I'm just drunk. Or dying. I won't cry. The thought startled her, because it was the first time in years that she had come close to tears. *No, not before this man who wanted me afraid as well as naked and humiliated. Not at all.*

The room began to rock slowly around her, and the lines of walls and floor lost definition. Alex closed her eyes, putting her feet apart to keep her balance.

"Come." The baron's voice was deep below the earth, muted and echoing. She felt his hand on her arm but she didn't have the strength to do more than lean on him as he led her the few paces to a couch. Her body folded like a ribbon as she fell to the silk cushions, and the baron lifted her legs to the couch. *A coffin, lined with silk.* Then the world grew dark as if Robert Demeresna had closed the lid over her face.

Robert rested an arm along the edge of the mantelpiece and stared into the fire, listening to the flames chew and crack the wood. He felt drained, and yet he had never needed to be more alert. Finally he turned and approached the couch.

He started to speak, then realized he didn't know the woman's name. The Black Mare, the court called her, and he wondered if she even had a name. Well, it didn't matter. He touched her jaw, turning her head lightly left and right, before he was sure she was unconscious.

"Give me a coverlet," he said.

Mayerd handed him one and he dropped it over the woman's naked body, tucking it around her. She was one of the most distracting sights he had ever seen, and he had to keep reminding himself who she was. At least now he could talk freely.

"What do you think?" He dropped into an armchair and gestured for Mayerd to do the same. Trained as the captain of his guard, Mayerd held the rigid discipline far too well.

Mayerd shrugged. "No weapons in the clothing, no wire loops in the hair. Of course, such measures may be too obvious for Lord Garnath."

They had searched every inch of the rooms for listening-holes, but Robert still felt sweat trace his spine. "I should have known something like this would happen—and the night before we left too. Still, no use complaining about it. The question is, what do I do with her? If she is an assassin, I'll have to keep her in shackles so she doesn't lay hands on a weapon. If she isn't, why would he give her to me?"

Mayerd rubbed one of his lateral lines. "You could give her to someone else, or release her."

"And if she's an assassin, she'll follow us." He thought of the four hundred miles to Dawnever, the long weeks of travel towards the east. The threat of ambush on the way didn't bother him. He had picked men-at-arms he trusted, and he half expected Stephen Garnath to stage an attack along the East Road anyway. What made his fists clench was the thought of one determined person trailing him back to his estate, a woman who could charm her way into any man's bed. And he didn't want her causing any trouble for his people.

"As for giving her to someone else, do you know anyone whom I hate that much?" he said.

Mayerd rarely smiled, but his eyes crinkled at the corners. "Besides, that would be an insult to Lord Garnath, wouldn't it? Who knows how he might take that?"

Robert sighed. "He didn't give her to me in good faith, Mayerd, I know that much."

"It isn't in the man to make a genuine gift?"

"No. More to the point, if he did parcel out mares, I wouldn't get the pride of his stable."

"She might have fallen from favor," Mayerd said. "You saw how he told her that she couldn't even take anything with her."

"Still, it doesn't make sense." Robert felt frustrated, because he had never been good at explaining why he felt certain things. He had known Mayerd long enough that it wasn't necessary, but he tried anyway. "Garnath isn't the kind of man to give a gift unless he thought he was getting something greater in value—and I've given him very little. Oh, I've made promises of support and troops from Dawnever, but promises are cheap. And Garnath made the whole thing sound very spur-of-the-moment, here you go, a last-minute present. Hell, even *she* looked shocked. But he never does anything without thinking it through."

"I suppose it could have been a staged act between the two of them," Mayerd said.

"Who knows?" Robert rubbed a thumb between his eyes. "I even wonder if she has some contagious disease and is in the early stages, before it shows."

Mayerd leaned forward. "Sir," he said quietly, "we could kill her."

Robert had guessed that option would be mentioned soon enough. Well, better to hear it now, from Mayerd, than later, from someone less trusted. "Can you put a blade through a naked, senseless woman? Because I can't."

"It doesn't have to be a blade." Mayerd's eyes and voice were flat, and he looked very Iternan, strange and withdrawn and dangerous. "If I had given her a little more of that—"

"No. Not for suspicion alone."

"Why not?"

At times like that, Robert wondered if Mayerd was testing him, to see if he was worth serving, or if Mayerd was testing himself, straining against whatever bonds a long-deserted Iternum had forged. He lowered his voice and did not once take his stare away from Mayerd's eyes as he spoke. "Because I'd be no better than the self-proclaimed Lord Garnath at that point. That kind of killing isn't execution, it's murder, and I won't have it on my hands. Understood?"

"Of course." Mayerd leaned back in his chair. The tension vanished, and once again he was the captain of the guard, steadfast and loyal. "So we take her with us tomorrow?"

Robert raked a hand through his hair and thought about all the things he had seen in Radiath, the city that was the core of Dagre. The city had withstood war and siege and magic, and from its eight towers, kings and the Quorum and the Governing Hand had summoned the people. Except that the kings were gone now, into the ashes of war and the dust of the past. The Quorum was reinforcing its walls, preparing for the storm that might break them. And the Governing Hand had been revealed for it was, a front for Stephen Garnath to rise to power as single ruler of a great land. One by one the dukes and prelates and merchant princes of the Hand had gone, like fingers cut cleanly off, and now there was only Lord Garnath, who held Radiath.

In a castle as unbreakable as an iron cage and more dangerous, Robert thought of his own house, eight miles from the growing town of Madelayn. But other images rose like smoke to blot it out. He saw the map of Dagre in Stephen Garnath's study, half of it shaded in the imperial red. He saw the crests of fallen provinces arrayed like trophies on the walls, and when he thought of the Demeresna emblem—the sign of the thunder's bolt—being added to them, he felt he would kill Garnath first, whether that put him on the usurper's level or not.

No, I won't succeed in that, not here and not yet. So he would return to Dawnever, having done his duty and obeyed the near-royal summons, grateful to still be alive but unable to believe that any of his deceptions had worked. He was hopeless at lying. Even when stories of his cruelty had spread, he felt alone on a stage, watched by the world, the boards creaking noisily under his feet. It was only with a sword in his hands or a map spread out before him that he would feel at all secure.

And soon enough, that's what I'll have. He had laid the foundations of his rebellion, and in Dawnever, he would build what he could on them. Garnath would not let him be; the provinces of Dagre had been polarized long before, either hunting with the hounds or fleeing with the hare. Except that Robert didn't intend to flee or hide for much longer.

Again he thought with longing of his home, but this time the image that blotted it out was that of a dark-haired woman, her eyes filled with the cold bitter fire of emeralds. He refused to look at her, even drugged and helpless. She was ill tidings of some sort, he just didn't know what. Black Mare, did they say? No, this one was a black cat, sent to cross his path with blood on her feet. And even sitting before the fire, he felt chilled, as if a wind had crept biting over his skin.

Stephen Garnath climbed the stairs to the Spiral Tower and selected a door carved with a line that curved and bent so that its ends moved out in opposite directions. He rapped sharply.

The door swung open and Stephen entered, not bothering to greet Ohallox, the Iternan magician he employed. Ohallox studied him in the same cool silence. His eyes were the color of water that had flowed over rotting leaves. There was a disconcerting, glassy quality to them, and his manner, silent as a lizard, made people more uncomfortable in his presence. Naturally, Stephen enjoyed reversing that.

"There's a setback." He pulled a chair out. "Demeresna also has an Iternan at his side."

Ohallox stared at him. "A Way practitioner?"

"How should I know?" Stephen tilted the chair back so that he could rest the sole of one boot on the edge of Ohallox's desk. "Isn't every Iternan, to some extent? Or if you mean someone who matches your talent, well, I can't tell that either. You should be able to."

Long hands touched the lateral lines that ridged each side of Ohallox's face. "I feel nothing," he said, frowning, "so he isn't employing whichever aspect of the Way he controls."

"At the moment," Stephen pointed out. "He could do so tomorrow—the day after—any time. Will he see into her?"

Ohallox lowered his hands, but not quickly enough to hide their clenching. "Yes, if he has mastered the Inward Way and if he suspects her of hiding anything. You have to find out."

Stephen shook his head. "Demeresna's been secretive about this man, kept him inside the chambers all this time. I suppose he thought that since he was taking his leave of me in the morning, there was no more need for secrecy. But if he was hiding his own magician, I doubt he'd be obliging enough to explain the man's training. Can't you sense it?"

"I can, but if I send out a broad probe, he'll feel it. The only kind of sensor he wouldn't notice would be a narrowed one, perhaps disguised as a fleeting memory, and those are impossible unless you know the target well enough to create a disguise that will deceive them."

"Let him feel it, then. It's an open secret that you work for me."

Ohallox's pale eyes stared through him. "Iternans don't like being touched by strangers. If he retaliates, I'll have a battle on my hands. Either he walks the Outward Way, and my books will fly off the shelves while the furniture spontaneously combusts—or he takes the Inward Way, and it will be a mental duel for which I'm not prepared. The answer is no. Not yet."

Stephen felt his eyes narrowing. No other sign of his anger showed, but he let the chair's tilted legs drop back. "Better that than the plan failing, Magician."

"It won't fail," Ohallox said sharply. "It cannot. He would have to be the Waymaster himself to undo the knots I've tied without springing the trap. She would kill him first."

"Or try to." Stephen considered. Perhaps he should make the mare act now. Yes, Robert Demeresna was still his guest and under his protection, but would he really lose so much? After all, he could have her executed after the murder; everyone would see that justice had been served. Demeresna didn't have a powerful family who would raise an army to avenge his death, or even connections to the Quorum.

But the Iternan magician was the baron's hidden card. Stephen felt his lips pull back from his teeth, because he couldn't risk the Iternan finding out what had been done to the mare. Ohallox could make her attack them both, but the baron was no weakling and might hold her off long enough for the magician to act. No, she had to catch them both off-guard, and neither of them was in the least distracted in his castle.

He said as much to Ohallox, who nodded. "Besides," he said, one finger tracing a lateral line in a rhythmic, soothing movement, "I touched her just now. She's sleeping. Even if you wanted her to act, there would be nothing she could do."

You do well to be wary, Baron, Stephen thought. *But as my star rises, yours shall fall. There's room for only one ruler here.*

"Let's see how much we can achieve," he said. "If the elimination can be arranged so that it appears another potential problem committed it—or better yet, if she throws blood on a Quorumlord's hands—that would be ideal. Keep listening, Ohallox. If the Iternan attempts to unravel what you've made, order her to strike. If not...there is potential in this."

Ohallox steepled his fingers. "There's a story in Iternum, about the great statue of a horse that was left for an enemy by a departing, seemingly defeated army. When the enemy took the gift past its gates, they learned their mistake; the horse was hollow, filled with soldiers."

Stephen grinned, rising to leave. "Of course, there's one great difference between that situation and mine."

"What's that?"

"I'm never even seemingly defeated."

Chapter Two:
In the House of Sorlia

Alex wondered for a drowsy moment why she had fallen asleep on the couch. She was never at her best when she had just woken, and her mind felt fuzzed-over. Then she turned her head and saw the room, which cleared her senses at once.

The embers of a fire smoldered, and a red glow touched the closed door of the baron's private bedchamber. Alex glanced at the figure of the Iternan sorcerer, apparently asleep on another couch. Carefully, she drew aside the wrap that covered her. Then she forced herself to look down at her naked body, something she rarely did even on the more normal days of her life.

No bruises. No cuts. In fact, no change at all. She couldn't feel any soreness between her thighs, and she wondered if the drug had canceled pain as well as consciousness. But if the baron had ridden her, there would have been evidence of it. Why drug her, then? Perhaps he was impotent and didn't want anyone to know it?

It doesn't matter. She looked at the outer door, longing to open it. Even if it had not been guarded by either Dagran men or Iternan magic, she had no clothes, no money, nothing at all. And her new master was a sadist. Life didn't get much better than that.

Unable to bear the stillness, she swung her legs off the couch, and the Iternan woke. Alex pulled the coverlet around herself. Had the soft thud of her feet hitting the floor disturbed him, or did magic alert him somehow? She held still as he sat up, looking as alert as if he had not slept.

"Must be early." He glanced at the baron's door. "You can wear some of my clothes."

He hooked a saddlebag with his foot and fished out a few garments, tossing them to her. Alex caught them out of reflex, too startled to thank him. And she hadn't thought an Iternan sorcerer would dress so poorly. The shirt's elbows were patched, and the cuffs frayed. The clothes were clean, but that was the only compliment she could have paid them. She wanted to laugh; she had gone from sheers and velvets to this. It seemed to be typical of her life to date.

Mayerd went to the main door, opening it to speak with the guards outside, and Alex took advantage of the brief but welcome moment of privacy to dress. Shabby as the clothes were, she had nothing else, so she pulled the trousers on and was slipping her arms into the shirt sleeves as the baron's door opened.

He was already dressed. The quality of his clothes was a step up from Mayerd's—leather boots were polished to a shine and the brass fasteners of his bear-pelt jerkin reflected the firelight—but his clothes had the same road-ready quality. She looked away as she finished buttoning the shirt.

"What..." The baron chuckled as he shut the door behind him. "Do you know how you look in Mayerd's clothes?"

Alex had a good idea. The shirt cuffs covered her fingers and the trouser legs folded around her feet. She was not a small woman, but Mayerd was so tall that she looked ludicrous in his clothes. Her face grew hot. Despite her station in life, being laughed at was something unexpected.

"I beg your pardon," the baron said stiffly. "No, don't roll the sleeves up, it's cold outside. As for the pants, just push them into a pair of boots—here, I have one."

Wondering what kind of a man burned a woman's clothes and then gave her boots, Alex accepted them with a formal thanks and found rags to stuff into the toes to help them fit. Servants set bread and preserved fruit out on a low table before the fire, pulling two chairs up to it before they bowed and left. Mayerd sat down and reached for the teapot.

"We need another chair," the baron said. He carried one out from his room, set it between his seat and Mayerd's, and looked at her. "Aren't you going to join us?"

Alex stayed where she was, certain he was mocking her. Even if he had not terrified and drugged her the night before, meals were not shared with one's inferiors. On the rare feast days or celebrations when she had been allowed to appear in public, she had sat at the lowest table, far removed from the nobility of the castle. Perhaps this was a test, to see if she would be insolent enough to try to rise above her place. The baron hadn't actually given her an order, after all.

And yet he kept looking at her. "If it pleases you, my lord," she said, her voice toneless and polite.

"Well, it would speed our departure. Sit down. Here, Mayerd, fill this." He handed the Iternan a cup.

That was definitely an order, so Alex obeyed. She kept her hands in her lap as the baron broke a loaf of bread and set a piece before her. Cautiously she took it, wishing that she could have stayed in the background, unwatched and peacefully ignored. The proximity to the two men was strangling her appetite.

The baron didn't seem to be especially hungry either and took a few bites of bread before getting up. Alex, her mouth full, started to rise too, but the baron only said, "I'll make my farewells fast, Mayerd. Be ready to start out."

Mayerd set his cup down. "I'll come with—"

"No." The baron's gaze flicked to her, and she understood. He didn't want his latest possession unguarded.

Mayerd hesitated. "Be careful."

"I don't intend to eat with him." The baron's voice had an edge. "Just to fulfill custom. The man's sheltered us, so I can hardly slip away before sunrise."

It was that early? Alex had been too nervous to feel tired, and now, as the baron left the room, she wondered why he was in such a hurry. He could have eaten a far better meal with Stephen in the great hall. Instead, he was all but running away. Still, it didn't concern her, and all she looked forward to was a single moment when no one watched her. She would find some way to escape, especially since she had travel-ready clothes now. Her spirits rose and she attacked the meal hungrily.

"How long have you lived here?" Mayerd asked.

Alex swallowed. "Since I was fourteen."

His eyes widened, but he said nothing. Alex hesitated, wondering if she should explain further. Why not? She had nothing to lose. "I wasn't a mare *then*."

Mayerd had been finishing his tea, and he choked, groping for a napkin. Alex handed him one quickly, wondering if he was angry, but when he could speak, he only said, "What were you?"

She shrugged. "My family had a farm, but we lost it during the Infestation. So I came to the city, and I became a maid here. Four years later Lord Garnath met me, and he offered to make me his paramour. I would never need to empty chamberpots or scrub the floors again, he said. That much was true."

Before Mayerd could reply, the baron entered, his mouth drawn to a line and his eyes narrowed. Alex knew there was trouble even before Mayerd rose. "Sir, is everything—"

"Let's go," the baron said. "No, he said nothing—other than wishing me a swift and safe journey back to Fulmion. I never told him the name of my house. We leave now."

If not for those few cryptic words—the sense that danger hung over them like a cloud—Alex would have been a little happier. She was finally escaping from a place she had loathed for years, leaving a city she had come to hate. Instead, as she followed the baron out of the keep, she was on edge. She tried to calm herself down, reasoning that a tyrant who led that kind of brutal life might very well be paranoid, constantly reading threats into the most innocuous words.

And she was right. When they entered the sunlit courtyard she saw only the long shadows of stables and storehouses, and the shivering that struck her was due only to the spring chill. There was a bay gelding for her, and when she swung herself into the saddle, the baron stared at her.

"Where did you learn to ride?" he asked.

Alex's hands tightened on the reins at his suspicious tone. "Riding is a favorite pastime of the nobility, my lord. I learned it through long association." Did he think she was a hothouse flower, unable to function outside a bed?

He raised an eyebrow. "Very well. Take your place."

Two of the guards flanked him, with the sorcerer directly behind him and four more guards brought up the rear. There was a space for her in the middle of the line, and she nudged the bay into it. The stablemaster blew two long notes on his horn—the signal that Lord Garnath's guests were about to leave.

The baron's white horse broke into a gallop, cutting across half of the inner ward before the echoes had died away. Alex let herself feel the wind on her face, the speed and strength of the horse under her. There was no pleasure in any of it—she knew she was going from one nightmare to another—but for those few moments, she could blank out her thoughts as her bay reached the opened gates of the inner ward. She heard the drumbeats of other hooves all around her, like pebbles dislodged in the first stage of an avalanche, and something made her glance over her shoulder at the castle she was leaving behind.

She saw nothing untoward, only a figure watching from the balcony of the Spiral Tower, too far away for her to recognize him. She turned, looking ahead to the outer gateway. As the baron's horse sped through it, she braced herself for something to happen—the portcullis to fall, an arrow to strike him.

Nothing happened. The horses thundered on, the ground thudding under their hooves, and she was out of the castle, her heart beating faster than the horses' gallop.

Before the sun had climbed much higher, they were out of Radiath. Its six-foot-thick granite walls had been built to repel invaders, and Alex felt sure that if the huge spike-studded gates had been shut, even the Bloody Baron would not have been able to get past them. No one had ever conquered Radiath, and she felt sure that no one ever would.

Therefore, it made sense that the baron should ally with Lord Garnath. Stephen had played his enemies off against each other, raising an army to crush anyone he distrusted, and she guessed that the only reason the baron might feel safer than the rest of the nobility was that Dawnever Province was on the land's edge, well beyond the Siege Circle. But that would make no difference eventually. When Stephen declared himself king, or some other title that meant the same thing, it would be all over for anyone who had failed to yield their full loyalty to him. If the baron fell into that chasm, he would never climb out, not even with an Iternan sorcerer by his side.

She might derive some benefit from such a situation. If she was still alive at that point, she could escape in the chaos. Of course, if Stephen ruled all of Dagre, she wasn't sure where she would escape to, which didn't help her mood.

Stop feeling sorry for yourself. Start thinking, planning, anything but waiting for the blow to fall. She held the bay to the same easy trot that kept it in pace with the other horses, looking around at the plowed earth that already showed a mist of green. Between the grain fields was the road of flat stones fitted closely together and mortared like a mosaic.

The Red Road had been built for trade and couriers and wealthy people. At a distant rumble, far ahead of them, the baron nudged his white horse to one side of the road as a coach drew nearer. She followed his example, wondering if the coach driver guessed that the man making way for him was a baron. Probably not. Robert Demeresna neither dressed nor acted like one, and it dawned on her again that he was being careful, leaving Radiath as quickly as he could and not flaunting his presence. He could have chartered a coach and traveled in luxury, but that would have been conspicuous.

Once the coach was gone, the horses once more had the Red Road to themselves, and they traveled well into the day. Now and then they passed wagons or carts, people carrying trade goods into the city, and the baron stopped to buy food from them. Alex felt grateful that she was wearing Mayerd's clothes rather than her own. People were surprised to see what they thought was a female soldier, but that was preferable to the looks of disgust bestowed upon a mare.

No one spoke, which Alex didn't mind at all. She liked being alone with her thoughts, deciding what to do. Obviously she couldn't just break into a run across the fields, and she had no resources that would let her survive alone in Dagre. She eyed the men's saddlebags enviously. If only she had a knife and a little money, they wouldn't even find the dust she raised.

The baron called a halt. They dismounted and led their horses off the road, into an uncultivated field thick with clover and dandelions, stopping by the side of a stream. The horses drank while Alex tried to think of how to request some privacy. She hoped the baron wouldn't humiliate her further by asking her to relieve herself before his men.

"May I go in there?" she finally said, gesturing at a stand of trees a few yards away.

It seemed to take a moment for her meaning to penetrate, and when it did, the baron turned to stare at the trees. Alex ignored the heaviness of her bladder and hoped that he wouldn't take much longer to make up his mind.

"Gavin," he said, and the man stepped forward. "Go into that thicket and make sure it's safe for her in there. Nothing out of the ordinary."

"At once, my lord." The man set off at a lope.

Alex watched him go, bewildered. Safe for her? It was out of character for the Bloody Baron to be concerned about a mare's safety from adders or poison poppies, and they were not on private land that would have been trapped against poachers. She resigned herself to being in the company of an unpredictable man, and thanked him when Gavin returned to pronounce the copse safe.

By the side of the stream, they shared the dried meat and fresh vegetables the baron had bought on the road. The horses grazed nearby, and if not for the tense silence, she would have enjoyed the day. The men-at-arms took their cue from the baron and left her alone, which was a relief. She felt sure that if he had planned to pass her around to his men, none of them would have treated her with that reserve.

Hundreds of miles remained and they had covered only twenty. She did not look around at the men who lay on the sunlit grass. Instead, she sat beside the stream, one arm wrapped around her legs, and killed a desire to gallop away as fast as she could.

"Any way to reach home without paying tolls?" Mayerd asked.

"Not until we're past the Siege Circle," the baron said. "This is a turnpike route, so we'll pay for the privilege of using the Red Road that the first King Alexander himself built."

Alex felt a twinge of amusement that never reached her face. That was the great ruler she had been named after, her mother had once told her.

"We should have such roads going to Madelayn, my lord," one of the men-at-arms said.

"I agree, Peter, but there's no way to enforce their building or upkeep, unless the people see value in them. The farmers have no money to pay tolls, and there's hardly any commerce so far east." The baron sat up, a new interest in his voice. "I've seen what happens to roads under those conditions. The farmers pull up the stones to build their houses and pasture walls. They need reasons to maintain the roads."

"Trade," Mayerd said, "best reason of all, except we have nothing to trade."

That cast a pall over the group, and Alex thought of the other reason commerce might have withdrawn from Dawnever Province: Who would do business with a man so brutal that he put a stake through an opponent's groin? She wasn't surprised that he was poor. She merely marveled that he thought he could thumb his nose at Stephen Garnath, Stephen who had the might of most of the Dagran cities behind him.

The two of them could tear each other apart. They deserved each other.

The baron rose, brushing pollen off his clothes. "Let's take the road again. I want to be under a roof before dusk."

They made good time, arriving at the village of Berry that evening, by which time Alex was saddle-sore and exhausted, too tired to escape even if she had been left alone. She was used to riding, but as a brief trot into the countryside, not a steady, relentless covering of miles that lasted all day. In the stable of the best inn of Berry, the men-at-arms rubbed down their lathered horses, but the most she could do was dismount and stay on her feet. From thighs to buttocks to hands she felt raw, in pain she thought she hid. Of course the baron noticed, stepping closer to take her arm.

"I'll have them draw a bath for you—"

"No!" Alex pulled away before she could think. Her legs gave way and she caught the stable door for balance. The desultory talk in the stable ceased as everyone stared at her, but she barely noticed them. Before her eyes rose a vision of the last bath she had taken, naked in a tub of scented water with Sir John Holleng, Stephen's minister of internal affairs. Holleng had eyes wide as a toad's, and he had not bathed in several months, so she suspected that Stephen had ordered the bath as a way to simply tolerate the man's presence in close quarters. The memory was vivid and nauseating, but she thrust it down with an effort and opened her eyes to see the baron turn away.

"As you wish," he said. "Mayerd, escort her to our rooms."

He went across the courtyard to the common room of the inn. Alex braced herself and let go of the door, thankful that the Iternan did not touch her. Outside, it was twilight, and servants lit small aromatic fires to dissuade insects. *If I can bear what Stephen considered amusement, I can walk on my own.*

She entered the inn, Mayerd keeping pace behind her. Beside the front door was the customary alcove that held an image of Sorlia, and Alex pretended to do obeisance before the shrine. She needed the moment to rest, to control the pain. She bent her head, breathing slowly, and never once looked at the image.

One hand gripping the banister until her knuckles stood out like tree roots, she managed to climb the stairs. Mayerd held a door open for her, and she almost pulled back again as she saw the three narrow beds, each placed against one side of the room.

"There isn't space for us to have private rooms." Mayerd shut the door behind her. "Better get used to it. Once we pass the Circle, we'll be sleeping on the ground."

As long as I'm not sleeping with either of you, Alex thought dully. She had to undress, but she couldn't make herself strip again.

The baron entered. "They're sending dinner up," he said with his usual abruptness, "and for you—what's your name?"

She looked up. "Alex. Alex Khayne...if it pleases my lord."

"Yes, fine. One of the servants will bring whatever balm or bandages you need later."

"Thank you," Alex said, but he had already crossed the room to stare out of the window at the night-quieted village. The sooner she healed and became accustomed to hard riding, the easier it would be to escape.

They left the inn early the next day. Alex dreaded riding again, chafing her wounds, but she walked downstairs with her face composed and her steps steady. Now she paused in the common room, as three of the men-at-arms went to the little alcove and knelt before the figure of Sorlia. The fourth man, Gavin, was already at the stables, bringing their horses out.

The baron stopped on the stairs beside her, obviously wondering why she had halted, and Alex disciplined her voice to calmness before she spoke. There was no chance of being left alone as long as the baron distrusted her. She had to lull his suspicions, to put him at ease somehow, and short of sharing his bed, the best way to do that would be to talk to him.

"Do you perform morning orison, my lord?" she asked, indicating the alcove.

The baron took a few slow steps down. "It would be the correct thing to do, I suppose. Especially to the goddess of travelers. Except that I'm tired of both the Quorum and the supernatural forces they claim to serve."

Alex looked around to see if anyone had heard him. Only Mayerd

Marian Perera

was nearby, and from the small smile on his face, that particular heresy was not new. "Why are you tired of them?"

"Because the Quorum hides in its strongholds, and the Benevolent Ones have always been resolutely silent." He strode towards the front door, and she had to follow, wondering about his views. The Quorum took a dim view of such criticism. On the other hand, of late the Quorum had become notoriously secretive and judgmental. She had heard Stephen damn them often enough, saying that had they allied themselves with him, he would have ruled Dagre in a matter of days.

"Can't you find and persuade their leaders?" she had asked. Questions to Stephen had to be posed carefully, when he was in a lenient mood, and even then she could not imply that he was weak in any way.

"I'd love to," Stephen had said. "But the High Quorum is established well beyond the Circle, and I don't want my hounds ranging too far. Besides...there are rumors the Quorum can call down powers that no other men wield."

"Powers?"

"Rumors, that's all there is to it. There's no record of the so-called Benevolent Ones sending earthquakes to destroy the unworthy. No, the Quorum's kept its grip on the common folk with its own minute order of knights, plus a stinking heap of superstitions to counteract whatever their swordsmen don't."

Alex remembered that as she passed by the alcove. When the men-at-arms rose and left, she had an unimpeded view of the statue of Sorlia. The woman's right hand was extended in greeting, but her left, held at her side, rested on a sword's hilt.

Benevolence plus a blade, and Alex could see which was more powerful. She walked out of the inn.

It took another two days for them to pass a lake which glittered in the afternoon sun. Alex saw fishermen taking advantage of the sudden glut of spring. She wished she could watch them, but the baron was rigid about his rules. During the day, they stopped for meals at set times, never for any other reason—hunger, pain and discomfort included.

She tried to ignore her aching body, looking at the fields and farmland unfolding around her. Every day, there was something new to see: people burning the wild grass to prepare the fields for planting, a roadside burial site for an unnamed traveler. She had spent so many indistinguishable days in the cage of Stephen's castle that it was a pleasure to travel through pastures sprinkled white with bleating lambs, with farmhouses built of yellow stones. They looked carved from cheese, she thought.

"How much longer until we reach the Siege Circle?" she asked the baron that evening, the first words she had spoken freely to him, with no purpose other than simple curiosity.

He frowned. "A week or longer. I'll confirm that with the nearest toll collector."

They passed the toll point the next afternoon, and Alex forced herself to look away as the baron counted out silver coins. She couldn't shut her ears to the jingling sound, and she hoped fervently that the Iternan couldn't read her thoughts. No chance of stealing unless there was some distraction, like a heath fire or a boar springing out of the forest. She sighed silently. In the relatively tame land within the Circle, neither was likely, and she certainly couldn't set a fire within the inns where they slept at night.

Half of the week passed without incident. Alex saw her body healing, her long legs toughening to match the bay's strength. The sores vanished to faint marks. She thought of reopening them, to ward off the baron, but he never made a move to touch her; he rarely even spoke to her. At night, she had dreams of her past existence and nightmares of the future, but she was always so tired that she never woke.

On the next day, the green shadow of Galvede Forest rose in the distance, far to the right, and Alex knew that they were close to the Circle's perimeter. It was on that day that she saw her first representative of the Quorum.

The baron drew his horse to a halt, raising a gloved hand. The sun stood directly overhead and she knew that he would have stopped for a meal at that time regardless. Mounted on a grey nag, the priest drew closer, returning the salute. Mayerd jerked on his horse's reins, but Alex nudged the bay closer, curious. In all her adult life, she had never before been so close to a member of the Quorum, even one so lowly.

The priest did not seem to be aware of his poor station. Despite his dusty robes and patched boots, his face was cheerful. "A fine day to you, sirs and madam, and may Sorlia watch over you on your journey," he called as he drew level with them, reining his horse in.

"Thank you," Robert said. "We were just about to stop for a meal. Will you join us?"

"I would be del—" The priest stopped, and for a moment Alex thought he had recognized her. Then she realized that he was staring past her. She turned and met Mayerd's dark eyes.

"You travel with an Iternan?" the priest asked Robert.

"Yes, I do." The reply came with no hesitation at all.

The priest paused, as if giving him time to reconsider. "A user of magic?"

Robert's gaze flicked over her, then returned to the priest. "All Iternans use magic."

Any trace of friendship disappeared. "I am sorry that you have chosen to defy the Third Mandate. *Magic is foreign to our ways and our nature; it is not to be trusted. Therefore, allow neither wizard nor witch to cast their shadows in your land.*"

Alex held her breath, waiting for the priest to call down power of his own and strike Mayerd, or vice versa. Either way, she could use the resulting mayhem to escape.

"I chose to give shelter to one who sought it," Robert said stiffly.

"The Quorum takes a more far-sighted view, I am afraid." The priest matched his tone. "And I am sorry that you have turned away from our guidance and strength."

"It also requires strength not to fear an Iternan. Who has done more for me than the Benevolent Ones, so far."

The priest fixed him with a long look. "They have given us gifts that you cannot imagine." He kicked his horse into a canter and before long, he had vanished into the distance.

"I'm sorry," Mayerd said flatly. "I should—"

"Shut up." The baron dismounted. "I'd rather eat with you than with any sanctimonious secret-hugger whose sum contribution to the betterment of our condition is reciting the Mandates."

Alex dismounted and led the bay off the road, wondering about the "gifts" the priest had mentioned. Were they so different from magic? Had the Quorum protected those gifts from Stephen as well? She was so preoccupied that their midday meal was over before she realized that one more opportunity for escape had gone.

34

A signpost by the roadside read *Hammer of Katash: 20 miles.* Alex kept her face blank, deciding not to show the baron that she was literate. He read the words for the benefit of his men, who looked relieved.

"That's the edge of the Circle, Lord Robert?" Peter asked.

The baron nodded. The Siege Circle had been born when the Infestation first threatened Dagre, with all the cities on its perimeter fortified and renamed to show their new purpose. The Circle had been broken, but never destroyed, and Alex knew that they were relatively safe within its perimeter. What happened when they passed beyond it was a different matter.

"We'll stay in the Hammer tonight," Robert said, "and I'll buy enough supplies to last on the East Road."

Alex felt a shiver under her skin at the thought of supplies and money. This was her chance to gather as much as she could before she escaped. Days on the road had toughened her, and she would survive, even in the land beyond the Circle.

They reached the Hammer of Katash. Alex drew a mental map of it as they rode down the public thoroughfare. That was her first time in the city, but she had heard enough to be familiar with it—the market, the college of history, the Church of Eternal Rest.

"Now to find an inn." Robert looked around.

Alex spoke without thinking. "The King's Hunt is on Half Moon Street."

"I thought you'd rarely been out of that castle." Robert frowned. "How did you—?"

"Lord Harold Croiros, the Duke of Rianx, owns businesses within this city, my lord," she said quickly. "He often spoke to me of them."

"Pillow talk," a man-at-arms muttered. It was true, so she said nothing, but Robert's face darkened. She wasn't sure if he was angrier with her or with the man who had spoken. Her stomach knotted, and her body braced itself reflexively.

"Another place was suggested to me at the gate," Robert said, and as they cut through the city, she told herself not to volunteer information again. The inn he chose was a crowded place called the Spent Bear, which Alex soon found was because it had once been an arena. A bear's skull was fixed to the front gate, and the ever-present image of Sorlia was missing an arm.

As always, she shared a room with the baron and his sorcerer, but that night, three of the men-at-arms were detailed to buy provisions. Two more were busy with the horses, since the inn had barely enough servants, let alone stablehands, and the last had been bitten by a viper along the way to the city, leaving his leg too swollen for him to walk. Alex sat on her narrow bed as the baron gave them orders, and after they had left, Mayerd offered to bring up dinner.

"May I help?" she asked.

The baron's gaze went to her at once, but he said nothing. Did he think she had said that so as to avoid being left alone with him? She bit her lip.

"Why not?" Mayerd said. "Save me making two trips, and I'll keep an eye on her."

You do that, Alex thought angrily as the baron nodded. She was starting to chafe under the constant watch. Obviously he had guessed she would escape, but he wasn't exactly giving her any reason to stay with him. A few men had treated her courteously despite her station, instead of watching her suspiciously or ignoring her.

That was all for the best. She would feel no regrets at doing whatever was necessary to escape from him.

She said nothing as she went downstairs with Mayerd, and he paid for their dinner. She would have to do without money, because the men were careful with what they had. They carried their coins in pouches tied to their belts, and at night, the small leather bags went under their pillows.

What she could take, however, was a knife, which was why she had offered to carry up a tray. The men kept a close watch on their weapons too, but a sharp little meat knife was different, and this place was just chaotic enough that she might be able to get away with it.

"Is there some celebration going on?" she asked Mayerd as they waited for the landlady's attention. She had to raise her voice to be heard over the din in the common room.

"From what I gather, there was a great offering-feast for the Benevolent Ones in the plaza this afternoon, to bring rain for the crops. It's been dry these past few weeks."

Alex thought of the sunny days of travel, then imagined squelching her way through miles of mud while rain poured down. She hoped the Benevolent Ones would be as indifferent to the feasters as they had always been to her.

The landlady, wiping her hands on an apron that bore many samples of the inn's dishes, finally thrust two trays at them, one covered with food, the other piled with crockery and cutlery. Mayerd reached for the first tray and Alex, secretly delighted, took the second. It was heavy, and the muscles in her bare forearms stood out like ropes. She made her way through the crowd, using the tray to push a path. From time to time, her eyes went to the longest knife in the untidy jumble of utensils.

"Alex, wait," Mayerd called from behind her, but she pretended not to hear him—in the commotion, that was not difficult. She quickened her pace towards the staircase. One moment of privacy was all she needed to take the knife.

She had nearly reached the stairs when Mayerd grabbed her sleeve. Caught off-balance, she tried to turn, but her foot slipped on a patch of grease and she dropped the tray as she fell. Plates smashed to pieces, spoons jingling on the floor, but she hardly heard that as she landed on one elbow.

"Are you hurt?" Mayerd put his own tray on the floor and bent over her, extending a hand.

She pushed it away, trying to sit up. "Leave me alone! Haven't you done enough already?" The knife was within her reach. She could ignore her hurt elbow, but she couldn't take her eyes away from the weapon.

"What's going on here?" The landlady pushed through a knot of staring farmers and gasped to see the broken plates.

"What did the Iternan *do* to her?" a man said.

Mayerd turned to face the crowd and that was all the distraction Alex needed to grab the knife, sliding it into her boot. A moment later, the baron's door opened and he took in the chaos with one glance.

"Pick up that tray and get back inside, Mayerd," he said, and Mayerd, with a cold look at the now-silent crowd, obeyed. Robert took the stairs with a pace as measured as if nothing had happened, then tossed the landlady a silver coin. "Enough to cover your costs, I think. Have someone bring us more plates." He turned to Alex and held out his arm, so she had no choice but to take it.

"You slipped?" he said when they were back in his room.

"It was my fault." Mayerd uncovered bowls of soup, but Alex's appetite was gone. "I startled her."

"I'm sorry." Alex kept her hands in her lap so that the baron couldn't see her fists clench.

"Are you badly hurt, Alex?"

It was the first time he had used her name, and she was surprised enough to reply, "No, my lord, just bruised." Inspiration struck her. "Perhaps I could go downstairs for some salve. That would convince people that your sorcerer didn't actually harm me."

"My wh... Oh. Very well. Be quick about it, or I'll send Mayerd down to find you. And here, take this." He gave her a copper coin. "In case they charge you."

Alex was gone at once, thankful that she was accustomed to pain. She paid the landlady for a striking-flint and a handful of supplies, then hurried to the stables. Perfect, she hadn't even needed to steal anything. She packed the food beneath her gelding's saddle and ran back to the inn. The baron would kill her if he knew what she was doing.

One hand gripping the stitch in her side, she reached the landing and saw that his door was closed. Good, so he hadn't noticed her absence yet. She looked around, but no men-at-arms were watching out for her.

Her heart pounded as she padded forward. *Don't do it. What if there's magic placed around the door? Well, too late already,* she thought as she pressed her ear against the wood.

"...King's Hunt?" Mayerd said. "You think that place was arranged between them?"

Arranged? Between whom?

"It might have been," Robert replied. "I couldn't take the risk. Besides, it's far too expensive."

Mayerd made a dubious sound. "The Black Mare's used to a finer stable."

"That's true. Still, a few days of grubbing with the likes of us won't kill her. Just don't hurt her deliberately."

"Not unless she gives me cause. I thought she would do something to that tray when I wasn't looking."

"Like what? I would have noticed powder or liquid in the bottom of my plate, I assure you."

They think I'd try to poison them? I see, just because I belonged to Stephen, I'm as treacherous as he is. She hadn't expected the Bloody

Baron to trust her, but that level of paranoia unsettled her. A man who thought she was so dangerous might take the precaution of ridding himself of her before she could anticipate it.

Still, she would be gone before many more days passed.

She paced quietly back, then strode forward, letting her boots thump on the floor before she knocked. Mayerd let her in, but the baron frowned. "You were gone a long time."

"I beg my lord's pardon." Alex dropped her gaze.

"Oh, never mind." They had started eating, and now he waved her to a chair. "Sit down. And after you're done, the maids will bring up a change of clothes."

Alex looked down at herself. After sprawling on the floor, she was filthy, and her borrowed clothes showed the grime of two weeks on the road. She had not minded the dirt, since the baron was less likely to want her if she looked like a pig, but now she found herself thinking wistfully of clean clothes.

"Would you like me to have them draw a bath?" Robert asked.

He sounded concerned, and she met his eyes. "Yes, my lord, I would, but..." She couldn't ask for privacy if he thought she was plotting murder.

"I'll ask them to bring in a screen. I'll have a bath as well. Finish your dinner."

Alex did so, and after two servants carried in the promised screen, she sank into the hot water with a sigh. Her clothes lay near the tub, where she could see the boot that hid her knife, and after she had scrubbed herself and washed out her hair, she felt much better.

It was only after she had put on a wrapper and stepped out from behind the screen that she saw the baron staring at her. Her hair, no longer dulled with dust and tied back, tumbled around her shoulders, and her skin felt clean, almost glowing. He looked away at once, but she had seen that kind of interest in men's eyes too many times before, and her skin crawled.

As the servants emptied and refilled the tub, she got into bed, facing the wall, and curled up into a knot. If he had touched her, her body would not have resisted, but he didn't. Anticipation scraped her nerves raw. She wished he would do it and get it over with; she was used to that. For a while she lay awake, longing to be anywhere but there.

A whore never became anything else, because men always looked at her and saw a body for their use. Stephen had told her that long ago, and now the words echoed through her head. Except she never even reached *that* standard, because if she had been paid to spread her legs, she would have earned enough to live on her own by now.

A grey weight settled on her like a thunderhead and chased her into an uneasy sleep.

They were outside the Siege Circle. Robert estimated that it would be another week before they reached Dawnever Province, and Alex waited for her chance of escape. It wouldn't be hard. That part of Dagre had first been devastated by war, then left to overgrow into a wilderness. Thorns thrust up between the stones of the East Road, and the sky grew grey overhead.

The first day passed with the baron on edge and she grew afraid again. If he caught her, it would all be over, so she had to succeed on her first try. He seemed to be watching her most of the time and she found his gaze unbearable. She kept the strain off her face; if he distrusted her enough, he might order her to be bound. Or drugged. *Smile.*

They slept under the open sky, and despite being stiff and sore the next day, she decided that she would escape that night. The sky was blotched and heavy with clouds that hung low overhead, and the air pressed down, stifling.

"Maybe there was something to that feast," Mayerd said.

Robert didn't look pleased. "If it always takes a feast for the Benevolent Ones to realize that their help is needed, they should send better harvests for us to afford all that food."

Alex hunched her shoulders and made herself as small as she could on the bay gelding. She agreed with the sentiment, but the baron's temper was beginning to show, and that scared her worse than any storm could have.

The storm. Think of that, forget everything else. Downpours of rain to hide my trail. Darkness to blind these men. And thunder to cover the sound of my escape.

The forest moved closer, trees pressing in on the right. To the left, cliffs jutted upwards, tree roots showing through broken stone. She hoped they would make shelter soon, but she disliked the look of this place.

A shape ahead loomed larger as they approached, blocky and dark against the sky. Gavin spurred his horse forward. "It's all right, sir," he called back. "It's a shrine."

"Light a torch before you go any closer," Robert said.

Mayerd scraped flint against steel and soon bundles of sticks were alight. Torches held high, the men spurred their horses and moved ahead. The baron took the reins of Alex's gelding, knotting them to his own horse's tethers, then prodded his mount forward to the shrine. Her heart thudded. Had he guessed her plan, or could the Iternan read minds? But he had done no magic so far, none at all.

The shrine was a wide, open area protected by three walls, the fourth unbuilt to welcome all who approached. At the end of the sheltered clearing was a huge image of Sorlia, thrice the size of a man, the features worn by weather to blankness. A bird had built its nest in the extended palm.

Alex couldn't help feeling relieved at that, and even the baron seemed to relax. "It's safe?" he said after his men had explored its interior.

"The shrines of Sorlia are sacred, my lord," Peter said.

"That's no answer," the baron replied, but he allowed the men to tie their horses at the right wall. Alex rubbed her gelding down, looking it over carefully as she did so and hoping it could outrun the others. The horses pulled at the tufts of grass which grew everywhere within the shrine, except around the praying stones. Those stood before the dais of Sorlia, clean flat stones the size of rugs. Alex guessed that they were only used in worship, and the men were careful not to step on them.

"Pity no one built a roof." Mayerd unrolled a length of waxed leather. Peter lit a fire beneath the shelter, as thunder rumbled overhead.

"Pity they didn't place that statue better." A frown appeared on the baron's face again.

The statue was twenty feet from the open side of the shrine, but Alex could see that it tilted slightly. Of course, its sheer weight would not let it fall, even in a gale.

"Probably the ground," Gavin said. "Must have shifted."

The baron shrugged. "Come, let's eat." He gestured towards the fire, and Alex knew that he disliked her staying near the horses, close to the open ground. The proximity to him would turn her stomach, but she couldn't afford to antagonize him now. She walked between the praying stones and crouched at the fire. Again the thunder sounded.

Mayerd had been tossing onions and dried meat into a stewpot, but he stilled, holding a hand up. "What's that sound?"

"What sound?" Robert's hand went to his sword, and Alex heard it too—hoofbeats, drowned out in the thunder and now approaching, loud enough to be heard over the rising wind.

"We're under attack!" Robert said, and one of the men started up, drawing his sword. His timing could not have been worse. Stones flew through the air and one struck his head, rebounding off his helm. The impact sent him reeling back.

Alex seized the moment. Bending over in a half-crouch, she ran across the shrine to the horses. She heard Robert shout, "Stop her!" and as she reached the bay gelding, lightning struck nearby. In the silver blast, she saw Gavin as he came after her.

He stepped on a praying stone. And it gave way under him.

In the crash of thunder that followed, Alex couldn't hear his scream, but she saw his body disappear into the pit trap. Her hands shook too badly to undo knots, so she pulled the knife from her boot and sawed at the reins. The gelding whinnied and strained against the tether. She saw the torches go out and knew why—the baron and his men were easy targets in the light, but a fiercer glow leaped up nearby as a tree, dried in the drought, started to burn. She worked the knife faster. The reins were almost cut through.

A hand seized her wrist, twisting, and she dropped the knife but kicked out as hard as she could. It was Mayerd, she saw when the next spear of lightning came down. Her heel struck his knee and he staggered back.

The knife, where was it? A scream rang out. She had to find the knife, but she couldn't take her eyes from Mayerd as he drew his longsword. She thought he carried that as part of his guardsman-disguise—she had never expected him to actually use it—

A crack like splitting rock nearly deafened her, and Mayerd spun around, pushing her to one side so that he could have the wall at his back. She fell, felt a blade under her palm and snatched the knife up, ducking into a corner of the open shrine. Then she looked up and saw the impossible happen.

The great granite statue of Sorlia rocked on its dais, swaying forwards. Alex watched in stunned disbelief. Even if Mayerd had spitted her on his sword in that moment, she wouldn't have been able to react. Then lightning flashed, and she saw the four men who stood behind the statue, on a ramp leading up to the wall, swinging a tree trunk like a battering ram. They shouted in chorus as they hurled the trunk forward, and it split against the statue.

Slowly, ponderously, the image of Sorlia toppled forward on to the shelter. It slammed the ground so hard that Alex felt the tremors in her bones.

Rain struck her face as she staggered to her feet, and the first man leaped down from the ramp. Three more followed him, knives in their hands. The fallen statue cut her and Mayerd off from the baron and his men—if they were still alive.

"Do something," she whispered to Mayerd. She wanted to cry out, but there was no air in her lungs. The brigands couldn't see his lateral lines in the dark and they wouldn't attack if they knew he was an Iternan. "Work your magic on them!"

The four men hesitated. She heard Mayerd's fast breathing.

"You *can't*." The realization burst on her colder than the rain. Either the brigands heard her or they reached that conclusion themselves, because they came forward, their knives gleaming in the rain.

Chapter Three:
Gathering Clouds

Alex pressed against the wall as the brigands closed in on Mayerd. Licks of flickering firelight played over their faces as they split up to flank him, and she knew they could take him down with sheer force of numbers. He backed away until his shoulders touched the wall, and they paced closer.

If they killed him, they would help themselves to her next. Only one thing to do.

She slipped her right arm behind her, pushing the knife into her belt. "Don't hurt me, please," she called out as her hands tore at the buttons of her shirt. "Please, I'll do *anything!*"

The fabric parted under her fingers and she pulled the shirt wide open as the brigands' collective stare darted to her, to the firm breasts that no half-decent woman would have shown a strange man. They were only distracted for a moment, but that was enough time for Mayerd. He sprang forward, his sword slashing in an arc that opened up the nearest man's throat, then twisted away from two other brigands as they stabbed at him. The fourth man raised his knife and turned on Alex.

"You bitch," he said and brought the blade down.

Alex shrank back, her right hand groping behind her back for her own knife, but she couldn't win in a fight. She tried to fling herself away, but the cramped corner of the House of Sorlia didn't favor maneuvers like that, and the ground was wet. She slipped, and as she went down, the brigand's knife drove into her left arm.

The pain was instant, burning like acid, and she bit back a scream as she fought to pull her own knife loose from her belt. It was stuck, and with her right arm trapped under her, she had no leverage. The man leaned forward, grabbing a handful of her hair. She tasted rain in her mouth as he hauled her head upward, and she knew he would cut her throat.

Instead, his blade slashed the air a few inches from her neck. Alex wrenched her own knife free as the man's body collapsed on her, and his weight took her knife up to the hilt.

She heard herself make involuntary sounds halfway between a whimper and a snarl as she struggled to get out from under the man's weight. Through her own runaway heartbeat and the slap of rain in her face, she realized that he wasn't moving. Was he dead? She remembered the other brigands and forced herself to lie still. If they thought she was another corpse, she would be safe. Steel clashed against steel nearby, followed by a choking scream.

Alex closed her eyes and opened them to look up into a sky black with clouds. Even the flames of the burning tree had died in the downpour of rain. Her cut arm throbbed, and she heard the agonized cry ring out again, but quieter that time. Then the body atop her was hauled off. In the next flicker of lightning, she saw the baron standing over her.

She froze, thinking of the stolen knife and her failed escape attempt as he went to one knee beside her. "Don't try to move just yet," he said. "Where are you injured?"

"Just my arm. My lord."

"All right, give me your hand."

The rain beat down on her, chilling her even further, but she couldn't disobey an order, so she held out her right hand. Gloved fingers closed on it and pulled her up. She stood, numbed and shivering, and saw at her feet the body of the man who had fallen on her. A deep gash opened his back.

So that was why he hadn't cut her throat. She was also grateful that the man lay face-down, hiding the stolen knife buried in his chest. Of course, Mayerd took two strides to the corpse and turned it over, exposing the knife.

"You stole that at the inn, didn't you?" He looked up at her, rainwater trailing along the twin ridges of his face.

Alex's stomach knotted. She had been so close, and if not for the brigands...

"Wrap this around your arm." The baron handed her a

handkerchief. "One of the bastards who attacked us is still alive, and I have a few questions for him."

Startled, she could only watch as he climbed over the statue. Mayerd got up, holding on to the granite sword of Sorlia for balance. His leather armor was slashed in places, a bruise darkening on his face.

"Let's go." He tilted his head towards the other side of the statue. "Robert didn't say you couldn't be present during the questioning, and I want to get out of the rain."

Alex thought again of escaping. Only Mayerd stood nearby, and he had no magic. She hesitated long enough for him to say quietly, "Robert can only be pushed so far. For now, he's willing to overlook your trying to run, because you saved my life. Don't do it again, because you'll never have another chance to earn his trust."

There was nothing good in a man who uses crucified criminals as arrow-targets, Alex thought, but she didn't have a choice. Her arm hurt fiercely and the rain had turned into a waterfall. She wouldn't survive long out in the wilderland, especially if other brigands waited there. Pushing back her wet hair, she buttoned her shirt again, then trudged around the statue, stepping over two more corpses. Mayerd followed her.

The statue had crushed one of the baron's men beneath it, and the others dug his body out while Robert kindled another fire beneath a makeshift tent. The drumming of rain on waxed hides was so loud that Alex couldn't hear what he was saying at first. Her attention fixed on a brigand who lay curled on his side, hands bound, the feathered fletching of an arrow protruding from his back. His face sweated in the firelight, and from the position of the arrow, she knew he wouldn't live.

And if the Bloody Baron had anything to do with it, he wouldn't want to. She trembled despite the warmth of the fire. Even after what Mayerd had said, she didn't believe the baron would let her get away with an escape attempt.

There was certainly nothing courteous or even reasonable in Robert Demeresna's face as he drew a dagger and pulled the brigand's head back by a fistful of hair. The blade pressed beneath a stubbled jaw as he said, "Do you know who I am?"

"Please..." the man gasped.

"I think you do." The dagger gleamed and a narrow red line traced the man's neck. "I think it's entirely too unusual that dogs like you should strike at a group of armed men."

"They set up the place, my lord," Peter said. "Those pit traps, the one that got Gavin, they have stakes buried in them."

The baron's eyes narrowed. "I don't believe that a pack of cowards would go to all that trouble to rob people." He brought the dagger up, then plunged it down. Alex shut her eyes as she heard the man's scream, but it went on for far too long, and when she dared to look, she saw the dagger buried to its hilt in the ground. Flecks of dirt covered the brigand's face.

"Be quiet." Mayerd pushed the protruding arrow-shaft with a finger, and the brigand fell silent. Robert jerked the dagger back up and touched its tip to the brigand's eyelid.

"Start talking." His tone was so calm that it made Alex wish she was anywhere else, including the castle of Radiath. "If you do, you'll die quickly and cleanly. If not, I'll be more creative."

"I—we were paid," the brigand whispered.

"By whom?" Robert asked. Alex leaned forward.

"I don't know his family's name, sir, please—"

"His own name, then."

"Jack. Tall, red hair—"

"Jack Iavas," Alex said, the name coming with no conscious thought. That was Stephen's aide, to whom she had been lent once. The brigand's terrified stare went to her.

"And he paid you to do what?" Robert turned the brigand's head with the flat of his dagger, so that the man was forced to look at him.

"Wait for a group of travelers on the East Road." The man's throat worked as he swallowed. "He—he said to kill all of you."

"Including her?"

Alex stiffened, her hands clenching—she would be dead if the brigand had been ordered to return her to Stephen—but the man whispered, "He didn't say about a woman..."

"All right." Robert looked up at his surviving men-at-arms. "Take him out and tree him."

The brigand screamed again, the sound cut off as a rag was shoved into his mouth, and Alex looked away as the man was dragged outside through the mud. To spill blood in a House of Sorlia brought bad luck, so the brigand would be hanged from the nearest tree. It was, she supposed, a quick enough death.

"Why would Stephen want to kill you?" she asked with little interest. She felt cold through to her bones, despite the fire.

"Garnath?" Robert frowned as he opened a saddlebag. "How are you so sure it was him?"

Alex shrugged. "I can't see Jack Iavas setting something like this into play without his lord's authority. Obviously it's Stephen. There are only two factions in Dagre now—Stephen Garnath and those who stand against him."

"Don't forget the Quorum." Robert took out a flask. "They're in the middle, and each side tries to sway them."

Alex hardly heard him as she stared at the flask, wondering if he would drug her again. He saw her fixed gaze. "It's just an alcoholic solution."

"I see." Was he trying to get her drunk?

"For your arm. Those weapons are none too clean."

She had forgotten about the wound, and when she looked down at her arm, she saw that his wadded handkerchief had turned crimson. Biting her lip, she let him cut away her torn sleeve. The wound was longer than she had expected, and would leave a scar.

"Doesn't seem too deep." Robert opened the flask.

Alex stared at the fire, pretending that she didn't notice his nearness and hoping that the goose pimples on her skin wouldn't give her away. She hated being so close to a man when she couldn't let herself go blank, her mind drifting as her body performed. Or better still, when she controlled the endeavor and remained coldly self-possessed, but here she could do neither.

"This is going to hurt," he said, and it was no lie. When he trickled fluid over her arm, the sting was like a wasp's touch, but she didn't make a sound. In the years of her service to Stephen, she had grown used to much worse than that.

Robert tied a clean handkerchief around her arm before he glanced at her face. "Keep that in place." He shook the flask, and she heard the firewater slosh inside. "Want some?"

Alex shook her head, aware that she had to keep her wits clear. They were not only outside the Siege Circle, but outside the law of the land as she knew it. Nothing was certain any more, and she couldn't afford to be drunk, no matter how tempting it might be to forget the past and the present and everything else.

"Thank you for your concern, my lord."

A nod was his only acknowledgment before he rose, his gaze going over her shoulder to the tree nearby. Wet earth moved under his feet as he left the shelter of the tent, and Alex leaned back against the stone wall of the ruined House of Sorlia.

"What happened to the signs?" Alex said.

The road forked, and the post that stood at its crux was conspicuously bare, the marks of broken wood showing. Within the Circle, that kind of defacement carried a silver penalty.

Robert only shrugged. "It was a harsh winter and the folk didn't have firewood. I don't blame them. I'm only surprised no one cut the post itself down."

Alex looked to her right, to the mass of trees called Galvede Forest. Even at that distance, she saw how thickly they grew in the spring.

"The Quorum owns that land." Robert's voice was hard.

Curious, she nudged the bay gelding to keep up with him. "Do they consider the trees sacred?"

His laugh was humorless. "Hardly. I've seen carts carrying trunks and logs away to their little strongholds."

They rode on, and before twilight they saw the first cottage, its walls a pollen-dust yellow. Since it was on the boundaries of the Quorum land, Alex guessed that the man who owned it fed his family through poaching, but he was kind-eyed and friendly, throwing open his tiny parlor to the men-at-arms and offering his even tinier bedroom to the baron. Supper that night was a pheasant stew, and Robert asked if the poacher, Sam Lisfent, had heard any news.

"About the Quorum, m'lord?" Sam shook his head. "No, all I saw was them dragging away wood, same as usual. Bloody thieves is all they are."

Alex looked down at her plate quickly to hide a grin. "Is that all they steal?" she asked when she had control of herself again. "No meat or fish or pelts?"

Sam frowned. "Now you bring that up, m'lady, I never saw them take none of those. But what they done, it's bad enough. The forest used to stretch all the way round my home."

That was true, Alex thought. The vegetable garden, with the first spikes of green pushing through the dark earth, was surrounded by the stumps of trees. Why would the Quorum only want wood, and so much of it that wide Galvede Forest had shrunk back? To build houses or castles? But surely anyone with that kind of wealth would choose stone.

"Where do they take the wood?" she asked.

"To the mountains." The poacher gestured, and Alex thought of the mountain range in the distance, peaks so high they were perpetually cloaked in clouds. Then, because she was tired after the long day, she put it out of her mind.

The East Road vanished under the horses' hooves. In the miles that stretched behind her, Alex saw the flat stones forced apart by weeds, but now the stones were gone. The only trail left was cut through the fields by the passage of horses and men, and it was too uneven for a coach to travel. Robert looked down at it with a faintly sour expression, but that soon faded.

She could see why. On the green hills that rose and fell in the distance were white tufts of sheep and Alex saw the black specks of dogs that lay watching. A shepherd waved, and the baron lifted a hand in reply. The hills sloped down to pasture fields where cows grazed among clover and plowed fields where tenant farmers worked in the chill winds of the sowing season. Many of them looked up and called greetings. Robert grinned back and spurred his white horse, riding past chestnut trees that still dripped with dew.

"There's Madelayn," he said eventually, pride evident in his voice. "Named after the first Baroness Demeresna."

Alex saw very little of the shops surrounding the town square or the twisted spire of a church. Instead, she thought how easy it would be for an army to march in force down the miles of the East Road and take the town. Madelayn was nowhere near large enough or armored enough to put up any resistance to Stephen Garnath's hounds.

They rode past the downs and the water-meadows, between the hedgerows that smelled of crushed hazel and green rain, to a house that was not the yellow of sandrock or the white of limestone. Alex raised her head, and the hounds blew from her mind like dust in the wind. She only thought how polished-steel the house looked, with its grey-tiled roof the color of silver beneath a cloud's shadow. On the horizon were beech coppices with black-slashed bark.

Robert spurred his horse into a gallop and the men-at-arms did the same, but Mayerd held back for a moment. "That's Fulmion, Robert's home," he said to her.

Fulmion. Alex remembered what little she had read of the ancient languages—that meant *lightning*. Then she flicked the bay gelding with her reins and it raced to the great iron gates where a lodgekeeper was already hurrying to welcome the lord of the land. Even at that distance she saw the concern on his face when he spoke, and as the gates swung open, Robert dismounted.

"*Who* came here?" she heard him say as her gelding halted.

"Quorumlords, my lord, two days ago to speak with you. Sorthry said that you were away on business, we didn't know when you would return, and thanks be that you—"

"Good." Robert took the white horse's reins in his hands. "Did the Quorumlords go back to the Mistmarch or did they seek shelter in Madelayn?"

The lodgekeeper looked at his patched knees, then at the house.

Robert's eyes widened. "In *my* house?"

"Yes, m'lord."

"They walked into my house in my absence? And squatted there for two days? I'd rather have a plague of rats!" The lodgekeeper cringed, and Alex didn't blame him. "What the hell do they...?" Robert paused, then turned to Mayerd. "You know what this means."

"Of course," Mayerd said. "They know of the meeting. Why be surprised? They have spies everywhere, walking the roads and listening in the cities."

"Damn them." With one sweep of his arm, Robert flung the reins at the wrought-iron gates worked with the sign of the lightning bolt. Alex's gelding snorted at the ring of metal on metal, but the white horse stood like a marble statue, only the heaving of its sides visible.

"I suppose the Quorumlords threatened to excommunicate my people if they didn't throw the doors open," he said. Alex saw the front doors of Fulmion open, but in the sound of the reins striking the gate, no one had heard it, and Robert had his back to the house. "And there's no way to rout them from their nest before the meeting is called."

"My lord..." the lodgekeeper began, his eyes fixed on the small procession. Down the drive they came, a figure in pallid robes escorted by two men in mail. And the crunch of gravel under their feet was loud enough for Robert to turn around.

Alex could guess how shameful it was for him to be met at the gates of his own estate by a Quorumlord, as if he were the stranger there, but there was a far greater concern at the moment. She kept her voice low but spoke urgently. "My lord, I should leave—if the Quorumlord finds out who I am—"

"No. This is my land, and I am the lord on it. I won't be ashamed of anything." Robert nodded at the lodgekeeper. "Open those gates wider. We're riding in once the Quorumlord steps off the drive. Or even before."

Alex's heart thudded unpleasantly. Somewhere on the long stretch of the road, she had lost her terror of the baron's temper, but she had no wish to be caught between him and the Quorum. Would this prelate, approaching like a ghost swathed in silk, recognize her as the Black Mare? No, of course not. She had never been presented to one of the Quorum. Still, what else could she be but a mare, when she wasn't dressed as a lady and she wore no marriage clasp? Robert, even humiliated and angry, owned the land he stood on. She had nothing.

Stonily, she held her head high and looked at the people who stopped at the end of the drive. The two men wore surcoats showing a spiked hammer raised to the sun. The Quorumlord raised gloved hands and slid back a cowl to reveal a woman's face.

"Welcome back, Lord Robert." She gave him a faint, superior smile. "My name is Victoria, and I represent the Quorum."

Alex stood at the window of the small room and wondered what she was to do now. Victoria's smile had vanished when she realized that the baron traveled with an Iternan and a woman not married to him. "Evidently you did not expect the Quorum's presence, Lord Robert. I must inform you that the Word of the High Quorum, who speaks for the Benevolent Ones themselves, awaits you and the other lords of the east. When you gather, he shall be present."

Robert swung himself back into the saddle, his mouth set in a hard line. "I hope the Quorum has made itself welcome in my house, Lady Victoria. Perhaps we can become better acquainted over supper." And he spurred his horse down the drive, leaving the Quorumlord in a cloud of dust.

Alex did not look forward to supper, but Robert had given the

1

order and she could hardly hide in her room, comfortable though it was. There was no connecting door to the lord's chamber, and there was no mirror reflecting the single bed. It was simply a guest's room, but she knew she was a prisoner there. What she disliked far more than being confined was the thought of facing Quorumlord Victoria across a table. There was a quality of purity about Victoria, highly bred and highly raised and very much aware of it. Alex knew the contrast between them was too striking.

But when the supper gong rang, the butler, George Sorthry, knocked on her door to say that the baron had been called away to Madelayn. An old cottager was dying, and Robert had ridden a fresh horse to the town to see the man. Alex no longer bled after a day's riding, but she was tired, and she could only imagine how the baron felt. The surprise showed in her face, because Sorthry said, "He's master of Dawnever, ma'am. When children are born, they're shown to the baron, so when men die, the baron must know of it. Still, it will be late before he returns, so he said that you might have a tray here."

"But will no one else be at supper?"

Sorthry's face never changed, but his eyes gleamed with amusement. "I think not, ma'am. I am afraid that the Quorumlords will have to dine alone."

"I think so too," Alex said. "Please send up a tray, and thank you."

"Lord Robert's orders, ma'am."

The next day there was a problem about which downs the sheep would graze on, and Robert was gone before breakfast. Once again Alex had a tray, but she ate poorly. Her sleep had been troubled again, with nightmares that she could not remember. Hoping that the fresh air and sunlight would help, she left her window open and later heard the stablehands talking. "And Lord Robert says to her, so polite, 'Lady Victoria, I am but a landowner, and landowners face such concerns. The sheep and the fields bring in money that puts food before you. So please forgive me your solitary meal.' Then he takes White Wind and he's gone."

Alex grinned. Robert had the correct approach—since the Quorumlords had commandeered his house, they were welcome to it. No one appreciated their presence except for the priest from Madelayn, who made a short visit. And even if she had not been confined, Alex would not have approached them.

She wished she could leave. The door was not locked, but when Robert had escorted her to the room, two of his men-at-arms following, he had told her, "Please stay here until I say otherwise." His voice had been firm and impersonally courteous. "The servants will bring your meals."

Food, but not freedom, Alex thought, so nothing was changed. And the writing desk was empty as an eggshell, so she had nothing to read. She tried to pass the time by devising ways to escape from the house, but any such attempt would be too risky. Even if she crept through Fulmion at night and stole a knife again, there were kennels, and she sometimes heard the dogs barking.

Still, no one had called for her or come to her bed so far. And to be waited on was a novel experience. Even when she rang the servants' bell and asked if she could have a bath and a change of clothing, she felt diffident. But the chance to talk to someone—anyone—couldn't be passed up, and Lucy, the maid who helped her undress, seemed friendly enough.

"Are the Quorumlords conducting devotional services, Lucy?" It was an innocent enough question, and leaving her room to attend a prayer had been one of her escape plans. She felt sure that the wishes of the High Quorum would trump even Robert's orders.

Lucy rang for more hot water. "No, ma'am. The priest in Madelayn, Brother Luke, he comes here for services." Alex understood that; the servants felt more comfortable praying with someone they knew. "And the Quorumlords keep to themselves." Her voice lowered in a confiding way. "Two of them are called Lord Desmond and Lady Victoria, but the third one, he's got no name. The Benevolent Ones claimed it as proof of his selfless nature."

They don't ask for a lot of evidence, do they? Alex wanted to say. The man pretended he had no name just to keep people uncertain and awed. She decided to change the subject. "Is it true, Lucy, that Lord Robert once ordered men to be crucified?"

"That's true, ma'am, but it was when a duke from the far city was visiting." Alex guessed that "the far city" was these people's term for Radiath. "And Lord Robert sent for the worst from Madelayn, who were to be hanged. Then the duke said they would have a wager on whose men were the better with longbows."

Alex's stomach turned over. "Lord Robert didn't refuse?"

"He didn't, ma'am." But there was no condemnation in the girl's face, only sadness. "He won the wager. There was blood running down into the ground. When the duke was gone, he ordered the crosses cut down and made into pyres for the dead men."

The hot water arrived, and she poured it into the tub as Alex began to scrub her skin. No wonder they had called him the Bloody Baron after that performance, and Stephen must have considered him a man after his own heart. Except someone as ambitious as Stephen could only be threatened—eventually—by a man who was too much like him.

"He's not...always so cruel." It was halfway between a question and a statement, and Lucy shook her head.

"My word, no, ma'am. He's a stern master, but he's never been unfair with us."

I wonder how fair he'll be with me. One thing was sure, he hadn't told the servants who she was, and she felt grateful for that. But at some point, the truth would come out. He couldn't keep an unmarried, unrelated woman in his house for long, and for the first time, she found herself regretting that she would have to leave Fulmion.

In the late afternoon, Alex, still fresh from her bath and wearing an old dress of grey wool, wondered what Robert's excuse for avoiding dinner would be. She hoped he would come back to Fulmion soon and make a decision regarding her, because this sort of existence couldn't go on for much longer. Everyone seemed to be waiting for something— the Quorumlords for Robert to arrive home while Robert, equally stubborn, was determined to wear them down. And she was just trying to tell which way the wind was blowing. After the hurry of the past weeks, the enforced inactivity was galling.

The wrought-iron gates creaked open, and she craned her neck, hoping that it was Robert; to her disappointment, it was a carriage crested with a poppy, the petals standing out in fans of vivid red. She had seen that sigil before, but where? She was still trying to remember when the second carriage arrived.

Robert wouldn't like more strangers here, she thought, then decided these were invited guests, since they hadn't spoken to request entry. And soon another carriage made its way up the drive. The light was fading, but she saw a woman step out of the carriage, a two-headed dog bounding after her. A maddog? Alex had heard the animals, bred in Lunacy, were loyal to the death, but she hadn't imagined that ladies traveled alone, with only such creatures as protection.

Stars glittered as the servants lit lanterns outside, but it was only after nightfall that the baron finally appeared, in the midst of a group of his men. Alex watched from the window as the stableboys led the horses away, their breath steaming in the cold air as the men entered the house. She wouldn't be allowed to dine with them, but she had to always look acceptable, so she was studying her reflection in a hand-mirror when Robert knocked at her door. He smelled of the outdoors—chill spring and earth, horses and leather.

"I trust you've been well treated in my absence?" He stood in the doorway.

Alex nodded. She was intensely curious about all the new arrivals, but perhaps he would be angry if she asked. After all, it was a presumptuous question from a mare. Yet he was more reasonable than she had expected, so, watching him carefully for any sign that she was on quicksand, she said, "In your absence, some visitors arrived at your house. Is this a new tactic against the Quorumlords?"

Robert peeled off his brown riding gloves. "I wish I'd thought of *some* tactic against them. No, my visitors are here for a meeting that I have planned for a long time."

Alex remembered what Mayerd had said—that the Quorum knew of "the meeting". "A meeting of people who oppose Stephen Garnath," she thought aloud.

His brows came together. "How did you know that?"

"What else could it be? My lord," she remembered to add. He was suspicious again but she could deal with that, and anyone who worked against Stephen had a right to be wary. "If you had called them together to discuss selling land, you would hardly be dismayed at the thought of the Quorum finding out—and the Quorum wouldn't bother anyway. For them to be involved, it has to be political, and the only political issue on anyone's mind is what Stephen will do next."

Robert shut the door. "Do you know?"

"I know he plans to be king of Dagre in all but name, but if you mean more specific plans, I'm afraid not. He didn't trust me that far." Alex tried to remember every bit of gossip she had heard, any chance boast that might help. "The last I heard, his hounds ranged out to Highfrost to put down a rebellion. Lord Raymond Quern came to the castle to complain about the army that had eaten their way through his land and demanded shelter from the sleet. I think he was afraid either the army or the rebels would put *him* out in the sleet. Stephen knew that, so Lord Raymond didn't get much compensation."

"Did he get you?" Robert said, his voice low.

Alex found that she didn't want to answer that, and a strange ache began in her chest. She looked away, at nothing.

"I apologize. I shouldn't have pried." Robert cleared his throat. "And my ill manners distract us from the point at hand, the information you have given me."

"My lord?" She glanced back at him.

"You can call me Robert, if you like." He sat down on the edge of a chair. "What you just told me, Alex—about the hounds in the north—I knew it already. I'd heard it from my cousin, who is a merchantwoman within the Siege Circle."

"Were you testing me?" Alex wasn't even sure whether to believe him, since she hadn't heard of a lady who descended to trade, or even considered that a lord of the land could have such relations.

He shrugged. "What would you do under the circumstances? I did have you as a gift from Garnath, after all."

That was true, and she could hardly fault him for his vigilance. "And you thought I was an assassin."

"And you nearly proved me right when you stole that knife." For a moment she thought she had gone too far, but then his eyes crinkled at the corners and she let herself draw another breath as he smiled. "Don't look so worried. I don't blame you for wanting to get away, since my reputation precedes me. Most of the time I like it that way, so Garnath doesn't think I'm the type to gather friends or organize resistance. But rumors are like rabbits—they spread quicker than you think."

"That's true," Alex said hesitantly. "Is it also true that you once impaled an opponent with a spike through his groin?"

"Yes. It was a duel I fought against a man called Gregory Forl, in the Scorpion Square of Empyrean, and he slashed my hand open." He held out his right hand, and she saw the scar that spanned it. "I dropped my sword and he kicked it away. I knew he'd spit me if I had no weapon. The spikes on the square-fence were rusty, so I broke one off and then he was on me. I went over on my back. He fell on top of me and his weight drove the spike in. I'll never forget the way he was screaming—or trying to."

Alex didn't know what to say. "Why did you have to fight him?"

"He tried to force himself on my cousin. I don't care if she goes unaccompanied into the merchant houses of the city, he had no right to lay a hand on her. Besides, I'm rather fond of her, and a wretch who tries anything of the sort has me to deal with. After that incident, she bought a maddog, and no one ever troubled her again."

Alex wished that she had someone to take care of her like that, but she kept a betraying look off her face—one didn't survive in Stephen's castle by wishing for what couldn't be. "Do you dine with your guests tonight, my l—Robert?"

"Oh yes. In fact, that's why I came up to see you. I want you to come downstairs and meet my guests."

"For what purpose, my lord?" Alex's heart sank like lead—did he plan to introduce her as the mare he had brought from Radiath? But she kept her tone pleasantly acquiescent. It didn't do to loudly proclaim dislike.

Robert looked uncertain, as though he had heard a few words of another language, and then the puzzled look vanished as his brows came together. "Let's get a few things straight, all right?" he said. "I'm not Stephen Garnath. I'm not going to pass you around to my family and friends like a plate of sweets. I'm also not going to tolerate any beating around the bush—if you have something to say, for all our sakes just say it. I hate guessing games. And I made that invitation to supper so that you could offer advice on our plans to escape Garnath's stranglehold. If you want to stay here, by all means do so, but I don't want you coming into the dining room and behaving like the main course."

Alex felt as if she had been slapped. Her cheeks burned, and that was something she couldn't control. She dropped her gaze, furious and embarrassed, trying to make herself murmur an appropriate apology. Robert rose, and she heard him sigh.

"I'm sorry," he said. "It's been a long day—but that's no excuse for my poor manners. Please forgive me, and I hope you'll do me the courtesy of being my guest this evening."

"I—of course." In all her life, she couldn't remember anyone apologizing to her, and that was unexpected enough for her to be off-guard. "I would be pleased to join you for supper." He looked relieved. "And I won't behave like the main course, or even dessert."

Robert smiled, offering her his arm. "Let's go, then."

Alex took his arm obediently, but she couldn't help saying, "If your guests include the Quorumlords, they won't enjoy eating with a mare."

Robert opened the door to her room. "That's their concern, not yours or mine. I'll warn you, Lord Desmond isn't too annoying, but you've met Lady Victoria, and she's a wolf in silk robes. As for the one without a name, the servants are afraid of him. They call him the Smiler, but we have to address him as 'Your Grace'."

The Smiler? Alex couldn't imagine a Quorumlord smiling too much, because the few prelates she had seen before had seemed solemn as the grave. She had no chance to hear any more before they were down the stairs, and a footman held the door of the dining room open.

Chapter Four:
The Quorum's Gift

Alex was too well trained to falter at the prospect of facing so many highborn and respected people, but she thought of the bareness of her arms and throat, with no marriage clasp and not even a ring or necklace to indicate her family's status. Even the clothes she stood in were not hers.

Then Robert led her into the dining room and the people seated around the table rose, except for the three Quorumlords in their pale robes. Robert went to the empty seat at the head of the table and a footman pulled out a chair on his right for Alex.

"May I introduce Alex Khayne, of Radiath?" he said to the gathered company. "Alex was a former recipient of Lord Garnath's hospitality, and she would like to participate in our work."

That brought a more relaxed look to many of the faces, and Alex memorized names as he introduced them. "My brother, Martin, and my cousin, Susanna Demeresna. Lord Nicholas Rauth."

Nicholas Rauth, Lord of the White Horn. Now she remembered where she had seen the poppy sigil before. Stephen had hoped, years ago, to gain the east by lending his support to one of its lesser provinces, what he called "impaling Dawnever on the Horn". But Nicholas Rauth was highborn to the bone and did not seem inclined to throw his lot in with an upjumped commoner like Stephen.

And sending me to him didn't help. Before she could even feign a response, Nicholas had said, "Tell Lord Garnath that I'd prefer a normal woman. One who can laugh or cry." He had given her a gold coin for her efforts regardless, but Stephen took it. Alex was relieved— that was better than Stephen trying to make her laugh or cry himself.

She wondered if Nicholas remembered her, but if he did, his blue eyes gave nothing away.

"Lawrence Chalcas." A man in black and gold bowed, but Alex noted the lack of a title or sigil. And whoever Lawrence Chalcas was, she would have heard his name before if he posed any significant threat to Stephen.

"Quorumlords Victoria and Desmond." Robert paused. "And His Grace, the Word of the High Quorum."

The three Quorumlords had taken places on Robert's other side, facing her across the table, and Robert had introduced his guests in the order that they were seated, starting opposite the Quorumlords so that they ended up last. Victoria's face looked carved from ice, but the Word of the High Quorum seemed not to have noticed, and that made Alex uneasy.

The butler poured wine and Alex took a generous portion of soup from a steaming tureen. Victoria had already been served, but she didn't seem any happier.

"Do you not give thanks for the meal, Lord Robert?" she said.

"Of course I do." Robert beckoned the butler over. "Sorthry, this looks excellent. My compliments to the kitchen staff." He glanced at Victoria. "May we eat now?"

Alex smiled inwardly, but the tension at the table didn't subside and there was very little talk as the fish was brought in, salmon from the river. Lady Victoria picked at it and plump Lord Desmond took a second helping, but the Word of the High Quorum ate nothing. Even his soup was untouched.

A roast goose was brought in and Robert carved the bird. Alex nibbled at the meat and listened to the desultory conversations around the table, which didn't include her. Victoria sat wrapped in affronted dignity, Desmond was too intent on eating, and the Word, a gaunt-faced man with eyes like copper coins embedded in his skull, was very still. He looked at Alex once or twice, long probing glances that unsettled her because he didn't look at her body. He stared into her eyes instead, as if he wanted to explore her thoughts rather than her flesh. *Still, he's not questioning me about what I did in Radiath.*

"Have you been long acquainted with Lord Garnath, Alex?" Victoria asked.

"Long enough," Alex said.

"In what capacity?"

"As his mistress."

The conversations stopped, and Alex was aware of the weight of all eyes on her. Robert put his glass down and wiped his mouth.

"You know, Lady Victoria," he said, "we have a saying about not asking questions when you're not prepared to hear the answers." Alex felt the weight slowly slip away as he continued, his steady gaze on the rest of his guests. "Garnath treated her as a kept woman and finally passed her on to me. She saved the life of the captain of my guard on our journey back—"

"Mistress?" Victoria said. "If I know Lord Garnath, he wouldn't think even that much of any woman. I believe that *she* is what was known as the whore of the hall—kept for the common use of any of the lord's guests, like a mat to wipe—"

"If you knew Lord Garnath, it wouldn't be half as intimately as I do." Alex's blood felt like liquid iron as it pounded in her temples, but she kept her voice level. "And while that's not something I'm proud of, it means I'm far more familiar with his tactics than you ever will be. You may call me a whore if you like—in fact, please call me whatever takes your fancy. But I intend to show Lord Garnath that injustice and ill use don't go unrepaid. And I certainly don't want him treating any other woman the way he treated me."

Victoria started to speak, but the Word raised a hand, then turned to Robert. His voice was quiet as the dripping of icy water. "If this girl is Garnath's slut, why did he give her to you?"

Robert shrugged. "Perhaps he tired of her."

"Perhaps she's a spy."

Alex's skin turned as cold as the Quorumlord's tone, but she raised her head. "I am not."

"You understand that the word of a whore is worth nothing." The Word's smile was as practiced as any of her sweet compliant expressions, and even less sincere.

Steady, don't let him frighten you. "How much is evidence worth?" Hidden in her lap, her hands tightened. "I came from Radiath with nothing, and on our journey to Fulmion, I was never alone. Even if I had somehow obtained writing materials, I had no chance to send messages to Lord Garnath."

"And she hasn't been out of this house since she arrived here," Robert said. "I've had her room watched."

"That is not evidence." The Word spoke with an assurance that made Alex press her nails into her skin, aware that he was no fool. "That is the absence of evidence, which is meaningless. You should be wary, Robert. This fallen child could be a knife in the night."

"An assassin?" Robert said. "I suppose that's possible. Alex, would you mind buttering your bread with a spoon?"

The Word's pleasant tone never changed. "You should be careful, Robert. A whore has no morality. She will use her body and her wiles to ensnare and corrupt you."

"That would indeed be a tragedy." Robert spoke as if discussing the weather. "More wine, Sorthry."

"Perhaps you should send her back to Garnath," Desmond said.

A softness deep as velvet filled the Word's voice. "Kindness, Desmond. In this case, kindness is called for. This bespoiled girl supposedly saved a man's life, so there may be some good in her." He gave Alex a slow measured look. "We could take her back to the Mistmarch with us, to teach—"

"No," Alex said, her manners and self-control vanishing together. Revealing her feelings might be a mistake, but she could think of few things worse than to be passed on to the Word.

Robert glanced at her, then turned back to the Quorumlords. "Aren't you afraid she would ensnare and corrupt you?"

"I think we are better prepared to deal with evil than you, Lord Robert." Victoria's expression suggested that either the evil or Lord Robert smelled slightly offensive. "And are you refusing a request of the High Quorum?"

"The High Quorum is welcome to my hospitality, but not to my household. She was given to me, so she stays here."

"And if the High Quorum takes an interest in improving the moral status of prostitutes," Nicholas said, "there are many more in Dagre."

The Word tilted his head. "True, if deplorable. But this one, my dear Robert, is in your house—and the High Quorum recognizes your importance to this land."

"What importance is that?" Robert nodded to the servants and they began to clear the table.

"What importance is that?" Victoria said. "Lord Robert, you do realize that only the east has not yet knelt to Lord Garnath, and you are the last bastion of this land?"

"I wouldn't go so far." Robert glanced at his other guests. "Lawrence Chalcas represents a powerful house, and Nicholas Rauth is Lord of the White Horn. They too oppose Garnath."

The Word laughed, a sound like dry leaves rubbing together. "No army would break its back on Chalcas Heights. As for the White Horn, it's too far to sway all the rest of the land. No, this holding is the plum of the orchard, and as easy to pluck. You're on level ground, poorly defended, and most of all, central to the east. Once the tyrant has Fulmion, half the battle is over."

That's what I thought. Alex was reluctant to believe anything the Smiler said, and yet she couldn't deny sense when she heard it. She waited for Robert's answer.

"Bring in the port, coffee and fruit, Sorthry," Robert said to the butler. "And send Mayerd in."

Alex looked up, surprised at the unusual request, but Robert didn't seem to notice. The servants brought a silver bowl of fruit and Mayerd carried the steaming pot of coffee just before the dining-room door swung shut.

"Sit down and help yourself," Robert said.

"What plans do we have?" Mayerd pulled out a chair, but he didn't touch the food. Beside the finely dressed Dagran nobility, he looked even more foreign and his studded leather armor gave him a crudely serviceable look.

"None as yet. The Quorumlord here warned us that our position would be difficult to defend against Garnath's hounds."

"I agree. What's the latest assessment of his army?"

"The rebellion in Highfrost is broken," Susanna said, "at small cost to the hounds. I've heard that Garnath's army still numbers nearly ten thousand. Of course, some of those are squires, servants and camp followers, not to mention heralds and scouts who won't do actual battle. Still, it's a daunting force."

Nicholas Rauth shook his head. "I can give you perhaps two hundred men, Robert. A quarter of them mounted."

"Thank you, but we don't make direct battle," Robert said. Alex let her breath out slowly, but she did not feel relieved. "Our combined forces would number less than a thousand, which is why I have no intention of making a stand at Fulmion."

"But you are the last bulwark of the east," Desmond said.

"I'm also a man who'd like to keep on living."

"Well, what do you plan to do then, if Garnath attacks?" Victoria asked.

"Fall back and burn everything," Robert said. "Garnath will find it difficult to keep so large an army supplied with food."

Mayerd nodded. "Especially if we cut his supply lines. We know the land, so we can set up ambushes and harrier parties."

Alex thought that was the best strategy they had, but Victoria shook her head. "You could defeat him, or at worst discourage him to the point where he retreats. Running is a coward's game."

"You ask us to engage in battle?" Robert looked incredulous. "Outnumbered ten to one, on land that your own superior has admitted is hard to defend? And you think *Alex* is the one working for Garnath?"

Someone chuckled, but the Word ignored that. "We need not *ask*, Robert. We could simply commandeer Fulmion and declare it a holding of the Quorum. Or we could withdraw the Quorum's sanction and the blessing of the Benevolent Ones from Dawnever Province. Then you could watch as the commonfolk fled your grounds."

Robert sipped his port before he spoke. "I will point out that you brought nine knights and twelve men-at-arms with you."

The Word's smile was wider than ever. "Indeed. Nine, for the number of the Benevolent Ones. Twelve, for the Mandates. And the Holy Order of the Knights of Katash counts three hundred."

"Then you could not take Fulmion, much less keep it." Icy courtesy edged Robert's voice. "And if you tried, the east would be so disrupted by infighting that it would soon fall to Garnath."

"It may fall to Garnath whether we're united or not," Nicholas Rauth said. "Isn't that why Aloewood hasn't joined our cause?"

Robert's lips tightened. "I sent a messenger to Lord Justin Vehessa, but he's more afraid of Garnath than of me."

"He should be more afraid of the Quorum than of either of you," the Word said. "But I am certain he will be inspired by your courage in defending this land."

"Why is it so necessary that we make a stand?" Alex asked.

"You will forgive me, my girl," the Word said. "I'm not accustomed to being questioned by a whore."

I'd like to dip you in honey and feed you to a bear. When Alex had been leered at or mocked by men, she had imagined such revenges, and the habit helped keep her voice pleasant. *Half a dozen bears.* "It is I who should ask for forgiveness, Your Grace. I only wish to understand the reasoning behind making a stand."

"Oh, that's simple enough." Mayerd spoke before the Word could answer. "If we fall back, if we play a game of hide-and-kill, that will deprive Garnath of a quick victory. So he'll look for easier prey—and he'll find it in the Mistmarch."

"What's the Mistmarch?" Alex asked.

"The mountain range we saw on the journey to Fulmion," Robert said. "That's where the Quorum keeps its own strongholds—I mean, monasteries."

"Oh, yes." Mistmarch was a fitting name too, since the mountain peaks were blurred and blue in the distance. "Is that where the Quorum takes all the wood it gathers from Galvede Forest—to these monasteries?"

Victoria's gaze swiveled like an owl's to her, but her voice was neutral. "That is where we take the wood. To repair and refurbish our monasteries."

Lawrence shook his head slowly. "If so, this repair has progressed for twenty years straight. They just burn it. When the wind blows from the west, it's always thick with smoke."

"Why is that, Lady Victoria?" Robert said. "Has it anything to do with the war effort?"

"Of course not," Victoria said. "And will you kindly stop discussing the Quorum?"

"No." Robert's voice was even. "In my house, we'll discuss anything we damn well please. And I don't see why the Quorum is so confident that I can make a stand here and survive, much less put up enough resistance to make Garnath think twice. So there is something you're hiding from us."

"I agree." Susanna turned to the Word. "Your Grace, you know our strength, which is a thousand men against Garnath's ten thousand. If we make a stand here, how will you even the scales?"

The Word showed her his teeth. "You will have the support of the Benevolent Ones."

"Shall I add nine to our total?" Robert said. "Even if you offer us the Knights of Katash, three hundred more men will make little difference. So we're back where we started, Your Grace. I will not make a suicidal stand here, and I will not order anyone else to do so either."

"You will. If you obey us, there shall be victory, and the bodies of our enemies shall lie like sheaves of wheat for the harvest." Alex grimaced before she could hide her distaste, and the Word saw that at once. "You feign delicacy, child?"

Thank you for giving me that opening, and I hope a plague of scratchskin infects you. Between your legs. "We will face an army several times our number, Your Grace, but you seem certain of victory. Is there something else, besides..." She paused, remembering the priest on the Red Road, and his boast about the blessing of the Benevolent Ones. *Gifts you cannot imagine.* Did the Quorum have secret powers? But they detested magic. Did they use it anyway and call it by some other name?

"You have some other way to defeat Stephen Garnath," she said, thinking aloud. "The question is, what?"

"That is no way to speak to the Word of the High Quorum." Victoria's voice flicked like a whip.

"Do forgive me. As it has been pointed out, I'm only a whore with no morality. I'm just curious as to why, if we adopted Lord Robert's original plan, the Quorum could not simply fall back to its monasteries and outlast a siege."

Desmond snorted. "The Quorum doesn't intend to skulk behind its walls. We have good weapons, so we'll use them."

Alex wasn't sure what weapons could hold back ten thousand men, but she set that aside. "Is it a question of supplies?"

Lawrence shook his head. "The monasteries aren't in any danger of starving. Two tributaries of the Stagwater flow down from the mountains, and I hear the Quorum has bought up plenty of supplies. Isn't that right, Susanna?"

"What sort of supplies?" Alex leaned forward before Susanna could reply. "Coal?"

"Right," Susanna said. "How did you know? The weather's growing warmer—the Quorum shouldn't need so much firing."

Alex's throat was dry, and she drained her glass of water, aware of the collective gaze on her. "Lady Victoria, would the Quorum be doing a great deal of smelting?"

"By hell," Lawrence said. "Is that why they felled the trees?"

"That doesn't make sense." Robert frowned. "They could simply buy weapons. They can afford it."

"But they're not forging ordinary weapons." Alex saw the Word's mouth twitch—the shape it formed was no longer a smile—and that stiffened her spine further. "Whatever secret strength the Quorum has, it's far cleverer than swords or spears."

"What else can you make with metal?" Robert asked. "And not something as mundane as armor. Come, Lawrence, you're closest to the Quorum's holdings. What have your men seen?"

Lawrence spread his hands. "Nothing, other than clouds of smoke and steam."

"Steam?" That made Alex think of laundry, not that she would have shown her low birth by saying so. "Could you use steam for anything?"

"Besides scalding someone, perhaps?" Martin asked. "I mean, it's just the vapors of boiling water. What more could it do?"

Robert chuckled. "You were always the good one, Martin, but I played tricks as a child. And once I fitted the end of a pig's cured guts over the spout of a boiling kettle. The cook came in and saw this swollen tube hissing and rising, and she thought it was a snake. I slept on my stomach that night, but it was worth it. So I have an idea what one could do with steam." He grinned at the Quorumlords, who looked back at him stonily. "Want to tell us more, Your Grace, or would you prefer to wait while we work out the rest of the Quorum's schemes? We can be here all night. There's plenty of coffee."

"Get these people out first," the Word said in a rasping whisper. "The whore and the Iternan. They're not to be trusted."

Robert leveled a look at Alex, and her skin warmed involuntarily under his gaze. "I think you've earned the right to be here, Alex. Would you like to stay?"

Alex could hardly believe he had offered her a choice. "Yes, I would. Thank you." Even then her training asserted itself, and her voice sounded as neutrally courteous as his.

Robert looked back at the Word. "Mayerd stays as well, and that's not open to debate."

The copper eyes studied him with the unblinking fixity of a snake. "The world is full of wickedness, and your refusal to heed sense is only one symptom of that disease. Nevertheless, we will be merciful. Victoria, my sister, you may speak."

Alex saw Victoria's throat work as she swallowed, but she spoke as if she was addressing a chapel full of penitents. "The scholars of the Quorum have conducted a number of experiments, and unlike any ridiculous pig's-bladder toys, our studies have focused on siege engines. Any such instrument that you use now will be powered by sheer strength of muscle. We wanted better machines of war and now we have them."

"But *are* they better?" Robert said. "Have you tested them?"

"The fire-rock cannons, yes." The matter-of-fact simplicity of Robert's tone seemed to have settled Victoria, and she spoke just as plainly. "Those could bring down a wall. The problem is moving them. They're heavy as boulders, and the steam-driven carriages aren't reliable. Steam lines leak, boilers overheat. One burst of its own accord—that was when we started implementing safety valves. Still, they're unsafe. I don't even need to mention the crude explosives."

You might not need to, but the rest of us wish you would, Alex thought. Now she understood the Quorum's secrecy.

"Could these machines actually destroy Garnath's army?" Nicholas Rauth asked. "Or even a single regiment?"

Victoria nodded. "If you could provoke their cavalry into a charge, for instance...and you poured blessed-fire directly into the midst of that battalion."

"Yes." The Word's smile grew as he continued. "Once a cannon was fired, those in the center of the charge would be unable to curb their momentum in time, and they would trample over the dead and dying. A second cannon would then spew destruction into *them*. Their horses might be used to arrows flying and swords slashing, but not to the thunder of a cannon's voice, nor to the smell of smoke and fire."

"Garnath's archers would hardly be idle during all this," Robert said.

"Hence the steam carriages," Victoria said triumphantly. "Those are spiked with steel. Drive such a carriage forward, and it will cut through any resistance."

As long as the ground wasn't soft or muddy. Alex felt uneasy. The scales had tilted during Victoria's confident recitation, and now the Quorum had the upper hand.

"If you bring these siege engines out of the monasteries," Lawrence said, "we could study them and construct more. Can you imagine—"

Victoria shook her head. "Unless an invasion of the east begins, the Quorum won't authorize any machines leaving our sanctuary."

"But why?" Lawrence said.

"Oh, please. If you copy their workings, just what will the Quorum be needed for?"

Robert laughed shortly. "I do admire frankness. Still, when the invasion of the east begins, how many machines will you give us?"

For the first time, Victoria looked uncertain, and the Word spoke instead. "Perhaps ten."

"Ten?" Robert might have looked less incredulous if the bowl of fruit had spoken to him. "Against an army of, what, ten thousand?"

"You won't be fighting them all at once," Desmond said irritably. "Besides, after they see the cannons belching steam and fire, they'll run."

Alex knew that wasn't likely. Stephen's officers would fall back, send small picked sorties, test the limits of what the new weaponry could do. Their columns would circle, probing for weak spots in the line of defense.

Robert obviously had the same thought. "I can't fight Garnath's army with only ten machines."

"Why, how many do you feel are necessary?" the Word said. "A hundred? Would you like a miracle from the Benevolent Ones as well?" In the taut silence, he continued. "We see no reason for your latest complaint. Now that we have promised you matchless technology, the war will not come to the Mistmarch. It will be settled here."

There was a new hardness to the set of Robert's mouth. "And if I refuse to court defeat and sacrifice myself? You'll use these machines to make war on me?"

"Why, no," the Word said pleasantly. "A better solution is to find some lord of the east who has both stomach and spine, who sees the prize that these weapons represent and who will be more than ready to use them in the land's defense. And if we gave the new bastion of the east our blessing, he might well decide to take Fulmion for himself." He tilted his head. "Unless he's already entitled to it?"

All eyes went to Martin Demeresna, and blood crept into the young man's face. "I couldn't do that."

"You could." The Word spoke as easily as if he was agreeing. "To save your land and your people. They need a leader whose strength—"

"You've made your point," Robert said, still steadily, not a hint of weakness in his tone. "If those are your terms, I will make a stand. And I have terms of my own—this stand will be carried out as I see best, which may not necessarily be as the Quorum wishes."

"Thanks be to the Benevolent Ones, who have granted you wisdom," the Word said. "As long as Garnath's hounds are breaking their backs on our combined forces, you may have as much of a say as you wish." Alex's heart sank like a stone, and all she saw was the gleam of moonlight on ten thousand helms.

"You said the weapons would be delivered to us if Garnath attacked," Mayerd said. "Would there be time to bring them here?"

Victoria nodded. "The quickest route to the east is past the edge of the Mistmarch, so our monasteries will see Garnath's army approach. Then we'll hurry the weapons to you on steam coach."

Robert's gaze was distant. "I wonder if he'll order the army to take another route—such as the Red Road."

Victoria shrugged. "News will still reach us in advance of the invasion. Garnath's troops are far too many in number to hide."

"True," Mayerd said. "But I don't think Garnath would trust solely to an army. Is it possible, Lady Victoria, that he might already know of what you've been telling us?"

"What are you saying?" For the first time since Victoria's revelation of the Quorum's secrets, there was hostility in her voice.

Mayerd didn't appear to notice. "It's something I would do. Plant a traitor in the enemy's ranks."

"That's impossible," Desmond said. "Oh, some inklings of our success have spread through the Quorum, but not details of the new weaponry. Why, the only people even allowed to leave the monasteries have been us and our escort guard, all trusted men."

And Stephen wouldn't use any of them. Alex felt sure that if he had spies, they would be inconspicuous and unobtrusive. Of course, such people would be unlikely to hear confidences from the Quorum, so she felt a little better.

Robert glanced at a time-candle carved in stripes. "It's late, so we had better end this meeting. I'm afraid I told the servants to retire after supper, since I didn't know how long that would last, but they will have provided water and fresh linen in all the guest rooms."

The Word rose. "Your hospitality is as great as your obedience to the gods, Robert, but we will return to the Mistmarch early tomorrow. One of us shall remain to watch over your household." A spy by any other name, Alex thought. "Victoria, my sister, the honor is yours."

Victoria bowed her head. "Of course, Your Grace." She left the room, Desmond panting his way after her and the Smiler.

Alex felt her hands fidgeting with each other and stopped them before they could pleat the edge of the tablecloth. Robert was no fool, but he was caught between the millstones of Stephen and the Quorum. He had no choice but to stand his ground and die on it. Then Stephen would take her back.

The Quorumlords' departure was apparently the signal for the supper to end. Mayerd held the door open for Susanna and the lords of the land. Her spine rigid, Alex stayed seated while hoping she could walk out too, but when she heard Mayerd close the door, that left her alone in the dining room with Robert. *Calm*, she thought, and made her hands relax.

"I'll say this for you, Alex." Robert poured more coffee. "The Quorumlords wouldn't have folded if you hadn't figured out their secret. That took brains."

If Alex had been told a month ago that she would be pleased to hear a compliment from a man, she would have laughed, but Robert's praise warmed her in a way she didn't expect, even though both his face and his tone were hard and serious. "Thank you." She hesitated. "You didn't mind my being angry with guests of yours, and Quorumlords into the bargain?"

"Anyone would have been. Though I don't expect anyone might have encouraged Victoria to call them anything that took her fancy. Good for you." Robert looked down at the tablecloth, then back at her. "But that doesn't change the fact that you are indirectly responsible for the Quorum's maneuvering me into making a suicidal stand."

All the warmth turned to ice. "I...that wasn't my intention."

"Nonetheless, that's what happened."

"You just complimented me on finding out about the Quorum's weapons." Alex's throat tightened.

If she had hoped her service would soften him, she would have been disappointed. "Those weapons have hedged me in like a wall of spears. Before Victoria told us about them, I might have waged a strike-and-run battle. If I try that now, the Quorum will call that cowardice and try to take advantage of it. Did you know about any of this?"

"No!" Alex forced herself to be calm. "I didn't. Do you think I was acting a role with the Smi—with His Grace?"

Robert shrugged. "Have you acted a role before?"

Alex swallowed through the constriction in her throat. Of course she had—she had played a part for every man to whom Stephen had sent her. She looked down at her coffee cup, thinking, *I won't show pain. I won't show anything.*

"I can't be sure of anything, damn it." When she glanced up, moving her eyes but not her head, she saw that Robert's fingers had tightened into a fist. The scar across his hand stood out in a ridge, but his voice was as controlled as ever. "Not of Garnath, not of the Quorum, and not of you. I wish I knew why he gave you to me."

Lifting her head, she looked straight into his eyes. "So do I." But she could guess. Stephen had wanted to hurt her, and he had known that even if the Bloody Baron wasn't as depraved as rumor had him to be, she would suffer nevertheless, seeing a halfway decent man and knowing that he would never trust her. "My lord," she continued, keeping her voice level, "what do you plan to do with me?"

For the first time that evening, Robert looked tired. "I'm not sure of that either. If we're defeated, I assume Garnath will take you back?"

Alex nodded. Robert had not laid a hand on her so far, but if he considered her his possession, he might want her to show obedience— if not loyalty—to him. She could hardly ask for her freedom in order to escape when the tide of battle turned against the insurgents.

"Well, he won't get you," Robert said. "I don't intend to have noncombatants trapped in Fulmion when the fighting begins, so you'll be sent to safety. What little safety remains in the east. That's a promise...unless you turn out to be a spy of any kind. But if you're as innocent in this matter as you claim to be, I'll give you what protection and hospitality I can."

Alex finished her coffee, to give herself time to think. "You can do that?"

"In my house, and on my land? Of course I can."

"I mean, I'm an unmarried woman, not related to you, living in your home." Alex lifted her chin. "Have you forgotten what the—His Grace said about my corruption of you?"

To her surprise, Robert's teeth gleamed through his beard. "Let's

call him the Smiler. It's so much more suitable than that pretentious
title. And I didn't believe a word of his honeyed poison, although I see
the reasoning behind what he said."

"You do?" Alex's heart felt like lead, and she braced herself to hear
that a mare knew nothing but carnal impulses.

"Yes. You might think that you have to pay for your room and
meals by offering me your...services. But that isn't necessary." He
looked as stiffly formal as Victoria, and more uncomfortable. "Since
Garnath gave you to me, I am responsible for you, so I'll make sure you
don't go cold or hungry."

Alex gathered her courage for one last time. "Do I have a choice
about any of this?"

Robert frowned. "What do you mean?"

"I mean, am I a prisoner here? You said I'm your responsibility.
Do I have to stay here even if I wish to leave?"

"Do you want any more coffee?" When she shook her head, he
filled his own cup and raised it to his face, inhaling the scent. "Alex,
I'm sorry, but I can't risk letting you leave Fulmion. I might have
considered it before, but not now. You know about the Quorum's
weaponry."

"And you think I'll send word to Stephen," Alex said tonelessly.

Robert set his cup down. "You even call him Stephen. Not Lord
Garnath."

"Because I've known him for eleven years and he was the first
man who ever..." Alex looked away, and this time she couldn't keep the
bitterness from her tone. "What does it matter? I'm your prisoner here,
just as I was his prisoner in Radiath. You even have my room watched.
I'm sure that if you had a cell, I'd be in it."

"You're not my prisoner." Robert's voice was hard. "You can leave
your room and go into the library or the garden if you like. I only ask
you not to wander any further."

"If that pleases you, my lord."

Robert sighed. "I'll take you to visit Madelayn tomorrow."

"If that pleases you."

"Don't be a bloody parrot."

He looked more exasperated than angry, but Alex decided she had
pushed him far enough. A lot of men might simply have hit her—and
had, for less. "I'm sorry. Do you have business in Madelayn?"

The moment of annoyance seemed to pass quickly as he smiled, almost to himself. "You'll see. Now it's well past midnight, so I'll show you to your room." He rose, taking a candelabrum from the table, and offered her his arm.

It was strange how he stayed courteous to her after a disagreement, and even the silence that fell between them as they climbed the stairs was unstressed. Still, she wondered if he would indeed keep his word and not try to bed her. That suspicion might never be far from her mind when she was alone with a man, but she hoped he wouldn't try, because she was too tired to pretend anything. *And I...I want to like him.*

Robert didn't try. He opened her door and handed her the branch of candles. "Sleep well. I'll see you at breakfast."

"Thank you," Alex said, which was not at all the correct reply, but she didn't care. It was what she felt towards the first man who had treated her as a lady, and who left her alone in her room. She undressed and slipped into bed, and when she realized that she was looking forward to breakfast, she smiled and blew out the candles.

"I see." Stephen Garnath heard his voice as if someone else in the room had spoken. Not surprising. He had had the shock of his life.

Ohallox shook his head. "I can hardly believe it either. Machines." He pronounced the foreign word dubiously—and as far as Stephen knew, there was no Iternan equivalent. Iternans had never needed siege engines. Magic accomplished everything in that particular land.

Dagre, however, was different, and he saw the alternate track down which the Quorum had forced the land. He supposed that eventually the Quorum might have unveiled its creations with much fanfare, announcing them as the gifts of the Benevolent Ones, and not to be mistaken for magic. But the threat of war revealed everything for what it truly was.

"And you heard everything clearly?" he asked.

Ohallox nodded. "I don't want to force sight transmission. That nearly always produces hallucinations. But hearing is a different matter, and the only symptoms of that are nightmares, which are hardly remarkable and which could be put down to the subject's own—"

Stephen held up a hand. "I'm not interested in the details. I just want to be sure of what they said."

"Well, I'm fairly sure. I was distracted once or twice—"

"Distracted?" He felt his temper slip its rein. Here he was with rebellion fermenting yet again—this time perhaps successfully—and the Iternan to whom he paid the fattest purse he had ever seen was waffling. His anger must have showed, because Ohallox straightened his shoulders.

"Yes, distracted." His eyes gleamed glassier than ever. "By the Iternan whom the Bloody Baron employs. Something is wrong there. He did not speak of either the Inward or the Outward Way, nor did anyone ask him of his talent. And his name... I have heard it before, except I can't remember who he is."

Stephen sighed. It was so like Ohallox to forget what was important. "Is he close to finding out what my mare will do?"

"No, he hasn't touched her at all." Ohallox's mouth crimped. "She appears to be under the protection of this baron."

"Oh, does she?" Stephen wished he could see the look on the baron's face when he realized who Alex really served, who listened through her ears and who would strike with her hands. "Well, there's no need to wait too much longer, unless..."

He thought fast. He needed a distraction, something to divert the apparently vigilant lords when his army marched into their land. A spectacular murder would do that.

"I have it," he said. "They expect the attack to come from the north or the west, don't they? I'll send orders to the army to march due south and then continue east. Off the Red Road, so that no passing couriers or traders will report their approach. They'll travel through Galvede Forest and use it for cover. Once my hounds cross the Stagwater, once they can be seen, order my mare to kill as many of the rebels as she can. Demeresna first. That will sow enough confusion to cover my army's approach."

"And the Quorumlord?"

"Not yet. I want to know all the secrets of the Quorum, but I don't intend to break my army on the mountains of the Mistmarch. This Victoria is a key to unlock the Quorum's door, and I won't have her harmed until I have what I need from her."

"It shall be done." There was a smile on Ohallox's lips, the shadow of a grin that never reached his eyes.

Chapter Five:
Hounds on the Scent

Ohallox steepled his fingers and frowned.

From outside, he heard the echo of the night watch's call sounding off the hours, a regular report from the outer wall of the castle. One of the patrols that Stephen had instituted, and completely useless against a trained Iternan.

That worried him. He kept wondering if the Bloody Baron's servant was as good as he himself was, as clever and highly trained. He couldn't detect probes or mental shadows aimed at his defenses, but did that mean Mayerd had not used any yet, or did it mean he was stealthy enough not to be caught? When Ohallox found himself leaving red dust on the floor to track any use of the Outward Way, he knew that he had to do something. Garnath hadn't given him any orders, but Garnath could hang himself. If Mayerd was as experienced a Wayshaper as Ohallox, Mayerd would lock minds with him sooner or later. So it might as well be sooner, rather than killing himself slowly with anticipation.

And if Mayerd was *not* as skillful—well, Ohallox wanted to know that too.

He considered using the mare against Mayerd, but decided against it. Acting through an intermediary, even one as finely prepared as the mare, was risky. Far more certain to use a probe—a direct vehicle that carried his distinctive signature. Let this silent Iternan know that he faced Ohallox, who had once been Submaster of Investigations in Nefance College, the great school of the Inward Way. As for what Mayerd had once been, that was a mystery Ohallox longed to unravel. He tried to recall in what context he had heard Mayerd's name, but all he felt certain of was that Mayerd had been associated with the College in some way.

Well, let's see, he thought. *Let's meet, on the Way.*

He sent out the probe, imagined it cutting through the distance between Radiath and Madelayn, shrinking the miles to stitches on a tapestry. He closed himself to all outside stimuli, feeling the probe move faster and faster as it sensed another Iternan, the mind for which it had searched, and it connected—

The impact slammed Ohallox back in his chair. His head rocked on his shoulders and his teeth snapped together. Desperately he withdrew the probe, wiping any traces it had left. Not that that helped, since Mayerd might force him on to the Way or simply attack him in reality, but it was one more precaution.

Small precaution, against so much skill. He covered his eyes. There was no need to make even a cursory examination of the probe, since he knew what had happened when it connected with Mayerd. It had crashed into a mental wall so strong that he was sure Mayerd had felt no pain at all. Forged from the power of the Inward Way, the wall had attracted his probe by its sheer might, and he had never seen anything like it. No one in Iternum, not even the Waymaster or Waymistress, put up such defenses. But then again, in Iternum, Way practitioners received silent messages from their friends and orders. If Mayerd was here, in a land that loathed both Iternans and magic, he would not expect any contact through the Inward Way—hence the wall that was stronger than steel.

And Ohallox could only imagine what talent it took to construct such a thing. He hoped beyond hope that Mayerd had felt nothing, that there would be no retaliation. And yet it made no sense. Why wasn't someone so powerful more well-known to him? Why hadn't Mayerd challenged him? Why hadn't Mayerd broken his hold on the mare?

Stop, just stop. He sank his teeth into his tongue to quell his rising terror. The new pain gave him a semblance of calm. *Now think. Yes, he has power that matches the Waymaster's, but you have talent and training too. Find a way to smash through those defenses and kill him. Because one thing is for certain—you will not be safe in Dagre as long as an Iternan so strong is your enemy.*

Alex woke with a start, her heart beating so hard that it seemed to fill her body with a single pulse. A nightmare again, but this time she remembered something of it. In the dream, she had stood before a great wall, clawing on it with her bare hands, finally biting it until blood flowed from her mouth. And all the time she had known, with the peculiar certainty of dreams, that what was behind the wall had been imprisoned for a reason, and she was letting it escape.

The image was so vivid, down to the coppery taste on her tongue, that she got out of bed. Careless of the cold floor under her feet, she caught up a mirror, flinging open the shutters with her free hand. Cocks crowed in the pale light outside as she looked at her face, relieved to see it unchanged. There were dark smudges under her eyes, but she felt sure that many people in Fulmion had not slept well.

Pushing her tousled hair back, she glanced out the window. The Word and Lord Desmond had already left, she realized, but Victoria and two of the knights knelt in the garden, praying with the priest from Madelayn. When they finished, the priest hurried away to a pony hitched near the stable. Alex thought that despite the distance from the town, it must have been a proud moment for the priest to greet the day with a Quorumlord.

And the morning meal was as pleasant as the supper had been tense. Robert's brother had left at dawn for Madelayn, and Nicholas was leaving too, to Alex's relief. She guessed he would not reveal that he had mounted the Black Mare, but she felt ill at ease with him. Nicholas was as coolly courteous as always, wishing her and Susanna farewell before he turned to Robert. "I've been away from the White Horn for too long. The bailiffs will be robbing me blind."

"Can't have that," Lawrence said. "Say you'll set the Bloody Baron on them."

"Better yet, the Quorum." Susanna picked her moment carefully, as Victoria was taking a large bite of bread.

"As long as it's not the toothless tig—" Lawrence cut himself off, but it was too late. Robert, who had got up from his chair to open the parlor door, turned around.

"Is that what you call him?" he said. Alex wondered what he meant, then realized that Lawrence had referred to Mayerd. The Iternan who could not work magic, a toothless tiger.

It was the first harsh note struck that morning, and to Alex's surprise, Victoria filled the breach. "That is how a great many people think of your friend, Lord Robert, and while it isn't complimentary, it is safe. Were your friend a sorcerer, he would risk having his throat cut, and you yourself would be much less popular. The Quorum is willing to conduct negotiations with you because we know you do not actually defy the Mandates. If you did..."

Robert shook his head. "Be that as it may, Lady Victoria, I will still not have Mayerd made fun of in my presence."

"I apologize," Lawrence said. "I let my tongue run away with me. He's a good man, Robert."

The simple truth of the last few words was enough, Alex saw. Robert nodded, opening the door, and Nicholas walked out to where his men-at-arms had assembled. Alex stood at the door, pretending not to notice that she wore the same grey dress that she had worn at dinner. She was well aware of both her lack of status and the fact that she was as much of a stranger here as Victoria. She didn't even belong elsewhere, with the commonfolk, and her heart felt heavy as she watched the red carriage clatter away.

In the yard, Robert turned from the cloud of dust and his eyes met hers before she could look away. With three quick strides he was at the steps that led up to the door.

"Want to come with us when we see Lawrence off, Alex?" he said. "It's a good ride up to the Downs."

After being indoors for so long Alex would have loved to ride out into the sunshine, but she shook her head. "I've no riding habit, but thank you."

"Oh, is that all?" He beckoned the housekeeper. "Find some riding clothes for her, Emily. And quickly."

Before she knew it, Alex was in the attic, with the housekeeper supervising a maid as she dug through a chest of stored clothes. "Whose were these?"

"Most Lady Anna's," Emily said. "She was my lord's mother, the Benevolent Ones watch over her. And some of Diana Besleter, who was to marry my lord."

"What happened to her?" Alex felt a little envious of any woman who could inspire men to marriage.

"She drowned in the Stagwater, my—ma'am. Lord Robert would have sent her belongings back to her family, but Diana was an only child and her parents refused them."

"They didn't want any reminders of her?"

"Yes. Shame, these clothes..." The housekeeper fell silent, but

Alex knew what she meant. The wardrobe looked not only beautiful but tasteful—no low-cut bodices, no sheers. And yet she couldn't wear them. Even the riding habit that the maid finally held up, as brown as an autumn leaf, was like a ring on someone else's hand. Alex admired it, but Emily had to urge her to put it on.

"Lord Robert won't like us being late," she grumbled, but as Alex hurried out of the grey dress, she unbent a little. "If you're staying here longer, ma'am, perhaps a seamstress can fit new clothes for you."

Alex shook her head with an effort. "I can't pay for that, Emily."

A softer look of understanding was in the housekeeper's eyes as she nodded. This house was certainly used to straight speaking, Alex thought as she slipped on a jacket and the maid laced up the boots. Her hair—the one thing she did own, thankfully—was pinned up neatly, and in moments she took the steps down to the stable yard, holding her skirts up with one gloved hand. Robert was tossing bits of meat to the maddog, and he dropped the whole handful of scraps when he saw her. The dog's heads began to fight over the meat, but Alex hardly noticed as she braced for an order to take off the clothes which had another woman's memory on them.

"Why, you look fetching," Lawrence said, and the moment was gone. Robert brushed his hands free of scraps.

"I've had the grooms saddle Tempest for you, Alex," he said as they walked out. A stableboy held the reins of a black horse as Alex mounted, and against its dark coat, the riding habit looked an even richer and glossier shade of brown.

"Won't Mayerd accompany us?" She looked around.

Robert's brows came together. "He didn't look well today. Mayerd's never ill—must be an Iternan trait—so I told him to rest. No point in his being too sick to carry out his duties."

"That's a pity," Alex said before she could think twice. She wished she could bite the words back, but Robert had heard them.

"Why?" He swung into the saddle of his white horse.

Alex cast about for inspiration, found none, and had to tell the truth. "I was curious about why he couldn't do magic." She gathered Tempest's reins in her hands and studied them. "I thought I might ask him."

She heard a quick exhalation that sounded like muted laughter, and when she looked up, the traces of a smile were just disappearing from Robert's face. "You're not afraid of him? No, I should think not, and it's to your credit that you'd ask him that instead of speculating behind his back." He paused. "But I doubt anything will come of it, Alex. I questioned Mayerd once before, but he doesn't say a word about what drove him out of Iternum."

"Did his people exile him because he couldn't do magic? I mean— is that lack of magic like a birth defect?"

"Oh, no. They wouldn't have let him take his first breath if that were the case."

The earth was soft with rain and fragrant with grass. Alex thought how different this place was from the castle, which she had been forbidden to leave unless some duke on Stephen's side took a fancy to riding.

"This is the northern boundary of Dawnever," Robert said to her, before he turned to Lawrence. "A safe journey. And I'll send a courier at the gallop if there's news."

Lawrence nodded. "If the worst comes, Robert, don't even think of standing at your post until they cut you down. Just take your people as far north as they can go. Garnath would be a fool to send his army into the Heights."

"The Heights aren't impassable in spring," Susanna said. "Perhaps they'd deter his army in winter, but not now."

"Let's not discuss this," Robert said firmly, "or he'll never get home."

"What do you raise there?" Alex knew Robert counted both commoners and nobles as his friends, but she didn't see how an untitled person could hold so much land.

"Oh, just enough vegetables to scrape by, mountain goats for skins." Lawrence took a quick sideways look at her and smiled. "Actually, my grandfather was penniless when he wandered into the Mistmarch, but in the mountains he found a copper vein that led to one of the richest lodes in Dagre. For twenty years he worked like a slave, saving every coin, knowing that if he once spoke of the wealth there, the nobility or the Quorum would snap up the land. Finally he had enough to buy it from the crown. By then he was too old and broken to do a day's work mining, but his sons developed the Chalcas Mines. Every child born on that land knows the price paid for it, and we will never let it go."

Trained as Alex was to show admiration to any man who wanted it, she found herself unable to speak now, to convey a feeling that was genuine for the first time. But Lawrence didn't seem to need it. He bowed to her and Susanna, and clasped Robert's hand before he rode off, his guards surrounding him.

Robert turned his horse. "It's nearly noon already. Let's get back home."

"Are we leaving for Madelayn afterwards?" Alex asked.

"What are you doing there?" Susanna said. "May I come too?"

"None of your concern, and no," Robert told her. "Mayerd won't be accompanying us, Alex, but I'll take a few of the men along." *Of course,* Alex thought resignedly, *in case I try to escape. And to forestall any rumors of immorality.*

An irrepressible gleam was in Susanna's eyes. "All right, be a clam. Alex, why don't we have tea together when you return? You must be bored to tears, with nothing to do in Bob's house."

Alex hoped that Stephen never saw this woman. "Of course, I'd love that. Thank you for asking me, Susanna." She wondered if Robert would forbid it, since he might not want his young cousin anywhere near a possible spy and certain mare, but he said nothing until after they had returned to Fulmion, left Susanna there and set out again.

"I hope you won't mind spending time with her, Alex." Robert had been firm and offhand with Susanna, but there was genuine concern in his voice now that she was no longer there to hear it. "She finds Fulmion dull, but I won't let her go back to the Siege Circle until I'm sure it's safe, and I certainly won't give Garnath the chance to use her as a hostage. Perhaps you can keep her occupied."

"Of course. Whatever you say." Accustomed to obeying orders immediately, Alex began thinking of ways to pass the time of a young lady who handled trade like a man. She had heard something from Lord Thomas Vallew about the rising price of wheat—would that be interesting?

"After we get back to Fulmion. For now, you enjoy yourself."

Enjoy myself doing what? She got her answer when they arrived at Madelayn and stopped before a seamstress's establishment. Robert smiled when she turned to him.

"Well, I did burn that...er...attractive gown you had on." He dismounted and held out his hands to help her from the saddle. "It's only fair that I should provide you with more clothes."

Alex longed to agree, but she shook her head. "Thank you, Robert, but I have no means of payment—"

"You paid me at dinner yesterday." A frown furrowed his brow. "Unless you really don't want anything new..."

Pride and wariness struggled with longing. She looked down into Robert's brown eyes, searching his face for any hint that he would deck her out as a mare, any lascivious indication that his tastes in clothing were similar to Stephen's, but she saw none. When she put her hands out, his grip was firm and impersonal.

And, as he had said, she even started to enjoy herself once she overcame her concern about the cost of everything. Stripped to petticoats, she stood while three seamstresses—all hastily recruited from whatever else they were doing when the lord of the land rode into the town—fluttered around with measuring string. In the front room, Robert gave orders as easily as if he was asking for glasses of water. "Morning and evening dresses, and a walking gown. Something suitable for supper—let them know if there's a particular style you like, Alex. Another riding habit—green, I think—and whatever's appropriate under all of those. Now, about boots...or do you like shoes better?"

"Oh, boots," Alex said. "They're more practical, surely."

His quick answering smile flashed out. "Practical they might be, but you need something fit for the house too. Evening slippers, but comfortable ones. Fetch the cobbler, ma'am."

The seamstress did as he asked, and Alex had her feet measured while Robert went out to make some other purchases. The seamstresses pressed a cup of tea on Alex and passed around a plate of biscuits while they asked carefully disguised questions about the Quorumlords, Stephen's plans and what she was doing in Fulmion. Accustomed to verbal fencing, Alex gave them cheerful, polite nonreplies and sipped her tea. When she finished, she was surprised to see that it was nearly dark outside, but Robert came back in moments later.

"Ready to leave?" He gave her his arm. "Madam Salinth, please have that wardrobe to Fulmion as soon as possible. Good day to you all." The seamstresses dipped curtseys, and Alex felt so happy that tears stung her eyes, but she knew she gave no indication of them.

"What a pleasant day." She mounted Tempest. "I hope you enjoyed yourself too."

Robert looked up at her, his smile as private and contented as that of a cat. "Oh, I daresay I did. Here." He handed her a long, narrow package wrapped in paper.

"Do you want me to open this?" Gifts were quite out of Alex's experience, so she only held it, the paper rustling under her hands.

"No, I want you to eat it. Open it, Alex—the damn thing's yours, you know." He shook his head, but by now she knew him well enough to understand the annoyance was only momentary, and she peeled away the paper. Inside was an ebony-handled riding whip, cool and smooth as silk, and her initials were painted on the black wood in white.

"You know," she said softly, "it would be a shame to eat this."

Robert chuckled. "May I presume that it meets with your approval?"

"It's beautiful. So this is what you did while I had my feet measured." To her own surprise, she found herself smiling at him. It seemed like the most natural thing to do, but she wondered in the back of her mind if he expected her to kiss him. No, certainly not with his men watching. "Thank you."

"It's my pleasure." Robert flicked his horse's reins. "Ready to ride? I believe there's wild duck for supper."

As soon as supper was over, Robert escorted Alex back to her room and left the house. His breath smoked out in one of the last cold nights of the year as he crossed the drive to the small buildings clustered close and set far to the right of Fulmion. No one noticed those unremarkable structures when the guesthouses, also to the right, were designed to be beautiful and built in yellow sandstone to catch the eye. The smaller buildings were where his household guard lived.

Even if Garnath had not made his bid for power, Robert would have maintained such a guard. Dawnever was too distant from the Siege Circle, too lawless. His guards were fewer in number than those of the Rauth estate or the Chalcas lands, but they were trained by raids from brigands in winter, and Mayerd had been their captain for three years.

He passed the first guesthouse, gravel clicking under his feet, and a man stepped out of the shadows. "My lord," he said with a slight bow.

Robert recognized the sun and hammer on the knight's surcoat.

Marian Perera

Victoria had consented to move into a guesthouse, to the relief of everyone, Victoria possibly included. "Are you guarding the place?"

"We maintain vigilance at all times, my lord."

Robert nodded and walked on. The single-minded dedication of the Katassian Knights was admirable, but he had nothing in common with men who never married, owned nothing but their armor and weapons, and supposedly inflicted wounds on themselves to increase their threshold for pain and make them finer soldiers.

On the other hand, he thought, except for the last trait, that could be Mayerd.

At the barracks, Robert met the sentry's salute before going to the largest building in the line. He paused in the unlighted hall to get his bearings and then knocked on the correct door.

"Come in," Mayerd's listless voice said.

He opened the door. Mayerd was off the narrow bed at once, his back spear-straight and his hands by his sides.

"Oh, at ease." Robert shut the door. "No, better still, sit down."

The small room contained the bed, a chair and a cabinet for Mayerd's few clothes. There was nothing else—no rug on the floor, no personal possessions, no indication that the room's occupant might be from another land. Robert had overheard the men joking that one reason the captain never had female company was because no woman felt comfortable in his cell of a room. Sitting on the battered chair, Robert understood that completely.

Mayerd sat on the edge of his bed and waited. His eyes were circled with sunken flesh, and while he showed no tension at all—no abrupt movements, no twisting hands—after twelve years, Robert had learned to spot subtler things.

"What happened?" he asked.

"Do you really want to know? An Iternan touched me."

Robert's first thought was for the security of his estate, and his second was for Mayerd's own safety. "Where?"

"Not that way. A mental touch—don't look so relieved, Robert, this is hardly good news. I don't know who or where he is. Or she."

"When did this happen?" Robert decided to take matters one step at a time.

"During the night. I suppose that was why I looked so ghastly this morning. I lay awake all night, waiting for the next blow."

86

"Were you in pain?"

Mayerd shrugged. "The initial touch was like an icicle pressing into my head. It wasn't so much painful as startling. Some Iternan is now aware of my existence, and I don't think he means me well."

Robert dredged up the little he knew of Iternan culture. "Is it one of those people who search for fugitives from Iternum? What do you call them—hunters?"

Mayerd's smile was bitter. "If a hunter tracks me down, I'll make a quick end to it myself on my sword. It would save us all a great deal of trouble. But a hunter wouldn't be this coy."

"Well then, who is it?" Robert realized even as he spoke that Mayerd had no idea. He raked a hand through his hair. "This is a fine flurry."

"I know. I want to do something—anything would be better than waiting."

"I'll speak to Alex. She mingled with the high nobility, so perhaps she heard about an Iternan one of them might employ."

"All right. As long as she doesn't have to force herself to tell you anything."

At moments like that, Robert wondered more than ever about the kind of existence Mayerd had endured in Iternum, but for now he had a more pressing concern. "By the way, speaking of Alex, did you know that Martin left Fulmion before breakfast? He told the servants that an old friend of his in Madelayn had sent an invitation. I was curious about that, so when I took Alex to Madelayn to be measured for some dresses, I looked for Martin. He was staying in an inn."

"Let me guess," Mayerd said. "He didn't want to share your house with a mare."

"Exactly. He agreed with the Smiler that a woman like her would be a bad influence. I asked what he thought she would do to me, and he hemmed and hawed before saying that a mare didn't even have to do anything to harm people—her nature alone was enough. I asked where we would be if she hadn't pieced together what the Quorum did in their strongholds. He said that if a murderer treated his friends well, did that excuse the crime? I said I didn't think anything Alex had done—or been forced to do, I'll warrant—was comparable to murder, and he asked if she had seduced me. That's when I...hit him."

Mayerd's eyes widened. "You did? Well done."

Robert shook his head. "It's not well done. It didn't solve the problem or convince Martin that he was wrong."

"Nothing will convince some people that they're wrong, so why bother? The most you can do is make your position clear, and I think you did. And please don't tell me you're going to apologize to him."

"I'm not sure," Robert said slowly. "If anything happens to me, Martin will inherit Dawnever. That's why I try to stay on the best terms I can with him, even if he does live near Joye and hardly ever visits. I want the next lord of this land to be schooled in its ways, and he won't be amenable to anything if we're at odds."

Mayerd spread his hands. "So what are you going to do—send Alex away?"

"No. None of this mess is her fault, and I prefer her company to Martin's, anyway."

"You like her?"

"She has a few admirable qualities." Robert had never been good at dissembling, so he cleared his throat and fished in his pocket. "Here." He handed over a small package.

"Admirable?" Mayerd's voice was amused, but he took the small parcel. "What is this?"

"What does it look like, a cow?"

Mayerd had always been difficult when it came to accepting gifts, and even if the gift was something practical, like a pair of gloves, he gave it quietly away later. Robert felt sure that this present would be as treasured as the others, so he got up as the wrapping dropped. Mayerd frowned.

"What *is* this?" he said again, holding up a toy. It seemed to have originally been a cube, but pieces of wood had been carved away so that while they were still held to a central core, they jutted out in all directions. Their jigsaw edges prevented them from being pushed in simultaneously to form a perfect cube.

"Where's this from, Robert?" Still frowning, Mayerd fitted one piece of wood in, then tried another, which refused to align. "Lunacy?"

"Looks that way, doesn't it?" It was the kind of thing that would have driven Robert crazy in five minutes. Mayerd studied the toy from all angles, then freed the first piece of wood and pushed in another, which fitted with the second but prevented the first from lying flat on the core.

"Well, you certainly know how to distract me from Iternum," he said.

And let's see you try to give that gift away, Robert thought as he left the room.

Three days later, the wardrobe arrived at Fulmion, so Alex spent the morning trying on dresses while Susanna advised her of the latest fashions. Some of her happiness vanished when she asked Robert if she could have notepaper to write her thanks to the seamstresses who had obviously worked day and night to prepare the clothes. He hesitated long enough for her to realize that paper and ink were a method of communication to Stephen.

"Never mind." She forced a pleasant expression, which felt like stretching muscles she had never used before. "Please convey my gratitude to them." Although she could no longer be angry at his understandable caution, she hated the constant cloud of suspicion that hung over her. She had started to venture through the house and into the garden, but she was not so much a guest there as a prisoner. It was ironic, but the only way she might have escaped the place entirely would have been if Stephen's army attacked it.

Except that she liked curling up with a book in the library, or choosing a rose from the garden to take back to her room in a slim vase. Fulmion was a gilded cage, but she found herself forgetting the bars occasionally. Still, even if Robert trusted her completely, what would she do? She couldn't leave, because she had nowhere to go.

So although the new evening dress fit perfectly, she went to supper feeling troubled. Robert had been out of the house at all hours in the last few days, as the spring lambing swept over Dawnever in a white flood, but he was in the parlor that evening.

He rose from his chair as she entered. "You look very well, Alex."

"Thank you," Alex said, pleased. She had heard plenty of eloquent compliments in Radiath, but they didn't seem as real or as welcome as a simple statement from Robert. "I hear Lady Victoria is joining us for supper."

"Ah, roast Victoria again?"

"More like pickled." Alex sat down. "She was in the garden yesterday and we spoke a little. She asked how you could possibly ignore the shadow of war that hangs over all our heads."

"Ignore?" Robert looked thunderstruck. "Is that what the silly co—

er, the Quorumlord thinks I'm doing?"

It took all her training to smother a grin. "Well, yes. Because you go about life as usual."

"If I didn't supervise the lambing, the wheat fields, the farm and the hundred other things involved in running an estate, who would? And the best way to calm people is to show them that not even Garnath can stop me from continuing my life as it was before I went to Radiath." His face set in hard lines. "I can hardly talk to a tenant farmer these days without being asked about a probable invasion. Ignoring the war is the last thing I could do even if I wanted to."

Alex nodded, feeling an unaccustomed sympathy. "Either way, you're in trouble. If you show fear or worry, the commonfolk will take their cues from that and be terrified, but if you put up a strong front, people think you're oblivious to reality."

"I hope no one else sees it as a front."

"I didn't mean—"

Robert put a hand lightly over hers, where it rested on the arm of her chair. "It's all right. You know a little more about our situation than most people do."

Alex fell silent, thinking ruefully that she could have been more tactful. She did know how vulnerable they were. Robert had asked her whether she knew of any Iternans in Dagre other than Mayerd, so she had told him of the sorcerer Stephen supposedly employed.

"It could just be a rumor about him, like those about you," she had said. "I never actually met the man." She wished she had. She might have been able to give Mayerd something he could use against the Iternan.

"May I pour you a glass of sherry?" Robert said, ending her preoccupation.

Alex nodded again, and he got up. "Just to be on the safe side, Alex, will you let me know if you see anything strange?"

"Such as what?" The strangest thing was that she'd felt no urge to pull away when he'd touched her hand.

Robert shrugged. "I know little about magic, but Mayerd says that one manifestation of it—the Outward Way—has to do with objects being moved or even flung around."

"Oh." Other than the infrequent nightmares, Alex's life was good, and there was not so much as a hair out of place in her room. She considered mentioning the dreams, but the butler showed Victoria into the parlor, and the moment was gone.

In the next two weeks, the spring weather grew warmer and Robert asked her to accompany him on rides around the surrounding land. She still couldn't leave the grounds of Fulmion alone, but that didn't matter as much when she saw the land and found that she liked spending time with Robert. She also felt more confident now that she actually owned the clothes she stood in.

Stephen's castle had been her whole world, so she was eager to see the Locking, a tributary of the Stagwater, and the high pastures. She enjoyed wandering among the trees and ferns, standing on the highest ridge of hills to look down at Fulmion and all the little satellite buildings around it. Robert showed her how to catch trout from the Locking and where the berries grew in shady hollows. In return, she introduced him to the power plays and secrets and hidden rivalries of the nobility of Dagre—things that he had never been aware of, since he had stayed away from Radiath until Stephen sent for him.

"It's a lunatic's game," he said after one of her stories. "Still, Stephen's allies seem cut from the same cloth—if he loses this bid for rulership, they'll desert him and begin an infighting for power that won't leave a single strong leader among them. That was what happened after the death of the last king—no heirs, so Stephen decided he could take that place."

"But who'll rule the land, then, if it isn't Stephen?" Alex answered her own question. "The Quorum, especially if they have all these magic-like inventions on their side."

Robert grimaced. "I don't care for that prospect either. Did Victoria speak of it to you?"

"No, but that reminds me—Victoria said that she had considered taking up residence in Madelayn. She feels she's presumed on your hospitality for too long now."

"Too long?" Robert raised his eyebrows. "Why, it's only been nineteen and a half days."

Alex laughed, astonishing herself, since she couldn't remember the last time she had laughed aloud. Robert regarded her with an amused look.

"So what does Victoria intend to do about her living quarters?"

"There's not much she can do." Alex had listened sympathetically to Victoria's concerns in that regard. "The Smiler allocated her very little money, and when she asked the priest in Madelayn if she and her knights could stay in the rectory, he pleaded a refusal. So you're stuck with her."

"That's all right, as long as she stays to herself and I get to show you the land." Robert studied her with an eye as keen as if he had been looking at a horse. "You know, Alex, the outdoors has been good to you. You used to have dark circles around your eyes when we were traveling to Fulmion."

"Oh." She was surprised he had noticed. "I...I didn't sleep well."

He frowned. "Do you still have that trouble?"

"No. I just have—had ill dreams at night."

All humor vanished from Robert's face. "You still have nightmares?"

Alex shook her head, not in negation but in a wish to change the subject. The last thing she wanted was his pity. "Nightmares are fine compared to some of the things I could have."

"Such as what?" Robert asked harshly.

"Diseases or scars." Alex's tone matched his. "Or bastard children." She stopped, shocked that she had gone so far. No man she knew would have liked a woman speaking in such a coarse way, so she looked away, struggling for composure.

"If Garnath had done nothing else, I'd still want to knock his teeth in for that." Robert's voice was taut with anger. "Is it him you dream of?"

"No." The nightmares were never so ordinary. In the last one, two days ago, she had traveled for hours on an endless road at night, while a creature followed her. She walked fast but it walked faster, until she felt its breath on the nape of her neck, and even then, she couldn't turn to see it. "The last dream was of a long road, Robert, that's all. Let's not talk about Stephen again."

"I won't mention him." He got to his feet, holding out his hand to her. "Come, let's ride down to the old mill. The last time I was there, a stray cat had kittens in the straw."

The army hid its pennants and put away its distinctive helms. No heralds announced its arrival. It moved through Galvede Forest like a scythe through weeds.

Stephen Garnath had not allocated great quantities of supplies for the men, but their general, Adam Nalle, was not overly perturbed. Scouts and outriders ranged out each day, finding cottages and homesteads that were quickly stripped of food, while the inhabitants— poachers and Quorum gamekeepers—were always killed. Lord Garnath's orders had been explicit: the hounds were to take the east by surprise. Lord Garnath had not, however, said anything about *when* their prisoners had to be killed, so the captured women stayed alive long enough to be passed around the troops. Nalle knew that such compensations made the crushing pace bearable.

Most of Galvede Forest was still untrodden land, heavy with moss and loamy earth. The horses had to find trails over the uneven ground, and the carts of supplies had to be taken safely through the green maze. There were boars in the undergrowth and snakes in the fern.

But after the Highfrost winter, the spring was warm and welcome, and Nalle pushed his troops as swiftly as they could go. Three weeks after Lord Garnath's orders had arrived, the eastern end of Galvede Forest was in sight, and another week took them to the banks of the Stagwater.

The huts of fisherfolk were quickly taken, and Nalle questioned the prisoners. Were any of them from Madelayn? Would they be missed? Were their supplies of fish or eels expected in the town? His greatest fear was that someone—a bailiff or a merchant—would approach the low-lying ground on the Stagwater's banks and see thousands of troops spread out where a handful of cottages had once been, tents pitched and fires lit, countless as the stars. The prisoners swore that no one was expected from the town and that they had had no visitors for weeks now—which Nalle guessed was somehow Lord Garnath's doing.

He sent a jackdaw back to Radiath, to report that he had arrived in Dawnever Province. Lord Garnath had assured him that when the troops marched into Madelayn, it would fall fast, and by the time they arrived at Fulmion, the Bloody Baron would be dead. An easy victory. He looked forward to it.

Ohallox looked up as Stephen walked in, a black bird held in one hand with its talons uppermost. He tossed a scrap of paper on the table, but Ohallox didn't need to pick it up to see the crude drawing of a stag's head.

"A sign?"

"Indeed. We agreed not to use words." Stephen grinned. "Be prepared, Ohallox. You know what to do."

Ohallox nodded. He had said nothing about the Iternan he had not been able to break or engage, and he hoped the hounds could take the man. Powerful as it was, the Inward Way would not heal a sword thrust through the heart.

"Good," Stephen said, as the jackdaw struggled to be free. He released it, and it deposited a white curl on the floor before it flew to the bookshelf. The bird's jet-bead eyes followed him as he walked out.

Ohallox leaned back in his chair and used a little of the Way. Spreading its wings, the jackdaw flew down and landed on the hearthrug. The flames played glossily over its plumage as it walked forward, into the fire.

The smell of roasting flesh and feathers was thick and reeking, but Ohallox did not notice. He was already within the mind of a mare, and four hundred miles away, Alex turned her head, looking at the swords that hung on the wall of Fulmion.

Part Two:

Shadowfall

Chapter Six:
Traitors

"I don't like the looks of that sky," Robert said at breakfast. "We'll have a cloudburst soon. I'm going to see that the flocks are moved from the water-meadows."

With the ease of long practice, Alex gave the impression that she was listening. Ordinarily, she would have looked forward to a glittering shower that made the grass smell fresh and polished the stone walls, but last night, the dreams had come again. She had woken early and now she ate mechanically. She was starting to dread going to sleep.

"Perhaps when better weather comes, Alex, you'd like to try your luck for salmon in the Locking." Robert got up from the table. "I'm sorry to leave you alone today. I'd ask Susanna to keep you company, but she's taken herself off to visit the Halforths."

"That's quite all right." Alex could tell that he saw something puzzling in her tone or demeanor, but before he could ask her what was wrong, Mayerd spoke.

"Robert, have you heard any superstitions about that river?" he asked.

Victoria had chosen to breakfast alone, so Mayerd had joined them, and Alex knew by now that he was more than simply the captain of the household guard. Still, he spoke so rarely that he seemed curt and standoffish.

Robert frowned. "The Stagwater? What kind of superstitions?"

"Ghosts." Mayerd's voice had an edge of contempt. "Those of drowning victims. They're supposed to come out of the water and search for the living. I heard it from Peter, who heard it from his sister in Madelayn. It's a new tale whispered in the town and it's having a bad effect on the people."

It sounds possible. Alex remembered that Robert's betrothed had drowned in the Stagwater, but she still found the rumor strange. People had known about that river for hundreds of years, so why had there been no stories of the water giving up its dead until now?

"Has anyone actually seen these ghosts, Mayerd?" she asked.

"Of course not." He looked even more dismissive—clearly magic was one thing, but ghosts were quite another. "Robert, I think there's nothing to this, but perhaps you can come to Madelayn and tell the people there's no worries. Or give me permission to take some of the men down to the river. When we come back, it will be the deathblow to this nonsense."

"Good idea," Robert said. "I'll ride into Madelayn with you as soon as I've made sure the sheep are moved. Would you like to come with us, Alex?"

Alex shook her head with real regret. "I'm sorry, Robert. Victoria invited me to see her before dinner today."

Robert raised a brow. "I'm surprised she unbent so far."

Alex wasn't surprised. After the first tentative greetings she had exchanged with Victoria following what Victoria called "that wretched supper", two things had worked in her favor. A long time ago, she had learned to be courteous and pleasant no matter what anyone had done or said to her. And she had learned to be a good listener.

Many of the men to whom Stephen had lent her didn't need a willing body as much as they did a sympathetic ear. They wanted someone who would listen as they poured out their grievances, someone who would understand—or pretend to, someone who would not interrupt to talk about other matters. Victoria was no exception, and since Alex didn't have to offer the usual bed services, she was happy to listen.

She was bored almost to sleep when Victoria talked about the Benevolent Ones, but she found subtle ways to steer the conversation to the Quorum's advances in technology. She longed to learn more about what the Quorum had discovered and now guarded fiercely, and Victoria was not averse to explaining. Like most people, she enjoyed expounding on a subject to an awed pupil, especially one who didn't seem either clever or powerful enough to do anything with the information. That day, she talked about the progress made in alchemy, leading to the use of fire-rocks, and what she called mechanical philosophy, which could even control natural phenomena.

"Like the weather?" Alex glanced at the grey sky beyond the window, recalling what Robert had said about a storm.

Victoria nodded. "To some extent. All the Quorum's properties, for example, are protected from lightning."

"Really?"

"Of course. Have you seen trees killed by silverbolts? The Quorum scholars realized that the Spears of Katash always seek a quick way to the earth. That's why they strike the tallest trees. But if you have a long metal rod nearby, the lightning prefers that to the wood, or to stone."

"Why is that, Lady Victoria?"

"Only metal is strong enough to bear the power of lightning without exploding or burning. But do you see the significance of this? If such a rod is fixed to the chimney of a house, extending to the ground, the lightning will use the rod as a conduit and the house itself will be unharmed."

Alex found that fascinating. "Yes, I see. But none of these houses, even Fulmion, have such precautions."

"Indeed." Victoria frowned. "Perhaps I shall send word to the Quorum, that a gift of copper lightning rods be made to Lord Robert as payment for his hospitality. Once he's won the war, of course."

"I'm sure he'll appreciate that, Lady Victoria. He is very generous."

Victoria studied her with a suddenly speculative look. "Alex, I hope you will not mind my saying so"—*whether I do or not, you would say it*, Alex thought—"but what is the nature of your acquaintance with Lord Robert? You must understand that the Quorum is willing to trust him with its most prized secrets and possessions because his honor is unquestioned and his behavior towards others has been exemplary." She flushed. "Of course, his manner of speaking is less than, shall we say, *refined*. I suppose it comes of his being a farmer. And his temperament could use some humility."

You could use some humility yourself. "I'm glad the Quorum has such a high opinion of him." She had to play for time, to make a suitable response. "Considering his reputation, I mean."

"As the so-called Bloody Baron?" Victoria looked magnanimous. "Well, the Quorum is privileged to know the truth that is hidden from less discerning eyes. We cannot approve of deceiving others, but we understand that he bought some peace in Dawnever by doing so, and we do not judge him harshly. I hope he is grateful for our leniency."

Alex imagined Robert listening and then replying to a speech like that, and she had to bite her tongue to keep from laughing.

"Nevertheless," Victoria continued, the word striking like a judge's gavel, "immorality is another matter. Lord Robert has never been guilty of that—unlike others whom I could name but will not—and there has only been one woman, his betrothed, whose name was linked with his. Until now. Whenever the priest from Madelayn comes here, he has some story about you and Lord Robert, some new tale that has spread through the town. The lord of the province is never held up to the same standards as those with less status, and the people will forgive him a great deal, but the Quorum feels differently. And his refusal to allow the Word of the High Quorum to take you into our safekeeping..."

"I understand. And I assure you that Robert's conduct towards me has been most correct."

"I hope it will remain that way."

Alex knew she should agree, but she was growing used to speaking her mind. "I am extremely grateful to Lord Robert for everything he has given me." She thought ruefully that she should have added his title the first time she had mentioned his name. "I wish that there was some way I could repay him for his kindness. And I certainly have no right to frown upon any of his actions."

She left the ambiguous words at that, seeing the satisfied look fade from Victoria's face. Good. Now any malicious gossip would be put down to her behavior rather than Robert's. Any dalliance could be blamed on her past and her character, and she didn't mind being a strumpet if that made Robert's position a little more secure.

"I see," Victoria said eventually, the pause and her tone indicating that she did not like the reply, but would leave it for now. Alex decided that Robert was right, a euphemism-filled talk could be a great waste of time. And what did Victoria expect her to do, anyway? She was a mare ridden for the pleasure of men. She wasn't as pure and high-minded as the Quorumlord and she never would be, so why pretend that she was?

Besides, I don't think I want to be, now. She flushed at the thought, pleaded a headache and took her leave.

The gravel crunched under her boots as she walked up the drive, and she found herself hoping that Robert had not returned yet. She wanted some time to be alone, to come to terms with the realization that she would not mind any advances he made.

I wouldn't mind at all. She looked up at Fulmion as if to see something, anything, to contradict her, and the clouds opened for a moment. The sun flashed out, white-hot, but Alex didn't drop her gaze. She felt far more blinded by the knowledge of her own warmth towards Robert.

Stepping off the drive, she walked into the garden. She didn't know when it had happened—wasn't attraction supposed to be something that struck like a thunderbolt? The first time she had seen Robert, she had been too terrified to notice much about him. And he wasn't handsome, not beside Mayerd's dark eyes and chiseled features or Nicholas Rauth's blond, aristocratic good looks. Robert's brown hair and brown eyes were plain and unremarkable, but she liked their color, which reminded her of crusty bread and autumn leaves just before they darkened fully.

But it took more than that to make a man pleasing—she knew because she had seen them all, from the ugliest to those considered a maiden's dream. And yet she preferred Robert. She liked the laugh lines that appeared around his steady eyes when he smiled, and she liked his hair, which was wind-tousled rather than slicked down with grease. And although he was not very tall, when she thought of the width of his shoulders, she wanted to smooth her hands over them and feel the muscles of his back under her palms.

Get a grip on yourself. Pressing her cheek to the cool moss on the bark of a tree, she closed her eyes. *This isn't happening.*

Except that didn't change anything, and she couldn't lie to herself. She hadn't felt attracted to any man since she had agreed to Stephen's proposal eleven years ago and then found out what he was like. There had been some men she found less objectionable than others, but she never had any choice about whether she would lie with them or not, so attraction had been irrelevant. Until now.

No, it still didn't matter, because even if she found Robert attractive she couldn't show it. He would be repelled by a mare, especially if there had been only one woman in his life previously, his betrothed. That was a long way away from her and all her experience.

And what if he wasn't yet convinced she was innocent of spying for Stephen? He might think she was coaxing him into a trap with her

Marian Perera

body. She sighed, rubbing her face to remove any traces of crushed moss. No, Robert needed a lady to wed and she needed someone who didn't know her as the Black Mare.

I'll go back to Fulmion and forget about all this. But she had not taken two steps before her boot struck the long handle of a garden tool on the ground. As she bent to pick it up, she saw that it was a pitchfork and her hand tightened involuntarily on the wooden handle, worn smooth from use.

She felt cold and strangely empty, a shell through which the wind had blown. For no reason that she understood, she kept staring at the sharp tines of the fork. Her hand would not loosen its grip on the handle, but that did not frighten her. She felt, in some visceral way, that this was *right*, she needed a weapon of some sort. There were enemies around her, there was danger, but now she was ready for it.

Then the impulse faded, and Alex released the pitchfork. She frowned, wondering why she had felt the need to protect herself from someone. She had had the same strange thought a day ago, when she had looked up at the antique swords over the mantelpiece.

Those aren't any good. Too heavy. I need a knife.

No, I don't. I'm safe here.

I will be safer when I have a weapon.

She went indoors, pausing in the kitchen. The cooks were at work and she couldn't take down a cleaver from the wall without being noticed, but she saw a skewer as long as her forearm. Slipping it unobtrusively into her sash, she went to her room.

It was odd, Robert thought. For three weeks he had expected a clear threat, the march of an army in the distance, but the worst that had happened was a strange vague fear in the town. Anyway, superstitions were easily dealt with. He would enter the town and declare that five of his men were going down to the Stagwater's banks. Peter would have to lead them there, because it took two days' journey and he wanted Mayerd close at hand in case news came of an invasion.

And thinking of Mayerd reminded him of the other Iternan's presence. "You haven't felt magic again, have you?"

"No." Riding alongside him on a grey hunter, Mayerd raised his voice to be heard over the thud of hooves. "But then again, I can't see Lord Garnath hiring an ordinary Iternan, with only basic knowledge of a Way. He's more likely to keep a trained Wayshaper, which means I

102

probably wouldn't notice a second attempt, and it might be successful."

Robert cursed silently. "Should I station one of the men to watch you?"

"No!" Mayerd said. "I don't like being stared at every minute of the day."

For a long moment, there was no sound except for the horses' hooves and the jingle of harnesses. "I apologize, Robert," Mayerd said finally. "I know you meant well—it's just that if you stationed a thousand men around me, there's little they could do. This Iternan follows the Inward Way, so if he's good enough with it, he could drive me insane. Even if he's not so skillful, he could send nightmares, hallucinations—"

"Nightmares?" Robert repeated. "Strange you should say that. Alex told me that she has nightmares sometimes. I thought they were of Garnath, but she said something about a road."

Mayerd turned his head. "The Inward Way always manifests itself as a road—that's one reason it's called the Way. Has this Iternan tried to get at her as well?"

"I don't know." Robert felt troubled. "She just said she has nightmares, and even that I had to wring out of her."

"Why didn't you tell me about this?"

"I didn't know nightmares were a sign of sorcery being used, Mayerd. You never talk about magic, you know."

"I know." Mayerd's voice was so quiet that Robert hardly heard the words. "But nightmares could be a sign of something specific—"

"We'll discuss it with Alex later, when we go back to Fulmion." They were almost at Madelayn, and he saw the weathervane on the church spire, the hens pecking outside a house. Once he was in the town square, everyone would come to see what brought him to town at the gallop, dust flying in his wake.

The horses thundered into the square and came to a halt. Robert swung out of the saddle and gave one of the Rynesser boys a penny to water the horses. Taking his time, he peeled off his gloves as Francesca Dira, the healer, came up to him.

"Is something wrong, Lord Robert?" She dropped a slight curtsey.

"Something about ghosts near the river." Robert kept his voice calm, but his temper simmered just below the surface. He didn't like being reminded of how Diana had drowned trying to cross the Stagwater. "Heard anything about it, Madam Dira?"

"I have." By now more people were gathering. "Rumors spread quickly, my lord, you know that."

"I do." Robert glanced over the crowd. Good, most of the men of the town were arriving. "But I'd like to know how this one started. From what Mayerd says, it doesn't sound like it's doing Madelayn any good."

"Business is down, my lord," an innkeeper agreed. "I serve a specialty, eels in cream, but that's stopped lately with no one wanting to go near the Stagwater."

Robert addressed the gathered men. "Is that a fact? Even though some of you have relatives who live near the river and fish it for a living, you're afraid to go anywhere near..."

He stopped, seeing the deserted Stagwater in his mind's eye, and the advancing army that he had been expecting for three weeks...but which had not come. Mayerd swore in Iternan, something he never did because it frightened people—they thought he was putting a curse on them—and Robert turned to him. "Send the word out."

"At once." Mayerd's face was hard and taut. "But shall we first find out who started this interesting rumor?"

"Oh yes." Robert remembered what Mayerd had told them, that Garnath would most likely have an informant. He turned to the crowd. "Who began this rumor? Let's start with you, miller. Where did you hear it?"

The miller had heard it from a farrier, who had heard it from Francesca. Robert raked a hand through his hair. "This will take too long, and I don't have the time—"

"Then let's pick another way." Mayerd's eyes narrowed. "A traitor would have to be someone with a little influence in the town, a person with reason to speak to everyone, a man to whom others would listen. And if I were to pick an informant, I'd choose someone who could move freely out of the town without being conspicuous."

"Even up to Fulmion, without being noticed," Robert said slowly. "Only one person from town has done that."

He turned on his heel and looked at Luke, the town's priest. Something flickered through Luke's eyes before he said, "Lord Robert? What's the matter?"

"Why did you turn down Lady Victoria's request for a room in the rectory?" Robert asked. "Anyone would be honored to put up a Quorumlord."

"And in any other case, Lord Robert, I would have. But Lady Victoria is a beautiful woman. The Mandates are clear on that point—immorality is to be eradicated, and I cannot do that if I am tempted by a guest within my own house."

"Then you could have moved out and given her the run of the place. You didn't, because you couldn't risk her finding out that you're Garnath's traitor."

Luke shook his head. "That is not true, my lord."

It was the honorific which snapped Robert's restraint—the politeness, coupled with the fact that the priest was simply wasting the little time they had left, stalling for Garnath's benefit. He took three steps towards Luke and grabbed a handful of the man's robes. There were exclamations from the crowd, but Robert knew that no one would lay a hand on him.

"Talk," he said briefly. "You haven't condemned this rumor, as the Quorum would normally do. You knew that the attack was coming from a direction we had never suspected."

Luke said nothing. After the first shock, his eyes were like dead lakes, calm and placid.

"Shall we take him back to Fulmion and work on him there?" Mayerd said.

Luke's lip curled. "I'm not surprised an Iternan would resort to torture. Do that if you like. You'll still lose."

"Will I?" Robert let him go.

Luke smoothed down the creases in his robes. "You and I both know that Lord Garnath's army can't be stopped. There's too many of them, far too many. Our only salvation lies in making peace with him, because a battle will result in our slaughter."

"And that's your response to a tyrant?" Robert wanted to wipe his hands clean. "You drop to your knees and do whatever he wants? Well, that isn't me, and it isn't anyone else in this town either."

There was a chorus of angry agreement from the townsfolk, but Luke's smile grew wider. "That's what you think."

"What's that supposed to mean?" The man's complacency was beginning to infuriate Robert.

"It means I'm not the only one who sees sense." Luke glanced at the gathered people. They stared back at him with hostility, and their muttering was louder. "It means that there is another who believes it's better to give in and live, rather than stand your ground and die as you want us to do."

"And who is that other traitor?" Francesca asked.

"Not one of us, Lord Robert," a magistrate said. "This man is lying to cause more trouble."

Luke shrugged. "Lord Garnath assured me that I was not the only one here who served him."

"Then *he* lied," Mayerd said. "I find that plausible enough."

Robert hesitated. He had overlooked something in the shock of the discovery, and now it came to him—what had made Garnath send his army through Galvede Forest, striking from the south, which no one had suspected? Certainly, it was clever, but the army was so large that surprise tactics should have been unnecessary—unless Garnath knew of the Quorum's weaponry. And how could he have known that? Robert didn't think that Victoria, for all her faults, would have confided the Quorum's plans to a priest who had not even opened his house to her.

Therefore, another person at the meeting was the second traitor. Not Lawrence or Susanna—he had known them for far too long—and for all their differences, Martin would never betray him. He also doubted that Nicholas could be bought off, and before Mayerd was a traitor, the sky would fall. That left only one person.

"We have to return to Fulmion," he said to Mayerd, then turned to the crowd. "Ordinarily, I would leave this man in the magistrate's custody, but we are on the cusp of battle. The town will be evacuated immediately. Taking prisoners along only increases the risk, and I won't have lawbreakers in my ranks."

Luke, suddenly understanding, took a step back from the gathered people. They began to move towards him.

"He betrayed us to the enemy." Robert mounted White Wind, then looked down at the crowd. "Whatever you mete out shall be justice."

Mayerd swung himself into the saddle, and as the priest tried to speak, his voice was drowned in the shouts from the crowd. The horses cantered out of the square, and Robert didn't look back.

"Alex," Mayerd shouted as they galloped out of the town. "You think it's her."

Robert didn't reply until they had put a little more distance between themselves and Madelayn, until he had a chance to get himself back under control. After he had come so close to trusting her completely... Well, now he knew why he had received Garnath's favorite mare as a gift.

"Who else could be the traitor?" He reined White Wind in and looked at Mayerd. "And this explains the attack on us in the shrine to Sorlia. That ambush was crude and it failed, but it did make me trust her enough not to hand her over to the Quorum."

Mayerd rubbed a lateral line. "I can't feel anything...yet."

"You think she's using magic?" Robert frowned.

"I think she could be acting as a pawn of that Iternan. It's possible, Robert, because if she was in Garnath's pay, she would never have revealed the Quorum's secret to you like that. Far more profitable to keep the knowledge to herself and approach the Quorumlords later. We have no evidence that she's a *willing* spy."

"That's true." Robert tried to give Alex the benefit of the doubt, then wondered if there was any doubt to begin with. "But she *is* a spy. Who else could have informed Garnath about the Quorum's weaponry?"

"I don't know, but why would she take his side? He's hardly honorable, so what's she getting from it?"

"Does he have some hold on her?" She had said she didn't have children, by Garnath or anyone else, and when Robert remembered her uncovered body, he decided that she had never borne a child. He also decided that he wouldn't think of her naked again, because the image was far too distracting. "A sibling or parent held hostage?"

"No. I spoke to her in the castle and she said she came to Radiath alone."

Alex's guilt, so obvious ten minutes ago, seemed less realistic now, Robert admitted to himself. "And she didn't behave like a traitor. She was edgy all the way from Radiath. If she was actively spying for Garnath, she should have been more cordial, to lull me into a sense of security."

Mayerd said slowly, "The Inward Way can be used to coerce people, to convince them to do things that they would not—"

"But she never even met Garnath's sorcerer."

"Oh, for crying aloud, Robert. If he could make her betray you, wiping her memory would be the easiest thing in the world."

Robert put that away with the little else he knew of Iternan magic. "All this is just speculation. We won't know until we return to Fulmion—the question is, should we? The last thing I need is to have myself made a puppet as I walk through the gates."

"You won't be." But Mayerd sounded doubtful. "That takes time, not to mention some proximity to the subject. The thing is, I don't know how much control this Iternan can exert over her. Is he looking through her eyes? That takes concentration, and he could do nothing else while he pulled her strings. And there might be a slight delay in her actions, while he considered what she would do in any given—"

"Mayerd..." Robert looked in the direction of Fulmion.

"Sorry. As I was saying, I can't think of any other way he could control her directly, so perhaps his control is more indirect. But if that's the case, it wouldn't affect you unless you were closer to her, unless she was interacting with you. And this Iternan wouldn't need to influence or control you."

"He wouldn't?"

"Not when he could kill you instead."

There was a knock at Alex's door. "Ma'am?" Lucy said. "Lady Victoria is downstairs, wishing to see you."

Alex thought of Victoria, the woman who had called her a whore. "Thank you, Lucy." Despite the knowledge of how much danger she was in, she liked the maid. "Lucy, would you go to the Home Farm and fetch me a pound of butter?"

"Ma'am?" Lucy stared at her.

"I think it would be good for you if you started out immediately." Alex looked straight into the maid's eyes. "It would be very good, Lucy, if you went now."

For a moment Lucy said nothing, then she bobbed a curtsey. "Of course. I'll go now." The puzzlement had faded from her face, and she looked serene. Alex knew that she would never even think about the order that had been impressed on her.

Orders were like that. She had to choose them carefully, but if she chose well, the subjects obeyed without fuss.

Now Victoria, the Quorum's bitch, and the dogs that panted at her heels—they were a different matter. Alex paused only to take the skewer from her room before she went downstairs. After all, she had to protect herself.

Don't kill Victoria.

The thought sprang cold and clear into her mind, as if a handful of icy water had struck her. Halfway down the stairs, she frowned, her fingers locking around the skewer.

Don't kill Victoria. Use her as a hostage.

Of course. She felt a brief surge of warmth before the world grew dark around her again, reminding her that she was on a dangerous road where wolves walked upright. Dropping her hand, she hid the skewer in the folds of her skirt and continued downstairs to the parlor. Inside, Victoria rose from a chair.

"Alex, you left in such a hurry that you forgot your reticule." She held it out.

"Why, thank you." Alex took the reticule with her free hand. One of the dogs in armor—like a crab in its shell—stood at the door, and the other was behind Victoria's chair, close enough.

"And I thought you might visit Madelayn with me this afternoon," Victoria said. "There are always questions about morality that a Quorumlord can answer, and it would do you good to be seen in my company." She paused. "What have you got—"

As Victoria's gaze fell to her right hand, Alex tightened her grip on the reticule and swung it with all her strength. It struck Victoria across her face. She gasped, stumbling back. Her knees struck the edge of her chair and she fell into it.

The knight behind her gave an exclamation and moved forward, interposing himself between her and Alex. If he didn't expect an attack—or thought it was just a fit of womanly pique—he was proven wrong at once. Alex's hand flashed up, and the knight was a moment too slow to block her strike. The point of the skewer drove into his eye with a squirting sound, like a grape bursting, and the skewer sank in for a third of its length. Alex threw her body at his, knocking him back against Victoria. He crumpled and she released the skewer, scrambling to her feet. Victoria screamed.

The second knight had time to draw his longsword, and he came forward, holding the blade ready. "Lady Victoria, are you all right?" he shouted, but his eyes, harder than the chainmail coif wrapping his head, were fixed on Alex.

This one was alert, but he could not frighten her. Raising her chin, she let her empty hands hang by her side as she returned the knight's stare. What a fool. Just as she had expected, he did not strike at an unarmed woman.

"Stand aside!" he ordered. Behind her, Victoria was trying to push away the dead weight of the first dog's body.

"Stand—" The word died away as Alex stepped forward. His eyes were wide, fixed hopelessly on hers, and he raised the point of his sword to his throat—

He broke the hypnotic hold. She could only imagine how much effort that had taken, but it was already too late. As he reeled with the shock of release, she bent and drew the dead knight's sword, which was heavier than she had expected. His body toppled as Victoria struggled out from under it, but Alex took no notice as she straightened and flung out an illusion.

The knight whirled and cut through the air five feet ahead of her, where the illusion of herself darted away. Even as he realized he had been tricked, Alex sprang behind him and slashed through the back of his leg. Hamstrung, the knight cried out and tried to turn, but only succeeded in falling to one knee. Alex drove the dripping blade into his mouth.

She heard a scream from the doorway, but she ignored it as the sword's point struck the back of the man's throat and punched through it. Gurgling noises filled the air, then died away.

Alex looked up, her mind as calm as ever, and saw the servants who crowded in the doorway, staring down at the scene, gaping at her. She dusted off her hands.

"You must clean up this mess." She met the servants' stunned or horrified eyes. "Emily, what's best for stains?"

"Milk, ma'am," the housekeeper said. "Or baking soda. But those rugs need to be soaked right away. I'll have the maids take care of them."

"Thank you," Alex said. Servants could not be trusted to be completely on your side, but they came in useful. As the maids rolled up the bloodstained rugs, she looked at the butler, then looked *into* him as the shock lowered weak Dagran defenses. "Sorthry, do you understand what has just happened?"

"Ma'am?" He was halfway there already, and she nudged a little more. "Please tell me."

"*Jevern.*" The Iternan title came to mind without conscious effort.

110

"I am your *jevern.* And my enemies will be here soon, so seal the windows and lock all the doors except one. Do nothing else, and do not obey anyone except me. Leon, tie this woman's hands."

Victoria got up as the servants said simultaneously, "Yes, *jevern,*" and when Alex turned to face her, the Quorumlord's face was pale as cheese except for a red mark where the reticule had struck her.

"What have you *done?*" she whispered.

"It's an ugly world," Alex said, shrugging, "and I do not intend to be victimized by it any longer."

"Alex, are you crazy?" Victoria looked faint. "John...Giles...what did they ever do to you?"

"They attacked me." Alex knelt beside a dead dog and took a dagger from its belt. "I simply protected myself."

Within the house, they heard the sounds of keys being turned in locks. Victoria shook her head. "How did they—how did you make them obey you?"

"It's called a frame shift." Alex slipped the dagger into her sash. "An alteration in perception. I redefined reality—your dogs are now a mess to be wiped up, and this house is an outpost to be defended—and they believed it, because the alteration is more comforting than the truth, and because my will that they should obey is stronger than theirs to resist."

Leon came in with a rope and Victoria tried to pull away from him, so Alex slapped her. She would have liked to use the Inward Way instead, but she remembered how the second dog had broken her hold. If servitors had such training, the Quorumlords probably knew more about resisting the Way, and she had no desire to waste her energy.

"You're doing very well," she said to Leon, and he smiled his thanks as he bound Victoria's hands and handed Alex the end of the rope. He remained standing in the middle of the parlor until she told him to bring two bottles of brandy to her room. Then she made her way to the stairs, hauling Victoria behind her. Upstairs, she took the brandy from Leon and ordered him to set a guard outside her door.

"What's that for?" There was another mark on Victoria's face, where she had fallen and struck the edge of a stair, but she didn't seem to notice it. "Taken to tippling?"

Her manner was so insolent that Alex lifted one of the bottles. "Would you like to see how this feels when it's inserted in you?"

Victoria's throat worked as she swallowed, then her eyes closed. She looked like a child caught in a trap, and Alex felt suddenly weary, an unseen weight settling on her shoulders.

"Oh, stop it," she said. "Don't be so gullible. This is for burning the house down."

"It's still there." Robert looked Fulmion over. The lodgekeeper opened the gates for them and the horses trotted down the drive. "I can't see anything wrong."

"That's the Inward Way for you," Mayerd said. "I feel it being used."

"Really?" Robert glanced at him. "What does it feel like?"

Mayerd traced one of his lateral lines with a fingertip. "These sting softly whenever power is in effect. And that's a natural feature of all Iternans—short of burning the nerves out, there's nothing anyone could do to take that ability away from me. Everything else..." He shrugged.

"So you won't be able to help at all?" Robert's heart sank.

Mayerd looked away. "I can try questioning her." He stopped, staring ahead at Fulmion. "That's odd. Why are the windows all shut?"

"I don't know." Robert reined White Wind in, wondering if the servants were preparing for the storm to break. But the day was still hot, so why didn't they let the fresh air into the house?

"The doors, too. Could word of Garnath's army have reached them?"

"If that were the case, people would be calling to us." Robert dismounted. "And at the lodge, we'd have been pelted with questions."

The house was as silent as a tomb. Robert looked around for inspiration, but saw only the gypsy's lace in the garden.

"Well, to hell with this." He could hardly expect the captain of his guard to walk into danger if he cowered from it. "The day won't come when I'm afraid to enter my own house. Let's go."

Mayerd's hand shot out and closed on his shoulder before he could move a step. That was betraying enough—Mayerd never touched anyone if he could help it. "Don't. We have no idea what's happening in there."

"We have no choice. What do you recommend doing?"

Mayerd glanced at the barracks. "I'll get some of the men."

That was so practical that Robert wished he had thought of it himself. "Yes, do that. As many as are on duty."

Mayerd hesitated. "I'd be careful of that, Robert. Some Way practitioners find it easier when many enemies are ranged against them. The mass of minds becomes protean, easy to shape, and group hypnosis is common, fostered by the—"

"Mayerd, we don't have time for this! Bring as few or as many of the men as you think best—just get a move on."

Mayerd thudded a heel into the grey's side and it galloped away. Robert watched him go, wondering what to do next. He wanted to walk up to the front door, as he had done nearly every day of his life, but he told himself that stealth would be a far better idea.

The problem was putting that approach into action. He glanced at Alex's window, but he couldn't see into it, and she might not be there anyway—too obvious. Even if she was in her room, he had no idea how to reach it other than climbing the stairs and following the landing. The ivy trailing across the walls would never support his weight. He considered leaning a ladder against the wall and climbing up to her window, for all the world like a lad gone courting, but if she had an ounce of sense, she would wait until he was nearly at the top and then dislodge the ladder.

And Alex had more than an ounce of sense. She was resourceful and clever, but it was more than that which tied his guts into a knot. She was damn near unbreakable. Even if the Black Mare had not been ridden by a hundred men, being handed over to him—tossed like an unwanted puppy into a pond—could not have been easy to bear. Alex had never cried or complained, even when he had burned her clothes and drugged her. The Smiler hadn't been able to crush her either. Now he finally admitted to himself how much he had liked and admired her.

I would give almost anything if she were not my enemy. If she were not a traitor sent into my home.

Hoofbeats drummed the ground, and he turned to see Mayerd approaching at a gallop. Behind him, the men kept pace as best they could, trying to avoid the earth flung up by the horse's hooves.

"I sent Andrew to warn the Quorumlord." Mayerd reined in and dismounted. "No one answered when we knocked at the guesthouse door."

Robert could only hope that Victoria had taken her leave of him and gone back to the Mistmarch. The last thing he needed was for a

Marian Perera

Quorumlord to be caught in this morass of traitors and surprise attacks and Iternan magic.

"I haven't told the men about what's happening," Mayerd continued quietly. "Do you want to speak to them?"

Robert shook his head. "When it comes to Iternan magic, you're the knowledgeable one."

The men drew up to them and, at a look from Mayerd, formed into ranks. Not that it did them any good, but Mayerd faced them as calmly as if he was conducting a drill.

"We have an interesting task ahead of us," he said. "Lord Garnath has just sunk to the low tactic of placing a spy in Fulmion."

"Who, sir?" Andrew demanded. The other men looked incredulous and angry.

"The question is how." Mayerd looked back at them like a teacher reciting a favorite lesson. "And the answer is magic. Garnath has employed a sorcerer for his filthy work, not that this magic can stand against good steel."

That seemed to raise their spirits. "Is the sorcerer actually in there, sir?" Peter asked.

"We'll find out when we escort Lord Robert in," Mayerd said. "He won't let any sorcerer hold Fulmion." The men nodded. "Just one thing. This magic may have overpowered some of the servants. They won't know what they're doing if they stand in your way. Try not to hurt them."

The men all wore armor of studded leather, with swords at their belts. Robert guessed it was that as much as Mayerd's insouciant tone that made them agree easily to what seemed like an amusing request.

"You're brave and well trained, all of you," Mayerd said. "Just be aware that you face magic—and this is called the Inward Way. Nothing may be what it seems. The Inward Way encompasses illusion, deception—"

"Mayerd." Robert didn't like interrupting, but the men were starting to look on edge, even if it was the first time in twelve years that Mayerd had had the chance to talk about magic.

"Yes." Mayerd blinked, seeming to return to reality. "If you don't mind, sir, I'll take the lead."

The men closed ranks as Mayerd set the pace towards the front door, and if Robert had entertained any hope that their fears were unfounded, it vanished. The approach of such a procession should have brought faces at the windows, but nothing happened as Mayerd drew his sword and turned the brass doorknob. The door opened.

Mayerd pushed it ajar with the tip of his sword, stepped inside and gestured at the men to follow. The entrance hall was empty, and the house quiet. Robert glanced around, and as his eyes adapted to the dim room, he saw the dark stains on the floor.

"What on Eden?" They looked like dried blood, but he didn't want to say that. The men were tense enough already.

"Could be real," Mayerd said. "On the other hand—"

A door opposite them opened, and the housekeeper stood in the doorway. A candelabrum burned in her hand, and she returned Robert's stare with no surprise.

"Emily, what's—" he began.

"I bring word from the *jevern*." Emily's face was calm and her eyes distant as a dream. "The soldiers will stay here, but you will go upstairs to her."

"What?" Robert said.

"*Jevern*." Mayerd shook his head. "That's the first Iternan word I've heard spoken by anyone other than myself in Dagre. It refers to one who walks the Way. If Alex is a *jevern*, this trap is worse than I thought."

"I still don't understand what she's done to them." Robert didn't take his eyes off Emily. "And I have no intention of going anywhere alone. Tell your je-whatever that."

Emily stepped away from the door and the butler came in with a silver tray, as if to press refreshments on the company. On the tray were the severed heads of Victoria's knights.

Robert jerked back, and the only sound he heard over the collective gasp of breath was the thud of his heart. He tasted bile, but he couldn't look away from those dead faces, from the bloodied eyes and sagging mouths. *Victoria. If her head is next...*

Sorthry didn't seem to notice what he carried, and there was no tension in the fingers that held the stained silver handles. "The *jevern* says that you would not wish her other guest to be inconvenienced."

"What's happened to you?" Peter asked.

"Leave him," Mayerd said. "No point in talking to anyone here— they won't hear you, or if they do, they won't respond."

Robert wrenched his attention away from the heads and looked at Mayerd. "The other guest—that must be Victoria."

Mayerd nodded. "It makes sense. Garnath wants the Quorum's machines, so it's in his best interests to keep Victoria alive."

"I don't understand, sir," Peter said. "Why are they doing this? Can't they see they've got Quorum knights dead—"

"If you really want an explanation of Iternan magic," Mayerd said, "they're influenced by the Inward Way. They see everything we do, but distorted, through a broken glass. That's why Victoria's death would be an 'inconvenience' to them."

"How could that happen?" Robert had a sudden terrifying vision of himself and the rest of his men ensnared in this madness, walking a nightmare road called the Inward Way themselves.

"The Way is very powerful." Mayerd still looked unaffected, as if he had seen the ugly scenario many times before. "Give it one starting-point—which would be Alex—and it extends itself from there. Its influence settles on everything within its vicinity, and every thought, memory and emotion is its food. And the longer you're exposed to it, the more effect it has on you, which means we need to finish this quickly."

Robert nodded. Mayerd's for-once-concise explanation had distracted the men from the ugly spectacle of the knights' heads, which was a good thing. "I'll go to Alex. Stay here and don't let anyone leave."

"You have your orders," Mayerd said to the men, then looked back at Robert. "But I'm going with you." Without waiting for an answer, he turned on his heel and crossed the entrance hall.

Robert saw a flicker of uncertainty touch his servants' eyes, but they stepped aside from Mayerd. He followed, ready to parry a blow, but neither Emily nor Sorthry seemed to see him. The faces of the dead knights had more expression.

He passed the mirror which hung from one wall of the entrance hall, and his reflection grinned at him. *Illusion. Don't look at it.* Mayerd held the door open for him, and the stairs were just ahead.

The rest of the servants stood on either side of the stairs, motionless as statues except for their heads, which turned in unison to observe Robert. A dustcloth was draped over the banister, and he found it hardest to look away from the reminder that a maid had recently been polishing the wood. It had been an ordinary day in his house, and now his entire staff stared at him with eyes as blank as ice.

"How did she *do* that to them?" he said.

"This is the Inward Way." Mayerd crossed the floor to the stairs. "And while Alex might be on it, she doesn't control it, which is why it's so dangerous. Garnath's Iternan friend might manipulate the Way from Radiath, but he's too far away—he's holding on to only one end of a snake. The Way is trying to establish itself here, to extend its influence, and we have to stop that before it takes us all into itself."

"Except you?" Robert couldn't help asking.

"Except me," Mayerd said, a bitter twist to his mouth. "Now hurry."

Robert took the stairs one at a time, ready for traps. Nothing happened, and the servants watched him like birds on the branches of a dead tree. Mayerd was ahead of him when they heard laughter—the giggles of a child as it rushed past them—except that no child was visible. Mayerd flung himself aside, his hip striking the banister.

"What is it?" Robert raised his hands in case Mayerd fell.

Mayerd looked away. "The Inward Way," he said dully, "when in force, can turn your own past against you, open the grave and resurrect every memory you have tried to bury. Remember that. Because I didn't."

Some day, my friend, Robert thought, *I'm going to make you tell me exactly why you fled Iternum. Just not today. And if we don't get to Alex in time, never.*

He hurried to the top of the stairs and followed the landing around to Alex's room, Mayerd a pace behind him, but he stopped when he saw her closed door. Two footmen stood before it, swords in their hands. He recognized the antique blades—they had hung on the walls of the parlor—but Geoffrey and Leon weren't trained in swordmastery. They could no more fight than they could fly. Robert hesitated, unsure whether to be relieved or to brace for a trap of some kind.

"Stand aside, Mayerd," Leon said. "Only the baron enters."

"No." Mayerd took a step closer, his own sword drawn and ready to parry. Incredibly, a slight smile touched his face, and for a moment Robert thought the Inward Way had taken him over as well. "To whom do I have the pleasure of speaking?"

Geoffrey's freckled face was slack, wiped clean of all emotion, but a strange light glowed in the depths of his eyes. "My name is Ohallox." He raised his own sword. "Have you heard it before?"

"No," Mayerd said. "But that will soon be the exception, rather than the rule."

"What do you mean?" Leon turned to present only the side of his body to Mayerd. Robert backed away, suddenly aware that two trained swordsmen had taken the place of his servants, and that he was armed with only a dagger.

"Simply that you'll go down in history, Ohallox, as the cause of the war between Dagre and Iternum," Mayerd said. Leon was on his left now, and Geoffrey on his right. "Or hasn't it occurred to you that Dagre will never countenance the use of the Way on its land?"

He feinted at Geoffrey, and as the man's blade came down, he whirled on his heel, slashing at Leon. Swift as his reflexes were, Leon's were as good, and steel rang against steel. Leon's breath hissed out between his teeth. Mayerd didn't even have time to grimace before he half-turned, getting his blade up in time to catch Geoffrey's. Again the clash sounded, and Robert's eardrums echoed with it.

"Dagre?" Geoffrey said. "Once its lords tear each other apart, Iternum can take this land. And I think I will be rewarded for my part in that."

Abruptly, Leon brought his sword in a fast arc towards Mayerd, a blow too powerful to be turned aside. In that instant of distraction, Geoffrey turned and charged at Robert. He saw the blade slice down towards him, with the footman's entire strength behind it.

There was no time to turn and run, no room to sidestep. Robert's arm flashed up, dagger in hand. His elbow locked, the muscles rigid, and the entire force of Geoffrey's blow struck the edge of the dagger's blade. Robert was driven to one knee with the impact, and his arm went numb before it flooded with pain.

And the sword snapped. It was an antique blade, beautiful in design and valuable, but its metal was not nearly as pure as that of the dagger, a newer and cruder weapon, but with a blade of the best steel. Geoffrey gasped, his hands still following the arc of the sword's swing, momentarily off-balance, and Robert slammed a fist into the man's belly. All the air left Geoffrey in a *whoof* and he crumpled. Robert tried to rise, the nerves along his other arm still singing.

Geoffrey raised his head, and Robert looked straight into Diana Besleter's face. He froze, the breath stopping in his chest. All he saw was the woman he had once loved, and her arms lifted to embrace him.

Someone gasped his name and struck out at Diana. Robert heard the thud of flesh striking flesh before a flailing limb knocked him to one side. A knife struck the floor and spun away. Then he rolled over and saw Leon stagger closer, a sword still clutched in his bloody hands. Mayerd, grappling with Geoffrey, saw nothing as Leon swung his sword down at them.

Robert caught a handful of Mayerd's collar and hauled him backwards just as the sword plunged down. The blade impaled Geoffrey's body and drove into the floor. Mayerd scrambled to his feet and drove his fist against Leon's jaw. There was an audible snap as the footman's teeth came together, and then his eyes rolled up in his head as he collapsed.

Mayerd caught him before he could fall, lowering him to the bloody floor. "Robert, are you all right?"

Robert nodded. "Did you see Diana—"

"The Inward Way used your memory of her."

"Thanks." Robert took a grip on a doorknob and pulled himself to his feet. "Leon disarmed you? How did he do that? No, wait, don't tell me. The Inward Way again."

Mayerd nodded. "In the far past, Iternans used weapons like this, and the Inward Way holds their memories too—"

"What did Ohallox mean about an Iternan invasion?" Robert asked abruptly. "Is that likely?"

Mayerd stooped to retrieve his sword. "It isn't. Iternum doesn't involve itself in the affairs of other lands, and under our law, Ohallox is a criminal for leaving Iternum without sanction. I think he's lonely enough to wish that his actions would be lauded by our homeland. Not that that makes him right."

And not that Mayerd would be considered much better under Iternan law, even though he was worth ten of Ohallox. Setting his teeth, Robert found his now-notched dagger on the floor.

"Open that door, Mayerd. Let's get it over with."

Mayerd reached for the handle of Alex's door, and when it swung open Robert saw them both. Victoria sat on the edge of Alex's bed, her head pulled back. Alex knelt just behind her, and the long line of a dagger against Victoria's throat was like a silver wire.

"You've lost, Robert," she said. "The Quorum will never help you after you let her be murdered in your house."

She raked the blade across Victoria's throat.

"No!" Robert rushed to the bed, but even as he caught Victoria, it was too late. Blood spurted from the deep mortal wound. He felt her body through the damp silk robes, but he felt nothing else as her life's blood spurted over him.

Illusion, he realized even as Victoria's weight crashed into him, knocking him off-balance. He stumbled and fell with her body atop his, and he heard her cry out as she was pulled away. A foot stamped down on his wrist to make him release the dagger, and Alex dropped into a crouch across his body. Her knee slammed his right arm to the floor.

"With the compliments of Ohallox," she said and smiled, her eyes empty and sad as the blade came down.

Chapter Seven:
Gathering Darkness

Robert saw the dagger plunge down to his chest. He was frozen, still stunned by the illusion of Victoria's death and there was no time to block the blow. "Alex, no!" Even as the words left him in a gasp, he knew they were the last he would ever speak.

The dagger drove into him, cutting through skin and muscle. He felt the shock of impact, but the sudden agony blazing up his left arm broke his paralysis. Alex's sprawled position—one knee on his stomach, the other pinning down his right arm—meant she was almost off-balance. Robert twisted to push her weight off him, and she pulled the dagger free. Desperately he lashed out, and his fist struck her cheek. The Inward Way overrode pain, he realized as she tried to stab him again.

And she gasped. Mayerd's fingers locked around her wrist, holding back the strike, and he tore the dagger out of her hand.

Blood scorched its way down Robert's arm. He forced himself to look, expecting to see a heartwound leaking his life away, but the pain stayed stubbornly in his left arm. Had she missed? She had been too close to miss by accident.

Keeping his grip on Alex's wrist, Mayerd pulled her to her feet. "How bad is it, Robert?"

"I'll live." Robert clamped his fingers over his arm. "Lady Victoria, are you—"

"Untie me and get me out of here." Victoria's voice was drained, but she appeared to have lost none of her charm.

Alex shook her head. Mayerd held her with one arm twisted

behind her back, but she didn't appear to be in pain. "Do you think this is over? I've only just begun."

Robert felt a sudden wrenching dislocation, as if he had been picked up and thrown out of the window. The room melted and flowed around him like stained currents, then peeled away in curtains of mist. He looked out over the familiar landscape of Fulmion.

Except that it was no longer familiar. A new standard flew from the house—a hound's head on a red field—and lines of chained people were being driven to work in the wheatrows. Even at the distance, he heard the crack of canes against flesh. The people were too far for him to see their faces, and he wondered why he couldn't hear them scream. Then he realized they were long past the point where they cried out with pain.

He began to step off the vantage point from which he watched, thinking only of stopping the brutality. Out of sheer instinct he glanced down, remembering that he was on the steep slopes of the Downs, and he noticed the path. Where he stood, the grass was trampled flat, smoothed down by unseen feet or hooves. He frowned, staring at the long makeshift road that extended as far as he could see—and which did not exist in the Downs as he knew them.

But none of that did, and none of it was real. It could happen—oh yes, if Garnath defeated him, it would—but it wasn't real yet.

The wind blew coldly about him as he hesitated, afraid to move. This was the Inward Way. And now the wind carried the sobbing pleas of his people to him; he even recognized their voices. A cane landed on a child's back and he heard a shriek.

It was an illusion. Robert closed his eyes. He didn't know what the Inward Way would show him next, only that none of it was real.

The screams grew louder, a chorus of torture. Were the slave drivers herding their victims towards him? The child's cries fell silent, and he nearly opened his eyes.

None of this is real, damn it!

"Alex," he whispered, not knowing if she was there, if she could hear him, if she even cared. "You're real. And you didn't kill me when you had the chance. Don't let this happen—"

Roiling confusion, as thick as nausea and as bitter, swept over him like a wave. It wiped away the screams and the wind on the Downs, leaving nothing behind but a great vacuum. He forgot what he was saying. He forgot his own name.

Nothingness was all around, and he felt empty space beneath his feet, waiting to suck him down. If he looked, he was lost, but he couldn't remember where he was—he *had* to look. His heart thudded with unreasoning terror.

No, he thought, fighting an impulse to open his eyes. In desperation, he grabbed his injured arm and clenched tightly.

The pain rocketed from a dull, throbbing ache into a teeth-grinding immolation. Robert threw his head back, struggling to hold on to the knowledge that the Inward Way had almost leached from him, struggling equally hard to stay conscious. His hand was wet with his own blood, but his eyes were still shut, and he knew what to do.

"Alex!" he shouted, not caring if anyone heard him. "Damn it, you wouldn't let either Garnath or me defeat you. Don't let this Ohallox do it either. And get me off this bridle path to nowhere. It's extremely boring." He wondered if the Inward Way would take that last remark as an insult. Did the Ways have feelings? He thought he was going crazy.

And solid ground formed under his feet. He felt warmth on his sweat-chilled skin, and there was the soft thud of a footfall nearby. His hands clenched, he waited, afraid to look and bracing himself for failure.

"Robert?"

It was Mayerd's voice. Robert still couldn't open his eyes.

"Where did we first meet, Mayerd?" he asked, his voice so tight with tension he barely recognized it as his own.

"On the edge of Rustwood. You were hunting a straig. You caught an Iternan instead."

Relief swept over Robert in a warm rush, wiping away the last remnants of the Inward Way's touch. He opened his eyes and saw the familiar territory of Alex's room. Mayerd had just finished untying Victoria. Alex was in a chair, her head buried in her hands, but when she looked up at him he saw the first tremulous joy in her eyes.

Robert's muscles relaxed, aching from the involuntary strain, and he sat down on the bed. "Mayerd, the Way—"

"You got off it," Mayerd said. "Well done."

"Robert." Alex got up, tears shining in her eyes. "I heard you call my name. I—that was real, and I saw everything clearly. I'm so sorry—"

"It's all right." Robert held out his hand but she didn't accept it.

Instead she sank to the floor and her head went down again, a lock of black hair spilling. Her shoulders shook.

"Alex—" He started to get up, intending to comfort her, and the sound penetrated. A muffled sob. She was crying.

Another sound echoed in his mind—the words he had called out earlier. *You wouldn't let either Garnath or me defeat you,* he had told her. And now here she was, weeping on the floor. If he had not been so taken aback, he would have acted instinctively, offering reassurance. But now he was thinking, wondering how likely it was that a woman who hadn't shed a tear at being given to the Bloody Baron would collapse and cry before him.

Alex raised her head, tear-stained skin glistening.

"Not likely at all," he said, staring at her.

"What—"

"Nice try. Just a little too melodramatic. I suppose you would have stalled me in this dreamland until Garnath's army arrived." Robert controlled himself, remembering what Mayerd had said—the Inward Way fed on emotion. "Enough is enough. I've passed the test. How much further do I have to go before the end?"

The room began to dissolve around him, and Mayerd spoke from the center of the fog, his voice recognizable, the words strange. "It's not up to you, *sarliren koit*—it never was. It's in the hands of the one who provided the starting point for the Inward Way."

"Ohallox?" Robert's heart sank.

"No," Alex said out of the grey blankness. "Me."

Everything shifted. Alex was sure she had won. She felt the man's heaving body under her—so familiar—and the face, it was that of every man who had ever used her, a dazzling mosaic that formed itself into one image, Stephen Garnath's. Her enemy. And she brought the dagger down.

"Alex, no!"

His voice rang in her ears, shattering the framework, shifting her perception, and for a moment she saw clearly, saw Robert's face drawn taut with shock and fear. Every muscle in her body wrenched, and the effort spent itself on the steel will of the Inward Way. *This must be done,* said the coiling emptiness within her mind. But her hand jerked. One small move was all that penetrated the unyielding control of the

Inward Way, but it drove the dagger into Robert's arm instead of his heart.

Pain flared in her face and then in her wrist as Mayerd twisted the dagger from her hand. He pulled her to her feet, but she no longer felt the floor under them. She was slipping back on to the Inward Way, the road she had walked in her dreams, except now she understood that there was no danger there, no more pain. And she knew that the man who faced her—whoever he was—did not want her to leave.

"Do you think this is over?" She welcomed the coolness as it closed around her. Odd how her thoughts didn't seem to reach her mouth. *It is over*, she thought, but heard herself say, "I've only just begun."

The room faded like a stain being washed out of cloth. *Safe. I'm not there any more, I'm not in a place where people hate me and inflict whatever pain they can on me.*

Robert didn't. The thought brushed her mind as lightly as a sigh and drifted away into the grey haze. Alex glanced down and saw a road of white stones, stretching as far as she could see in two directions.

She looked at the mist that swirled on either side of the road, and it was a blanket ready to wrap her in a sleep that would last forever. But something—a shred of curiosity, a last wish to see the world before her eyes closed—made her start to walk along the road. Around her, the mist formed spirals, blurred, made spirals again. She kept walking and tried not to look at them, because her head began to throb dully.

Behind her, the footsteps started. They kept pace with hers so well that she was never sure if it was an echo—an echo that grew louder—or if she was being followed. *Don't turn around. Keep walking. Faster.*

If I stepped into the mist I could lose my pursuer, she thought, but as she began to veer off the road she saw the crossroads in the distance. She hurried closer, only to find that the straight white road met another straight white road and the signpost was blank. In the road ahead of her, a tree grew, pushing itself from between the stones as she watched. In the road that crossed her path, a snake coiled forward.

It was the growth of the tree—years of branches unfolding in seconds—that stopped her in her tracks. *This is only another nightmare. None of it is real. I want to wake up, I don't want to be here any longer.*

Marian Perera

The tree grew flowers and they turned to glossy fruit as the snake slid closer, tongue flickering. Alex stared at it, willing herself to run, but nothing happened. Behind her, the footsteps came closer. She was trapped between the snake and her unseen pursuer.

The snake was so close that she could have stepped on it if she had been capable of movement—and if she had not been so afraid. It was as long as she was tall, and as thick as her wrist. Its head lifted to the level of her face.

"Alex," it whispered.

The voice was Mayerd's, but she wasn't surprised. This was, after all, a nightmare—anything could happen, and anything would. She stared at the snake with a numb lack of interest.

"Don't detach from the Way," the snake said. The mist thickened, turned into pulsing grey clouds. "*Use* it instead."

Lightning flickered between the clouds overhead.

"How?" A fruit fell from the tree and smashed on the path, spilling seeds and a winy smell. She ignored it.

"The Way feeds off your mind and your emotions. But you were its stepping stone, so you can use it to find Ohallox, the one who—"

Lightning speared down, striking the snake. Alex gasped, flinging herself back as the snake's body exploded into ash. Too late she remembered the pursuer, just behind her. She turned, scrabbling to rise, and she saw what stood in the road.

It was herself, staring straight at her with eyes as green as glass. And when the thunder roared, her mirror image vanished.

I could have stepped off the Way. I could have lost myself in a dream that lasted forever—because I was trying to run from myself.

She turned, seeing the lightning bleach fallen fruit to skulls as it stabbed the path here and there, as if trying to strike an invisible enemy. A wind stripped the leaves from the tree so that only black branches jutted into the air. "Ohallox," she said, raising her voice to a shout that matched the wind. "You're on the Way too. And I will hunt you down."

For a moment the storm paused, seemed to flinch, and Alex wondered what she had said. Had it simply been her defiance, something that no one would expect from a mare trained to obey all her life? Well, no more. She was going to find Ohallox, and if Mayerd had said she could use the Way, she would. As a hunter—not one of

126

Stephen's hounds, but something quicker and fiercer by far—

She felt her clothes vanish like dust in the wind, felt her body change, a snarl starting in the depths of her throat. Dropping to all four paws, she scented the man who watched her.

He sent the lightning. Tear the clouds apart. I want to see him.

The clouds ripped. She had one glimpse of a man's startled face— the lateral line on each cheek was all she needed to see—and then he struck back, forcing terror and revulsion and blinding panic into her. But she had felt it all before as a mare ridden and used, and she controlled herself, suppressing the roil of emotion. Since she wasn't an Iternan, she couldn't make Ohallox feel the same way, so she did the next best thing.

I want to get at him. And tear out his throat.

The Inward Way arched. Alex sprang forward, following the white curve that looked like a satin ribbon whipping in the gale. She climbed higher than the twisted tree, higher than the clouds, and even over the howl of the storm, she heard Ohallox's startled gasp as she reached him.

He flung lightning at her. Her reflexes were good, but the Inward Way was too narrow to maneuver on, and the white-hot bolt struck her foreleg. She dropped to the Way, muscles spasming, her lips drawing back from her fangs as she stared at him. He was already retreating into the clouds. His image grew smaller as if he was a puppet drawn back by some great unseen hand, and she knew that he was detaching—safely—from the Inward Way.

Oh no, you don't. She struggled up, only to find her leg folding under her. *All right, then. If I can't go to you, you'll come to me.*

The Inward Way extended like a whiplash, sliding under Ohallox's feet, contracting and coiling in on itself to pull him closer. She saw his face twist with shock, then rage flared in his eyes, making them swell and gleam yellow. His mouth lengthened into a muzzle. She stared at the Inward Way that was pulling a dragon towards her.

Terror filled her, but she gritted her fangs together. The dragon was an illusion, nothing was real, and even the lightning had only hurt her because she had believed it could.

The dragon spat a gout of fire at her. Nothing was real—except the Inward Way. Flames filled her vision, but they brought neither pain nor heat, and Alex let them play over her, refusing to move from her secure position. Then she shrank the Way.

Marian Perera

The road narrowed from a ribbon to a thread, and Ohallox choked off his fire as he struggled to keep his balance. Alex, swaying on the tightrope of the Inward Way, had a smaller size and better reflexes to keep her steady as she bent the Inward Way again. It flicked around Ohallox in loops and coils, constricting closer and tighter around him. The dragon roared again, this time in panic.

If the Inward Way feeds on emotions, I have a banquet for it. Alex poured out every nightmare that Ohallox had inflicted on her, the choking fear and misery, and imagined it all being given to him. The Inward Way used her greedily, and the sky around her was no longer grey, but a black deeper than a grave. Ohallox screamed, the sound shivering in her bones. She knew that he was no longer in control of the Way, that he couldn't *get* control of it. Perhaps it didn't like being twisted to serve his ends. Perhaps it had some sense of justice too.

With the last of his strength, Ohallox reached into her. An arm extended from the tangling spider web of the Inward Way, and even as she snapped her jaws, he pulled something out of her. She saw a bloody fist holding a burden that pulsed and twitched, and then the Way began to sink down through the midnight sky, leaving Ohallox far beyond her.

Go now, a cold voice said out of the darkness, and when she looked down, she saw that her clothes had reappeared, on her own body. *Go. You no longer have the ability to walk the Way.*

Thank you for that, Alex thought as the road vanished. The mist peeled back and the floor of her room was solid beneath her. Mayerd knelt beside her, holding her hand tightly.

"You did it." He released her fingers. They were numb from his grip, but she hardly noticed. His usually cool, closed-off gaze burned and his face was filled with longing. Had it been for her, she would have turned away, but she knew that it was for the thrill of walking the Way, the power of controlling it.

"How could you have been there if you can't—"

"I wasn't there, Alex. I just spoke—well, shouted at you and hoped with all my heart that you heard. And I hoped Ohallox would focus on me instead of you."

"The snake," Alex said, understanding.

"Is that what it looked like?" He smiled. "The Way controls a great deal, but it can't block all stimuli from reality—not when they come from someone with a drop of the Way themselves."

128

Alex nodded. "I couldn't have done it without your help, Mayerd—but I still don't know why the Way let me go."

"Did Ohallox manipulate you in any—"

"Yes!" She remembered his hand reaching into her, pulling a twitching thing out. "Was that what he—"

"—used to control you, yes, and because of that, because of the trap he built in your mind—"

"—which I saw as real, because that's what the Inward Way does, it gives form to the formless—"

"Exactly. And the activated trap connected you to Ohallox, so he couldn't leave the Way while you were on it."

"So he had to free me to save himself," Alex said. "And I called myself a hunter, but he didn't like the word—"

"I'm not surprised." Mayerd grinned. "Hunters are people who track down rogue Iter—"

"*Mayerd!*"

Robert's voice cut through the room and Alex raised her head, startled. She saw the bloodstains on Robert's shirt and she saw Victoria, her face drawn, rubbing at the red marks on her wrists. The events of the past few hours flew through her mind and she remembered everything she had done, from the murder of Victoria's knights to her influence over the household, culminating in an attempt to kill Robert. And she had nearly succeeded. She looked back on the whole nightmare with the stunned clarity of a sane person watching a mad one.

And she had nearly murdered Victoria. The Quorum would never grant the use of their inventions now. She had been the spy within the gates, which meant the war was lost before it had begun. She couldn't meet Robert's eyes—or Victoria's, for that matter—and she stared at the floor, wishing it would open up and swallow her. It didn't, and no one spoke, so she looked straight at Robert once more. Tears rose in her throat and she bit them back.

"I take the responsibility for what I have done, my lord." She derived a small comfort from the fact that her voice did not shake. "Whatever consequences you decide are appropriate for my actions, I will accept."

The moon was a glow-worm smudge behind thick clouds as

Robert leaned against the front door of Fulmion, tired down to his bones. His arm was numb from a poultice, and he wished the rest of his body felt that way. When he opened his eyes and looked out over the grounds of his house, he saw more glow-worms, fallen stars flickering gold. He blinked the exhaustion out of his eyes and the light resolved itself into small cooking fires—twenty or thirty of them. The evacuation of Madelayn had proceeded well.

Not that it'll do any good. Garnath's army was on the march towards the town. The townsfolk had laid traps within Madelayn, to the extent of poisoning the wells, but he knew that such tactics were only a pebble on the road to such a large army. By tomorrow, the hounds would be at Fulmion.

Without the Quorum's weaponry or knights, he had to fall back. He had sent messengers on the gallop to the Rauth and Chalcas estates, to the villages for miles around, but he was afraid to call them all together, one sheaf for Garnath's reaping. Would it be better to keep all the free people of the east separated and that much harder to pick off? But even that would only delay their defeat.

Garnath didn't even need an Iternan sorcerer with an army of ten thousand at his disposal. Victoria had left on a swift horse that afternoon, carrying the heads of her knights in saddlebags. Robert had watched her ride away, and her horse had crushed his last hope under its hooves.

He was still the baron of Dawnever, so he had to plan a course of action to save his people. And he had no idea what to do. Fall back? How far could they fall back—fifty miles to the Sea of Slaughter? What then? The Sea might earn its name a second time.

Exhausted but unable to sleep, he walked around the house, only to stop when he saw a figure seated on the edge of a stone sink in which water lilies grew. The man looked up.

"Hello, Robert."

It was Mayerd, and Robert felt a little better. He retrieved a lantern, bringing it to the sink so that firelight glimmered off the dark water.

"What's that for?" Mayerd asked.

"So no one else sees you sitting in the dark. They'll think you're spinning witchcraft."

"Mmm." Mayerd's gaze wandered away.

"What are you thinking about?" Robert asked, on impulse.

Mayerd usually ignored questions like that, or replied with sarcasm intended to make the questioner feel as small as possible. Now he smiled. "Just wishing I could have seen Ohallox's face when Alex was pounding him—and using the Way to do it."

"Nothing much happened to me when I was on the Way. Other than two nasty situations—it certainly wasn't this pitched battle that you and Alex were talking about."

Mayerd's smile faded to a gentleness about his usually taut mouth. "Well, I mean no offense, Robert, but you're not very imaginative. Alex is—that's why she was able to manipulate the Way—and don't forget that she and Ohallox were linked anyway, thanks to the trap that he built in her. The Way intensifies all mental devices of the kind—"

"All right, thanks for the explanation." The last thing Robert needed to think about was the trap that had walked into his house, the snare laid for him in a woman for whom he had come to care.

"You know she never intended any of this to happen." Mayerd paused. "Don't you?"

"No, I don't." He couldn't be sure of anything. "How do I know this isn't another trick, like that ambush Garnath set up in the shrine?"

Mayerd frowned. "That made sense, because he wanted to lull you into a sense of security before the Way was unleashed. What kind of deception do you think he'll try now? And why would he even bother? He has the upper hand."

Robert hesitated. "You're right about that last part..."

"And if you're afraid of the Inward Way, you needn't be. Ohallox had to disconnect himself completely from her. He couldn't coerce her again."

"I'm not afraid of sorcery." Robert tried to keep the bitterness out of his voice.

"Then what is it?"

"*It* is the fact that two Katassian Knights were butchered in my parlor and one of my footmen slaughtered on the landing, a Quorumlord nearly had her throat cut, and there's an army advancing on Madelayn. This hasn't been the best day of my life."

"Must have been a wretched one for Alex as well." Mayerd gazed out into the night. "I wonder what'll happen to her."

The words were a jarring blow that connected with Robert's

stomach and traveled up to his throat. He hadn't thought of Alex since he had locked her into her room hours ago, as much for her own safety as for his servants' peace of mind. Alex was distinctly unpopular in Fulmion now.

So if *he* felt alone and afraid, how did she feel? Once again, she had been used by Garnath, and now that he saw how powerful Iternan magic was, he knew they were lucky not to have suffered worse. Except that for Alex, it was bad enough. She had taken the blame for what Garnath had forced her to do, as it had been for most of her life, and she was too proud to make excuses for herself.

It still didn't change the fact that two men had died at her hands. Even if Mayerd felt she wasn't likely to do it again, no one had seen Ohallox or the Inward Way—they had only seen Alex.

"What shall I do?" he said finally, thinking that that always happened when it came to Alex—he didn't know what to do with her. She was the most unsettling gift he had ever been given. "I can't just let her out and expect everything to be all right. The servants are afraid of her now."

"Are you?" Mayerd said.

"No."

His answer came so naturally that it took Robert aback. Alex had carried a magical trap into his household and had attacked him, and yet it was the truth. He wasn't afraid of her. If she couldn't kill him when she was controlled by the Inward Way, then she was even less likely to harm him otherwise.

And he couldn't keep her locked up any longer. He was sure of that too. He still didn't know what to do with her—no matter how clever she was, she wouldn't be able to convince anyone else to trust her again. There was no way to rebuild the ruins of the war effort either. But she had stood between him and the Inward Way, so he owed her that much of a chance.

He got up and went indoors.

Alex noticed nothing after her room was locked. She stayed on the floor, her knees drawn up and her arms around them, determined not to think about why the happiest time of her life had been so short and ended so badly. Instead, she pretended she was back in the castle, being called for, and it worked. Her mind went blank, wiped clean as a dinner plate, and she did not feel the hardness of the floor beneath her. She drifted until the key turned in the lock again.

Startled, she turned, wincing as her cramped muscles and stiff joints made their presence felt. The door opened, and she straightened her features as Robert entered. He frowned when he saw her, and her heart sank.

"What are you doing on the floor, Alex?"

Alex managed a shrug. She had been on the floor earlier, and it had seemed best not to move from there.

Robert shut the door and held his hand out. Uncertainly, Alex took it, and he drew her to her feet. She clenched her teeth to keep from making any sound.

"Sit down." He indicated the bed so she obeyed, wishing he would just turn her out of the house and be done with it. *Steady*, she thought. *Calm.* He sat beside her and studied her, as if watching for a sign of weakness, so she straightened her back and stared ahead.

Looking away from her for the first time since he had entered, Robert fished a small jar from a pocket. When he uncorked it, Alex smelled a sharp medicinal odor. He dabbed a finger in the contents and said, "Hold still."

You have no idea how still I can hold. But she was glad she hadn't said that when he smeared the salve across the bruise on her cheek.

"I'm sorry I hit you." His touch was light and careful, and she didn't need to pretend that she felt no pain. "I've never struck a woman before, if you believe that."

"Why shouldn't I believe it?" Alex was surprised into turning to face him. "And you don't need to apologize."

"Of course I do." Robert pushed a hand through his hair. "I'm not good with speeches, so I'll just say this. What happened was Garnath's doing, and I'll make him pay for it. But you're not to blame, and I won't hold you responsible for it any longer."

"Thank you," Alex replied with trained courtesy, but on some level she *did* feel grateful. He could have had her formally charged with witchcraft, which had worse consequences than being a spy. Now that she was certain she would live, she clasped her hands in her lap and prepared to hear the bad news.

Robert looked at her. "You don't believe me."

"I do." Alex was even more taken aback. "Why wouldn't I? I'm just waiting for you to say what I *am* going to be held responsible for."

"What you—" Robert stopped and rubbed the heel of one hand between his eyes. "I told you, none of this was your fault. We have consequences to deal with, but we can think about that tomorrow."

Alex felt the ice around her heart crack. It was the last thing she had expected him to say. "But you..." *Don't get your hopes high, it'll only make the landing harder.* "There's no evidence that Stephen did anything. The only person implicated here is me."

Robert frowned again. "Excuse my language, but that's bollocks. Everyone knows you don't normally give orders to nail the windows shut, or dishonor the dead, for that matter. It's Garnath. Who else could it be? What would *you* gain from threatening Victoria?"

"It doesn't matter. Your household still won't want anything to do with me, because the servants didn't see Stephen or Ohallox. They only saw me."

"I don't care what they saw." The set of Robert's jaw was stubborn. "I still won't have you ill-treated because Garnath used you for one last time. You're having supper with me tonight, since I forgot to eat earlier, and tomorrow we'll plan our next step." He stopped, studying her face again, and he sounded a little worried. "Unless...was there something else you wanted to do?"

Alex looked away quickly, feeling her restraint crumble, and she thought of Stephen as she struggled to collect herself. She had believed that no matter what he did to her body, he wouldn't be able to touch her mind. Well, now he had. He had used her thoughts as much as her flesh. And Robert knew that, so why did he keep on behaving like that towards her? After all she had lost, there was nothing left to give him. The desolation swept back, stronger this time, implacable, and she buried her face in her hands.

She felt Robert take her shoulders and draw her close, his arms going around her. His hand pressed her head down on his shoulder, and she felt the softness of his jacket under her cheek.

She didn't cry. After her twenty-fifth birthday, Stephen had never succeeded in making her cry, and she would not break that rule she had given herself. Not that it was any easier to hold back the tears with Robert's arms surrounding her and the warmth of his body soothing hers, but she told herself that hysteria was the last thing she needed at the moment, and her body relaxed slowly. She realized through a haze that she had gripped the lapels of Robert's jacket, holding on as if to a lifeline, but he didn't give any indication that he noticed, other than resting his face against her hair.

This won't benefit either of us.

It feels good.

Not in the long run, Alex. Remember what you are.

She released his jacket, letting her palms flatten against his chest for a moment, before she sat back. "Thank you, Robert," she said, keeping her voice low and steady, "but I'm quite all right now."

Robert looked skeptical, but he didn't press the issue. "Then would you like to have dinner?"

"Oh...yes." Alex had forgotten about food, but now her stomach came to growling life. "Downstairs?"

"Yes. I'll wait outside, if you want to change."

Her dress was bloodstained, crumpled and damp with sweat. No if about it, Alex thought as she washed and changed quickly. Robert gave her his arm as he led the way downstairs.

"The servants are all asleep, so I'm afraid it's just a small meal laid in the parlor."

Alex was grateful for that. Facing the servants would be hard enough, and she had no more energy left. "Is—is Victoria—"

"She left." Robert held the door open.

The smell of roast beef filled the air, but Alex no longer felt hungry. She had hoped that Victoria would understand and forgive her, that the hours they had spent talking would have some effect, any effect. Apparently not.

"I'm sorry," she said. "I know how much we needed the Quorum."

Robert pulled her chair out and said nothing until he was seated as well. "Is there any way to get them back into the fold?"

Alex bit her lip. If she could only persuade the Quorum to relent, Robert might not be staring defeat in the face, but how was she supposed to do that? No flash of insight occurred to her.

"I don't suppose it would make any difference if you turned me over to them, as His Grace requested you do?" After that day, even the prospect of being a prisoner of the Quorum couldn't penetrate her shell, and she spoke as normally as always.

Robert shook his head. "I'm sorry, but not after what happened. The Quorum has no way to be certain that you're free from the Inward Way." He paused. "But let's not discuss it any further tonight. I brought you down to have supper, so we'll eat—and we'll talk about

135

Marian Perera

something else."

Alex wasn't sure what would be worse—discussing the battle they had lost before it even began, or determinedly ignoring that topic. Still, if a man wanted to talk she was always prepared to listen attentively.

"What shall we talk about?" she said as he poured cold white wine.

Robert sipped the wine, and to her surprise a smile spread across his face. "I'll tell you how I first met Mayerd, and how he tried to make me kill him."

The story was intriguing enough to distract Alex from what had happened, but it ended all too soon and she lay awake that night, trying to think. They couldn't fight or negotiate or even flee. The Inward Way was all roads and paths, but reality was walls closing in on her. No wonder people preferred the illusion.

"I'm expecting word from Lawrence," Robert said the next morning. "Mayerd sent a message to him as soon as we heard the news about Garnath's army. If Lawrence agrees, I want people to start traveling to Chalcas Heights. The mountains will slow down the hounds, and give us enough time to plan a counterattack."

"Have they already reached Madelayn?"

"They're within a day's march of it. And when they see it's been emptied, they'll come at the gallop to Fulmion." His face was drawn and tired, even in the early morning. "I suggest you pack whatever you need after breakfast."

That took only a few minutes, but Alex stayed in her room after it was done. She longed to do something—no task would have been too distasteful—but she knew the servants wanted nothing to do with her. So she stayed alone until the bell rang for the midday meal, at which point she straightened her spine and walked downstairs.

Robert was already in the dining room, and he told her that the flocks of sheep had been dispatched north, along with enough men to watch them. "A pity about the wheat. It would have been a good harvest. Alex, could you pour the wine? Lawrence just arrived, and since I can't take the contents of the cellar along with us, we might as well enjoy them now."

"And I'd like a brandy." Susanna came in, pulling off her hat and tossing it on a chair. Robert's brows drew together, but he said nothing, and Alex saw why. Susanna's eyes were sunken, her mouth

136

taut with exhaustion.

"What have you been doing, Susanna?" she asked.

"Making sure the refugees from Madelayn have enough food and shelter." Susanna rubbed the back of her neck. "I counted nearly two hundred people, and—"

"Are they ready to move?" Robert said, with a nod for Lawrence as he came in.

"Yes, but where?" Susanna said. "There are twenty-eight children under the age of six. They can't keep running, Bob."

Lawrence accepted a glass of wine from Alex and smiled up at her. "Heard about your fracas yesterday."

"Did you?" Alex said.

"I did too, and I'm glad you're all right." Susanna folded her napkin into a bird shape. "I was wondering, Alex—do you think that might have influenced Lord Garnath in any way?"

Alex sat in her place next to Robert. "Yes. He'll be furious."

"I meant, might he be willing to negotiate with us now?"

"Negotiate?" Lawrence said, raising his voice. "Susanna, my girl, one does not negotiate with a tyrant."

Susanna took a gulp of brandy, her eyes flaring. "Well, what precisely do you plan to do? We can't fight him and we can't run from him like a troop of gypsies!"

Robert rang the bell for the soup. None of the servants had been permitted to stay in the room, since the already low morale would become nonexistent if people realized that those in charge were undecided on a course of action.

"You *can* escape." Lawrence turned to Robert. "My holdings are open to you—just keep me apprised of your movements so that we can make the place inhospitable to Garnath's army when it approaches."

"*When* it approaches." Susanna paused as the soup was served, and when the door closed, she continued. "Again, Larry, where does this end? The Mistmarch isn't impregnable. And Garnath has enough troops that he can afford to lose hundreds finding a safe path to your mines. We're only delaying the inevitable."

"We can't negotiate with Stephen," Alex said.

Susanna's jaw jutted, and for a moment she looked very much like Robert, beauty notwithstanding. "I've bargained with the hardest merchants in—"

"And you've had guilds and magistrates and the merchants' own reputations to back up the contracts," Alex cut in. "Who will make Stephen keep his word?"

"Alex is right," Robert said, but there was no spirit in his eyes or his voice. "And yes, Sus, most of these people will die through harriers or disease or hunger. But I saw what our lives would be like as Garnath's slaves, and I'd rather face any kind of death than that."

"I'd rather face no kind of death at all," Susanna said. "But I suppose that's not—"

The dining-room door opened, and Robert looked up, frowning. Alex knew that the servants would not have interrupted unless it was an emergency.

"Lady Victoria of the Quorum," the butler announced.

Robert got up so abruptly that he knocked over a glass, and Alex caught it out of sheer reflex, before it could break. Victoria walked in, nodding at the butler with her usual coolness and he shut the door.

"Welcome back." Robert's voice was wary. "Do you wish to join us for dinner, Lady Victoria?"

"I might as well." Victoria seated herself. "I'll have a glass of wine, Alex. It may be a mocker of men, but the Addendums to the Mandates mention its restorative properties. Why are you all staring at me?"

Alex poured the wine with hands that trembled only a little, and handed Victoria the glass. "Because," she said quietly, "after you were bound, threatened and forced to watch your guards being killed, I didn't expect you to return here."

Victoria sniffed. "You must think the Quorum to be made up of babes in arms, or cowards at the worst."

"Well, it certainly isn't made up of—" Robert began, then stopped as Alex kicked his ankle under the table. "I mean, um, the affront to your dignity, not to mention the shock of what happened—I assumed that was why you left in such a hurry."

"I must apologize, Lady Victoria," Alex began.

"My dear Alex," Victoria said, "I am not quite such an imbecile that I cannot discern either Lord Garnath or Iternan magic. And the blatant use of sorcery in this land is something the Quorum will never countenance. Then I learned that Garnath's troops had approached from a direction we did not expect. Understanding that time was of the essence, I proceeded to warn the Quorum."

"But you couldn't have." Alex felt that she needed another drink. "It would take a few days' travel for you to reach the Mistmarch, and then to return—"

Victoria smiled. "Again, the Quorum's power worked in our favor. I rode perhaps twenty miles away, to a camp which the Quorum has set up. There we have stored a method of communication that allows us to speak instantly to each other."

"How do you do that?" Susanna said.

"I'm afraid I cannot reveal our methods. Suffice to say, I conveyed the situation to the High Quorum, and I was told that a select few of the weapons of war would be dispatched to you."

"Thank you," Robert said. "Unfortunately, by the time those devices are conveyed here, we'll all be a-moldering."

"Don't forget the steam-powered carriages." Victoria helped herself to soup.

"Can they bring the machines here soon enough?" Alex asked.

"I think so. But it's in the hands of the Benevolent Ones now."

"So once again we are prevented from doing the practical thing and retreating," Robert said. "The Quorum's insistence on my making a stand is likely to result in our massacre."

Victoria's voice was distinctly cold. "I would hardly be here if I expected a wholesale defeat, Lord Robert."

As if you would be fighting. Alex could see Robert longing to give Victoria a similar reply, so she said, "Could the Quorum invite the refugees to proceed to the Mistmarch, Lady Victoria?"

"I'm afraid not. As I said, we wish you all to fight for the land you hold."

"Hence the *select few* machines," Robert said. "The Quorum doesn't want the battle to be on *their* land, so they give us just enough weaponry to keep us dug in and holding on. Garnath's hounds will face weapons that they have never encountered before, and that may induce them to break off the attack."

"Not likely." Alex knew General Nalle. "They won't give in."

"Of course," Robert said. "It's far more likely that despite these *select few* siege engines, we'll be overrun and defeated through sheer force of numbers. However, we will have dissuaded the hounds from marching to the Quorum, because they will have seen the power that the Quorum commands."

Marian Perera

"But the machines." Lawrence frowned. "If we're dead, they can take the machines."

Robert shrugged. "The Knights of Katash are probably ordered to destroy the inventions before letting them fall into anyone else's hands. Am I right, Lady Victoria?"

Victoria looked down at her soup and continued eating.

"I'll take that as a yes. The Quorum is concerned with its own safety. We are merely a front-line strung to provide the first obstacle, and we are not expected to survive. Isn't that right, Lady Victoria? Answer me when you're under my roof and eating at my table."

"I'm beginning to regret coming back here," Victoria said through her teeth.

"Well, that makes two of us."

"Bob." Susanna spoke with resignation. "Please. At least now we'll have weapons."

"It's not much," Robert said.

"It's more than we had a few minutes ago."

Alex said nothing. If she was going to die, she wanted to take as many of the hounds with her as she could, and the Quorum's machines looked like an ideal way to do that. On the other hand, she was in full agreement with Susanna that dying was to be avoided if at all possible, so she stayed silent as Robert rang for the rest of the courses. Conversation at the meal was stilted in any case, and once it was over, Alex hurried to her room. Robert knocked on the door soon afterwards.

"May I sit down?" he asked.

"Yes, please do." Alex frowned. "Nothing worse happened after I left, did it?"

"No, it's just that...well, Victoria said the machines would be here by tomorrow evening at the latest. That's cutting it fine—Garnath's army has almost reached Madelayn. And I won't trust completely in the Quorum's generosity or Victoria's confidence, so I'm sending the children and women to the north. Can you help Susanna with getting them ready for the journey? Mayerd's organizing the men to build fortifications."

"Of course," Alex said, and left the room.

She came back to Fulmion late at night. The children had been sent north, some of Lawrence's men-at-arms riding with them. Buckets of water were drawn and sacks gathered to beat out fires from lighted arrows. Every cart and wagon was prepared for sudden flight—axles tested for soundness and wheels greased. Mayerd posted sentries in a wide crescent around the house and strung them like beads along the Madelayn road, ready to ride back as soon as Garnath's army was within sight. Fulmion was ready for battle, and clouds hung over the makeshift breastworks. Alex was glad to be inside, even though she had missed supper.

To her relief, Susanna told her there was a tray for her in the parlor. "No time for a proper supper, so the servants just laid out plenty of cold things."

Alex thanked her and went in to have a solitary meal of bread and cheese and chicken pie. Despite the work, she was far too afraid of the approaching army to feel weariness.

What is it about our strategy that worries me? Apart from the fact that it's hopeless. As she picked her way through a bowl of blackberries, she realized they were doing nothing that Stephen did not expect. He knew the Quorum had powerful new weapons. He knew Victoria had been sympathetic towards the insurgents and might continue to be, especially now that the Quorum's other enemy, sorcery, had come into play. Therefore, they had no more surprises.

Disturbed, she made her way upstairs. They had to find some way to even the odds—something other than the Quorum's machines. She thought of discussing it with Robert.

To any other man, she would have said nothing, because any other man might have told her to stop complaining, or might have been reluctant to speak to a woman about matters of war. But Robert would listen, and speaking to him always left her feeling better. Rounding the corner of the landing, she stopped, with the door of the master's room on her left. At the end of the passage, Robert was in a window seat, looking down over the crude fortifications, but he turned to see her.

"Come and sit." He swung his leg off the window seat to make room for her. "Is anything wrong?"

"Everything's fine." As fine as it could be under the circumstances. Alex felt awkward, because the window seat was short enough that she would be very close to Robert, but her body had already moved to obey and she seated herself.

"Not everything, or you wouldn't have come looking for me. What is it?"

Now that Alex was closer, she saw the tired lines on his face and knew he had enough to worry about without her adding to it. But she couldn't just sit in silence, and the polite meaningless chatter that had come to her so easily in Stephen's castle was out of place here.

"I agree with Susanna about one thing," she said. "We can't win even a war of attrition, and if we flee to the Mistmarch, all Stephen has to do is to cut our supply lines and wait for winter. Then he could walk in and pick the skeletons clean."

Robert sighed. "We can't win *any* war, Alex. We don't have the numbers. The Benevolent Ones favor large armies—I learned that much from my history lessons."

"So you think we could all die?"

"I think that's a distinct possibility, but one I'd like to forestall for as long as possible." He did not look either terrified or bitter, and when he raised an eyebrow, it was an almost teasing gesture. "Is this how you imagined your life might end, fighting a battle with a band of renegades?"

Alex nearly smiled. "Renegade" was not a word she would ever have applied to Robert. "This isn't too bad. How did you think you would die?"

"Oh, in bed at the age of eighty, with a big family clustered around me, bickering over who got what in my will. And from time to time, I'd hold my breath and stare at the roof, wait a minute and then sit up yelling, 'Praise the gods, I'm still alive!' until my family got so tired of it that they would hit me with a poker just to end the farce."

That time she laughed—it was preposterous and funny and so much what she had come to expect from Robert. For a moment she could forget about the battle and the fact that he would die in the trampled, bloody mud outside Fulmion, if he was lucky.

"You're a morbid woman," Robert said, "giggling at a deathbed scene."

"I don't giggle." Alex pretended to be offended. "Young girls may, but ladies do not giggle."

Robert's face grew serious. "Ladies also wouldn't be caught in a window seat with a man to whom they weren't joined. Did you know that?"

"Yes." Alex wasn't sure whether to meet his gaze or to look away.

She could take a punch or even a beating, but she felt balanced on a tightrope, and one word from him would push her over.

"I thought you did." Robert paused. "So why are you really here? Be honest with me, Alex—not only does it save time, but I hate guessing games. I don't know how you feel about them."

"I've never played." Alex's voice was suddenly hoarse, so she cleared her throat and looked at her skirts. It was true, she hadn't. If a man wanted her, he asked Stephen, and if Stephen had something to gain, she undressed and did whatever was required. She had no idea how to convey her own interest, because she had rarely felt it before, and because it had been quite irrelevant when she did.

I'm making a spectacle of myself. I can't just say out loud that I— that I want him. What if he still thinks I'm a spy, not to be trusted? And why should he be attracted to a mare?

The last word slapped cold sense back into her, because no respectable man would want a woman who had been used by countless other men. She swallowed, composed herself and looked back at Robert.

"Very well, I'll be honest with you," she said, her voice as strong as ever. "I think I was a fool to come here, not to mention forward and indelicate. I apologize for disturbing you." She rose to leave.

Robert took her hand, his fingers closing around her wrist. Alex froze, uncertain whether to pull away or pretend that she hadn't noticed.

"Sit down, Alex." She obeyed, but he didn't release her hand. "Forward and indelicate—what does that mean, exactly? What did you have in mind?"

Robert, don't do this to me! She stopped herself blurting that out with an effort of will, and she hoped he couldn't feel the corresponding rise in her pulse rate. Fine, if there was a battle to be fought, she could start it right now.

"What did I have in mind?" She glanced down at his hand. "Nothing that wasn't in yours, obviously."

He smiled, and she felt him stroke the back of her wrist with his thumb. "I've always liked that about you, Alex—you don't crumble at the first tap."

"You call that a tap?" Alex tried to ignore the light, rhythmic movements along her skin. She had taken threats and blows and magic, so she wouldn't let Robert disconcert her again.

143

"What do you consider a tap?" His voice was low and husky, and Alex felt her thoughts disappear while her skin prickled. She had to make him stop stroking her.

She grasped his hand and lifted it off her wrist, only to find that she couldn't let go. The ridged scar and the calluses on his palm felt rough against her fingertips, but his touch had been as gentle as if she were a kitten. Slowly, feeling that this was a dream which might end unless she was careful not to disturb it, she raised his hand and held it to her cheek. His palm curved to cup her face.

"That's a tap," she said.

"And are you close to crumbling?"

"Oh, no." She had never felt so nervous, and her heart thudded wildly. "That takes more than just one tap, remember?"

"I remember." Robert tilted her jaw upwards as he leaned closer. "May I give you another?"

Alex couldn't reply. She could barely think any longer, not when Robert was so close that she could have tipped her head forward and met his lips with hers, and in the next moment, that was what she did. Her eyes lidded as she simply let herself feel him, the tickle of his beard against her skin, the firm straight mouth against hers. It was the most chaste kiss she had ever had. Then he deepened it.

Alex gasped at the first touch of his tongue on her lips, lightly flicking against them, and when her mouth opened, Robert kissed her harder. His arm went around her waist, drawing her against his chest, and she felt the sudden softness of his hair under her hands as she buried her fingers in it, holding him to her. When his tongue brushed hers, she shuddered in startled pleasure, then returned the slow intimate touch with a desire that was rapidly burning out of control.

Most men had not bothered to kiss her first, but Robert did, tasting and exploring her mouth hungrily. And with any other man, that would have left Alex cold and untouched, but now her own passion met and matched Robert's. There was no need to feign her reaction. She slanted her mouth beneath his to take his tongue deep, drowning in the heat, a low longing sound in the back of her throat.

Robert broke the kiss, gasping, but before Alex, equally breathless, could recover, he was kissing her again. The corner of her mouth, her cheek, her earlobe, which he took into his mouth. She moaned when he found her ear, breathing into it, his beard brushing her skin like a fox's pelt. Then his mouth covered hers again and Alex softly sucked his lower lip. She heard him groan even as he pushed her away gently.

"We have to stop," he said.

All her desire chilled. "Why?"

Robert swallowed hard and looked away. "Alex, I don't want you to think you have to do this. You don't owe me anything."

Alex privately disagreed, but she only said, "Why do you think I kissed you?"

He shrugged.

"Because I'm a mare? Because I know no other way to relate to a man? Do let me know, Robert. I hate guessing games."

Robert smiled, a little reluctantly. "Alex, I have no illusions about myself. You're one of the most beautiful women I've ever seen, but I'm at the other end of the scale as far as looks go. So if you don't want to be with me—well, I'd rather you didn't pretend. I know I've shown interest, but that doesn't mean you have to reciprocate."

"Do you want me?" For once, Alex's voice wasn't velvet with coyness as she asked what had always been a rhetorical question.

"I should think that was obvious."

She glanced at his lap and smiled. "It is. Robert, I didn't come here because I felt an obligation, or even because I wanted to make love before we're all 'a-moldering'. I've wanted you for a long time now, but you never made the first move."

Robert raised an eyebrow. "I almost didn't tonight. That's why I pushed you so hard—I was hoping you would do it yourself."

"It would have served you right if I had walked away," Alex said, annoyed.

"You may yet regret not doing that."

"What's that supposed to mean?"

Robert flushed. "I'm afraid I'm...not very skilled...in bed. I only had one lover in the past, and that was five years ago, and...damn, this is hard to say—"

"Not as hard as *that*, from the looks of it."

He went even redder. "You're a big help, Alex."

"Not as big as—"

"Oh, shut up. Sometimes I think women have it easier than men— you don't have to work to please us, you don't fear that you might hurt us, you never worry that you might finish too quickly—"

Alex burst out laughing. She would have liked to respond solemnly to such a heartfelt confession, but every time she glanced at Robert's face, she had to bite back her mirth.

"I take it you're more amused than aroused?" But the corners of his mouth turned up, despite the mock-severity of his tone. He slipped an arm around her waist. "Put your legs up."

Alex did so with a sigh. After being on her feet all day, it felt good to rest them on the window seat. She leaned back against Robert's broad, hard chest, and felt his arm tighten around her stomach, holding her snugly against him.

"Mmm." She rubbed her cheek against his jacket. "Now what?"

Robert kissed the top of her head, burying his face in her hair. "There was one other thing," he said, his voice muffled.

"What?"

"I want you to be Alex with me, not the Black Mare." She turned halfway, propping her elbow on his thigh, and looked up into his eyes. "I didn't want you to think of me as any of the men who used you before."

"Robert, I could never..." Her voice trembled, and she paused to control it. "I thought that was why you didn't take me to your bed, because you knew I'd been with so many other men."

"But you didn't want them." Robert brushed his lips over her forehead. "Even if you had, what would it matter? You're not with them now. You're with me."

Alex kissed him then. She had never thought any man would overlook her past, but Robert had, and she wanted him more than ever—his tenderness, his strength, and most of all, his acceptance of her. She kissed him deeply, trembling with desire as he slipped his arms beneath her knees and shoulders and carried her into his room.

She didn't hear the door close behind them—she was still breathless from the long sweet kiss—but when Robert laid her down on his bed, she sat up, not wanting to be apart from him. Still looking at her as if memorizing her with his eyes, he began to undress.

"Let me." Alex knew all about men's clothing, but when she began to unfasten his jacket, he pulled her closer, kissing her again as he undid the buttons on her dress. She skimmed her palms up his chest, freeing the jacket, and Robert shrugged it to the floor. Alex pulled her dress away from her arms and let it drop. Then she was in Robert's arms again, and his hand slid up her side as she unbuckled his belt.

He took his mouth away from hers and glanced down. Alex looked down too, but she saw nothing apart from his hand cupping her breast, making her flesh tingle.

"What's wrong?" she said.

"I can't feel anything." Robert's thumb brushed lightly over her breast, searching for a nipple. "How many petticoats are you wearing?"

Alex chuckled and drew away, pulling garment after garment over her head with more speed than seductiveness. There had been too many times in the castle when she had worn nothing under her dress. Her hair tumbled down as she dropped the last petticoat and stood in her camisole. Robert took in the discarded clothing with a look.

"This isn't much." She unbuttoned his shirt. "Susanna told me that the latest fashion is whalebone vests to make one's waist narrower."

"If I wanted whalebone, I'd court a whale." Robert drew the last few pins from her hair, then pulled her close, pressing her against the length of his body.

Alex gasped. With only the silk of her camisole covering her, she felt every inch of his body, the hard muscles of his arms and thighs, and the harder heat of his erection against her belly. She squirmed, rubbing herself against it, and Robert's body jolted. He stepped back, slipping the camisole off her shoulders, and as it dropped, his gaze roamed over her.

The slow caressing look was hot as a brush of fire, setting her alight wherever it rested. "Alex, you're so lovely," he whispered, and her nipples hardened, aching for his mouth.

"I can't wait." She was trembling with a need that pooled between her thighs and made her wet and tingling. She reached out to his trousers, but he brushed her hand away.

"I can't wait much longer either." He undid the buttons himself as Alex backed towards the bed and folded on it, her knees shaking. When Robert kicked his last clothing away, she held her arms out and he covered her body with his, pressing her down against the single great fur that served as a bedspread.

Alex's head fell back as he kissed his way down her throat, nuzzling and lightly sucking the soft flesh there. The mat of hair on his chest rubbed against her nipples, making them stiffen even further, and then he shifted slightly to cup her breast. She buried her hands in his hair and pulled his head to her, longing for more of his hard, sensitive mouth and searching tongue. His thigh pressed between her legs, and she opened them. Robert groaned into her mouth and pushed her thighs wider apart, his hand lingering on the inside of one long leg.

"Alex." He finally dragged his mouth away from hers. "Show me what you like."

"Anything." Alex kissed the corner of his mouth, his firm jaw. She drew a fingertip lightly around the bandage on his left arm, then ran her hands over his shoulders and found the small of his back.

Robert sighed. "I mean it. Not anything. Do you like to be kissed here?"

His thumb circled one nipple, and Alex managed a nod. She closed her eyes when she felt the soft scratch of his beard against the puckered, sensitive flesh.

"Take it in your mouth," she said breathlessly, and gasped when he did. He lashed her nipple with his tongue before he sucked, and her back arched towards him. Alex tossed her head, and she heard herself saying his name through her teeth. Robert stroked the hair back from her forehead and bent to take her other nipple into his mouth. She whimpered as he teased, prolonging her need before he suckled and made her hips buck upwards.

"You're a fast learner," she whispered when she could speak again.

Slowly his hand moved up her thigh until he cupped the damp curls, rubbing his palm against them. It was maddening, and Alex tried to arch again, to push herself closer to him.

"Next lesson." His teeth grazed her ear.

She couldn't wait. She reached down, guiding his finger into her folds and to the small bud hidden in them, showing him how to rub it.

"Like this?"

He began to circle it slowly, playing with her by taking his finger away to slide deeply into her, returning to caress in slick rhythmic strokes that made her gasp. A deep clenching tension mounted in her, making her hands tighten on his back. She was rocking against him, pressing against his finger, nothing mattered but what he was doing to her, and then her need exploded in convulsions of pleasure so intense that she cried out, again and again, her head falling back with the force of it, and Robert kissed her throat.

"See?" he said. "It wasn't just 'anything', it was something, except I'd never have *found* the damn thing if you hadn't pointed it out."

Alex's laughter was shaky. "You—you can take your hand away now."

"I thought you liked it."

"Yes, but it's your turn." She traced the long line of his spine with her finger, feeling the shiver that followed it, and then gripped his buttocks, kneading the hard muscles. He gasped and rolled over on his back, pulling her on top of him.

Alex suddenly found herself sitting astride him, and she went still. Her knees registered the softness of a fur spread, but the rest of her body noted one thing only—a man beneath her. Too many times in the past, she had seen a man like that—naked, reclining, erect, expecting a service from her. She thought nothing, but her body behaved impeccably, and her hands trailed along his belly as she bent to take him in her mouth.

And she found herself flat on her back in the fur, her hands pinned above her head by his good arm. "What—" she began.

Robert's weight held her down. "Alex," he said quietly, their faces inches apart, "what happened to you?"

Alex swallowed. "I don't remember. Did I—did I do something you didn't like?"

"Please don't talk like that. Your face went blank and I thought you were on the Inward Way again. Then you started..." He flushed.

Alex closed her eyes. "I'm sorry," she said dully. "It wasn't the Inward Way—just force of habit." To her horror, she thought she would cry. She clenched her teeth and waited for the impulse to pass.

Robert let go of her arms and held her instead. "You don't have to do anything you don't want." He stroked her hair. "You know that, don't you?"

Alex nodded, resting her face against his shoulder, listening to his heartbeat. She might know that but her training didn't, and what if it made her give another such polished performance? Steeling herself, she looked up to meet his gaze.

His brown eyes were soft as velvet, caressing her with a single look, steadfast and utterly without condemnation or disgust. Alex felt a hard knot within her melt and vanish under that gentleness, and she drew his face down to hers for a kiss that burned through her like wine. This was Robert, whom she wanted with all of her body and her mind, the lover for whom she had waited all her life. There was no room between them for the past, only for the pleasure that they gave each other.

Robert turned on to his back, his hands still holding her, but Alex felt them clench as she reached down. She straddled him, enjoying it now as she felt his body shudder beneath her, his face taut as he struggled for control. Sliding her hand slowly, she explored and fondled him, until he groaned and drew her closer to take her nipple in his mouth.

Alex bit down a cry. She was close again; as his erection throbbed in her hand, her thighs clenched in counterpoint. "I want you," she whispered, and when he rolled over on her, his weight warm and solid, exciting her further, she locked her legs around his waist. "Inside me, now."

"Alex, no—"

Alex could have screamed. "Why the hell not?"

"You might conceive!" His hips jerked forward, obviously involuntarily, because he swore as he closed his eyes.

Tears stung her eyes again, and this time she couldn't hold them back. "I won't. Robert, please—" It was all she had time to say before he kissed her again, hungrily, and she felt him sliding into her, thick and hot and hard. Her arms held him tightly and her hips arched to take in more of him, all of him. He made a choked sound, low in his throat, and slipped a hand under her buttocks, pulling her up to meet his thrusts.

The rhythm was slow at first, rocking her, and then it quickened, rising faster and harder. Alex caught her breath as he released her mouth, and she heard him gasping her name as he pushed in and out of her. The slick friction was exquisite, unbearable. She felt her body pull taut, and when she shuddered in wrenching, sobbing spasms, the last thing she heard was Robert's growl of pleasure as he buried his face in her hair.

"I wasn't that bad, was I?" Robert said in her ear.

Alex smiled, rubbing tears away with the back of her wrist. Robert slid off her on to his back, and she lay curled beside him, her leg thrown across his. "No, you weren't. I didn't mean to cry."

"Oh, good. I thought it was something I did, or failed to do."

"Why would that make me cry?" Alex said, and Robert rolled his eyes. But his expression quickly grew serious again.

"That reminds me." He hesitated, looking uncomfortable. "Why were you sure that you wouldn't conceive? Because I don't think you had anything...well, inserted."

All her amusement vanished. "Have you ever heard of cantharis? No, I didn't think you had. It's an aphrodisiac, and I was sometimes made to consume it." She spoke tonelessly, as if reading a text on mathematics aloud. "It causes infertility."

Robert's face hardened. "Of course, it was to Garnath's advantage that you didn't have children. And—Alex, when I made you drink that dragora, you must have thought—"

"It's all right...and don't bring this up again, Robert, please. It's in the past now."

He kissed her forehead and said nothing. Alex sighed, rubbing her cheek against the hair on his chest. In his arms, in his bed, the past grew easier and easier to forget.

"May I ask you something?" she said, to change the subject.

"Certainly."

"Why is it that you've only been with one other woman? I mean, a man in your station has surely come into contact with many ladies who would be happy to share your bed."

"I doubt there are as many as you'd think." Robert stroked her back, his hand moving in long warm lines. "And even if there were, I'm choosy about women."

Alex eyed him carefully, waiting for some indication it was a joke. If not for the fact that he had had only one woman of whom everyone knew, she would have laughed.

"I know what you're thinking," Robert said. "That I've just said the most ironic thing you ever heard."

"How would you know that?"

"It's obvious. You have this 'if only someone else could hear you, Robert' expression on your face."

Alex had never had any difficulty hiding her thoughts before. Except with Robert, because with him, she was never afraid that speaking her mind would lead to a fist in her stomach. She closed her fingers on his.

He glanced at their joined hands. "It's true, you know. I can't abide girls who faint at the drop of a hat, or birds of paradise who are all show and twitter. I like women who say what they think and who aren't afraid to stand up for what's right. You see, I am choosy. And while I'm not much to look at, I do appreciate attractive women."

Alex smiled. "And you think I'm attractive?"

"Passably." Robert made a back-and-forth gesture with his free hand. "You do have beautiful eyes—they look like deep forest pools, and they almost glow when you smile."

"Why, how poetic." This warm, relaxed talk was something new, and she would have been happy to do it all night, but her practical streak intervened. "Robert, much as I enjoy being here with you, we both need to sleep. I should leave."

"I suppose so." He sighed. "I could make love to you all night."

"Good thing you don't have to prove that."

"Safer for everyone if I don't. Can you imagine me trying to work one of the Quorum's inventions after a night with you and no sleep at all?"

Alex slipped her camisole over her head. "They'd never let you near the machines, and I could see why, after Victoria explained the working mechanism to me."

"Oh?" Robert propped himself up on an elbow. "Lawrence is very curious about those machines. What did Victoria say?"

Alex frowned. "We just talked about the cannons. The fire-rocks are called carbide of calcium. When you add water to them they produce a gas, and that catches fire easily. Actually, it explodes, and that propels a projectile out of the cannon, which is shaped like a cylinder."

"At speed?"

"Of course, at speed."

Robert grinned. "It's a shame Garnath isn't leading that army. I'd love to fire one of those cannons straight at him."

Alex reached for her petticoats. "So would I. But he'd never come out of that castle..."

She froze, then straightened up. When she turned to face Robert, his smile faded.

"The castle," he said quietly. "No one's ever taken it by force, have they, Alex?"

"No." Alex spoke just as softly. "The walls are too strong to be broken easily. By the time besiegers dug in and began sapping, Stephen would have time to alert his army or allies."

Robert nodded. "The garrison?"

"Is small—perhaps seventy men. It doesn't need to be any larger, because no one would ever attack the city."

"But we could smash the walls with those fire-rock cannons. And with the steam carriages—"

"—we can stay ahead of the army." Still, there was something about the plan Alex didn't like.

"Right." Robert sat up. "The hounds are just outside Madelayn. If we circle around them, we can reach the East Road, and from there make all speed to Radiath."

"And when we reach it?"

Robert looked puzzled. "We attack, of course."

Alex pulled on her petticoats. "That's what Stephen would expect us to do."

"What else can we do? Go to Radiath and say that we were just passing through on our way to Lunacy?"

"No. Negotiate." Reaching for her dress, she continued speaking to forestall his objection. "Not with Stephen, with his allies. Keep him penned up while we lure them away to our side. Derek Argilow, the Duke of Goldwood, believes he has a claim to the throne because his grandmother was King Colin's bastard daughter. He told me about that once. He might consider throwing his lot in with us if he believes we can offer him more than Stephen can."

"I see."

"Would you help me with my dress?" Alex turned so that he could do up the buttons. "One or two of them could even be intimidated into joining us, and I know which ones. Especially if they know that you're fighting fair, with good Dagran weaponry, while Stephen uses magic." She imagined Stephen's allies wondering if their loyalty to him came from their own free will or from Iternan sorcery influencing their minds.

"I see," Robert said again.

The reply didn't sound very encouraging and his voice had changed as well, but his fingers were busy with her buttons so she couldn't turn back around. She thought over what she had just said.

Of course, Stephen's army will still be pursuing us. I didn't take that into account.

"Even if we evade the army, they'll know soon enough where we're headed," she said as Robert picked up his own clothes. "General Nalle is no fool. And if we don't stop him, he'll follow us to Radiath, so we may not have the time to extend offers to Stephen's allies."

"Then we'll attack Radiath instead."

He sounded confident about that, but Alex was a little more skeptical—partly because she had lived in Radiath long enough to know its defenses. "The difficulty will be in taking it. We'll have to be close enough to use our weapons, and the city will be pounding us all the time."

Robert had finished dressing while she spoke, and now he straightened the rumpled fur over the bed. "What do you suggest?"

Alex considered. "We should weaken Radiath before we attack. Once we're past the Stagwater, you could send a few picked troops ahead on the fastest horses. If they weren't flying your colors or carrying obvious weapons, they could slip into Radiath—the gates will only be closed once Stephen's been warned of our approach. They can't poison the water supply, but they could set fire to storehouses and bridges."

"No," Robert said.

"What?" Alex didn't expect him to nod like a pigeon to everything she said, but she hadn't anticipated a flat rejection either.

"I said no. I'm not going to do anything so underhanded."

"Underhanded? Robert, this is war."

"I'm well aware of that." Robert came out from behind the bed and faced her. "But even in war, there are principles to be observed. I'm not going to resort to deceitful schemes like poisoning the water supply."

Alex was used to shrugging off insults, but now heat flooded her face. "You let the townsmen do that in Madelayn."

"To defend their homes." Robert's mouth set in a hard line. "But I'm not going to deliberately kill hundreds of innocent people, even to defeat Garnath. I'll win this war honorably or not at all."

How can you be so unrealistic? "Tell me, was it honorable to set yourself up as the Bloody Baron and make people think you'd committed all kinds of atrocities?"

"That's not the same thing. I may be a liar but I'm not a

murderer."

You'll still need to be as resourceful and ruthless as Stephen to win this war, Alex thought, but she made her tone conciliatory. "You're right. The war doesn't stop with Stephen's defeat, because you'll need to win over the people and the other lords of the land. And one thing which will sway them to you is your honor. No matter what happens during the battle, once it's over, you'll be the leader they can respect and follow."

Robert looked as if he was wondering whether to order her out of the room or to leave himself—through the window if necessary. "If that's a roundabout way of telling me that I can put my principles on the shelf until Garnath's defeated, don't waste your breath."

Alex's restraint began to fray. "We're not in such a secure position that we can afford the luxury of you indulging your honor."

"The people who know me are following me *because* of my honor, in case you haven't noticed!" Robert didn't raise his voice, but that only made his taut control of it more obvious. "Do you think Nicholas would have agreed to fight side-by-side with a commoner like Lawrence otherwise? Do you think Mayerd would have sworn his service to any Dagran who paid him?"

"Do you think that's all you'll need to break Radiath?" Alex said. "I believe you said earlier that the Benevolent Ones favored the largest army, not the most impra—upright general."

There was nothing gentle in Robert's eyes now. "What did you just say?"

Alex braced herself. If she had endured it when he had ordered her to undress and then given her a drug, she could continue to stand up to him. "I said you're being impractical. I see how the new weaponry and a clever scheme could help us, but I can't see how honor will prevail against an army that outnumbers us, a city that has never fallen and an Iternan sorcerer. If you can show me how, I'll listen."

"I wouldn't bother," Robert said. "There's no point in discussing honor with someone who can't understand it."

Alex felt as if she had just been slapped—which had happened before, except that then the impact had only hurt her face. The last warmth of their lovemaking drained away. "I see." She matched his intonation. "In that case, I'll take my leave of you."

She went to the door, wondering if he would tell her he hadn't meant it. There was no sound from behind her so she walked out. She stood in the corridor for a little while to give herself time to recover; it had nothing to do with hoping Robert would call her back and waiting as long as she could for that to happen. Finally she went to her room and locked the door.

Chapter Eight:
Over Hill, Over Dale

"What is the meaning of this?" Victoria demanded.

Robert looked up from a loaded cart. He had supervised the guardsmen as they packed supplies, and now he tied the last rope over the cover before giving Victoria his full attention. "I assume you refer to—"

"To the robbery of the Quorum's property." Victoria's eyes bored into his. "And the unlawful treatment of its servants."

You've certainly got your priorities straight, Robert thought but did not say. He knew that Victoria had every right to be angry.

"Let me speak to her." Lawrence came forward, with a wary look at the knights who stood behind Victoria. "If you're inclined to blame anyone, Lady Victoria, blame me. My men had orders to ride out to your encampment and take whatever they could find. They also had orders not to harm any of the Quorum's servants or engineers, and if such orders were disobeyed, my punishment would be worse than the Quorum's."

Victoria stared at him with open dislike that slowly appeared to subside. "None of our servants were harmed. Only that has saved you, Master Chalcas. Now return everything you took, and this crime will be overlooked."

"No."

Her voice was suddenly quiet. "Would you repeat that?"

"If you wish," Lawrence said. "No."

"Do you refuse to return stolen property to a Quorumlord?"

"Yes. Would you like to know why? It's because I'm tired of the

Quorum doling its power out drop by drop, when we need all the help we can get. So I will not give back anything we took. The Quorum owes us some help."

Victoria glanced at the carts—identical under their roped-down covers—and Robert said, "Don't, Lady Victoria. You wouldn't know where they were, and what would you do with loops of wires and magnets, anyway? Carry them away with you when we strike out from Fulmion? Leave it for now. After the fighting's over, if we're alive, you can ask for—"

"Do you countenance this, Lord Robert?" Victoria's ire was suddenly redirected. "You promised the Quorum that you would stand your ground here, but I allowed you to go back on your word and follow an alternate plan. Do you repay me by abetting this crime?"

Robert groaned inwardly, though he was glad that she hadn't asked how Lawrence had found the camp in the first place. He was sure Susanna's damned dog had smelled its way there.

"I think we have a battle to fight." He kept his tone as tactful as possible and hoped Victoria would recall whatever the Mandates said about forgiveness.

She was still smoldering. "The weapons of war that the Quorum promised to you—"

"Are still on their way here," Lawrence said. "I'm afraid that your telegraph worker couldn't send a message in time. He smashed the machine instead."

A tight smile curled the corners of Victoria's mouth.

That seemed to harden Lawrence's own resolve. "If people were starving, I wouldn't hand each of them a crust of bread. I would give them as much food as they needed, but more to the point, I would find out why they had no work or no harvests, and I would try to correct that, or show them how to do it."

"It is stealing." Victoria spoke through her teeth.

Robert shifted his weight, not knowing whose side to take. Lawrence was his friend, and always tried to do the best for the people who trusted him. But Victoria had a point—once you started disobeying any laws you didn't like, where did you end up? Like Stephen Garnath?

On the other hand, he had no right to judge anyone, since he hadn't exactly been abstinent in his desires the night before. He wished he had been. If he had taken Alex back to her room rather than kissing her, he wouldn't feel as if he had been thrown from a horse's back and was waiting to hit the ground.

"This isn't accomplishing anything." He addressed the space between Lawrence and Victoria. "Could we put our differences aside for now? Once the battle's over, there can be a full inquiry, but now we're running out of time."

Victoria's stance relaxed at the mention of an inquiry. "When the Quorum finds they can no longer communicate with me, they will take action. And once peace is restored, an inquisitor will be dispatched to settle this matter." She gave Lawrence the kind of look she might have bestowed on an earthworm, and left.

"Oh, good," Lawrence said. "Now I have something to look forward to."

"I suppose I'll be called as a witness." Robert began to walk back to Fulmion.

"Don't look so concerned, Robert." Lawrence kept pace with him. "The heyday of the Quorum is over."

Not while they have machines that we can barely understand. Much as Robert appreciated having so many allies, their internal dissension could tear them apart before Garnath's hounds did, and he said so, concluding with the request that Lawrence beg Victoria's pardon for his rudeness, if not for anything else. Lawrence agreed so easily that Robert knew it meant nothing to him. Impending death certainly dwarfed any fear of the Quorum.

Nicholas Rauth had arrived, with two hundred men-at-arms, and Robert was relieved to see them, even though the sudden jump in the population of Fulmion strained the food supplies. The men wore the crest of the White Horn, and their horses were harnessed in red leather.

We need something to unify our forces, a banner we can all stand beneath. Robert considered that as he went indoors for dinner. Alex was already at the table and she seemed cool and unruffled, as if the past night had never happened—except she didn't look at him.

He had to take her with them to Radiath, he realized. Not only did she know the city, he could hardly leave her behind. She didn't even have a family who would protect her.

He wondered if she would want that of him now that he had made love to her. No, surely not. If she were a lady born and bred, she would expect a proposal of marriage—that is, if he were cad enough not to bring it up himself. But she was a mare.

That hadn't deterred him the night before, since she had hardly chosen to be one, but why did she seem so indifferent to her past that she could name names in his bedroom? He had lain awake for a long time, imagining the Duke of Goldwood doing to Alex what he had just done. The thought of it made him want to take a sword to something or comfort her or both, but Alex didn't seem to want or need comforting. Instead she was so closed-off that he had to struggle to stay detached too. Even that hadn't worked, since he had lost his temper and started an argument that he'd spent the night regretting.

On the other hand, maybe that was a good thing. He was used to Alex's manipulative streak—she couldn't have survived by being docile and honest—but on top of everything else, she was barren. Robert had never longed for a houseful of children, because he led a dangerous life working against Garnath and he couldn't endanger a wife or children by dragging them into that life. But he had always expected to marry some day, and he had taken the subsequent production of a son for granted. Alex didn't fit into that family portrait at all. *What a mess,* he thought and stabbed at the cold venison as though it had been Stephen Garnath.

"Robert?" Nicholas leaned forward. "Did you hear me?"

"I beg your pardon." Robert set his knife down. "I was woolgathering. What did you say?"

"I was asking you about this plan. We would circle around Madelayn, isn't that correct, and then take the stone bridge across the Stagwater? But if Garnath's army reaches that bridge first, they can hold it forever, and we won't be able to cross the river."

"I hope they haven't reached it already," Victoria said.

"Doubtful," Robert said. "They don't expect us to run towards Radiath, after all. And they came here from the south, avoiding the roads. They must have crossed the Stagwater at the old bridge fifty miles downstream."

"Fifty miles isn't too long for a column to split off from the army." Alex spoke as she always did, and Robert began to relax a little. Perhaps she had decided to put last night behind her. "Nalle has divided his troops before, and he may well have sent some at the gallop to secure the Stagwater. A column might consist of only five hundred men—but they'll attack like five thousand, with horns howling and the element of surprise on their side."

"Well, this time, we have the element of surprise," Robert said, trying to bolster his own confidence. "And we—"

There was a knock and Mayerd was in the dining room before Robert could give permission for entry. "Sir, there's word. The hounds have taken the town."

The sky was heavy with compressed clouds, and when the storm broke, the rain would descend in a cascade that turned the ground to mud. Alex had an ugly vision of the wheels of steam carriages buried hub-deep. Of course, if Nalle simply struck now, before the machines reached Fulmion, all that would be irrelevant. The only reason he didn't attack was because eight miles separated Fulmion and the town, because he didn't know what was happening across that distance. He had defeated armies, but he had never faced cannons.

She went into the garden and saw Mayerd fiddling with an odd wooden toy, but he stopped as soon as she was within earshot. "Oh, it's you." He put the toy away quickly. "My nerves are on edge."

"Everyone's are," Alex said listlessly. "Waiting for battle has that effect."

"As long as that's all it is. You don't have any ill-effects from *jevesaen*—walking the Way?"

"*Riye*," Alex said, and he smiled. "I mean, no. Mayerd, will I do that often—speaking Iternan when I don't intend to?"

Mayerd shook his head. "Iternan magic may have branded you, but you won't see that unless you come into contact with more Iternan magic. Power calls to power."

"But..." Alex hesitated. "I thought you didn't have any, and that was why you couldn't step on to the Way."

He looked away from her, and the muscles in his face grew tense.

"I didn't mean to pry." Alex was suddenly tense as well. She trusted Mayerd but her training mandated that she make men feel comfortable with her. "You don't need to tell me anything."

"I wouldn't have told anyone else." Mayerd's voice was colorless as ice. "But you know what it's like, and you're as much of an outsider here as I am. All right, here it is. I used to take the Outward Way, but then it was walled off from me, sealed in my mind. If I were starving to death, I couldn't lift a crust of bread to my mouth."

"Was that why you wanted Robert to kill you, when the two of you first met?"

He shook his head. "I wanted to die because I'd murdered the person who crippled me."

Alex had often believed her own life was unhappy, but no murders haunted her. She didn't know what to say, so she settled for, "You don't still want to die, do you?"

"No." Mayerd's dark eyes met hers. "But that's not the same as wanting to live."

Alex thought of asking why he had been crippled in the first place, but perhaps she had questioned enough for one day. Still, she might never get the chance again, and it was a distraction from her brooding. She started to speak just as the rumble of heavy wheels sounded.

"The Quorum's machines." Mayerd went to the garden gate.

Alex hurried to the drive as the huge carriages trundled closer. They were reinforced with riveted steel and bristled with spikes. Blackened chimneys belched smoke and smeared the rest of the carriages with soot, but for all their ugliness, they looked powerful. She only hoped that their function lived up to their appearance.

Robert came out and stood on the steps. "Those look intimidating enough," he said to Mayerd. "But I'd prefer it if the helmsmen were protected too. I know they have to see where they're steering, but one bolt into the front of the carriage..."

"True." Mayerd frowned as the first carriage halted. "What's that painted on its side?"

"Khovostil's Chariot." Lawrence stood to one side of the steps, angling his head for a better look.

"Khovostil never rode anything so noisy," Robert said.

"Oh, it gets better," Victoria said from behind them. "It can scream like a soul in agony."

"Can you make it scream now?" Alex thought that a long, unearthly wail might lower the morale of the hounds.

"Well, the boiler..." Victoria hesitated. "I shouldn't tell you any of this. Excuse me." She walked away to the Chariot.

"Robert, I don't know about you, but I can't take this much longer." Lawrence dug the toes of his boots into the gravel in short arcs. "I don't mind Iternans being secretive about their magic. We couldn't do anything with it even if they revealed everything to us. But this is Dagran, and we deserve it as much as the Quorum does."

"They devised it on their own, Lawrence," Robert said.

Lawrence gave the steam carriages one last look. "Do you know what causes improvements? Competition."

He went back into the house before anyone could reply. Robert looked ready to do the same, but the Katassian Knights were riding up the drive while the seven carriages disgorged men who wore much humbler clothes. The knight in the lead dismounted, tossing his reins to a squire, and came up to Robert.

"I am Michael Frew, Commander of the Holy Order of Katash," he said, with a bow. "Our supplies were depleted in our journey here. We need as much coal or wood as you have, and clean water, filtered if possible."

"Why do you need filtered water?" Robert asked.

"May we have the supplies?"

Just let him have them, Alex thought. *We've no time to waste.* She was relieved when he gave the orders and strode indoors, not only because she felt more at ease away from him, but because Lawrence's parting words had made her think. And she was afraid Robert would guess what was in her mind, simply by assuming the worst of her.

"Competition" meant that Lawrence wanted to build machines of his own, perhaps better ones. Alex was all in favor of that—assuming they survived the war—but only the Quorum knew of the machines' workings. The coal made the carriages move somehow, and the water gave rise to steam, but everything else was a mystery. If she could find out and take that information to Lawrence, would it put some coin in her purse for the future?

She considered approaching the knights, but dismissed that idea. On the other hand, the commonfolk who rode in the carriages would not be too proud to talk and, more importantly, would not be celibate. Few men could resist explaining something to a woman who looked at them with wide-eyed interest. If that worked, she wouldn't have to depend on a man who despised her.

She felt a little better, until the last carriage lumbered into the drive and disgorged the Word of the High Quorum. With three guards beside him, he entered the house in search of Robert but Mayerd slipped in through a side door and Alex knew he would be present at the meeting. He came out a little while later.

"What happened?" she said.

"The Smiler said Robert had broken his promise, and Robert said

163

his promise was that he would make a stand against Garnath. He just hadn't said where he'd do so. Then the Smiler said he would accompany us—I think he called himself a beacon in the night or some such nonsense."

Alex couldn't see what use the Word would be, especially since Victoria was there to lead the Katassian Knights, but they couldn't leave him behind either. In the next hour, Mayerd's scouts brought word that General Nalle had indeed split up his army, cavalry columns peeling off, moving in a great pincer that extended for miles. There was a living line across the land now, to cut the insurgents off from the River Stagwater. The battle for the east had begun.

"Why are they doing that?" Michael Frew asked. "It makes no sense to string their cavalry out."

"It does." Mayerd stood a little apart from the rest of them. "That army is advancing, making a giant scoop across the land."

"I see," Nicholas said. "If they simply marched ahead, in an arrow-like line, we could escape easily."

"Exactly." Robert slashed a red arc on the map. "This way, it's far less likely. The cordon extends from the edge of the Downs to the slope of Sulling Quarry. And it's moving closer. We'll have to head due north to avoid it."

"They'll have a system of communication." Alex thought of the miles that the hounds would cover. "Some way that individual units can inform the rest of the line that they've seen us. Especially now that it's dark."

"If we knew what that system of communication was," Lawrence said, "do you think we could sneak past them?"

"Why sneak?" Victoria asked. "Couldn't we break the line?"

Robert considered. "Can the cannons be used on the move?"

"No," Michael Frew admitted. "They have to be rolled off the carriages and set up on wooden trestles first."

"We're not limited to cannons," Victoria said. "We have explosive compounds."

Robert shook his head. "Once we start fighting, the individual units only need to hold us long enough for the rest of their army to come to their rescue. And that wouldn't be long. They might even cut us off before we reach the river. No, we have to slip past the cordon."

The Word said nothing, and that made Alex uneasy, but there was no time for any more talk when a guardsman brought news that Fulmion had been evacuated. A stableboy saddled Tempest for her, but once she had mounted she held the horse back from the head of the crowd, where Robert rode with Nicholas and Lawrence. She couldn't ride with the rank-and-file either, so she felt caught between them, out of place and conspicuous.

The air was oven-warm, tingling with the foretaste of a storm, and Robert had ordered that no torches be lit. The only good thing about the darkness was that it hid the blanket of smoke that rose from the steam carriages.

Mayerd took up a position beside the column. That gave him the freedom to go where he chose without breaking out of the ranks, and he joined her to say, "Why aren't you riding with Robert?"

"I can hear him if he calls for me, and it looks better if he doesn't have a mare at his side." It was true enough, but Alex changed the subject quickly. "We'll need some way to deal with Nalle's cordon if they see us."

"Robert's got a thought about that. Good thing it hasn't rained in a week." Before she could ask him what he meant by that, Robert gave the order to fall out, and the horses broke into a swift trot, out of the gates of Fulmion.

"You failed?" There was an edge of anticipation in Stephen's voice, a prelude to violence.

Ohallox had put off informing him for as long as possible. He had to recover from the shock of being beaten on the Inward Way itself, by a Dagran bitch who shouldn't even have been able to resist the trap he had built in her. Except that first she had fought against the coercion, then she had ignored the Way's illusions, and finally she had turned the Way against him. It had seemed ravenous. He wondered if that was because it had grown strong in Fulmion, unleashed and unchecked, feeding off minds with no one to control it. That would make an interesting case study, not that he could ever publish it in Iternum.

But first he had to survive his report to Stephen Garnath.

"She was weak, my lord—"

"Bollocks." Stephen's lip curled. "My mare had many faults, but weakness wasn't one of them. I'm not quite the fool you take me for."

Sweat broke out on Ohallox's skin. He began a gentle wave of calmness and persuasion, sending it unobtrusively in Stephen's direction.

"You're right." He looked down. "She was actually strong enough to resist a lot of what the Way attempted to do. I wish we had started with a more docile creature."

Stephen's sneer smoothed into a half-smile. "Oh, I have those, but they would have bored the Bloody Baron. If she's still alive I'll take her back, as long as she wasn't permanently disfigured or anything like that."

Not for the first time, Ohallox saw how Stephen had gained so much control over Dagre. Feeding plausibility into the power that flowed out like mist, he continued, "Had she stood alone, she would have failed, but you recall the baron's Waywalker—he helped her to resist my compulsion. I was distracted through dealing with him."

"So you killed him?" Stephen leaned a shoulder against the door's frame, but the guards behind him never changed their ready stances.

"I tried to." Ohallox sent the suggestion that he could even control the rest of the insurgents once they were close enough, as he had originally done with the mare. He would work like a slave to do so. "The man is clever enough not to give direct battle, but now that I'm aware of his tactics, I can—"

"You will destroy him," Stephen said. "Understand?" Ohallox nodded, and he knew that his use of the Way had worked when Stephen continued, "And what is the Bloody Baron planning now?"

Ohallox's mind raced. He couldn't say that he had broken his connection with the mare to save his sanity, but he had to answer. "He isn't confiding in her any longer. After she tried to kill him, I mean. They have fled his house, but she isn't aware of their destination."

"It doesn't matter. Nalle will outmaneuver them wherever they run." Stephen's eyes gleamed. "Have they been intimate?"

Ohallox had no idea which answer would be more pleasing. "No. The baron intended to, when she stabbed him."

Stephen laughed. "Good. Very well, I'll leave you to it. And these men will stay outside your quarters."

"What?"

"Just a precaution. You won't even notice them, Ohallox, since you'll be too busy, working like a slave." The door slammed shut behind him.

Robert's plan was to strike out north, skirting the Downs—the carriages could not make the climb to the grassy slopes where the earth rolled down in dust after the long dry days. From there, it would be due west, using the cover of Dreadwood, a patch of forest that was Dawnever land. The trees were unfelled, but they were neither beautiful nor valuable. They were called mourning trees, Alex had heard, because they were supposedly haunted by the children who had starved there during the Infestation. Dreadwood was the last place that a sane person would approach, so Robert headed there.

"We'll slip past the end of the cordon," he said. The harnesses of horses jingled, while the carriages creaked and trundled as they kept the pace; water boiled and steam hissed. To one side of the column rode the Word and his elite guards.

They passed farms and meadows and pastures, and Alex heard faint horn-calls, short regular peals with an occasional long tone. The night was so still and windless that sound carried for a long distance, but she tensed anyway.

"Pick up the pace," Robert said, spurring White Wind.

"Not easy, on this uneven land," Mayerd said. "For now, those carriages are more of a liability than anything else."

Alex agreed silently. The carriages were large and unwieldy, and she wondered what would happen if the hounds, more quick and maneuverable on their horses, surrounded them. The carriages couldn't fire projectiles or turn easily. It would be interesting to improve the design and develop a machine that could, but she knew no one would have the chance while the Quorum kept its secrets.

Time passed. The night was full of sounds, closing in on them, and the horn-calls from the cordon grew louder. Now she could decipher them—the short, repeated bursts swept down the line from one end to another. That was a "here I am", so any unit that was ambushed would be missed. A longer tone meant that a unit was held up, on rough ground. Nudging Tempest to keep up with Robert, she knew their fast pace would work. Nalle had expected them to stay and fight.

"Mayerd, tell them to hurry." Robert glanced back into the darkness. "I can't hear those carriages—they must be thirty yards away. We're close to Dreadwood. We have to keep together."

Alex began to hope—if they were near Dreadwood, they had

evaded the hounds, and the dead forest would shield them as they rode west. She liked the idea of using General Nalle's own trick against him. By the time he realized what had happened, it would be too late.

Hooves thudded nearby and the Word asked, "Did I hear you say, Robert, that we have successfully avoided Garnath's hounds?"

"Apparently so." Robert had not slackened his pace, and the sound of horns grew fainter, fading behind them.

"It's best to make certain of that." Before anyone could ask what he meant, the Word turned his horse and spurred it, his guards following.

Robert reined White Wind in as the drumming hooves died away. "What is that idiot doing?"

"Heading back down our column," Mayerd said. "In Iternum, someone like that would have been quietly buried a long time ago."

"Well, we try to be a bit more civilized here," Lawrence said. "Rather than killing people out of hand."

"Who said anything about killing?"

Lawrence ignored that. "He might want to bring up the rear."

"Since when has a Quorumlord put himself in danger to benefit us?" Robert said. "More likely he's checking that our troops are in place."

"Whatever he's doing, we can't waste any more time," Nicholas said. They had heralds to sound the alarm, but there was no way to pass a quick silent message from one end of the line to another, to inform the lead of what the Word was doing. And the moving column had nearly come to a halt, so Robert lashed White Wind's reins.

The peal of horns broke out far behind them, sharp calls piercing the night. A tremor shot down the length of the column, and Alex knew that the hounds had found them.

"What—" Lawrence began.

"He did that!" Before Robert could say anything more, thunder drowned out the horns. It was an earsplitting roar from the same direction as the hounds' alarm. If the horns had startled the column, the sudden blast nearly sent it into headlong flight. Horses whinnied, some bolting from their positions. Alex heard shocked exclamations and the maddog began to snarl.

"Bobby, quiet!" Susanna said.

She named her dog after Robert? Alex shook her head, feeling stunned, disoriented by the thunder and the terror which filled the column. "What was that noise?"

The advancing ranks had stopped. The enemy horns broke out in long howls as the cordon began to converge on their position.

"Move out!" Mayerd said.

"No." Michael Frew rode closer. "We will not leave without the Word of the High Quorum."

The clouds parted and a haze of moonlight turned Robert's knuckles to ivory as they tightened on the reins, but before he could give an order the Word came up at a gallop. His horse was white-eyed and lathered.

"What on Eden have you done?" Robert turned on him. "You gave us away to them—"

"To serve a greater good," the Word said, speaking loudly to be heard over the commotion. "Now they will be sure to follow us, instead of pillaging the countryside. And thanks to our efforts, one of their units has gone to the judgment."

"I'll deal with you later." Robert raised his voice to a shout. "All speed to Dreadwood—sound the march now!"

Susanna's bay broke into a gallop. Heralds sounded the order for flight and Alex gave Tempest his head, but Robert's horse was like carved marble in the moonlight, standing still as the enemy horns rose in screams. Waiting to make sure that everyone reached Dreadwood, she thought. For a moment she wanted to be with him, to keep him safe, but she knew he wouldn't want her there. She hunched over Tempest's back and let the black horse follow Susanna's bay.

Her bones jarred from the impact of hooves as Tempest began to outdistance the column. The clouds hid the moon again, but she heard the maddog's barks ahead, and the sound of horns rose behind her. Then light flared ahead and she saw Susanna's face illuminated in the spurt of fire from a torch.

The mourning trees of Dreadwood loomed up and Tempest halted, his sides heaving. Susanna threw another torch to her and Alex caught it from sheer reflex as she nudged Tempest into a canter.

"This way!" Susanna shouted and Alex saw what she meant—a trail led through the forest. The ground was uneven with roots and fallen branches, but there was enough space for the carriages to maneuver their bulk through.

Shouts echoed from far away and a shiver, like a ripple through a black pond, passed through the wood. The firelight made the clotted shadows beneath the trees seem even darker in comparison. The twisted trees wore moss coats long since dead, but there was movement among them—the gleam of tiny eyes in a hole, the twitch of claws beneath a protruding root. Alex told herself that it was only the ground, that this forest had sprung up on a chalk bed which stunted the trees, but she couldn't move.

"Come on, Alex." Susanna's free hand clenched around the reins of her horse. "Don't be afraid."

There are six hundred men behind us. Alex drove her heels into Tempest's side, and the horse bolted forward. Susanna's bay joined it, plunging ahead into a maze of trees, and the men followed close behind them. The trail led on through the wood, and echoing through the night was the cry of horns, strident with victory. She reminded herself that that was a favorite tactic of Nalle's, to make his enemies believe the hosts of heaven were descending on them, but that didn't stop her heart pounding. Sweat trailed down the nape of her neck.

"We should be out soon," Susanna said as a fork in the trail came into sight. She picked the left trail and the maddog loped ahead, a streak of red in the firelight. They were moving so fast that Alex barely had time to see the trail ahead, to duck from low branches that stretched out to rake her. They were moving so fast the hound just missed her.

She had a glimpse of him as he darted out from behind a tree, and steel flashed at her. The shudder that shook Tempest told her where the blade had bitten instead, and the black hunter broke into flight so frantic that Alex hauled on the reins before she could be separated from the rest of the insurgents. Tempest snorted, wheeling on the trail. Skeletal leaves flew up like dust. Another horse screamed behind her and more hounds emerged from the shadows of the wood.

Alex had not dropped the torch she held. Tightening her knees, she urged Tempest forward, at the hounds. One of them grabbed at her reins and she brought the torch down at his extended arm. The man fell back, and as he raised the sword in his other hand, Tempest reared up and brought two iron-shod hooves down.

The man's halfhelm was shaped like a hound's head, the long canines on either side of his eyes, but one hoof struck the helm so hard that something crunched beneath the steel. The man dropped.

Nearly dislodged by the horse's bucking, Alex clung on with all her strength before Tempest struck earth again and galloped back to the column. She heard Mayerd shout a warning, not to let any of the hounds escape, but it was already too late. The trees provided them with enough cover.

Ahead of her, the few hounds who had not escaped were outnumbered, but the trail was so narrow that they could fight the forerunners, rather than every man who brought up the column. And they had the advantage of surprise. Susanna's horse went down, the bones of its foreleg shattering under a mace. The maddog struggled free from the crumpled body of another man just as a hound drove his dagger into Susanna's chest.

The world wavered around Alex, hot with blood and screams and the distant baying of horns. The maddog leaped at the man who had stabbed Susanna, its jaws closing on his arm and shoulder as Alex pulled Tempest to a halt and swung herself down. Susanna grabbed the maddog's collar as she tried to rise.

Alex dropped to one knee. "Lie still, you'll bleed to..." She stopped as she saw that despite the blood all around, there was none on Susanna. When she put her hand to Susanna's torn bodice and pulled it aside, careless of the men all around, metal gleamed beneath the silk.

"Chainmail." Susanna struggled to sit up, wincing. "You didn't think I'd run into battle without some kind of armor, did you? The catamite just drove those links into me."

"I thought you were dead!" Alex said.

"It'll take more than that to kill a Demeresna," Susanna said, and Mayerd helped her up as the Word and his guards approached at a more leisurely pace. Alex wondered if he could be prevented from causing trouble again and leaving the rest of them to take the consequences. Probably not, so she just wished a sepulcher spider would lay her eggs in his mouth. Though that would poison all the little spiders.

To her relief, the men-at-arms drew quickly back from the trail and White Wind shone like pale gold in the firelight as Robert galloped to the forefront. "I thought the attack would come from behind." His mouth twisted. "How many were hurt?"

"Four dead," Mayerd said, "twelve injured. They took us by surprise."

"It's typical of General Nalle," Alex said with resignation. "He either sent hounds into the forest or had them stationed here all along."

Mayerd nodded. "We killed six, but some got away. And they'll hurry the news of our location back to the general."

"Or to whoever's closest to Dreadwood," Alex said. One of Nalle's great strengths was that he knew how to delegate authority. His captains responded independently to threats, so in the heartbeat-fast developments on a battlefield, news did not have to reach the general for the army to react—but she saw how that speed could be turned against the hounds.

"Quick," she said to Mayerd. "We might still throw them off the scent. Take their helms."

"Their helms—" Mayerd's eyes widened. "And armor. Peter, find six men who speak without an eastern accent."

"Hurry," Robert said. "They're chasing us from behind too. The men bringing up our rear are setting a few traps with that wire Lawrence stole—they'll string it across the trail at neck height—but it won't delay the hounds for too long."

Alex inspected a corpse, rubbing away blood from the sigils on the dead man's armor as Mayerd wrenched off the houndhelm. The marks were odd combinations of lines, meaningless to anyone who was unfamiliar with the army.

"They belonged to the Eighth Regiment." She glanced up at the men. "When you ride away from here, search for hounds from another regiment—they'll wear different sigils. They'll be less likely to recognize you."

"How did you know all that?" Susanna asked.

The Word smiled. "I'd call her a turncoat, if she maintained any garments to turn."

Alex couldn't reply. She had endured nights with General Nalle that had left her bruised and bleeding, unable to walk afterwards. Lying in bed encouraging him to talk about the army had often been the only thing that staved off another session.

"We don't have time for talk now," Robert said harshly. "Mayerd, get the men ready and be quick. They'll have this wood surrounded in no time."

The men hurried to obey as Alex heard the steam carriages, slow as always, trundle down the trail. Ignoring the Word—which she could tell disgruntled him—she checked the wound on Tempest's flank, then straightened. "Someone else can ride this horse. It's injured."

The friendliness left Susanna's face. "I'll take him. If you don't want one of our horses, there are always the steam carriages."

Alex put on a taken-aback expression but nodded reluctantly. The Word might be suspicious of her being near the Quorum machines, but the idea hadn't come from her.

Mayerd turned to the men who now wore the distinctive helms and armor. "Split up and give conflicting reports. We headed north, we're dug into the wood to use the cover of the trees, we never went into the wood at all and this is a distraction from a suicide force, buying the rest of us time to escape to the White Horn."

"How do we throw the rest of them off our trail?" Alex asked him.

"We'll set the forest alight."

We'll have to make all speed out of it. As the rest of the column reformed, she hurried towards the nearest carriage, the Sleeping Dragon. Victoria had chosen Khovostil's Chariot, so this carriage was safe. She hammered at the door until it opened and a gangplank slid down. Before she could climb more than halfway up it, someone pulled her in and slammed the door. Lantern-flaps slid back, and she saw the men and knights around her.

"Who are you?" one of them asked. He wore drab clothing, stained with coal and grease and sweat. Alex wasn't surprised. The interior of the carriage was large, but with so many people crowded inside, not to mention the steam—Victoria had mentioned a boiler, she remembered—she was sweating herself.

"I'm Lord Robert's cousin." She smiled. "My name is Alexis. And to whom do I have the pleasure of speaking?"

The man bowed. "Philip Celagos, the master mechanic."

Alex tilted her head, and he nodded to a crate on the floor. "Sorry our accommodations aren't any better, my lady. You should have been in the Chariot, with Lady Victoria."

"No time," Alex said. The men sat around the huge wrapped shape of a cannon and barrels of supplies. Doors separated them from what she guessed were the helmsman's room, to the front, and the boiler at the back.

Philip Celagos tensed as a shout rang out, carried down the line.

"There we go. Full steam, and may the Benevolent Ones watch over us."

Alex felt the carriage lurch beneath her. "I wish I was out there," she said, raising her voice to be heard over the thuds as everything in the carriage moved with it. From behind the second door came hissing steam and the grind of machinery.

Philip sat beside her. "Don't be afraid, my lady. We won't choke—there are ventilation slats cut into the Dragon."

"But what if something happens to the boiler?"

"How do you know about that?" a knight asked.

"Lady Victoria told me." Alex turned innocent eyes on him.

"Oh," Philip said. "Well, boilers do all right as long as dirt doesn't collect in them. The only way dirt gets in is through the water, and we make sure it's clean."

That was why they had asked Robert for filtered water. Alex wondered where he was, then forced herself to concentrate. He was no concern of hers.

"And they need to have enough water," Philip said. "Keep the level above a certain point. You ever left a kettle on the fire too long?"

Alex started to say yes, then remembered that she was supposed to be a lady. "No, but I can guess. The water boils away and the bottom of the kettle becomes red hot."

"And if you put any water in it then?"

Alex pretended to consider as she heard the distant crackle of flames. "The water would boil all at once?"

"Right," Philip said. "And the sudden rise of steam would burst the boiler. Course, there's a fusible plug that stops that happening, but it puts out the fire in the firebox, so the carriage halts and is useless for a good hour or so."

"Is that the fire?" Alex was unable to think of anything else now. "The one outside, I mean. Robert said that Dreadwood would be fired to deter the scum pursuing us. Are we clear of it, Master Celagos?"

Philip looked pleased at the title. "Well, we're in the lead, my lady, so we should be safe, but you can take a look."

"Oh, now, wait a moment," a knight began.

"She's a lady, Sir Charles," Philip said. "She's not going to carry the coal away on her back. I'll just open a shutter."

Alex followed him past the cannon, which was tied to the side of

174

the carriage in case it shifted and crushed someone. He swung back the rear door and a cloud of smoke and steam billowed out. Gasping, he drew her inside and shut the door.

"This is the engine room." He raised his voice. "Be careful of your dress, my lady, you don't want it caught on anything. Come this way."

There was very little "way" to go, Alex thought, nearly choking in the heat. The room was cramped and the floor covered with coal dust, gritty chunks breaking under her boots. The men shoveling more coal into a furnace were vague shapes in the near-darkness, and the clank of machinery was now that much louder. Water gurgled like the sound of her own blood in her ears. She staggered to Philip, the only recognizable thing in the place, and he threw open a shutter. Alex thrust her head out, breathing in the air greedily, and then she saw the forest.

The fire leaped like a leopard from black trunk to black trunk, and they exploded in sheets of glowing, liquid flame. The stars vanished behind curtains of smoke. She saw nothing beside the fire and the carriages that rolled at full speed away from it, so fast that their spikes tore through dead trees a minute before the fire completed the destruction. She imagined the hounds in the blazing wood, cooked before they could find a way out.

"We'll be safe, my lady. Your cousin is a fine commander."

Alex nodded, blotting her face. "How fast are we traveling, Master Celagos?"

"As fast as a horse canters, my lady." He shook his head. "I travel with my heart in my boots, expecting a wheel to break—the coppertops weren't meant to carry so much weight."

"Coppertops?"

"The boilers have brass covers for their steam domes. So we call the carriages coppertops."

"I see." Alex didn't see at all. How could she ask him more? "I would never have thought steam could push a carriage. I mean, it's just boiling water."

Philip grinned. "It is, my lady, but when steam turns to water it leaves an empty space, because a gas always fills more space than a liquid. That empty space pulls down a piston, and when more steam enters the piston chamber, the piston goes up again. And it's connected to a bar, which propels the wheels."

"That's fascinating." Alex put training as well as truth into her

175

face. "How much of it did you design?"

Philip tried and failed to look modest. "Now that you mention it, my lady, my father designed the engine governor, to regulate the steam flowing into the piston chamber. I learned my craft in his workshop. Now we'd better return to the main room."

Alex followed him and accepted water from a knight who cast an amused look at her damp and stained clothes. She was too pleased to care. The principle of the steam carriage wasn't hard to grasp—it made sense, rather than being a mysterious, incomprehensible gift from the Benevolent Ones. And if the carriage was taken apart into its separate components, she felt sure that she could guess the functions of some of the different parts. She liked being aware of something that not many other people knew—especially if she might be paid for it later.

If there is a later. If we outrun the fire. Then there was nothing more to occupy her so she waited, her hands clenched in her lap, for the carriage to stop.

Robert drew a lighted torch in a line across the ground.

Dry leaves ignited instantly. Moss burned and fire licked at dead branches. Fixing the torch beneath the roots of a tree, Robert wet his finger and held it up, checking that the wind would fan the flames due south. Two of his men fired burning arrows into the distance, while the third splashed rum on the flames.

"We're done," he said.

The fire grew swiftly. By the time he was in White Wind's saddle, the entire trail was blocked by a sheeting wall of flame. He heard the horns in the distance and thought, let them follow. The woods were burning, and they would cremate anything within them. He drove his knees into White Wind's sides, and the horse galloped down the trail.

The wind changed. Bent on a safe escape, Robert only realized that it had shifted when his nostrils were suddenly full of smoke. He crouched over White Wind's neck and heard the crackle of flames close behind them. The panicked horses raced on. *All right, we can still escape as long as they don't put a hoof down a rabbit hole.* He saw open sky ahead—the trees were growing thinner—and the fire roared behind him, all around him.

And the hounds burst from the curtains of flame. Robert knew at once that Nalle's captains had sent in scouts after hearing conflicting reports, and this was what had happened to the men so chosen. Even burned half to death, they did their work. One body, wreathed in fire, fell thrashing beneath the hooves of a bay, which reared and toppled its rider. Another hound, his armor smoldering, plunged from the shadows ahead and blocked the path.

Robert had only one chance, and he took it. As White Wind streaked past, he slipped his feet from the stirrups and threw himself off the saddle. He crashed into the hound, driving the man backwards against a black oak. Bones snapped, and the hound's twitching body crumpled over the tree's roots. Robert got to his knees, but before he could recover a mailed hand fastened on his collar and twisted it, jerking him backwards. He tried to draw his dagger and the hound kicked out. A boot struck his elbow, and the nerves in his arm went into a frenzy. He saw the line of a sword raised over his body as the stranglehold tightened. Choking, a red fog forming before his eyes, he got one foot against the bole of the tree and pushed against it with all his strength.

He drove his own weight back against the hound's legs as the blade came down. It missed him by inches, and the grip around his neck loosened as the hound staggered. Robert grabbed the hound's wrist, halting the sword for the moment it took Mayerd to reach him and drive his own sword through the hound's throat.

Robert struggled to his feet, the sweat on his skin drying at once from the nearness of the fire. "Is everyone—" He coughed, unable to continue.

Mayerd thrust the reins into his hands—he could hardly see White Wind over the smoke—and he mounted. An owl hurtled overhead, its feathers aflame, and dropped at the horse's hooves. Robert shuddered and gave White Wind his head.

They burst from Dreadwood at the gallop, just ahead of an inferno that swallowed the wood, and Robert tried to concentrate on where they were. A low stone wall marked the start of the common fields that were so poor in soil that they were not used for crops—the Breakstone Fields, they were called. How far were they from the Stagwater? Forty miles or fifty, he wasn't sure, but the hounds were off their trail. He thought of the men he had lost and promised himself silently that their deaths would not be in vain.

They caught up with the steam carriages far ahead, and he slowed White Wind to a trot, not wanting the horse to end up broken-winded. Mayerd glanced at him. "You need a rest."

"We all do." Robert had never felt more tired. "When we can't see Dreadwood any longer, we'll stop."

The carriages rumbled ahead, and behind them, the forest was a torch in the night. It took a long time for the glow to fade from sight, and when it finally did, Robert called a halt by a well. Mayerd rode to stop the column.

"Our losses aren't bad," he said when he returned, by which time Robert had watered White Wind. "Fewer than twenty men, and we seem to have thrown them off our tracks."

Robert nodded. "But I think we'll see them again."

"What happened between you and Alex?"

There was a moment's pause, during which Robert entertained a pleasant vision of tipping Mayerd headfirst into the well. That helped him to get his features back under control. "It's none of your concern."

"I know. I just don't want her to be so upset that she doesn't contribute to our effort."

"She will. She hates Garnath, of that I'm sure. She knows on which side she's better off."

Mayerd drew up a bucket for his horse. "I'd play it safe and offer her something more, like a home after the battle's over."

Robert knew why he was suggesting that. Mayerd had found a safe place in Fulmion, but it had taken him years to be accepted on the estate, and even an Iternan who couldn't work magic was better than a mare. He swung himself back into the saddle. "I'd have to think about it. And since the future's a little uncertain right now, I won't waste time worrying about the end of a battle that we may well lose."

"In Iternum, there's a description for what happens when you see something clearly for the first time. That's the instant when lightning strikes, the moment of lightning."

Here we go again with the Iternan talk, but thankfully he isn't doing it in front of the men. "And what do you think it is that I need to see?"

Mayerd didn't speak. His gaze was fixed on the horizon behind them, but when Robert turned, he saw only the ridge of hills in the distance, black as humped wolves. "What was it?"

"A man on a horse." Mayerd mounted his own horse. "Let's go. We're not alone in wanting to reach that bridge."

Alex knew they were being followed before they had traveled more than five miles—not just by scouts, but by an organized army that was drawing itself together. The sound of horns rose in the night behind them, calling the units together to form regiments and the regiments together to form the pack.

Everyone, from the mechanics to the men-at-arms to the knights, knew that the hounds were on their trail again, and Alex began to wish she was mounted. She could have spurred the horse ahead...if it hadn't been exhausted from the grueling ride through the night. The carriages didn't need rest, and as long as they had enough coal they could keep moving indefinitely. All that time she had only thought of selling information, but suddenly she thought of selling a carriage itself.

Some of the knights got out to lighten the carriage's load, and Alex caught a glimpse of their position through the open door. The fields stretched on either side for miles, but the East Road was forming beneath the wheels, and time ticked by in the steady clopping of horses' hooves on cobblestones. Behind them, the pauses between the horn-calls grew longer and longer over the hours before they stopped.

Robert sent a man to call her to the column's head, so she had no choice but to go, and the man helped her mount a grey cob. "I'd like you close at hand, if you don't mind," Robert said. "With the hounds so near, I would rather not risk the delay of passing messages."

He might have been cold, but she could freeze all the steam in the carriages. She produced her most gracious tones. "I quite understand. Was there anything in particular you wanted me for?"

Robert's lips tightened. "Why did they fall silent?"

Abandoning her attempt to bait him, Alex considered. "I'd love to say that something's happened to them, but more likely Nalle has realized that we're not scared of the sound—we're more unnerved by the silence." Men edged closer to hear, and she raised her voice. "They don't need to coordinate their positions any more. They're in formation, and they're heading to us at the gallop."

The pace picked up at once, the Word positioning himself prudently near the head of the column. "Twenty miles to the river," Robert muttered. "We have to stop them from giving chase, and that bridge is the only way to do so."

"If the horses weren't so tired, we could harness them to the piers," Mayerd said.

"I have a better idea." Lawrence had not said much before, but he watched the carriages like a hunting hawk. "Use the Quorum's explosives. Remember Victoria mentioned those? And I'll wager anything that's how the Smiler attracted the hounds' attention in the first place."

"That sound of thunder?" Alex asked. If the Quorum's invention had indeed killed an entire unit of the hounds, it might even take down a bridge.

"I hope we get a chance to use these explosives, whatever they are," Robert said. She knew what he meant. A thread of fear ran through the column, stretching it taut as wire, and the horses were slowing despite cracks of the whip. They had been on the move for too long, too fast, but no one looked back. They could only ride as hard as possible towards the bridge. Sheet lightning flickered over the hills to the right.

What felt like hours passed, until Alex felt sure it had to be dawn, but the blanket of clouds allowed little light to filter down. Only when the lightning struck again did she dare to turn around. A few miles behind them, the sloping land was black.

The hounds, packed close, coming after us. Her mouth went dry. If they caught up to Robert's army, they would win through sheer force of numbers. Then Nalle would take her back to Stephen if she was fortunate and give her to his men if she wasn't.

"Don't worry," Robert said. "The Stagwater's close. Can you hear it?"

Ignoring the thudding of her heart, Alex focused on the distant rumble of water. The East Road was complete now, so the carriages put on a final burst of steam and plowed ahead. Horses stumbled out of their way. Robert let them pass, but hoped aloud that they didn't bring the bridge down.

Behind them was the drum of hooves, as distant as the water. She dug her heels into the grey cob's sides, and as she covered the last mile towards the bridge, she saw a steam carriage cross it. The passengers had hurried over first, so that their combined weight didn't strain the bridge. The Word and his guards crossed as Alex reined in and stared at the Stagwater.

It roared down in a froth of foam that gushed around the piers of the bridge. She remembered what she had heard about storms in the Mistmarch, but she hadn't realized what the end result of those storms were. The swollen river threw spray over the surface of the bridge, and the stones gleamed like ice.

Anyone falls into that, it's all over, she thought as the last steam carriage crossed it. A wheel slipped into a rut in the bridge and the axle cracked. Robert set his teeth and ordered the men-at-arms to push it the rest of the way. They did so eagerly—anything to be as far from the hounds as possible. When Alex looked behind, lightning flickered on the helms of the cavalry, so numerous that they looked like stars.

They were still far away. Still a few miles.

The carriages were over, and they drew up into a semicircle that faced the bridge. Lawrence and his men-at-arms crossed, and the Stagwater seethed beneath them.

"You go next," Robert said, and Alex knew he wouldn't move until everyone was safe. The rest of Robert's men followed her as she rode across the thirty-yard-long bridge. Safe in the crescent of the carriages, she dismounted and hurried to Victoria, who was unlocking a chest while a group of men watched her. Nicholas Rauth and his men were crossing the bridge.

"Take six," one of the men ordered as Victoria opened the chest, revealing what looked like sausages wrapped in sacking. Long thin cords ran from each of them. The man coughed, and Alex could hardly hear his rasping voice over the Stagwater's torrent.

"One for each corner of the bridge," he said, "but best to have a little more than you'll need. Find cracks in that bridge and insert the packages."

Alex watched as two men gathered the correct number of tuberlike packets, wishing she knew how those were supposed to destroy the bridge. "Can the bridge be pulled down before the hounds reach it?"

"I believe so, my lady." The man who had given the orders turned to face her. "I am William Flerrin, chief alchemist to the Quorum, and we have spent many years developing those explosives."

The horn-calls broke out again, but to her relief, White Wind was almost over the bridge. The hounds were less than half a mile away, and as Robert swung out of the saddle, he said, "Why are they howling?"

Alex had no idea. Foolish bravado wasn't Nalle's style, and she saw the hounds spurring their horses into a frenzied gallop. Nalle didn't need horns screaming to the sky to demoralize anyone.

"How will those packets bring the bridge down, Master Alchemist?" she asked. "They're so small."

On the far end of the bridge, fire glowed as the men flipped open a lantern. William Flerrin smiled at her. "In those packages is a powerful explosive, my lady, trinitrate of glycerol. Once it's fired by lighting the wicks, it will destroy that bridge."

The two men ran back to the other end of the bridge and bent to light the other two wicks. Panting, they stepped off the bridge and hurried closer, the two unused packages in their hands. The first hounds leaped up on to the wet stones.

"When will those explode?" the Word asked. "The ones I used earlier detonated with no delay."

The horses must have been exhausted, but whips cracked and they lurched forward. The men in the lead gained the middle of the bridge and the rest of the army followed at a gallop.

"William!" Victoria said. "Why does that bridge not fall?"

"The wicks..." William Flerrin's eyes widened. The hounds had nearly reached the end of the bridge, and the men-at-arms and knights drew their swords to intercept them, faces grim and set. "The spray from the river, it extinguished them!"

"A fire arrow—" Victoria looked around desperately.

"No time!" the Word snapped. "Use one of the explosives instead!"

Robert pulled a dagger and plucked a package from an alchemist's slackened grip. Before the man could snatch it back, he sliced off most of the long wick and dipped the remaining stub into the open lantern.

"Get rid of that!" William shouted, spreading his arms as if to shield the Quorumlords. The flame had disappeared into the sacking as Robert threw it straight at the bridge. It flew through the air, sliding under the hooves of a red charger, and a quakelike blast split the night. The hounds and their horses disappeared in a seething cloud of ash and scorched flesh, and an instant later, four other explosions broke out as the other packages were triggered. Stone shattered with multiple cracks. The bridge crumbled away before their eyes, and the screams of men and animals were drowned in the roar of the Stagwater.

A giant invisible hand struck Alex, knocking her to the ground as a wave of heated air swept over the riverbank. The horses screamed.

Her heart pounding, she stayed face-down in the mud until Robert crouched beside her.

"Are you hurt?" he asked.

"I'm all right." She staggered up. The alchemists and the Quorumlords had also been thrown down, and they picked themselves up, looking dazed. Debris was everywhere—bits of armor, broken stone—but one of the little packages also lay in the mud nearby.

The sixth one, Alex thought, it must have fallen from that alchemist's hand. If it had exploded too...

Two hounds had gained the other bank, but the force of the explosion toppled them and a dozen swords cut them to pieces. As the alchemists struggled to their feet, Alex took a few steps away and went to her knees, pretending to lace up her boot. Her fingers shook as she took up the package and slipped it into her sash. She hoped Robert hadn't seen her. Not meeting his moral standards was one thing, but he might insist she give the explosive back.

"The bridge is down," Victoria said. Mud plastered her robes, but she was triumphant. Alex felt only apprehension as she stared across the Stagwater, hearing thunder rumble overhead. The ground trembled, and a horn-call rang out.

"Something's wrong." She turned to Robert. "Nalle has a trick planned."

"But what can he do, from that side of the riv—"

A scream rang out from beyond the semicircle of the steam carriages. Alex heard an answering horn-call, but it came from their side of the river.

"He left a regiment here," she said through numb lips. "He left a thousand men back here, just in case."

"That was why the hounds howled, to warn their reserves," Robert said, and she heard the drum of horses' hooves—fresh horses, ridden by men who were pleasantly surprised they would be part of the battle. The noise had been drowned before, in the destruction of the bridge, but now she realized they were caught with their backs to the Stagwater.

Victoria spun around. "Get ready." The knights moved to obey. "Do not let a single one of those apostates take what is ours. We won't run this time. We have a battle to fight."

Part Three:

The Moment Of Lightning

Chapter Nine:
The Road to Radiath

"Tell the men to fall back," Robert said to Mayerd. "Use the steam carriages as cover—they're bristling like hedgehogs, and the hounds would have to be mad to attack them."

Mayerd was off at once, but even over the sound of the river and the rain, Victoria had heard. "You don't intend to fight?" she said.

"Not a surprise battle in hellish weather against who knows how many men! I'm going to seek cover, evaluate the situation and then make a plan—which is what generals do, Lady Victoria, if they don't want to lose their entire force."

Despite her faults, Victoria seemed to know sense when she heard it, and she followed him to the carriage he chose. It was not the largest, but it stood squarely on the East Road and was likely to move fast if they were routed. The horns howled again, and horses' hooves pounded the heat-baked earth, heading towards them from the south as the rain began to fall. *Wonderful, on top of everything else, we'll be fighting in the slush.*

Alex had already reached the steam carriage, pulling open the door as the rain turned into a sheeting cascade. Lawrence and Nicholas hurried up to him, and Nicholas raised his voice to be heard. "What's the plan, Robert?"

"Is your cavalry ready?" Robert said.

Nicholas nodded. "But how best to deploy them? The attack's coming from the south, but we don't know how many—"

"We won't deploy anything yet." Robert climbed into the carriage. "We need a plan of action."

Lawrence hesitated. "It sounds a little late for that."

"Don't be silly, Larry," Susanna said from inside the carriage. "They were nowhere near us—they probably dug in well away from the East Road, so that no one would see them. What you hear is just the advance—the cavalry—and they can't run us down if we're sitting close around these carriages."

"The rest of them will be coming up fast." Lawrence was still chafing at the bit, but he entered the carriage. Rain splattered down, drumming against the roof.

Victoria sat on the edge of a crate, but her usual straight-spined position looked rigidly tense rather than dignified. "Whatever they do, we can't run. The wheels of the carriages will stick in the mud."

The door opened and Mayerd came in, dripping from head to foot and oblivious to it. "They've reached us."

Michael Frew grasped the hilt of his sword, then released it. "I presume, Iternan, that you would not be so complacent were they actually attacking?"

"His name's Mayerd," Robert said. "Try to use it."

Susanna gave him a sharp not-now look. "If they're not attacking, what are they doing?"

"They have lances, and their first charge picked off a few men who were away from the carriages. They're still making the occasional lunge, but we're prepared, and we unhorsed two of them." Mayerd handed Alex two scraps of leather. "Here's what they wore."

"The Ninth." Alex's voice grew hard. "Their cavalry numbers nearly two hundred, a quarter of their full strength. And their commander won't stop until we're all dead. This regiment will fight to the end."

"Isn't that something they would all do?" Victoria said.

"Not really." Alex's smile was faint. "You see, the regiment's commander is a woman."

There were stares all around, but Nicholas snapped his fingers. "Of course. I've heard of her—Celia Trovart. She's supposed to have earned her rank by being the general's cousin."

"She's also supposed to have earned it by less savory means." The smile faded. "But military skill runs in that family. Nalle would never have promoted someone who didn't know how to command troops. Still, one thing works in our favor—many men don't want to serve under a woman, so the Ninth is a small regiment. But because she constantly has to prove herself to the rest of the army, Celia Trovart won't withdraw her troops. We have to defeat them."

"Sir Michael, inform your men of this," the Word said. "They will not be defeated by a woman, even one so unwomanly as to participate in the arts of war."

"Just one thing." Robert had no objections to inspiring words of any kind, but he had hoped for something solid and practical to back up such a speech. "How exactly do we defeat them?"

"A cavalry charge?" Frew sounded doubtful.

Robert knew why. "Two hundred of their horsemen against perhaps three hundred of ours. No plans or strategy, which means it's simple force against force. How many of our men will be left to take this battle to Radiath?"

There was a pause, during which Robert heard shouts from outside, carrying over the hammer of rain. Mayerd got up to investigate, while Alex broke the silence. "We have to do something quickly. The cavalry will make feints to keep us close together."

"I see," Lawrence said through his teeth. "They'll rely on the darkness and the filthy weather to prevent us from giving open battle, and they'll buy time for their bowmen to arrive. Bunched up, we'll be easy targets even in the dark."

Before anyone could reply, Mayerd came back in. "They're taunting us, and some of the men are yelling back."

"They're trying to provoke us." Victoria's fists clenched. "They know that once they engage us in battle, they'll win."

"Or else," Robert said, "they want us to reveal our weapons. They've heard of the Quorum's power, but they don't know what it can do as yet. Is there any weapon that can repel a company of archers under these circumstances, Lady Victoria?"

Victoria hesitated, which was all the answer he needed. "Do you know how many bowmen this regiment possesses, Alex?" she said.

"Perhaps a hundred and fifty. But they have crossbows."

Robert barely had time to imagine the bolts piercing armor and flesh before a man spoke up. His clothing was filthy, but he had a look of authority and Victoria had not asked him to leave the carriage. "If those hit the boilers, they'll be destroyed."

"Aren't they protected by the carriages, Philip?" Victoria asked.

"I'm afraid not, Lady Victoria. If the Dragon's boiler was hit now, it would explode and we would all be, well, killed."

Susanna and Nicholas started up. Lawrence didn't notice, since he was almost salivating at the closed door that hid what Robert guessed was the boiler. Victoria made a warding gesture that incorporated the names of three of the Benevolent Ones, and the Word's smile drained off his face.

Alex looked mildly interested. "Shame we couldn't lure them in here and then shoot a quarrel at the boiler."

"We don't have any crossbows." Robert's flicker of hope went out as if drowned by the rain. "They're bulky, slow and expensive. A few of our men have longbows."

Philip frowned. "If we have to destroy the boilers, it'd be better to remove their fusibles and block their safety valves. Let the water run out and the interior parts'll overheat. Then throw some more water in and watch the whole thing go up."

Victoria nodded. "Do that, then. It won't remove many of them, but—"

A cough interrupted her, and the man who had destroyed the bridge spoke. "I have a thought, Lady Victoria." Despite his scarred hands and thready voice, there was nothing weak about his demeanor as he looked around at the gathered people. "William Flerrin, chief alchemist to the Quorum. I have sat here thinking how best to use the explosives against our enemies. There are enough packages to cause damage, but this rain will wet the wicks before they can ignite the contents."

"You could cut them shorter." Alex frowned. "But that's dangerous, isn't it? They could ignite before you're ready."

"You're right, my lady," Flerrin agreed. "However, there is a safer method of both applying the explosives and destroying the boiler."

"You mean to set them off in here," Victoria said slowly.

Flerrin coughed again. "That is safest, is it not? For everyone concerned except the helmsman."

Victoria shook her head. "We can't afford to lose you. I'll appoint another—"

"No, thank you, Lady Victoria." Flerrin's voice was firm, and Robert didn't know whether to admire his bravery or try to save him from his suicidal urge. "There are others whom I have trained, and all my work is documented. You can afford to let me play a part in our victory."

"We can drive the Dragon out as if to attack them," Michael Frew said. "Then, when it bogs down, the cavalry will naturally close in to attack."

"And pack some kegs with nails, caltrops, whatever we can find," Lawrence said. "So that when the carriage explodes, it showers all that in the vicinity."

Victoria looked in his direction. "That is...somewhat clever. Sir Michael, give the orders."

Robert got up. "Susanna, let's get the supplies out of here. Lawrence, you're in charge of filling it with projectiles. This carriage is called the Sleeping Dragon, isn't it? Let's wake it up."

Alex brushed the wet hair from her eyes and looked at the carriages. The semicircle they had formed was still in place. Armored men crouched between the carriages, weapons bared, forming a solid line that protected the people behind them. She couldn't see the hounds clearly, but she caught flickers of movement in the rain.

"If only their horses sank into this wretched bog," Victoria said. "You'd think anything deep enough to hold our carriages would hinder their horses too."

"The horses weigh less than these overloaded steam coaches." Nicholas stepped back as Lawrence's men carried boxes into the carriage.

Alex waited for them to leave. "I must speak to Master Flerrin before they begin. Please excuse me."

She hurried back into the carriage, where William Flerrin was arranging barrels around the chest of explosives. He looked up as she entered.

"I'm going to seal the doors, my lady." He coughed again. "You had best leave."

"Thank you," Alex said through a constriction in her throat. She liked this man who had treated her with courtesy and whose knowledge—something she respected—would be splattered over the landscape in the next minutes.

"For what?" Flerrin said. "You have many more years of health before you. I don't. I regret nothing about my choice of profession, but few men remain unscathed by alchemy. If not without, then within,

191

from poisonous fumes or tasting unknown substances to identify them. I did not look forward to living out another decade with my health destroyed, unable to even talk without a shortness of breath."

"If you have no regrets, Master Flerrin, that is good enough." Alex hoped she could say the same eventually. "I'll leave now."

She shut the door. The knights drew away from the carriage, except for a few who crowded into the helmsman's deck, just enough to give the impression that the vehicle bulged with living cargo. A plume of steam screamed up from the top of the carriage, so loudly that Alex jerked back, nearly slipping in the mud. It drowned the sound of hooves as Mayerd galloped up.

"Better start." He didn't bother to dismount. "The bowmen have reached us."

"Pull out," Frew ordered, and the Dragon moved. Alex watched as it rolled down the road, away from the cavalry.

"Why is it going in the wrong direction?" she asked.

"It will build up speed that way." Philip Celagos sounded tired, but he was still the master mechanic. "Once it gets into the mud, that will be the end."

The cavalry had stopped their swift weaving moves and the horns silenced. They watched the Dragon in what Alex hoped was growing unease, and she heard the first shouts when the Dragon turned, off the East Road. The flat ground had contributed to its speed and the space around gave it plenty of room to maneuver despite its bulk. Spikes gleaming in the rain, it trundled straight at the cavalry, out of Alex's line of sight.

She hurried to the side of a stalled carriage, using it as cover to look out, and crouched beside a wheel that was nearly half her height. The spike on its hub was the length of her forearm. Crossbow bolts flew, but the quarrels were directed at the Dragon rather than the other carriages and the Dragon's boiler was fortunately not hit. The knights were not so lucky, and one of them dropped. Three others leaped down from the Dragon.

"Good," Victoria said tensely. "Give them another target."

Alex understood what she meant. The Dragon was still thirty yards from the cavalry, which pulled back in the center, forming a pincer to surround the carriage. The knights drew their swords in a last futile gesture before the quarrels cut them down. The Dragon lurched forward in a final spurt and a bolt drove into the helmsman's throat with such force that it pinned him upright to the back of the deck, like a butterfly.

Mud rose around the Dragon's wheels, sucking them down, and the carriage stopped. Its wheels vibrated, motive power straining, but the effort spent itself uselessly. Whoops arose from the cavalry as they surged around the trapped carriage.

"Get ready," Robert said. "Hit them at speed."

"We're ready." Frew's voice was a single breath, gelid as ice.

The door to the carriage opened and the cavalry halted. "What is he doing?" the Word said in a harsh whisper. "That wasn't in the plan!"

No, Alex thought, as William Flerrin slipped out of the carriage. "We surrender," he shouted in his cracked, rasping voice. "Please—show us mercy—"

He vanished from sight as the cavalry drove forward in a wave of glee. They surrounded the Dragon, ripping open slats and doors. And the carriage exploded. Alex crouched, hearing debris clang off the carriage that sheltered her as the call to battle rang out.

"Destroy them!" Frew shouted, swinging his warhorse around to lead the charge.

Nothing like an unexpected blow to even the odds, Alex thought as she looked back out. Her stomach turned; accustomed as she was to unpleasantness, this went far beyond her experience. Men and horses lay in the mud, which turned a vivid purple in the lightning. Their screams were worse to hear than the explosion had been, and the stench was a mixture of burned flesh, smoke and blood. The Dragon had disappeared, and bits of wreckage lay strewn about—not enough to construct a chicken coop, much less a steam carriage.

With a shout, the knights led the strike, their horses breaking from the line of steam carriages. They slanted their charge around the reduced mass of the cavalry, aiming for the men behind them. Half the bowmen broke and ran, but the rest fired. Horses crumpled, slewing up mud from their momentum, but the crossbows took too long to nock again, and each bowman could get off only a single shot before the knights struck them. Even as the cavalry tried to regroup, the men-at-arms were on them. The insurgents were not as well trained, but they didn't need to be, not against a force that had been halved and terrified.

The battle was over quickly, and the heralds called again, this time to regroup the insurgents and lead them further south, in the direction from which the bowmen had arrived. "That's the only thing we can do, isn't it?" Victoria said. "We can hardly continue to Radiath if the rest of this regiment pursues us down the East Road."

Alex knew why she might want to be convinced of that. A small contingent of men picked their way through the battlefield, killing wounded enemies or horses too injured to save. Some of those horses were their own, broken-winded after the night gallop to the bridge. A cart was filled with the spoils of war.

"I'll have to help find their camp." Susanna rubbed her arms as if banishing gooseflesh. "My dog can smell the way in case they hide."

Robert sighed. "Just stay close to Mayerd and don't take any undue risks."

Alex walked to the space where the bridge had been, telling herself she was glad that no one imposed any strictures on her or insisted that some man accompany her. She had half expected to see Nalle making a brilliant plan to cross the Stagwater, but the river's bank was as empty as if the hounds had never been there.

Footsteps crunched on the sludge and debris, and Robert came to stand beside her at a careful distance. "Will they try to rebuild the bridge?" he said.

"I doubt it. I don't think Nalle brought engineers—who would have thought a stone bridge would fall so fast? Besides, the river's so wide that building another bridge would take too long, especially since they'd have to go some distance for timber."

"True. So they would have gone downstream to the old bridge which they took to get over the river." Robert paused. "I'll send a few men to fire it before they reach it."

You don't need to tell me your plans, Alex thought and said nothing. She heard Robert clear his throat. "The Smiler's leaving us."

"Really?" Alex was surprised out of her silence. "To go where?"

"Back to the Mistmarch, of course, now that he's set Garnath's army on our trail. He can follow the Stagwater north—safer than staying with us now."

I suppose Victoria can be our beacon in the night. She's not as bad as that snake. The rain had stopped, so Alex excused herself and went to put on dry clothes. She helped with the cooking until the knights returned and Susanna's dog ran up to her. When she gave it a bone the heads began to fight over that, but it broke in two, so they both gnawed happily.

"Sir Michael, what news?" Victoria said.

The knight commander dismounted. "We burned their camp, Lady Victoria, and left a warning for the rest of the pack should they find their way across the river."

"Very good," the Word said, smiling. "What losses?"

"Nearly fifty." Victoria's eyes widened, and Frew said quickly, "Those are acceptable losses when outnumbered, Lady Victoria."

"I know, Sir Michael, but considering the small size of our forces to begin with..."

Robert nodded. "We have to conserve our strength for the assault on Radiath. So after the men have eaten and the horses have been watered, I suggest a meeting, Lady Victoria. We have matters to discuss."

Victoria hesitated. "Very well." She gestured to Frew and they rejoined the rest of the knights.

Mayerd approached them, and when Alex saw the flat withdrawn look in his eyes she went closer. "Is there any water?" he said.

Robert produced a flask. "What's wrong?" His voice grew tense. "Were you or Susanna hurt?"

"No." Mayerd rinsed out his mouth. "There wasn't any water at the camp—the hounds destroyed their supplies when they knew we had won. What we had went to the injured."

"Then why do you look as though you've seen a ghost?"

Mayerd began to unsaddle his horse, keeping his eyes on the harness. "Sir Michael is a skilled swordsman. He took on the regiment's commander and defeated her. Then he had a pot of wax set on a fire."

Alex had heard of that signature before, from Stephen's more brutal cohorts. She breathed out slowly. "That's what Sir Michael meant about a warning. He had her head dipped in it."

"Yes," Mayerd said. "But most people would have killed her first. Then he put her head on a pike and set it outside the camp."

Susanna came up to them, her dog at her heels. "I know this is war, but is it necessary to torture anyone?"

"No," Robert said. "I'm sorry you had to see that. And I'm glad I thought of the meeting. Nicholas, could you find a secluded location and secure it? Mayerd, pick five men, give them the best horses and send them to the bridge downstream. They are to destroy it before the hounds cross it. I know that army has a head start, but there's no point in going through all this just to have them after us again. Now, let's meet with the Quorumlords."

"What's this about?" Victoria asked. "I'd like to finish burying our dead and then move away from the river before we finally get some rest."

Alex was tired as well, but she felt the undercurrent of tension that began with Robert and flowed through the group of people, making them as wary as Victoria. She crossed her arms and felt the slight bulge of the explosive package under her sash.

Robert addressed the gathering. "We survived yesternight's attack. But if we're to stay together until we reach Radiath, we should unite our forces into one army, with one commander. As it is, we have too many different troops."

The unspoken "with different loyalties" settled into the silence. Victoria broke it first. "I suppose you would want to be this commander."

"Was there someone else you had in mind, Lady Victoria?" Robert managed to make it sound like a question rather than a challenge.

Victoria looked a little taken aback. "Well, I..." She glanced at the Word. "Your Grace?"

The Word's eyes glittered like scales in the sunlight. "You are wise beyond your years to suggest that I lead our victorious army. However, the good news must be taken to the High Quorum, and since my presence here is no longer required, I will take my leave."

Typical, but we'll be safer without him. Alex waited for Victoria's farewell.

"Why, Your Grace, there has been some mistake." Victoria's voice was cordial and her eyes were steel augers. "Your presence is indeed required here. You are a beacon of hope to our army. And when the gates of Radiath are breached, you should be with us, bringing light to the darkness."

For a moment Alex thought that she was hallucinating from sheer weariness, but the startled expressions around her were proof enough that everyone else had heard the same speech. Only Michael Frew nodded in agreement with Victoria. The Word's smile had frozen, and he looked like a puppet, stiff and wooden.

Then he rallied. "You are a fit representative of the Quorum, Victoria, my sister. I may be your superior, but it was my fondest hope that you would one day succeed to my place, and this is an excellent first triumph for you."

Victoria raised her eyebrows. "But, Your Grace, I am a woman and should not participate in such unwomanly arts as those of war. The troops would be more heartened by a man at their head."

Even the roar of the river seemed to have died down, and no one spoke in the silence that fell. The Word's smile had peeled off his face. Frew broke the stalemate.

"Lady Victoria is right, Your Grace." He paused when the Word turned molten-copper eyes to him, but continued awkwardly. "The— the Knights of Katash would prefer their leaders to be men, and their morale would be even higher were you to bless us with your presence."

"Look!" Victoria pointed at the sky. "A rainbow! The Benevolent Ones approve of what we have proposed."

"Please allow me to interpret signs from the Benevolent Ones," the Word said, but Frew had already raised his hands in thanks.

"A sign," he agreed.

The Word let the silence stretch to the breaking point before he spoke. "Very well. I shall see this holy war to its just conclusion. Now, are we finished?"

"Why, no, Your Grace. We were discussing who would command our joined forces." Victoria turned to Robert. "I suppose you would not be incompetent, Lord Robert. As long as His Grace and I are able to override any order you give."

Her voice hardened on the addendum, but Robert nodded. Alex guessed why he had given in—on the battlefield, there would most likely be no time for them to countermand an order.

Victoria looked mollified. "Now, about the uniting of our troops. The Katassian Knights cannot be lowered to the level of common infantry."

"I wouldn't dream of altering the status of the Katassian Knights," Robert said. In either direction, Alex thought. "However, I believe that we should be joined under a single banner."

"And I suppose you want to use your own family's sigil?"

"Why not?" Susanna said. "It's not fancy, so we can sew the banners along the way."

197

Robert went down on one knee and smoothed the earth. He spoke quietly but with pride. "The Demeresna emblem, the sign of the storm, has no more been given to tyrants than has the lightning itself."

He sketched a zigzag in the ground—a lightning stroke—and Alex remembered the long-ago day when Victoria had worried about a storm and said that Fulmion might have copper rods to conduct the lightning safely. Lawrence nodded his assent and Nicholas shrugged. Robert brushed his hands clean. "Then in this sign, we will conquer. No matter what enemies we face."

His voice was steady and confident, but it didn't make Alex feel any better, not after she had seen the vastness of the army after them. And if General Nalle discovered his cousin's death, he would make them all pay for it. But Victoria agreed and walked back to the makeshift camp, escorted by Michael Frew, while the Word stalked away after darting a venomous look at her back.

"That's a sign from the Benevolent Ones, all right." Lawrence grinned up at the rainbow. "They like to talk to people just after it rains."

"What was that all about?" Susanna said. "Why did she want him to stay with us? She must know he hates her now."

"Perhaps she hopes he'll be killed," Nicholas said. "That would leave a nice empty space in the upper echelons of the Quorum."

Robert groaned. "Damn the both of them. As if we didn't have enough problems already, we get two feuding Quorumlords."

Divisions in the ranks no matter what Robert does to unite them, Alex thought as people began to drift back to the camp. She went as well, and when no one was looking, she helped herself to a dagger. The package of explosive felt like a coiled snake against her stomach and she hoped fervently that it was only affected by fire, rather than by her body's warmth or the dagger's blade as she slipped that into her sash.

Then Robert gave the command and the march began again.

The good weather held while they broke camp and struck out again. They stayed on the move for hours and Susanna set up a schedule of riding in the steam carriages, to ease the burden on the horses. Not that there was anything pleasant about being in the steam carriages. Even disregarding their cramped, smoke-fumed interiors, anyone riding in them had to work, so Alex helped make the new banners while Susanna cut up linen for bandages. Each day was filled with tiring work which never quite stopped. The only consolation was that the duty of cooking for five hundred men did not fall on her, since the knights had brought along a contingent of menials who chopped wood, drew water, prepared meals and groomed horses.

She was grateful that nothing untoward appeared as they marched down the miles of the East Road. Each day she looked behind them for the hounds, and each night she listened for horns in the distance, but she neither heard nor saw anything. Not that that was good news, since the men whom Robert had sent to destroy the old bridge had not been seen again either.

"They had to cover the distance to the bridge and back, and we have a head start," Victoria said when Alex found herself alone in a jolting carriage with her. "I wouldn't speak about it. We have to keep morale high."

Alex didn't mention that she had no one to whom she could say anything. Mayerd treated her the same, but he was too busy to do more than exchange a few words. Susanna had picked up on the tension between her and Robert and, despite not knowing what it was about, had evidently sided with Robert, since she was polite but no longer friendly. So Alex threaded another needle and changed the subject. "Will His Grace hold a prayer service soon, Lady Victoria? I imagine that would improve morale too."

Victoria's white robes were stained with smut from the coal, but she seemed not to notice that, and the stare she bent on Alex was cold. "I was unaware that you were faithful in your prayers, Alex."

"I would be, if that made His Grace leave."

Victoria thawed a little. "I'm sure everyone wonders why I asked him to remain with us."

"Yes." Alex decided to be honest. "You know that he bears you ill will for that."

Victoria closed the ventilation slats. "Oh, I know. I'm not exactly taken in by all the Victoria-my-sister. And I've watched my step ever since I played my hand."

Alex frowned as she knotted the thread. "What exactly do you hope will happen, Lady Victoria? He could be a liability when we take Radiath."

"Indeed. But before then, he will show the knights his true colors."

"Which are?"

Victoria fanned herself. "My dear Alex, surely you're enough of a judge of men to deduce that. He may be clever, but he's an opportunistic coward. He can dominate people in the Quorum halls, but there's no bullying the walls of Radiath. Sooner or later he will break, and I want witnesses to that. When the High Quorum hears of it, he will be demoted."

And Victoria would take his place, Alex guessed. She could only hope that the Word didn't break when they were fighting their way through Radiath, when they could least afford a display of cowardice.

She kept her disquiet to herself, but considered taking the news to Robert. Stephen had been pleased when she brought him whispers from pillow talk, though she had been careful not to do that often. There was a line between being a useful tool and being a dangerous liability who knew too much.

But he hadn't minded her methods at all, whereas Robert might. A dog that would fetch a bone would carry a bone. Then again, what did it matter now? At least that way, she was still useful...and he should know.

So when they made camp that evening, she went to Robert's tent.

Robert knew he wasn't very good at devising methods to counter magic, but what he had heard of Iternan laws had given him an idea. Leaving that land without sanction carried a death penalty, which meant that very few Iternans became involved in the wars or politics of other lands. That was a great relief, given what Garnath had done with only one sorcerer, but now Robert wondered if he could enlist Iternan help in dealing with Ohallox.

It didn't matter that the land was a thousand miles away. He'd heard that the most powerful sorcery could take an Iternan from one city to another in three paces—but he wasn't at all sure how that was done, and imagined the Iternan with some kind of seven-league boots. He waited until they made camp that evening and sent word that he wanted to see Mayerd. Iternan bounty hunters, or whatever they were called, would make it so easy.

Except when the guards at his tent let Mayerd in and he heard the plan, he looked at Robert with mild surprise. "They know about Ohallox already."

"Oh." Robert felt deflated.

"Of course." Mayerd found a tinderbox and lit the lanterns. "You didn't really think the Lexterra or the Mirrors needed us to send word of Ohallox, did you? When his trace would have appeared on the spatial map of the Inward Way the moment he first used it here?"

"In other words, they know about Ohallox already." Robert thought that for someone who had fled Iternum in rags and who couldn't even do magic, Mayerd certainly knew a great deal about its workings. Another oddity about him. "Why don't they do something, then? They must know he's trying to wreak havoc on Garnath's behalf."

"Because they also know he's under Garnath's protection, so they can't simply charge in here. Hunters wait until their prey least expects it. Anyway, no hunter would ever come to Dagre on your request—it would look like they're choosing sides."

Robert gave up on Iternum as a lost cause. "All right. But there must be something we can do about this sorcerer. Perhaps find a way to tell when magic is being used against us?"

Mayerd looked dubious. "Unless the Inward Way acts against me and my lateral lines detect it, there's no detection system."

Robert supposed that was why it was called the Inward Way—no one could see what was happening inside something. "What about the other one? The Outward Way?"

"That's different. You could use red dust—that forms patterns when it's near the influence of the Outward Way."

Robert nearly started to ask why the dust had to be red, then decided against it—Iternan magic seemed to be as arbitrary as Iternan law, and he didn't really need to know how it operated. He was beginning to wish he'd never brought up the subject. Mayerd was probably a little perplexed, at best, at the spectacle of a Dagran fumbling his way around Iternan sorcery.

"I wouldn't worry about it yet," Mayerd said. "The Inward Way can't act over great distances unless it's got someone or something to act as a stepping stone."

"Something?" Until then, Robert had thought magic needed minds to influence. He found a bottle of wine that had been cushioned in straw and poured a healthy dose into battered tin cups.

"I shouldn't have said that." Mayerd accepted a cup. "I heard in the College that it's possible to prepare an object to hold the Way. But that's more than dangerous—it's suicidal. A living stepping stone can fight back if the Way shows signs of growing out of control, but an

201

inanimate receptacle can't. No Way practitioner would risk it. Why, even—even Ohallox wouldn't do that."

Robert knew that Mayerd had almost said another name, but had used Ohallox's at the last moment. He thought of asking what Mayerd was hiding, whether it was something Ohallox could use against him, and a bell clanged outside. Mayerd turned at once.

"The meal's ready. I'll bring yours in." He slipped out of the tent at speed.

Wonderful. Robert would have questioned Mayerd at length when they had first met, except at the time Mayerd had been starving and unable to speak Dagran. As a result, Robert only knew the obvious—that the fugitive he'd found had been brutalized in Iternum and needed help. *And by the time he picked up enough of our language, it was too late. He had my measure and knew that just being reticent wouldn't get him beaten or thrown out.*

Still, Mayerd would not have betrayed him for even a pardoned return to Iternum, and that counted for a great deal. He fitted the stopper back into the bottle and was rewrapping it as the tent flap was flung open behind him.

"Anyway, we can be sure Garnath didn't give us any such receptacles." He put the bottle back into its crate as he heard Mayerd enter. Bowls rattled softly against a tray. "Alex didn't bring anything with her out of Radiath. Good thing I burned her clothes."

He turned to take the tray and saw Alex standing beside Mayerd.

Robert's throat closed as if knotted shut. All the good manners he had thought were second nature to him flew through his mind, but didn't make their way out of his mouth. Mayerd set the tray down.

"Alex came to speak with you about something." He left the tent, pulling the flaps closed behind him.

Like all of them, Alex showed the hardships of the daily march—her boots were muddy, her skirts smeared with dust and tendrils of hair escaped from the knot at the back of her neck. Only her eyes hadn't changed. Like gemstones in the ground, cold and valuable and unbreakable.

"I beg your pardon." Robert cleared his throat. "We were discussing how inanimate objects can be used in magic. I didn't mean to imply I was happy that I'd burned your—"

"It's quite all right." Alex would have spoken the same way if he had made a small gaffe, like knocking over a glass of water. "I've spoken with Lady Victoria about her insisting that His Grace remain with us. She hopes he'll give way at some critical point and shame himself before their knights, so she can take his place eventually."

Robert's first thought was that Alex wasn't wasting any time with pleasantries. His second thought was, *Just as Nicholas predicted.* It made him uneasy. A chair could stand even if one leg of it was nearly sawn through, because the others would bear more than their share of weight, but kick the weakened leg hard enough—

"I'll just have to keep him out of harm's way." He only realized after the fact that he had spoken to Alex as if she was a confidante again. Too late to take back the words when she was looking at him with a faintly puzzled expression. "It's one thing to hope for a man's public failure, but it's another thing entirely when that man controls Quorum machines and commands troops."

Alex nodded. "Or you could let him slip away at night. Give him an escort and let him go back to the Mistmarch."

"If he can reach it." Robert didn't think General Nalle would expect such a retreat and send troops to intercept it, but Nalle was by no means the only threat. "We can't tell who might be a sympathizer of Garnath's. If the Smiler's captured...well, he knows about our weapons. We can't lose the advantage of surprise."

"Of course." Alex had gone back to being polite, and Robert thought of asking her to continue bringing him such reports. *And what can I give her in return?* He couldn't even ask her to stay and share his meal—it was one thing to ignore custom in the relative privacy of his house and another to do so in the middle of an army camp.

"I'll take my leave of you then." Alex walked out, but when Robert heard her speak to someone outside, he realized that she hadn't gone very far. He couldn't make out the words, but he heard Mayerd reply.

For the first time in his life he was jealous of Mayerd, even though he knew he had no competition from that quarter. Mayerd had never shown any interest in Dagran women, and wouldn't start with one who had been given to his friend and liege lord. That made Robert feel both relieved and ashamed, as did the silence outside when Alex left. She wasn't spending too much time with Mayerd. They just had a few things in common, that was all.

He would find a woman with whom he had something in common as well. Someone like Diana. Even if such a woman hadn't ridden in his ranks and come to him the night before a battle, she would still be a good wife—and fertile, he had to remember that.

The comfort was cold, much like his meal when he finally ate.

They had traveled for well over a week, and the Hammer of Katash was only two days away. Robert sent men into the city to buy coal, thinking that he would rather have a good horse than one of the carriages any day. They were noisy, constantly in danger of failure, couldn't move in the mud, ate expensive fuel and belched clouds of smoke. He couldn't understand Lawrence's fascination with them.

The good weather held as they passed the Hammer and continued down the Red Road, and he was so focused on the city at the end of that road that he rarely thought about Alex during the day. It was only at night that he remembered showing her the land, hearing her laugh, making love to her. Common sense and longing fought a constant battle, and he told himself to be grateful for the distance between Alex and himself. If she had been sweet or confiding, she could have tipped the scales in one direction with a single touch.

Now she was going west on the road the same way she had gone east on it: cool, distrustful of him, and not volunteering information. He also suspected she was plotting something behind that mask of a face—not because he had any evidence of it, but because it was safe to assume that at her quietest and most reserved, Alex was at her most speculative.

So he was not at his best on the evening when Peter came to his tent to say that the Word of the High Quorum was outside. He tried to think of some excuse to avoid the visit, but it also occurred to him that the Word had not sought a private meeting since they had left Fulmion, so he nodded. The Word entered and seated himself on a pile of blankets.

"Thank you for your time, my son."

The next time he addresses me in that condescending way, I'll ask if he's calling my mother an adulteress. "Is there anything I can do for you, Your Grace?"

The Word studied him without any trace of a smile. "I am determined that we should win this war."

Robert was a little taken aback. The Word was technically on their side, but he seemed to value his own skin more than anything else. Still, perhaps he had come to see that there were other priorities, and Robert supposed there was no harm in giving allies the benefit of the doubt. "So am I."

"Good. Since we are of one mind, perhaps you will share the strategy you will use to defeat Radiath. One that will take Garnath's army into account if they do catch up with us before we have forced a surrender from the city."

Robert had never heard such an unwelcome speech before. Trying to make the gesture look like natural courtesy rather than an attempt to buy time, he poured two goblets of wine. The Word waved his away.

"Your Grace," Robert said after a long draught from his cup, "our weapons would be more than adequate against the gates of Radiath." He hoped they would also be intimidating enough to convince the city's population not to raise arms against his troops. "Once we have gained a foothold, it's only a matter of fighting our way to the castle."

There was a pause as the Word waited for him to continue. "That is your strategy?"

Robert decided to be blunt. "It's a simple plan. Those are more likely to be understood by everyone and less likely to fail. Besides, I can't see any other way to breach the city."

"Can't you?"

"No. A siege or sapping will take too long, and we'll be attacked on all sides while we do it." Including from inside their heads, when Garnath's sorcerer acted. "What else do you have in mind, aside from a frontal assault?"

The Word shrugged. "I would not presume to instruct you on matters of war. However, I will say this." He paused again. "There is no point in a victory that leaves us as weakened as our enemies. If you conquer Radiath but have only a handful of soldiers remaining, one or more of Garnath's allies will wipe you from the face of Eden. The weapons of war are one wheel, Robert, not the entire conveyance. I leave it up to you to find the other two or three wheels, or we will be halted long before we breach the city walls. And do not be too concerned about sparing the lives of our enemies. I could place you under a moral dispensation until the war is won."

"Do you believe your sanction makes any difference to me?" Robert said.

"The sanction of the Benevolent Ones."

"If I wanted to break a law, Your Grace, I wouldn't need their permission to do so. And if I wanted to keep one, all nine of them couldn't offer me anything worth changing my mind."

The Word drew in a long breath and released it before rising to his full height, which brought the top of his head scraping against the tent. "There is a time for honor and a time to crush the enemy by any means necessary, and a good leader can tell the difference between the two. I have already spoken to Nicholas Rauth and Lawrence Chalcas, who are inclined to agree."

"Well, you'd better pray for a bloody miracle then. In your own tent, if you don't mind." Robert thought that might lead to further castigation, but it was clear that the Word could tell when he had won. He grinned, eyes and teeth bright even in the dimness of the tent, and walked out. Robert reached for the untouched goblet and drained it at a gulp. He needed alcoholic fortification for his next engagement.

"Peter?" he said.

"Yes, my lord?"

"Bring Alex Khayne here."

Alex slept in an empty carriage that felt emptier when she was in it, so rather than retire she went to see Mayerd. He was too close to Robert's tent for her liking, but she knew he wouldn't turn her away. He sat by a fire alone, his dark head bent over something in his hands, and she heard the clack of wood.

She walked closer. "Are you repairing something?"

Mayerd started as if he had been hit with a snowball and tried to hide what he held under his blanket.

"What was that?" Alex didn't reach for whatever it was, because she remembered how fiercely she had held on to her few possessions when she had lived in Stephen's castle.

Mayerd rubbed the back of his neck in an embarrassed way. "I suppose you won't tease me about it."

"*Riye.*" Alex took the toy when he handed it to her. "From Lunacy?"

"*Iyein.* Think you could solve it?"

Alex worked at the projecting slats of wood, but it was like trying to put together a jigsaw with no picture on the pieces. The slats bent, slanted and even revolved on an axis, but they never all fit together to form a cube. Finally, feeling that the toy had drained her far more than making the lightning-bolt banners, she handed it back.

"Definitely Lunacy. Do you think it can even be solved?"

206

Mayerd looked doubtful, then indignant. "It would be just like Robert to give me a puzzle with no solution. This is his way of repaying me for the other gifts that I didn't keep."

Alex couldn't help laughing. "Oh, keep working at it. Who knows, you might find the right combination—"

"Pardon me, sir." A shadow fell across the firelit ground and she looked up to see Peter. "Lord Robert asked me to bring her to his tent."

Bring her? As if she were a child, so he didn't need to ask her permission or speak directly to her? Alex would have said that if she hadn't noticed the men nearby glance in her direction. There was enough attention on her already without starting an argument—and Peter wasn't the one who deserved that argument—so she stood and smoothed the wrinkles out of her skirts.

"I think he's more scared of you than you are of him," Mayerd said in Iternan.

"I am *not*... He's what?" Alex realized she had spoken in the wrong language and turned on her heel while she still had most of her dignity intact. Peter looked bewildered but led her to Robert's tent and held the flap back for her.

Inside, two lanterns glowed on a wooden chest and in their light she looked warily at Robert. He seemed much the same as he had been in Fulmion, except for the faint hollows under his eyes.

"That was quick." He looked faintly surprised, and Alex hoped he didn't think she had been wandering about near his tent like a lost puppy. "I mean, I expected Peter to take longer to find you. Would you like to sit down?"

"No, thank you." Alex had been with more men than she wanted to remember, but she had never felt so constricted in one's presence. She might have been wearing one of the whalebone vests Susanna had mentioned. With other men, knowing them intimately made her aware of their failures and shortcomings. With Robert, it worked in the other direction, and he knew her too deeply for her own good.

"Then would you like a drink?"

Why was he doing that, after telling her he hated beating around the bush? "Of what, dragora? Or wait, would you like me to undress first?"

Robert sat down on a pile of blankets, rubbing his thumb between his eyebrows. "No, I wouldn't." He dropped his hand and his gaze was so direct that she longed to look away, except that would have been a sign of weakness. "I'm sorry about what I said earlier. I should never have insulted you like that."

The ground shifted under Alex's feet. Robert could take her aback with something as simple as an apology, but a dull ache also began in her chest as she realized he wouldn't have called her to his tent only to apologize. He looked tired and vulnerable—so much so that she couldn't tell him to just get on with what he wanted—but she wouldn't be fool enough to let her guard down with him again.

"Well, that makes everything better then," she said.

Her voice sounded wooden, and Robert flushed, but his bearing was as stiff as ever and reminded her of the lord of the land extending a gloved hand to a mendicant. "Words are better than nothing and deeds are better than words. So if there's anything I can do to make amends—"

"Would you mind telling me what you need from me?"

Robert sighed. "His Grace the Word of the High Quorum told me that he wanted some way to take Radiath with minimal losses."

"You mean, he wants us to have a strategy in mind first?"

"I did have— Well, he wants something less straightforward than what I'd planned to do."

"Oh, my," Alex said. "It sounds as if he wants to try something underhanded. How dishonorable. I hope you put him in his place."

Robert's mouth tightened. "There are times you deserve a slap or two."

"Well, go ahead." Alex turned her face sideways. "Some men enjoy that kind of thing."

In the pause that followed, she heard Robert's breathing. "Are you quite finished?"

"No, Robert, I haven't even started." Something in the pit of her stomach cringed into a cold knot and told her not to be stupid, he could very well hit her if he wanted to, but her mouth seemed to be moving of its own volition. "When I suggested we do something other than simply throwing ourselves at the gates, you called me dishonorable and deceitful. But I'd rather that than be on a tall pedestal like you, because it's a long way to the ground from your lofty height."

Robert got up as if the pile of blankets had bitten him. "I didn't mean that!"

"Then why did you say it?"

"Because you were talking about the Duke of Goldwood."

The conversation had taken a turn into uncharted waters. Alex thought back over whatever she had told him about the duke, trying to remember if she had said anything offensive. "Is he a friend of yours? Did I insult him?"

Robert lowered his face into his hands. Alex felt even more uncertain, but it was easy to keep her face blank when she had no idea how to react. "Let's just put this aside for now," he said. "Would you?"

He hadn't hit her when she had been sarcastic, and if he was going to speak normally to her, Alex thought she had to stop resenting him. She had remained on more or less amiable terms with a dozen men who had asked for her whether she wanted it or not, so the least she could do was extend the same courtesy to Robert.

"We need to capture that city with most of our men alive." She went to the chest, took the lanterns off it and sat down. "The cannon could do that, but if we keep them at any distance from Radiath, they'll be flattened by the catapults on the walls."

"And if we roll them closer, they'll be flattened anyway," Robert said. "The cityfolk just won't need the catapults then."

"Right. They'll use burning oil too. What if we built a reinforced cover for the cannons?"

Robert shook his head. "Even if we construct one which can withstand strikes from a catapult, that will take time. And any shield for cannon will be large, so we'll have to build it once we reach Radiath—we won't make much progress dragging it behind us."

"There's Nalle's army as well. How close are they?"

"I don't know, but I'll leave a man behind in the Hammer to watch for news. Safest to assume that they're close." When he sat, it looked less like relaxation than like giving way under a burden. "I don't want us to be caught between that army and that city, between a hammer and anvil."

The image was so vivid that it made Alex wonder if they could just move out of the way, letting the hammer and anvil break each other. "Could we make General Nalle attack Radiath instead of us?"

"Why would he do that?" Robert frowned. "Unless we had already captured the city."

"Or he thought we had."

The frown vanished. "I see. What kind of evidence would work?"

That would be a problem. "We can smash the city gates and get well out of sight, but that's still not convincing. What if we disguised a few people as refugees and sent them to tell the hounds that Radiath fell?"

Robert looked dubious. "I wouldn't attack a city unless an enemy standard was flying over it."

"We might do that too. If we slip some men into the city, we could order them to get to a vantage point and raise your banner over it when they hear the army approach."

"They'd be sacrificing their own lives to do that."

"They'd sacrifice them anyway if we face Nalle in battle. Offer them whatever it takes—lands or wealth or a knighthood." Alex considered. "I'd wait until Nalle's army is less than half a day behind us and stage the attack in the afternoon, so they arrive at Radiath when it's evening. They'll see less that way."

"It's a risky plan," Robert said. "If it fails..."

Alex started to lean back before she remembered she was in a tent. "Then I suppose you'll wait a while before asking me for advice again. But I don't expect Radiath and Nalle to wipe each other off the face of Eden for us. The best we can hope for is to reduce their numbers—take bits and bites out of them until we weaken them."

"If they're weakened enough, we could even face them in battle," Robert said. "When I visited Radiath, I stopped at a monastery miles south of the city, on high ground. Fortified too."

"And staunch supporters of Stephen, no doubt."

"Oh, they praised him high and low while trying to hide the spaces on the shelves where their silver candlesticks had been." Robert smiled, and Alex pretended that that hadn't made her heart turn over. "I think they'll shelter us."

"We could retreat there after we prepare the stage. If Nalle discovers the trick and follows us, we can fight without the city providing cover fire for him. But is that monastery large enough for all of us?"

Robert shook his head. "Have to split up our forces. I'll speak to Lawrence and Nicholas about that. The Quorumlords as well." He hesitated. "I won't be able to tell them you suggested it."

"No one will ever hear about it from me."

"But it's not that I'm not grateful," Robert said hastily. "I do appreciate your help. Very much."

Don't feel anything, Alex thought. His courtesy was worse than her cold reserve. Her response was a mask, but Robert wasn't as good a liar, so she was seeing what he actually felt for her—a dutiful politeness. Just being alone with him made her think of the night they had made love, made her remember the strength of his arms around her and the softness of his hair against her skin, but he didn't seem to want her any more than he had on the night they had first met.

"And if it works," Robert said, "if your plan helps us win this war, just ask me for whatever you want and it's yours."

Alex's pride was the only thing that had sustained her through so many empty years, the only thing that kept her from believing she was as worthless as the world thought she was. It was still there, as stiff-necked as ever, and it made her reply, "Nothing."

"I beg your pardon?"

"You heard me." Alex rose. "I don't want your charity."

"Benevolent Ones, it isn't charity!" Robert got up as well. "I just want to do what's right."

What a noble sentiment. "Whatever coin you would have tossed at me, give it to the poor and destitute in Madelayn. I have other ways of supporting myself."

Robert's brows went up. "Such as?"

"I've learned about those machines from the Quorum mechanics."

"Oh, so that's what you've been doing with..." Robert reached for a bottle of wine. "Are you sure you don't want a drink? Because I need one."

"Another one," Alex said, looking at the empty goblets. "And how did you know I spent time with the mechanics? Did you order your men to watch me?"

She expected her tone to rile him, but as usual he took her by surprise when one corner of his mouth went up. "You know, Alex, you're clever about many things." He set the bottle down unopened. "But there's one matter you're not so smart on."

"And what's that?"

"Men."

She couldn't have heard right. "You're joking."

"I'm not. You don't understand men as well as you think you do."

211

"That's ridiculous." If all she had done was lie on her back, rather than listening and speaking to men as well as she pleasured them, no one would have known who the Black Mare was. "And coming from you... Do you think you understand women?"

"No. But I know I don't. That's the difference."

"I don't have to take insults from you."

"True. You can leave that way if you want to."

Even a glance at the tent flap might have made her look nervous, so she dug her feet into the rug and kept her posture straight. "What do you mean, I don't understand men?" If Robert was trying to keep her off-balance, she could return the favor. "You think I'm stupid, so spell it out."

"Damn it, Alex, I don't think you're stupid." That got some reaction other than peculiar remarks, but he paced forward as he spoke, and she wished he would keep his distance. "I think too much of you for my own good."

Alex felt even more confused. "What does *that* mean?"

"It means I miss you," Robert said quietly. He was so close that a flush spread through her skin, as if neither his clothes nor hers existed and his body could warm hers even if they stood apart. "I don't know if you..."

If I... Before she could complete that thought, Robert touched her shoulder. She flinched, and he drew his hand back at once. "I'm sorry, I didn't mean to scare you."

"I'm not scared." Move*, so you don't prove it by looking paralyzed,* she thought but her feet took a step forward. When she tore her gaze from his, she found herself looking at his mouth instead, and she couldn't think any further when his hands slid up her arms. That time, she didn't start so much as shiver, and she knew Robert had felt the movement when he lowered his head.

Alex closed her eyes as his lips brushed hers, but even as her mouth opened, Robert's body went still. He raised his head and released her.

"I shouldn't have done that." His voice was controlled. "It was wrong of me to make advances without offering you any promise or pledge. I—it won't happen again."

Alex felt as if she had swallowed a stone. How polite, to pretend this was all somehow due to his failing. She had thought that being treated as a mare was bad, but there was something worse, not being wanted even for that function by a man she longed for. He might talk about missing her, but those were just more empty pretty words.

"You're right, it won't happen again." She was glad she sounded even calmer than he did. "Because I'm tired of this now-I-want-her-now-I-don't game. There are a lot of men here who don't behave like nervous boys with their trousers sewed shut." That, she saw, made heat flare in his eyes, but before he could reply she walked out.

Robert sent one of his most trusted men, Hugh Senneith, into the Hammer, then held the meeting a few hours later. They would stage a frontal assault, he said, but it would be a diversion.

"That's when we send a small group of picked men in through a side gate. Or even by the river. They'll raise our banner over the city at the crucial moment. If it works, Garnath's army will strike the city before anyone within can reveal our trick. If it doesn't, we'll be not much worse off."

The Word nodded. "Our army will be held in reserve until Garnath's forces have smashed themselves against the walls of Radiath."

"I spoke to the Quorum mechanics," Victoria said. "We have just enough explosives left for a subterranean detonation device—a land mine, they call it. I believe the river will be watched, because it's an easier way to enter the city, but the side gate won't be heavily guarded if we draw defenders away from it with an attack elsewhere. And more importantly, the road leading to the side gate won't be paved."

Unpaved road, subterranean detonation device, however the two worked together... Robert longed to call Garnath out to a duel and end the war right there. No big words and machines needed. "I don't understand, Lady Victoria."

"It's very simple." Victoria spoke slowly, as though he was just as simple. "Under cover of the attack, our elite infiltration force can dig a cavity under the gate to deposit the land mine."

"But by the time they do that, the guards at the gates will hear the sound. If they don't try to kill our troops, they'll simply grab your device from the other side of the gate."

"I hope so," Victoria said. "There's a conveniently placed handle."

"It's a trick?" Lawrence said.

"Of course. The handle drives a flint on to steel. That ignites the last of our explosives. I believe those devices work even more effectively if they're underground and the flint is connected to a tripwire."

"I see." Robert thought that if the Quorum ever wanted to punish him for his sins, they could simply string a few tripwires up on his land. They wouldn't even need to connect the wires to devices first. "That should get our men in."

"And from then?" the Word said.

Robert had decided that he, the Quorumlords and their machines would go south to the monastery while Nicholas led the other half of the army north. As he had expected, Nicholas approved. It would be his chance at glory and spoils, since Garnath's army was far more likely to pursue the machines than to give chase to him.

"I'll press any advantage I see," he said.

"Don't do anything rash," Robert said. "You'll have less than a thousand men under your command."

"A smaller army is a more maneuverable one," Nicholas said. "But what of you?"

"We'll fall back to the monastery a few miles south of Radiath." Robert tried to remember what the monks called the place. "The House of, um." Susanna, sitting in a corner where no one else could see her, quickly held up three fingers and put the other palm flat on the top of her head. "The House of the Third Blessing. From there, we'll plan our next step."

No one asked any more questions but once they had all gone, Susanna got up. "We'll have to stop running sooner or later."

"Sooner," Robert said. "The more time we give Garnath, the more time he has to call on reinforcements and the more time Nalle has to defeat us. I'd give a lot for some way to lead him into a surer trap. From what I've heard, that army would lose a lot of its spine if he was gone."

"You could have asked Alex. I'll bet she'd have come up with something cleverer." Susanna whistled for her dog and wished him a good night before she left.

The next day, Robert chose what Victoria called the elite infiltration force and what he thought of as the poor brave bastards whom they would never see again. Secure high ground, he told them, and raise my banner when you hear the hounds. He also gave them more silver than any of them had seen before, hoping they could use it to bribe their way out of difficulty, but it felt like blood money. Victoria looked askance at the payment, evidently thinking of other uses to which it might be put. Then she blessed the men after reminding them that the Benevolent Ones saw whatever they did, and would not be so benevolent if they ran from their duty.

Another week of hard riding took Robert and his men well past the Siege Circle, and towards the end of that time, he knew they would reach Radiath in a day or two. During that night Hugh Senneith staggered into camp, his feet bloody. The entire camp roused, but Hugh had already spoken his news by then.

"Nalle." His voice was flayed with exhaustion. "Reached the Hammer. He's after us."

"How far behind us?" Victoria said.

"A day perhaps."

"Then let's go," Robert said, and Mayerd alerted the troops. The herald's long peal sounded, a call to flight, a charge towards a city that had never fallen in war, from an army that had never been defeated. The battle of Radiath had begun.

Chapter Ten:
Gathering Thunder

"Burn everything in need of repair," Robert said. "Tents too. We won't need them now."

At any other time, Alex would have slipped into a steam carriage, but she would be more nervous if she didn't know what was happening outside. She hurried to the area fenced in by a captured stagecoach and the carts, where the horses had been tethered to the wheels, and she stroked Tempest before she fastened a saddle on his back. She wished she had a carrot for him, but their food supplies were low again.

A man-at-arms—she didn't know whose estate he served, because he wore a crudely bent sign of lightning—inspected the stagecoach and shook his head. "This wheel is ready to split. Stand back. I'll put it to the torch."

Alex nudged Tempest away as the fire grew, licking at the stagecoach. They still had the six steam carriages, but those delayed them while the fires were lit and the water boiled, building up a head of steam. They shrieked as valves opened to release the excess steam, and within moments, the herald sounded the last call. At the head of the column, Robert was flanked by two men who carried lightning-bolt banners.

"No need for secrecy," he said to Nicholas. "We fly our colors, and we stop for nothing. Strike out."

The forced ride lasted throughout the night, at a pace Alex would never have believed possible. At morning, Robert called a halt, and for the first time she was glad of a strong drink—a raw red wine. It burned her stomach, but sent new strength into her aching limbs, and then the ride began again.

They passed through deserted fields and pastures, where men had dropped their hoes and run for cover at the sight of an approaching army. A land opened up before them, civilized yet empty of its inhabitants, and they saw Radiath in the distance. It was impossible to tell the time, since the clouds had thickened to block out the sun.

Alex sweated as much from the heat as from fear, and the afternoon seemed like twilight. Steadily Radiath grew in size, and when Robert called a halt again, the day was almost over. She slipped out of the saddle and laid her face against Tempest's flank. The only relief was that the hounds were still not in sight.

"I don't suppose General Nalle would agree to a challenge of single combat?" Robert said from beside her. Alex glanced up, so startled that she didn't refuse when he put a strip of dried beef in her hand. "Chew on that while you're thinking."

Sighing, she obeyed. "I don't need to think long. He might agree, but..." *Don't say he's a highly skilled swordsman. Robert will just take that as a challenge. Who says I don't understand men?* "...but he'll wear armor." She looked pointedly at Robert's brown velvet jacket and brown breeches. "And he won't fight fairly."

That was a lie, but Robert had no way of knowing it, so he only handed her another flask half-full of gut-burning wine. She finished it and climbed into the saddle while he adjusted a stirrup.

"Have you seen Mayerd anywhere?" he said quietly.

Now that her attention was brought to his absence, she knew she hadn't. "You don't think he's...missing?"

Robert grimaced. "He wouldn't desert. There's no place for him to go, even if he did. I'll ask the men."

The answer came that the captain had not felt well since that morning, and was in a carriage. There had been enough injuries to result in a number of wounded who rode in the carriages. But Mayerd's excuse was far too vague, and Alex knew they could never expect the men to fight bravely if their captain was absent.

"Tell him to join us." Robert started the ride even before the man could reach the carriage. A breeze sifted the grass, and by the time Mayerd's horse drew level with them, the wind had snapped the banners out straight. Mayerd didn't appear to notice anything, and his gaze was fixed between his horse's ears.

217

"You took your damn time." Robert's voice was a whipcrack. "What is it?"

A cold warning curled Alex's skin. "It's the Inward Way."

Nudging his grey to keep pace with them, Mayerd said, "Ohallox." His voice sounded flat and tired, as if he was stating a fact they all knew. "He's a presence growing stronger in my mind, but I don't know what he's doing."

"No signs at all?" Alex asked. "Hallucinations or hints of coercion?"

"*Riym.*" Mayerd caught a strange look from Robert and clarified. "Neither. I think he's simply...probing. And that's frightening, because I don't know what he'll do when he strikes."

Robert nodded. "You did well to keep this silent. Just stay as safe as you—"

"Wait." For the first time, Alex felt neither the jolts of the road through her body nor the fear of hounds in the distance. "There's one thing he can't do. He can't take you on to the Inward Way, isn't that right? He can't use you as a stepping stone for it."

"Yes," Mayerd said. "But that's because the Inward and the Outward Ways don't mesh easily, and I walked the Outward Way to begin with."

"Does Ohallox know that?"

Mayerd stared down, but Alex saw his eyes swivel from side to side. "He doesn't know. Why should he? He left Iternum before everything went wrong and Elinah became Waymistress. And I've never heard of anyone being punished like this—anyone who was would have died a long time ago, especially here!" His hands clenched. "Ohallox must think I'm a practitioner of the Inward Way. He wouldn't play it so cautious otherwise."

Robert frowned. "Why would he think you walk the Inward Way, when you don't?"

"Because my heartmist—" Mayerd took a deep breath. "The person who crippled me used the Inward Way to build a wall in my mind. It's *that* he senses, that drop of the Inward Way, and like any wall it stops him from seeing anything behind it."

Alex said nothing, even when Robert looked at her to ask if she understood any of that. She turned a single word over, the word Mayerd had almost spoken. *Heartmistress.* The woman whom he had loved—and she had crippled him.

Which meant he had killed her.

Which explained why he had escaped from Iternum, and why he had loathed himself enough to want to die.

Suddenly her life didn't look so bad in comparison. She heard her name spoken over the clops of the horses' hooves, and looked up. "I'm sorry. What did you say?"

Mayerd's eyes shone, and she didn't know if it was with joy or tears. "Ohallox is strong enough to destroy that wall, Alex, I know he is. If he does—"

"You could walk the Outward Way again?"

He had already moved on to other thoughts, speaking aloud to himself. "But I don't know what traps Elinah built into the barrier. Its destruction could kill me." He paused. "That might not be so bad— especially if I can take *him* with me. But the results might be worse. And how to trick him into attacking it in the first place?"

The last question was something Robert could handle. "Make him think you're growing stronger."

"How?" Mayerd asked.

"We're only a few miles from Radiath," Alex said. "Perhaps the closer we get, the more nervous he'll be—until he strikes."

"That's not enough," Mayerd said. "I can sense him in my mind, and my lateral lines feel like two open wounds. He's making no efforts to hide this time, and if I don't act, if I don't retaliate, he'll guess that I can't—"

"Get a grip on yourself!" Robert said. Mayerd's voice had started to rise, and the men nearest them edged forward to listen. He continued more quietly, but with iron force. "Don't lose control, Mayerd, because that's the only weapon you have left. And if you show fear, it'll spread to the men quicker than—"

Mayerd's head came up. "That's it."

Robert pushed a hand through his hair and glanced at Alex, but she shrugged to show that she didn't understand either. Behind them wheels trundled and harnesses jingled, but Mayerd released the reins, careless of the horse stopping in its tracks. Robert held up a gloved hand, and the column came to a halt, orders shouted down the line to the carriages.

"This may not work," Mayerd said.

"*What* may not work? For all our sakes—"

"Listen." Mayerd was suddenly calm, none of the bleakness or febrile intensity in his face. "I am going to project as much of the Inward Way as I can upon you."

Alex blinked. "Us?"

"Yes. Starting with you, Alex, since you're the most receptive. But I'll mark each person here with as much of the Way as I can—from the barrier."

Robert shook his head as if brushing away cobwebs. "I don't understand, Mayerd. First you said you can't use the Way. What will this do for us?"

Mayerd started to speak, looked around at Lawrence and Susanna as they rode up, then at the Word's bright copper eyes. "Alex, help me here."

Alex considered. "It's like a cat. When a cat marks its territory, that doesn't alter the cat. But its scent is left everywhere, and if you're sensitive to cats, you'll feel its presence even after it's gone."

"Right," Mayerd said. "And while I can't shift the barrier that was formed from the power of the Inward Way, I can rub a minute scent of it off on everyone else."

"You are speaking of sorcery," the Word said. "The Quorum will not countenance it."

"His Grace is quite right," Frew said. "Lord Robert, we were told that this man was not a sorcerer. Was that incorrect?"

Robert sighed. "He's no sorcerer, but do you see anyone here who knows more about magic? What about yourself, Sir Michael? Would you like to face Garnath's sorcerer alone?" The knight commander hesitated. "Don't waste your good steel on that coward. Let's turn his own magic against him instead."

"You can do that?" Victoria asked Mayerd. "Without harming us?"

Mayerd nodded. "Nothing will change for you, because I can't do a complete projection. It's the lightest of touches, just enough to transfer some of my scent—like a cat rubbing against you, think of it that way."

"But Ohallox will think that you're extending the barrier to protect everyone," Alex said.

"Yes. And if that doesn't frighten him, if that doesn't make him act immediately, nothing will." Mayerd dismounted. "If you don't agree, I cannot be held responsible for what this sorcerer does—and his talents are impressive even by Iternan standards."

Victoria wavered. "You will not twist us with magic?"

"I give you my word."

"The word of a—" the Word began.

But Victoria interrupted. "Your Grace, the army that pursues us is visible from the Chariot. We have no time left. You, being seniormost among us, should remain unaffected by this man, so that even if he twists us with magic, you may be able to save us."

Clever, Alex thought. She watched as Victoria set her shoulders back and stepped up to Mayerd as if she approached a gallows.

"Very well," she said.

Mayerd took her hand and held it for a moment before releasing it. Victoria looked at her hand, turned it over and inspected it again. "Was that all?"

"Yes," Mayerd said. "Contact and willingness are enough to transfer the Inward Way. And I have only one aspect of it. An unbreakable wall. To Garnath's sorcerer, it is forming around you as we speak."

"Then hurry." Victoria swallowed hard as she spoke, but it was still an order. The knights stepped forward, one by one, and for the first time in their lives Alex saw them allow the touch of an Iternan.

Ohallox frowned, not understanding. His first probe had detected the other Iternan easily. Then he had braced himself for the inevitable counterassault, which never came. He didn't know why, because he sensed that Mayerd was powerful. It was like the old practice of dowsing for water—the hazel twig shuddered near an underground source. Similarly, his probe reacted to Mayerd's strength, but that strength was never used.

At first he thought that Mayerd had not even noticed his touch, not with a defense so strong. Or was that what Mayerd wanted him to think? Was he being toyed with, baited into committing to an attack from which there would be no turning aside? Especially since Mayerd was familiar with the Inward Way too. Ohallox had known that as soon as he saw his enemy help the mare while staying off the Way himself. The Way had put his voice into a serpent, the keeper of knowledge and bringer of death, and Ohallox did not like the implications of that.

With growing desperation, Ohallox began his attack, driving

against the wall with increasing force—it was as much as he could do while off the Inward Way itself. When facing a stronger enemy, it was safer to stay in reality. He knew that Mayerd sensed his assault now, and again he waited for a backlash which never came.

Then news reached them on a jackdaw's wings—Demeresna's army was on its way to Radiath. Somehow they had slipped past the hounds, who were giving chase. So that was why Mayerd did not retaliate; he was biding his time, waiting for a close confrontation. Ohallox opened the windows of his study and despite a sky full of clouds, he felt better. The baron's forces would be crushed between the city and the army. Perhaps he could simply leave Mayerd, because the hounds would tear any Iternan to pieces.

But that might be dangerous for him as well. The guards Stephen had assigned to him were outside, and Stephen expected him to act. If he simply sat back while Mayerd mesmerized half the hounds into attacking the other half, he would need to escape or kill Stephen or both. He would not balk at killing Stephen, but he had no illusions about his future in Dagre if he did, especially with a hostile Way practitioner so close at hand. So he returned to his task.

And that was when he realized that the wall had grown. Of course, that was a feature of the Inward Way—it spread like mold on bread wherever it could—but what was Mayerd thinking, extending his protection over Dagrans—

Ohallox went rigid in his chair. He imagined the city gates flung open, the castle left undefended as the garrison became convinced that the people outside were friendly. Then the slaughter would begin. And when the victors marched up the stairs of the Spiral Tower with swords drawn, his power would shatter against the walls that protected them. They could hold his attacks off for the moments it took to kill him.

It had never occurred to him that Mayerd might defend the insurgents with his own power, because no Iternan would have done so much for a Dagran. Now he was truly afraid.

No. I can still defeat him. He gathered his strength, gathered every drop of hatred he felt for the Iternan who challenged him so carelessly, and formed it into a bolt of power so concentrated that it felt like acid in his mouth. When he rammed it against Mayerd's defenses, he thought, *Die or go insane.* Then he was caught up in the raging storm, and he was beyond thought.

They were so close to Radiath that Robert saw people running for the city, and he slowed White Wind to a trot as the great iron-banded gates began to close. The defenders on the walls of Radiath swarmed like ants.

One of the gibbet cages that hung from them crashed to the ground, splintering. The others soon followed, to deny his troops any easy way to climb the walls. The gates slammed shut and he was close enough to hear jeers and laughter from the two gatehouses as the column came to a shuddering stop.

Robert sprang off White Wind as the defenders on the walls wrested catapults into position. "Get the coaches and carts in front to shield the cannon!" he shouted to the men.

"We're getting into position," Michael Frew replied. The first carriage came to a shuddering halt ten yards from the gates, and a handful of knights hauled the cannon out. The two catapults on the walls were already winched back, and Robert ordered his archers to move well away from the cannons and take down as many of the defenders as they could. The cannons were swathed in stained hides and didn't have the impressive size of a siege engine, but he couldn't risk them drawing any fire from Radiath.

And Radiath seemed to have more than enough fire for all of them. Heat waves shimmered up from a bright blur to the north, and he realized that the dockyards at the river's mouth were burning. Oil rained down from the walls, and the trampled ground just before the gates turned to a leaping sheet of flame. The broken gibbet cages became a pyre for whoever had died in them. Bricks and rubble flew from the walls as well, and he heard cries of pain from his ranks as he crouched behind a cart.

"Hurry it up," he said to the knight commander.

"We're moving as fast as we can," Frew snapped back. Stolen carts came in useful now, ranged to form a slight defensive barrier with the cannons poking out from between them. One steam carriage lumbered ahead through the fire until it rammed spikes-first into the gates of Radiath. The helmsman scrambled out, coughing, but before he could rejoin the ranks, a pot of liquid flame swallowed him up.

"The boiler should go at any moment." Triumph filled Frew's voice. "And he's bought us that much more time. The Wrath of Katash is almost prepared."

"What?" Robert said, before he realized the man was speaking about the cannon. "Almost?"

"This is the last one, my lord." A knight poured water into a funnel at the rear of a cannon, then snapped a lid over the funnel.

Red pennants flew from the castle, a sign of siege. Under the clouds they looked like slashes of clotted blood, like the smears on the battlefield where the catapults had let fly and men had not fled in time. A chunk of broken masonry struck the cart behind which Robert's archers took cover, crushing three of them. The steam carriage that had rammed into the gate was alight, the roof weeping copper tears in the intense heat.

With a burst like thunder, the carriage blew apart—not as destructively as the Dragon had, for it contained no explosives—but it was enough to send the spiked foreparts of the carriage punching into the wood of the gates. There was a stunned silence from the walls, and Robert took advantage of their shock to climb up on to a cart's wheel. He glanced back, but there was still no sign of the hounds or the outriders he had left along the Red Road.

There was also no sign of much order in the ranks of his own army—impossible to keep lines straight when all the fire came from above—but Nicholas and his personal guard had already started moving to the north. A boulder nearly as large as White Wind hurtled overhead and smashed into the last steam carriage, crunching it like an egg. Robert all but fell off the wheel, his heart hammering.

"Give the reaction a moment longer," the knight said. "And they have provided us with fire. The Benevolent Ones do watch over us."

He produced a handful of sticks and slipped to one side to dip them in a pool of fire. Robert tried to remember the principle behind the fire-rock cannon—something that produced an explosive gas. Of course, the fire would ignite that. He hoped it would do enough damage to the gates.

The knight screamed. As he had left the front line, he had been a more-or-less easy target, and a crossbow bolt drove into his leg. He fell sprawling, and a second bolt transfixed his arm. Robert dragged him back to shelter, but the knight twisted around enough to shove the burning sticks into his hands. "In the touch-hole," he gasped.

"What?"

"The orifice just before the funnel! Now!"

The menials who had pushed the cannons into place waved him over. Robert hurried to the nearest cannon and saw the lid beside the funnel. When he flipped it up, he heard a hiss of escaping vapor. He dropped a burning stick into it and slammed the lid back down.

The explosion drove the cannon backward and knocked him to the ground. He started up, wincing as another stick burned his hand, and then stared at the smoking rent in the gate. His ears rang, and he had not heard the projectile smash through the iron-banded wood.

"Quick!" Even wounded, the knight was in charge, and he gestured to the cannon crew. "Remove the firing chamber and reload, then get it back into the carriage. Second cannon, prepare to fire!"

That means me. Robert repeated the procedure with the next cannon, this time remembering to stand back. A wooden trestle elevated the cannon so that when it fired, the second projectile hit the gate just above the first, shattering the wood in a shower of smoke and splinters.

"Let's take those down." Robert gestured at the packed gatehouses. *We can do that. We can destroy the walls of Radiath with something smaller than a trebuchet, by doing nothing more than tipping a flame into it.*

The knight nodded. "Use the fourth cannon from the end, my lord. It's elevated the highest. You—" His gaze flicked to the menials. "Beat out those fires."

Another knight pushed his way to the front. "Lady Victoria gives word that we're ready."

The poor brave sacrifices are in position, Robert knew. The side gate of Radiath would also be a smoking ruin at any moment. "Prepare to fall back." The knights hurried the cannon back into the remaining carriages. "Sound the—"

The explosion at the side gate was muffled, but it thudded through the ground. White Wind snorted and shied. The herald pealed the retreat, and the mass of insurgents divided like waves, flowing away from the city.

The sound of thunder echoed in the closed carriage.

Alex rocked back on her heels, but the convulsion that shook Mayerd was greater. He lay on the Chariot's floor, his hands bound and secured to one wall. They had agreed that if he was coerced by Ohallox, he had to be prevented from harming anyone, and Alex, remembering how she had been controlled to the point where she had enjoyed what she did, had understood completely.

The smell of blood rose hot and coppery into the air. The ropes were wrapped with rags, to restrain rather than hurt, but Mayerd's mouth was free in case he needed to speak. He had bitten his lower lip, and when he turned his head a red trail ran down his face.

Alex wiped it away with a handkerchief. She wouldn't have believed it before, but it was harder to see someone else being tortured than to go through it herself.

"Is there anything I can do?" she asked.

"Elinah..." Mayerd's hair stuck to his brow, and when her fingertips brushed the ridged surface of a lateral line, she felt it throb with a pulse of its own. "She must have given the barrier the ability to fight back against whatever threatened it." He closed his eyes. "Why isn't it fighting?"

Victoria, the only other person in the Chariot with them, caught Alex's eye and mouthed, "Who is Elinah?"

Alex shrugged. She knew who that was—Mayerd's dead lover, who had obviously been a skilled Way-user—but some things were best left secrets.

Mayerd's body arched off the floor, and when his eyes snapped open, they showed no recognition, only terror. "No," he whispered.

"It's giving way?" Alex asked.

"Way," he repeated, and she realized what he meant. That was how the barrier fought back. The Inward Way, held quiet for so long, given only the tiny foothold of a wall in his mind, was finally spreading out from him. She wasn't sure if Ohallox's assault had broken a leash that had held the Way in check, or if Elinah had planned that all along, in case Mayerd tried to fight the stranglehold. The only thing she knew was that whether Mayerd liked it or not, the Inward Way was starting to grow in him.

What am I going to do? Ohallox thought.

He couldn't seem to affect Mayerd in reality. Ascend to the Way, then? No, his caution advised against it.

The more he thought about it, though, the more he wanted to do it. *If I reach the Way first, I can take him by surprise. Mayerd knows I'm not as skilled as he is, so he won't expect me to rise to the Way, to attack from an unexpected angle.*

There was something wrong with that reasoning, but the mental pull was too strong by then and he ascended to the Way. He would have had to face Mayerd there sooner or later, he thought and dismissed the slight doubts he felt. It wouldn't do to be anything less than self-confident now.

Every person who walked the Inward Way had their own place within it, and Ohallox's was in the sky, where Alex had surprised him earlier. Now he strengthened his own shields, which appeared as grey thunderheads. Because Mayerd still did not ascend to the Way, he saw no enemy behind a stone wall, but now he sensed that barrier buckling under the strain. Finally. He hoped that Mayerd was in agony. As for the people who shared that wall, they were not even Iternan, so they would be driven mad when the wall broke. That would take care of any attack on Radiath.

He looked down at the shifting web of the Way, crossroads upon crossroads. One of them rose to him, shaping itself into a snake like a shaft of moonlight, and Ohallox checked that it did not have Mayerd's scent.

The Inward Way is deception and illusion, the serpent said and sank back down.

I know, Ohallox thought. *But what has that to do with Mayerd? He hasn't deceived me, because I know nothing about him.*

What happens when an irresistible force meets an immovable object? the Inward Way whispered, and he felt sure it was laughing at him. Because Mayerd's crumbling defenses might still not be destroyed in time. He redoubled his attack, wishing that Mayerd would do something, anything, to give away his own strategy.

Mayerd. Mayerd. The name was more familiar than ever, yet it eluded him.

Well, why should it? he thought angrily. *I am on the Inward Way now, and it holds the memories of anyone who has ever walked it. Mayerd is a Way practitioner, so I can find his distinctive pattern here and learn why he doesn't give battle.*

With practiced ease, Ohallox separated a corner of his consciousness from the continuous battering against a wall that bent and trembled but still refused to give way. He searched the Inward Way quickly and found nothing of Mayerd. Could he have wiped his traces from the Way itself? That smelled of power greater than any except a Waymaster's or—

Of course, Ohallox thought, thankful to have found an answer to one of the questions Mayerd posed. An attempt to access the memories of living Way practitioners would alert those people to his existence, and Ohallox didn't need that. But there was one who could not attack him, one who would have kept close watch on anyone so powerful. Ohallox had been in Dagre when it happened, but even he had heard of the Waymistress's death—and she had taken the Inward Way.

He sent a swift search along the path to the past, over the limitless miles of the Inward Way, for any traces of Elinah, the dead Waymistress of Iternum.

Three hundred, give or take, Robert thought. The walls of Radiath had taken their toll on his troops, and there were more injured in the carts and carriages. But they were out of the catapults' range now, making speed along a dusty road that led to the House of the Third Blessing. The plumes of smoke gusting from the steam carriages trailed like banners and were sign enough of their passage, even with a dark blanket of clouds pressing down overhead.

Still, they were safe for the moment. The city might even be lulled into a false sense of security at the hounds' arrival, even if the defenders wouldn't obligingly lower their defenses and allow Nicholas to strike. He asked Peter if there was any change in Mayerd's condition, but from the look on the man's face, Mayerd was worse than before.

The Quorumlords overheard. "Your Iternan is drawing that sorcerer's magic to himself," Victoria said. "It's an honorable sacrifice."

"It's not a sacrifice, Lady Victoria, because he's not going to die."

"Of course not," the Word said. "And we'll find a comfortable place for him outside the monastery."

Robert nearly reined White Wind in. "Outside?"

The Word hailed Michael Frew and went to speak with him, leaving Victoria to look uncomfortable as she explained that the monastery itself could not provide sanctuary to a sorcerer. "It's holy ground. If he could wait outside..."

"I'm sure he'll enjoy that. And we can toss him a few bones from our meal."

Victoria asked him who could more reasonably be requested to give way—one foreigner or dozens of their own people on their own land—and since Robert had no answer to that, all he could do was press his horse faster. The lit windows of the monastery came into sight, visible even in the gloom since it was on a hill, and he sent a rider ahead to announce their arrival.

The man returned in minutes, saying a monk had met him at the gates to let him know they were welcome. The outer gates swung open as Robert dismounted and led White Wind up the well-trampled road. That was steep enough without putting more strain on the horse. The steam carriages likewise had to be emptied, and both knights and men-at-arms set their shoulders to the carriages to push them past the gates. Two monks waited just within. Robert wondered where their servants were, then guessed that Garnath had bled the place for as much as he could get, probably taking domestics after the monks ran out of silver.

He looked around as the steam carriages rolled past the gates and into the outer cloister. The monastery loomed up ahead, tall and imposing, lights blazing in its windows. Stained-glass windows, he thought, very pretty. He'd trade them all for a deep ditch filled with spikes, and arrow slits in the walls. And men enough to guard the place. The outer cloister filled up rapidly with his troops, but the only monks in sight were the two who had given them entrance.

"I thank you for your hospitality," he said to the monks. "I know the risk you run by sheltering us, and we will defend this place if it comes under attack."

"The—the House of the Third Blessing was named for a risk, Lord Robert," one of the monks replied. "You are welcome here, and so are all your troops." Well, all except one, Robert thought. "The abbot is waiting within to..."

His voice trailed off as he stared past Robert's shoulder. Robert turned, but all he saw was the Word descending from a steam carriage—bloody hell, he hadn't even bothered getting down from that to lighten the load. Setting his teeth, he said nothing as the Word came up to pronounce a brief blessing on the two young monks. They both looked stunned into silence at being in the presence of a Quorumlord, and Robert was glad his own troops were more practical; Peter had ordered the men to make sure the area was secure, and to see to the wounded.

"May we see the abbot?" he said when the Word had finished.

"Father Julian asked to meet only the leaders of your army," the monk said. "He's waiting within. Perhaps Your Grace will pray further with us here?"

The Word smiled. "I will indeed, but a representative of the Quorum should be present at any council, even that of war."

I don't have time to waste with this. "Lawrence?"

Lawrence came over to them, and Robert glanced at the Chariot, but there was no sign of Mayerd and he couldn't risk asking. Best to secure their welcome with the abbot before bringing up the presence of Iternan sorcery. "Let's go, then," he said, and the two monks hauled open the monastery doors.

Those were of heavy iron and oak, Robert noticed as he stepped into the empty reception hall. Maybe the place wouldn't be too difficult to defend, and the windows might be more useful than arrow slits. His men could roll the cannons up to them if the monastery was attacked.

"Where are they?" Lawrence said. Doors led off to what Robert guessed were the chapel and the public rooms, but the reception hall was empty. "We don't have time to waste."

"True, but let's be pleasant," Robert said softly, as the Word seated himself on a bench that ran nearly the length of the hall. His three guards stayed close around him. "If a few of these monks dress like common folk and run to tell the hounds that the city fell, they'll be more convincing than our own men. They don't have eastern accents."

Lawrence nodded. "Good thing Garnath didn't anticipate us falling back here—"

He stopped, his eyes widening, but it was already too late. On their left and right doors opened, and armed men strode in with swords drawn. Robert pulled his own blade, but a man leaped up from behind the abbot's dais. He wore a houndhelm, and when he raised his crossbow, it pointed at Robert's chest.

The past opened up before him. Ohallox hurtled into it, falling deeper and deeper into a life that Elinah had hidden from everyone she had known. No one had seen how her initial happiness with Mayerd had turned into misery and loathing for each of them. And when Mayerd gave her what she hated most—contempt, then indifference, followed by a wish to end their marriage—she did the one thing that nearly broke him. She had his children and taught them to despise him.

How had either of them presented even a semblance of a normal life to the world while they ripped each other apart in privacy? Of course, that must have been harder for Elinah, since she was the

Waymistress while Mayerd was a nobody who didn't even walk the same Way as she did. *No wonder he didn't try to meet me on the—*

Cold realization drove through him. The pieces of the puzzle fell into place, and Ohallox reeled with the understanding. Mayerd had never walked the Inward Way—in fact, he could not walk either of the Ways, and the wall, the barrier that Elinah had placed in him... *I tried to break it.* Ohallox's throat went dry as sand.

He detached from the attack immediately.

Or tried to. Nothing happened. In fact, he could sense nothing at all. The grey clouds around him had thickened to the point where they cut off his ever-present view of the shifting pattern of the Inward Way. What had happened?

In rising fear, he probed and saw immediately. The Inward Way had sprung from Mayerd, planted by a seed Elinah had sown twelve years ago and which he had now wakened. The Way had established itself with its customary speed, and it did that by dominating people to whom its source was connected. Most of the time, those were the people nearest to the source by physical proximity. But the Way was not limited by distance, and it could control people who were connected to the source through mental closeness. And Ohallox's relentless attack had brought him closer to Mayerd than anyone else in Dagre had ever been.

The Inward Way had spread to him and had revealed Mayerd's past as the one thing that would get his own barriers down, have him gawking while it did its work unnoticed. He had been prepared for a counterstrike from Mayerd, but he had never expected the Way itself to turn against him, making him just another stepping stone.

He tried to regain control of it too late. That was the trap Elinah had built into the barrier, the unfettered growth of the Inward Way—it was something Mayerd could never have controlled—and now Ohallox failed to assert his power over it. Or had he? What if that was an illusion of the Way? Perhaps he did control it, but it made him think he had not. But if he had, then he would *know* that he had. He shook his head, trying to collect himself, and the Inward Way struck again.

Fear and forgetfulness washed over him. Images flew past him like rags in a gale—random memories from hundreds of people. He knew he was close to stepping off the Way without truly detaching himself from it, which meant he would wander forever in its depths, except that would be peaceful and quiet, a refuge from the howling maelstrom—

No!

He couldn't fight the Way alone, so he tried a last desperate tactic, extending his power in a rapidly spun web over the castle. Every mind within it was a potential outpost of the Way, but he claimed them first, turning the force of their combined will against the Way. Ohallox had mesmerized Alex into oblivion but he had no time to do that now, so the castle's inhabitants knew that it was he who gnawed into their thoughts like a worm into an apple. He saw everything, from a kitchen maid's prayer for their victory to Stephen Garnath's farewell as his wife and son began their escape from the city, and he felt their collective hatred of him as they fought against his touch.

But the plan worked. The Way found no fertile ground and sank away from him. Ohallox saw the familiar pattern of crossroads, and he began to detach. The impact was brutal, nearly splintering his consciousness into coma, but he was still alive, and more importantly, sane. And he left the Inward Way.

He heard the serpent's laughter a moment later, but the clouds vanished and he was in his study, his clothes damp with sweat. Then the door flew open, and one of the guards looked inside, his face twisted with rage. The other guard drew a sword.

Ohallox stared at them with a numb lack of interest, wondering why the Way had mocked him at the last. Hadn't he won? Was he still on the Way? *I'm going mad.*

"You filthy bastard," the first man said, drawing his own sword. "You were in my head. Like a spider crawling in my skull."

What had he done wrong? He was no longer on the Way, but there was something he had forgotten—

The sword slashed down in a vicious arc. Except the guard pivoted on his heel as he did so, and the blade cut through his companion's throat. Ohallox used the surviving guard's own shock to plant self-loathing and horror in him, and the guard screamed, dropping to his knees.

After what you've done, you don't deserve to live.

Fingers fumbled at a dagger's hilt and closed around it.

"Put it down," Stephen said from the doorway. The words were directed at the guard, but his eyes were on Ohallox, and a crossbow was in his hands. "Make me feel anything, and there'll be a bolt in your belly. Understand?"

Ohallox nodded slowly and released the guard, who scrambled up, eyes nearly starting from his head. "My lord, he made me—"

"I know," Stephen said. "I felt him too. But there's one reason that you'll live, Ohallox, only one reason. Do you know what it is?"

"No, my lord," Ohallox managed to say.

"When you did that little trick of getting into my head, I heard something interesting." There was a smile at the corners of Stephen's mouth, which could mean either good news or bad. "It was my mare speaking of that monastery. I knew they would run there once they saw they couldn't take Radiath, but even if they overcome the men there, they won't have time to secure it."

Ohallox frowned. Unsurprising that Stephen had outwitted his enemies, but what confused him was how Stephen had heard Alex.

"Speak to Nalle," Stephen said. "You know how to do that. Tell him to make for that monastery with all speed—"

"How could you hear her...?" Ohallox stopped, as the one thing he had forgotten burst on him like a fall of icy water. The only way that Stephen could have listened to Alex was if he had—temporarily—exchanged sense perception with someone near her. That happened sometimes; the Inward Way was a road that went in two directions, not a river that flowed downstream. And the only person among the rebels who had actually had anything to do with the Way was Mayerd.

But if there was a connection between us strong enough for the Inward Way to spread from him to me, strong enough for Stephen to exchange sense perception, we were joined as strongly as I was to the mare, Ohallox thought. *And when I detached myself from the Way...*

When he had faced Alex on the Way, he had broken the connection between them by tearing the trap out of her. That permitted him to detach from the Way without dragging her along with him like a shadow. With Mayerd, with the revelations and subsequent terror, that had slipped his mind.

I did not break the link that bound me to Mayerd, which means that whatever happened to me happened to him as well. No. I couldn't *have destroyed the Way's shackle-hold on him along with its grip on me.*

"Ohallox?" Stephen said sharply. "What is it?"

"Go, Stephen." Ohallox slumped in his chair, careless of a nocked crossbow. "It would take too long to explain. Go and kill them all... We'll speak afterwards."

"Drop your sword."

The man in the houndhelm sighted along the line of the crossbow. All right, Robert thought and threw his blade down as hard as he could. The clang would be alert enough for any of his men near the monastery doors, though it wasn't likely to do him or Lawrence any good.

He heard a shout of warning outside, but the houndhelm shouted back that the first man to enter would have a baron's blood on his hands, not to mention a Quorumlord's. The Word rose, but he seemed too petrified to order his guards to attack, and their only duty was to protect him. When the houndhelm ordered the two monks to close the doors, they moved to comply and Robert knew there was nothing his men could do about it. Still, Alex and Susanna were outside and safe— as safe as they could be when he had walked into a trap.

"Wait!" the man in the houndhelm said suddenly. The monks had bolted one door, driving a thin iron bar into a slot in the floor, but the other was still half open. "Call them in first. The other Quorumlords and your captains."

"Very well." Robert raised his voice. "Anyone who wants to walk in here and die is welcome to do so!"

The man's brows disappeared beyond the upper edge of his helm. "Isn't there anyone willing to trade their life for yours, Lord Robert? I could accept that. An exchange of hostages—"

"Don't waste any more of my time." Robert's mouth was dry, his heart thudding so hard that it hurt. "Go on. Loose. But none of you will leave this place alive if you do."

"Then we'll take you with us," the houndhelm said, and his finger tightened on the trigger. The prods snapped forward with a *whang.*

And the bolt broke in three, the pieces pattering to the floor. The man's gasp was lost as the props cracked, and the bowstring whipped back to lash him across the face. For an instant Robert thought he was dreaming, and the men-at-arms looked too stunned to react as well.

The houndhelm ignored the blood running down his face and snatched his sword free. "Kill them!"

That broke the spell. The men-at-arms obeyed, rushing forward, and steel hissed against wool-lined wood as Lawrence drew his own blade. There was a struggle behind them, as the monks tried to close the last door, but the men-at-arms reached Robert, a dozen of them against him and Lawrence.

A bench flipped itself off the ground like a twig kicked by a child's foot and flew through the air. Robert flung himself down. The bench sailed over his head and smashed into a handful of the men-at-arms, driving them to the ground. Without pausing, it whirled end over end and rammed into the other men-at-arms, so hard that when the edge of it struck one of them in the face, bone splintered from the impact.

The houndhelm charged. Lawrence blocked his way for one moment before swords rang and clashed off each other, and suddenly Lawrence reeled aside with blood leaking from an arm. That was enough time for Robert to grab his fallen sword and get to his feet, meeting the houndhelm's steel with his own.

The man was stronger than he had expected, and fast as well. Robert blocked, slashed, stepped over a moaning body, parried. Sweat ran down his brow.

Are you one of the swine who had Alex before I did? He twisted to one side abruptly. The hound's blade sliced into his jacket, scoring a line of fire along his side, but he felt no pain at all as he drove his own sword forward. It crunched through mail and flesh and grated on bone, and the mad light of battle went out of the hound's eyes as he slumped to the floor.

The Katassian Knights and his own men surrounded him, two supporting Lawrence and eight more clustering around the Word. The wounded men-at-arms were finished off, and Robert heard Peter tell more men to go into the monastery, flush out any hounds and see what had happened to the abbot and the monks. He knew it would be a few minutes before he could give orders himself. All he saw was the bloodied bench and the scraps of the crossbow.

"How did that happen?" he said, not even knowing to whom he spoke.

"It was a miracle." A knight wiped his sword on a dead man's clothes, then rose. "A reward for refusing to yield to evil. On sacred ground, the Benevolent Ones protect—"

"It was nothing so holy, Sir Edmund," Victoria said from the doorway. Something in her face warned Robert, and he made his way to the doors. Beyond her the Chariot's gangplank was extended, and Mayerd stood on it.

"Iternan magic?"

Robert wasn't sure who said that, or who made the initial warding signs, but Mayerd seemed to neither notice nor care. "It's difficult." His voice was drained. "I thought this would be one of the sweetest moments of my life, but it's not. More like using a muscle that's withered."

The knights turned away. Victoria's face was troubled, and Robert hesitated, unsure of a word of thanks that would have come so easily if Mayerd had used a sword instead.

"You did well," Alex said. "Keep working at it, but don't push yourself too hard."

"Like this?" Mayerd took the wooden Lunatic toy from his pocket and flung it into the middle of the circle of knights who had drawn away from him. They flinched, hands going to sword hilts, but the toy only hung suspended in the air, turning over as if invisible fingers worked at it. Then the slats of wood clattered and snapped against each other as they fitted together, slapping back when they didn't. They moved faster and faster, blurring with the speed, and clicked into place a few moments later, each of them sliding into the correct slot. The toy fell to earth in a puff of ash, a small and perfect cube.

The knights stared at it, then turned to look at Mayerd. But the door of the Chariot was already closed.

The horse was blown, foam dripping from its mouth, and the outrider didn't even dismount before he spoke. "They'll be at the city in an hour's time. Maybe sooner."

Alex's fingers tightened on the edge of the Chariot's door until there was no feeling in them. Robert's men had freed the monks, and a few of them agreed to go, in disguise, to Radiath at the gallop. Then Robert ordered Mayerd to accompany them.

Mayerd nodded, but after he shut the Chariot door his lip curled. "I wasn't good enough for their sacred soil. But now that I can walk the Way again, they need me."

Alex offered him a flask of wine, but he shook his head and then winced. "Water." His voice was raw, and that didn't change even after he had drunk deeply. She wanted to ask what he could do besides moving things without touching them, but there was no more time and from the way Mayerd looked, everything he had kept controlled for twelve years was ready to explode from him at the slightest provocation.

The lantern's light gleamed off the silverbolt on his sword's hilt, but the sight didn't reassure Alex. The surface trappings might have been Dagran, but everything below that was Iternan, and there was a lot beneath the surface.

She stayed alone in the Chariot until she heard horses' hooves thud outside, growing quieter and fading into the distance. Then she left the carriage and stepped on to the monastery ground for the first time.

The place was nearly unrecognizable. Robert's few surviving archers crouched along the walls as the first line of defense, and the cannon were arrayed along the windows as the second. Alex wished there was something she could do as well. There had been plenty to occupy her on the journey, but here the monks were busy with the wounded and serving out what little food they had. She crossed the reception hall, trying not to look at the bloody smears on the floor where Robert had fought for his life, and went into the dining room. Trestle tables were set up and a fire roared in the hearth, so she accepted a plate and took a seat at the end of Robert's table.

No one noticed her, to her relief, because all attention was on the Word. "Our troops should have accompanied the Iternan," he said. "His sorcery and our steel would have ended this war far from holy ground."

Far from you, you mean. Alex guessed it was the first time the Word had been in fear for his life, and it seemed to have shaken him badly.

"He'll do what he can and then report to us," Robert said. There were dark stains on his jacket, but to her relief, he didn't look badly hurt. "The troops are needed here to defend us in case Lord Garnath tries another such trick."

The Word's eyes narrowed. "Should that happen, it would be best if the women and noncombatants had some way to reach safety." There was a crunch as Susanna brought a knife down on an apple, splitting it in half, but the Word ignored that. "Father Julian?"

"There's a postern gate behind the kitchen wall," the abbot said. "The land slopes down steeply towards a tributary of the Hound, so anyone taking that path must travel in single file, but it can be done and the hounds wouldn't know."

"The women and yourself may stay within unless we're in danger of defeat, then," Robert said, and Alex kept her dismay off her face. She wanted nothing more than to escape outside to the Chariot; the monastery felt like a trap. *And whatever happens to Robert outside, you won't know about it. That's how it should be, so get used to it.*

The Word said nothing more and Alex bolted her meal. She couldn't taste the food and she only wanted to get it over with so she could leave. There were fifty men in the dining hall, but she was aware of only one.

There was no privacy in the guest chambers or the inner cloister, and low chanting came from the chapel, so she sat in a nearby alcove which held a poorly daubed painting of a man looking at three boxes. From the pale rectangle on the wall below it, she guessed a plaque had once hung there. No doubt that had been more valuable than the painting.

"Have you heard that story?" someone said from outside the alcove.

It was the abbot, so Alex gave him what she thought of as her sweet-but-distant smile. "What story?"

He pointed at the painting. "The tale of the Third Blessing. Nydir once descended to Eden and gave a poor man a choice of three boxes. The first held great wealth and the second the key to the heart of a woman who would love him all his life. The man asked what was in the third box, and Nydir said that was a blessing greater than both the others, so the man chose the third box."

"And what was inside it?" Alex said.

"Nothing. After that, the man traveled through Dagre speaking of how he had gained a blessing greater than money or love."

"But he didn't."

Father Julian shrugged. "I think he learned he had the courage to choose the unknown rather than the known. But the story is open to interpretation."

My interpretation is that Nydir had a vicious sense of humor. "Is there a prayer service in the chapel?"

"Yes, His Grace is conducting it." Father Julian paused. "I have asked him to pray for your safety. There is no place for women during a battle."

Alex thought of the images of Katash—spear in one hand, hammer in the other, and faceless in her fury. Still, the old abbot had spoken kindly to her, so she didn't contradict him and he went to pray with the men. The Word might have been conducting a service in the chapel, but Father Julian went to pray with the menials by the cannon and the sentries outside. Distracted by watching him, she noticed a movement nearby too late, and when she turned she saw Robert walk towards her. There was no chance to get away.

"May I speak with you?" He stopped outside the alcove.

He sounded cold and detached, but after what she had said to him at their last meeting, she couldn't expect anything more. "Of course." She pressed her shoulders against the wall of the alcove so there would be more room for him.

Robert didn't step inside. "I'd like you to watch for the Smiler. I think he'll try to slip away now that he knows the escape route. He looked terrified when Garnath's men surprised us and I don't trust him to stand fast. Susanna's loitering by the kitchens and I have two men at the foot of the path, but I'd like you to keep an eye open for him as well."

Alex glanced outside to make sure the Word was nowhere in sight. "Does it make a difference if he runs? Stephen knows about our machines now."

"True, and I couldn't stop him if he struck out for the Mistmarch. I'd just like to be aware of it. If you don't mind." The formality rankled, but she forced herself to nod. "And I'd rather he *not* be aware of it, so stay out of sight."

"No fear of that." Alex knew at once that she had said too much, but it was too late. Robert frowned.

"What is it?" His eyes searched her face.

Alex wished he would pretend he hadn't heard. It was her fault for not saying merely yes or no. She had meant to, but whenever she was near Robert, all her good intentions went awry.

"Just the way he looked at me in Fulmion." She tried to shrug it off. She had not been afraid to be alone with Mayerd in the Chariot, but she didn't want the Word to corner her anywhere.

"I could assign one of the men to be with you."

"No, they're needed at the walls." In case he suggested one of the injured men, she continued quickly. "I'll be fine. I can take care of myself."

"Yes." Robert's eyes were still keen, but something had closed off within them. "You'll always do that."

"What does that mean?"

"Just that you can take whatever any man gives you. Garnath, the Smiler, the Duke of Goldwood... It doesn't matter who. They either insult you or use you, but you brush it off."

"Do you think I should cry or slap them instead?" Alex said. He didn't reply, which frustrated her even more. "As if you haven't done the same. Or worse. Say what you like about Derek, he wouldn't have insulted me if I'd mentioned you to him."

"Because he couldn't have cared less about whoever else had you! And I never used you. You came to me willingly."

"We all make mistakes." Alex kept her tone casual. "And you've got another thing in common with Stephen and his friends. None of them ever promised me anything after riding me either."

Robert's face hardened. "Maybe you're not the kind of woman men marry."

That was like being trodden on. All her training snapped into position as fast and hard as a crossbow's prods—*it's the truth, I can bear it*—and she knew her face would show nothing as she turned away and studied a painting that looked like a blur. She thought she heard Robert say something else but she didn't hear it, and a moment later he was gone.

General Nalle set a crushing pace for the army, covering dozens of miles each day. If he had not witnessed the destruction of the Stagwater Bridge, he would not have been concerned. The insurgents didn't have the numbers to take Radiath, but they had Quorum weaponry.

The few survivors of the Stagwater battle could tell him very little about those weapons, so he gave orders to take the Quorumlords and the captains of the insurgents alive if possible. He was less than a day's travel from Radiath when his advance scouts galloped up to say that the insurgents had reached the city.

Nalle's gut clenched. He wanted to sound the charge, but he knew what had happened when his men had rushed ahead to the Stagwater Bridge. Clouds gathered overhead as his army marched on, and when the flicker of fire came into sight, it looked even brighter in the gloom. The dockyards were burning and the scouts reported that the gates were smashed, the gatehouses turned to rubble and pulped flesh.

"Have they taken the city?" Nalle asked, fingers so tight around the reins that he could no longer feel them. He was in the vanguard, heralds and bannermen before him, and he didn't need to look back to see an army so numerous that it stretched for miles.

"No sounds of battle from within, sir," a scout said. "Lord Garnath's banner still flies over the castle."

"Then where are they?" said Ned Treych, his second-in-command. Nalle would have liked to know that himself. A battle had taken place outside—there were boulders, smashed carts and smashed bodies, some burned beyond recognition and some lying crumpled at the foot of the walls. Not so many bodies that they could hope all their enemies had died there.

He knew the insurgents had laid a trap, but what was it? And the city was so quiet that he distrusted it. What if the insurgents had swarmed in through the smashed gates and overwhelmed even Radiath's defenses? They could be waiting for his men to walk into the city's maw.

"I want three men to ride up to the gates." He wheeled his horse to speak to the captains who rode behind him. "Not the scouts." They wore no armor, to be as unnoticeable as possible, and he wanted armed soldiers with their distinctive hounds' heads. "Take our banner—"

"Sir!" A scout on a horse trotted up to them, herding two men before her. One limped, and the clothes of both were smeared with dirt and blood.

"They smashed the gates," the limper said. "They came in on all sides—"

"Are they in Radiath?" Nalle said. The other man nodded as if the gesture took the last of his strength.

In the city, maintaining a mask of normalcy to lure his men in. And yet, could the city have fallen so fast, with no sounds of war from within and not even word sent to him from Lord Garnath? Something was wrong.

"Keep them under guard," he ordered. "Now we ride."

The horns sang out in a peal that he knew the city heard, and his banners streamed out in the wind. The army moved ahead, not at the gallop that had led them into the teeth of the Stagwater trap but at a steady, measured advance that had crushed everything in its path.

The city came into sight, although the men on the walls were only dark shapes. Horns sounded from its walls, three blasts that were the signal for safety, and a great cheer rose from the people within. Nalle's spirits soared as well. Either their prisoners were lying or the insurgents had indeed swarmed into the city and had been crushed there, cut down in the streets—

The cheers were so loud that he never heard the heavy *whack* as the catapult's arm snapped forward. He only saw a movement high on the city's wall and a boulder flew through the air. At first he thought he was dreaming, that weeks of hard travel and little sleep had made him imagine things. Then he heard his troops go silent a moment before they shouted.

They were too closely packed, drawn up into ranks that would have surged ahead in tightly disciplined power but which could not avoid attacks from above. The boulder hurtled over his head and smashed into the forefront of the First Regiment, crushing men and horses who were trying to wheel about. The stalk of a banner snapped under the impact.

The second catapult released before Nalle could turn to see it. The ranks towards the rear scattered, fighting to get out of its way, and screams ended abruptly as the boulder landed. The screams that started up again were far more terrifying. Spheres of fire blossomed on the walls and Nalle knew that the next strike would be pitch.

He started to shout orders to sound the charge, and the cry died in his throat as a new banner raised itself over the city, so high that it seemed planted in air, higher even than Garnath's standard. The lightning bolt on it was molten silver in the firelight. Nalle's mouth went dry.

"Sir!" Ned Treych shouted, and the sound jolted him out of his shock. The army had paused, staring at the insurgents' banner raised over Radiath, and in the silence Nalle heard a *snap-thud* as the catapults sounded. He drove his heels into his horse's sides and galloped away before a great globe of pitch plowed into the ground where he had been. It rolled to set alight anything in its path.

Nalle smelled burning grass and burning flesh. He snapped out orders and the heralds' horns sang, but the second pitchstrike slammed into his baggage train and into the camp followers who had not yet fled.

"Reform the line," he said through his teeth.

In the light of the fires, he saw the horn trembling, but the herald blew a long, strong call. By some mercy of the Benevolent Ones, the catapults went still and as he rode forward his army milled behind him, moving to make ranks behind their standards. He ignored the boulders, the pitch, the cries of the injured.

"Archers to the fore!" he said. The walls of Radiath swarmed, knots of activity clustering around the catapults, and he guessed they were preparing the next strike. He wouldn't give them time for it. "When we ride, pick them off."

He didn't want to enter Radiath without knowing what was within, but they couldn't fight from outside. The flat land provided no cover from the catapults and they had no siege engines. They would ride through the gates instead, relying on their numbers to crush anyone in their way.

"Sound the charge," he ordered.

The horn pealed again, and the army answered with a roar as surviving men and horses broke into a run. He thought he heard the traitors on the walls howl, but the sound was lost under the drum of hooves. He reined his horse in at the last moment, just outside the gates, and his army surged around him and into the city.

The companies of archers peeled off from the army's flanks. Stones and chunks of broken masonry flew overhead, but they didn't slow his troops down as they plunged ahead of him, past the broken gates. Nalle looked out over the battlefield, watching arrow-spitted men drop from the walls. No thunderclaps, no Quorum traps, and yet something had made him stop. His heartbeat was a drum echoing through his mind. The echo moved out of step and grew faster.

Nalle's body jerked as an unseen hand shoved him—hard enough to push him into a place he had never seen. He was in a narrow dark room, and all he knew for certain was that another presence crouched in the chamber beside him.

"*Your senses temporarily implode,*" a voice whispered. "*Nothing to be afraid of. Just listen.*"

"Who are you?" Nalle said.

"*My name is Ohallox and I serve Lord Garnath. As you do.*"

Nalle felt as though he had drunk vinegar. He had heard rumors about a sorcerer working for Lord Garnath, but there was vile talk about anyone in a position of power. Until that moment he had not believed the tales, because Garnath had allies over most of Dagre, as well as an army at his command.

"*That army is slaughtering your own people!*" Ohallox said. "*The rebels tricked you.*"

"How could they raise that banner—" Nalle stopped. Had the Iternan heard his thoughts? Did the Iternan know whatever he was thinking?

"*Never mind that now,*" Ohallox said. "*They tricked you. They're hiding in the monastery south. Break off your attack now. That is Lord Garnath's order.*"

"How do I know—" Nalle was aware of people asking him what was wrong, who he was speaking to, but their voices were a long distance away.

"*Lord Garnath hopes you like the priests he gave you.*"

When he had risen to command, Nalle had needed priests to provide rites for the dying, but he didn't want anyone who would put the Quorum Mandates before his own orders. Soon he had some devouts who openly disapproved of Lord Garnath to show that their loyalties lay with the Quorum. He doubted anyone knew that the priests were all in Garnath's pockets.

"*Very well,*" he thought. "*But don't ever do this to me again. Understand? If you have to speak with me, possess someone else.*" It wasn't just his distrust of magic, it was the simple fact that while an Iternan sorcerer occupied his head, he was useless on the battlefield, not to mention a source of new fear for his troops. "*I'll have some servant beside me for you to use—*"

"*You're all servants to me. Now go. I'll watch over you.*"

Nalle had never heard anything less reassuring, but before he could reply his mind slammed back into his body like a fist into a gauntlet. His personal guard and two of his captains were nearby, but careful to keep their distance from him in case his strange speech was a sign of incipient madness. And he couldn't tell them that Lord Garnath was using a sorcerer. They would watch him like hawks, trying to tell if someone else looked out through his eyes. And it might be reason enough for the ambitious ones like Raymond Varifor or Arthur Lyng to foment mutiny.

"Report," he said. "What's been done?"

That took them aback, but he knew they were less likely to challenge him about his behavior if he pretended it had never happened. The battle was nearly won, Ned reported, they had a beachhead at the gates and no one within had put up any fight. Fire arrows had set the catapults alight. When he heard that, Nalle turned his horse again and rode out where he could see the battle-ravaged city and the sky above it. The silverbolt banner was gone.

"There's no sign of any rebels in Radiath, is there?" he said.

"There isn't," Lyng said. With the walls abandoned, he had called back the companies of archers who served in the Second Regiment. Nalle could only hope that the rain would begin soon, extinguishing the fires and washing away the blood that trickled down the stones. "I didn't see much of whoever we took down from the walls, but none of them wear the rebels' sigil."

"They've tricked us." Nalle still watched the sky. Sheet lightning flickered to the north, over the hills through which the River Hound flowed down into Radiath. Where it flowed out, bodies bobbed on the wash. *I'll make them pay for this.*

He gave orders to sound the retreat before anyone could ask how he knew the rebels had tricked them. Before the army reformed on the battlefield, he had dragged the truth out of the men who had contributed to the pretense. Monks, so Ohallox had not been lying. He wiped his dagger clean and ordered two regiments to secure the city and deal with the injured while the rest of them rode to the monastery. Reporting to Lord Garnath that most of the Radiath militia was dead and the city's defenses smashed would be easier if he could present Lord Garnath with the people who were responsible. Or at least with their heads.

Nalle set his heels into his horse's sides and began the ride south, close enough to Radiath that the burning catapults cast flickering light across his path. That was enough for him to see the man who sat on a slab of fallen granite near the wall. The man's head was bent, hands to his face.

Jeremy Rostelinek, who commanded the scouts, spurred his horse on, shouting a command to the man to stay where he was. The words were lost in a whipcrack sound, and part of the wall broke away.

Nalle's horse shied and the men nearest the wall pushed and trampled as they tried to get away. Chunks of stone clipped the ones who were not fast enough and smashed a horse to the ground. Nalle turned away from the cloud of dust and saw bare ground before the army.

"Where did he go?" He had to raise his voice to be heard.

"I..." Jeremy stood in the stirrups and stared out over the battlefield. His eyes could see a fly on a horse's back at fifteen yards, but finally he sank back into the saddle. "There was a rebel sign on his sword's hilt, sir."

"Did you see where he went?" Nalle said.

"No. I just looked away for... Even if he ran, how could he drag that stone with him?"

Nalle had no answer, and he saw how unsettled his troops were. They had fought tenacious opponents and assailed walled fortresses, but now they faced enemies who tricked them at every turn without giving battle. Could the Quorum weaponry have failed the rebels? Or was it still waiting to be unleashed?

It doesn't matter. I'll find them, I'll defeat them, I'll take their leaders alive and before they die, they will confess how they did this. He gestured at the heralds and the army's ride began again, towards the south and away from the ruined walls of Radiath.

Mayerd lay across the block of stone, its broken edges digging into his belly. Dry retches burned his throat. It would be all over if he dropped, he thought as he stared down at Garnath's army, swarming south below the stone suspended in the air. Nothing else was visible through the blur of his vision. He might even take a few of them with him.

Except that might not kill him. He longed to break the ground apart, but in his condition, the most that would split would be his head.

At first he had enjoyed it. Sitting unnoticed at a short distance from the walls, he looked up at the catapults and imagined them moving, pictured ropes breaking and the massive arms snapping forward. The Outward Way reached out and did as he wanted.

He had been alone in Dagre, trying to hold his own against Dagrans, but now the Outward Way was with him and he smashed them like ants. A pulse hammered at the insides of his temples, the effect of trying to use too much magic too quickly, but he ignored it. They spit on Iternan sorcery—well, let them see what it can do. Fire. The huge balls of pitch ignited. Lift and drop. They obeyed, slamming into the catapults' cups and soaring out over the battlefield.

The screams were distant, not that it would have made any difference had they been near. He had been half-dead for a dozen years, but now he was alive and strong. He still felt neither joy nor peace of mind, but the power rising in him made up for that.

Then the pain overrode even the intoxication of riding the Way again, and it all ended abruptly when Ohallox sensed him. There was no wall between them any longer. Ohallox could not enter his mind, but the Inward Way could do far more than that. Terror and revulsion shattered his thoughts and racked his body. It was all he could do to lift the stone into the air when the army came upon him.

His lateral lines burned fiercer than if claws had raked his face open, and he knew Ohallox was preparing another strike. Move, he thought with all the force of will he had left, and the block of stone sailed through the sky like a kite. Move move *move. Just get me away.* Too late he realized that the Outward Way had responded only to his desperation and was taking him north, away from Garnath's army.

Mayerd twisted awkwardly until he was sitting upright. When he glanced down, he saw silver ripples far beneath as the block of stone followed the river upstream, and the sound of thunder was closer as the storm moved towards Radiath. He felt a jagged shape beneath his palm and realized that he was gripping the hilt of his sword, but he knew he could not go south.

I have to warn Robert. But the thought stopped before it could leave his mind. He didn't have the strength to stop an army, especially if Ohallox was on that army's side. *If I have to choose between Robert's life and victory...*

The clouds were dark clots, and the wind parted around him as he flew north.

The sky was like a hand cupped over the monastery, making everything beneath it still and airless. Alex sat motionless on a stone bench in a corner of the inner cloister, where she had a view of the walkway that led from the chapel to the common buildings. She wasn't sure if the Word would desert them, but if she saw him and his guards slip away, she would send a servant to Robert with the news.

She was not going to be alone with him again. It was so rare for her to lose her temper that she always took a long time to return to indifference. If any other man had hurt her, she would have imagined a humiliating experience inflicted on him and that would have soothed her battered pride, but the trick failed when it came to Robert. Even the thought of him being ill-treated made something tighten in her chest. She was fine with him missing her or being unhappy about what he had said to her, but she didn't want anyone else hurting him.

The chanting from the chapel stopped, and Alex stiffened. The night was nowhere near silent—horses stamped and whinnied in the stables, fires crackled in the kitchen—and farther away was a distant rumble that she guessed was the approaching storm. But the chapel was quiet until a man emerged from it.

Alex stayed where she was, knowing that in the shadows of the cloister she wasn't easily visible, but the man was shorter than the Word and wore a breastplate. One of the Word's guards, then. She watched as he strode along the walkway and disappeared into the kitchens.

She waited for him to emerge with food for the Word, but he didn't. Was he eating in there or trying to sneak away alone? She couldn't leave her post to find out, and there was no one else in sight. Turning, she rested an elbow on the lichen-overgrown back of the bench and stared at the chapel door.

"Alex?"

The voice made her start. Susanna stood nearby, her hat at an angle with its fashionable veil hooked around the brim.

"What is it?" Alex said.

"I was watching the kitchen gate in case the Smiler took it into his head to say his farewells to us, but his guard went out that way."

Alex frowned. "You mean, ran off?"

"I suppose so. I waited for him to come back, but he didn't. My dog's at the gate, and he'll bark his heads off if anyone tries to leave, but I don't know if I should tell Bob about this."

"Well, what orders did Bob give you?"

She regretted the tone of her voice at once, but Susanna's mouth had already tightened. "Whatever you're snippy about, could it please wait until we're in a safer place? My cousin has enough on his mind without anyone adding to it."

Alex took a breath and forced her emotions down. "All right. There are two choices here—the guard is either obeying orders or he isn't. If he isn't, he's deserting. If he is, then the Smiler ordered him to leave." She wondered if the guard had gone to scout out a safe path or have horses waiting for the Word when he sneaked out as well. Perhaps they had arranged some sort of sign to show when the time was ripe.

"What should we do?" Susanna said. "Bob said to let him know if the Smiler left, but he didn't say anything about the guards."

"Tell him anyway." Alex wasn't sure if that would be useful, but better to bring too much news than not enough. "I'll keep watching."

Susanna started towards the other end of the cloister. Before she could reach it, two of Robert's men swung open the huge doors. The clang was so loud that if Alex had not been listening for soft footsteps in the chapel, she would not have heard them. The Word stood on the chapel steps, watching as Robert and Lawrence walked into the cloister courtyard, their captains and Victoria following. Robert waited until silence fell.

"Our scouts have fallen back, and Garnath's army is on its way." The indrawn breaths sounded like a sigh, but he continued to speak. "We're prepared for them. We're on higher ground, and we have better weapons."

"Quorum weaponry," Victoria said. "And the blessing of the Benevolent Ones."

Robert nodded. "We defeated them at the Stagwater. Twice. We'll do it again—"

"Where's your sorcerer?" the Word said.

His voice was quiet but it cut off Robert's speech like a strangler's wire. The gathering crowd turned to him as he stepped down from the chapel, but Robert replied before the Word could reach the courtyard.

"Mayerd did his best," he said. "He's bought us time and—"

"He's betrayed us."

The Word hadn't spoken. That was another man in the crowd, but before anyone could identify him, the Word replied, "Even if he didn't, his sorcery failed us and he couldn't even return to warn us." He paused. "We have lost."

"We haven't!" Robert's teeth showed white through his beard when he spoke. "I'm not one for stirring speeches before the battle, so this will have to do. I'll fight Garnath until my last breath and I'll defend anyone who follows me. Even if—"

"You're right." The Word smiled, but the movement was as devoid of expression as a ripple spreading across a pond, and Alex suddenly realized what people often saw when they looked at her. "You're not one for stirring speeches. And it makes no difference when we're so badly outnumbered."

"We have the Quorum weapons, Your Grace," Michael Frew said.

"We need more," the Word said. "I warned you, Robert. I told you we needed a strategy that would defeat them. Yours failed. I see no reason why your decision to stay here and die should have better results."

"You are free to leave at any time. Your Grace." Robert's voice was icy and contemptuous. "I'm certain you can use the cover of battle to run. And anyone who wants to accompany you is free to do so. The women and noncombatants, as you said earlier."

Susanna shook her head, making the lace veil sway. "I'm with you."

Victoria looked around at the gathered men, clearly challenging any of them to claim less courage than a woman. "You could always go alone, Your Grace."

"I'm not a fool," the Word said.

"Then shut up and let us do our work." Robert turned on his heel before the Word could reply. *Not that he seemed capable of doing so,* Alex thought with some pleasure. As the crowd dispersed, she waited to see if he would take Robert's advice and leave, but he only went back into the chapel.

Father Julian began a prayer in the cloister courtyard with the servants and men-at-arms who were not at the walls, and Victoria joined them; Alex guessed that it was too dangerous for her outside. The howl of horns rode on the wind to sound the army's approach, and she longed to cover her ears. Susanna retrieved her dog, which seemed to feel the same way, because its lips drew back from its teeth and it kept looking in two directions at once.

A timekeeper monk told them that it was eleven of the clock, and one of Robert's men came in to say that the army was in sight, three thousand of them. By midnight Father Julian's prayer was over and Nalle's army had reached the foot of the hill, but they didn't seem in a hurry to attack. With the storm almost upon them, Nalle wouldn't be fool enough to throw his men into an uphill attack through the mud and cannon fire.

If only we had a way out, Alex thought. The people gathered in the courtyard went back to their duties, but she hardly noticed the ones who walked past her. She touched the little package of explosive beneath her sash, but it didn't provide much inspiration.

"What have you got there, Alex?" Victoria said.

Alex hadn't noticed her nearby. "My dagger." She pulled the weapon free with a flourish to draw Victoria's attention away from her waist. "Not that it could do much here."

"Then do put it away."

Remembering that Victoria probably had bad memories of her and a dagger, Alex pushed it back into her sash and nearly pierced the package of explosive. Can't risk that, she thought and slipped the dagger into her sash at the back, against her spine. The maddog snarled at Victoria, so Susanna led it off into one of the guestrooms.

The horns sang out, so close that Alex gripped the edge of the bench. Lichens gritted under her nails. Next came a thousand-throated shout as the attack began and the cannons roared. There was a thunderclap as a steam carriage exploded, and Alex imagined its spikes driving deep into the mass of Nalle's army. The night rang with cries of pain.

And someone screamed on the other side of the cloister. Alex spun around as the kitchen door flew open. A servant stumbled out, clutching his side where blood pumped between his fingers. He collapsed slowly and Alex saw the axe shaft which stood up from his back.

The hounds poured out from the kitchen doorway—a dozen, two dozen, fifty of them. Alex bolted up but before she could run to the doors at the other side of the cloister, they were on her. One man whipped a mailed arm around her and put a blade to her throat. Another one knocked Victoria to the ground.

A few of the men-at-arms drew swords and yelled for help before they died. Half the hounds overpowered the monks and servants, dragging them to one side of the courtyard, while the other half disappeared into the public rooms that lined the cloister. Alex held still. *They won't kill me right away. They're taking hostages instead, so just stay calm.* The edge of steel against her neck moved a little with each breath she took.

Blood soaked into the beds of herbs as Robert's soldiers and the Katassian Knights rushed into the courtyard, but the sight of hostages stopped them even before a hound put a horn to his lips. He blew three short blasts on it. Another man emerged from a guest chamber, dragging Susanna, and shoved her to her knees in the courtyard. Alex guessed they had killed the maddog, and she thought she would die too when she saw the man who came to stand in the midst of the hounds.

She thought of jerking her head forward and slashing her throat open on the blade's edge, but before she could do it, Robert pushed his way through the knights. Susanna's breathing caught as General Nalle stopped behind her and drew his sword.

The blade hissed through the air and her hat flew halfway across the courtyard. Nalle rested the flat of the blade on Susanna's shoulder and its edge touched the pulse in her throat.

"Do you surrender, Lord Robert?" he said.

Robert didn't even seem to hear that, but when the chapel door creaked open, the sound seemed to jolt him out of his shock.

"How did you—" he began.

"*He* did that," Alex heard herself say as she looked at the chapel door. She knew now why one of the Word's guards had slipped out. If only she had guessed what he was going to do.

"You gave me no choice." The Word crossed the chapel steps quickly and went to Nalle's troops, his guards keeping pace with him.

"You knew Garnath would want good reason to keep you alive." Robert's eyes were hot with fury. "Betraying us all was reason enough."

Victoria stared at the Word as though she wanted to spit in his face but was too well bred to do so. "When the Quorum hears of this, you won't just be stripped of your position. You'll be excommunicated. You'll be—"

"You'll be raped," the Word said. Victoria stopped with her mouth half-open and the Word continued. "We would have lost this war regardless. This way, one of us can live."

"Are you going to surrender, Lord Robert?" Nalle said. "Or shall I begin with these women?" He gestured, and the arm around Alex's body was suddenly gone. A foot drove into the backs of her knees and a hard grip pushed her down beside Susanna.

"Dog?" she said, trying not to move her lips.

Susanna's reply was nothing more than a shallow exhalation. "Hole."

A priest's hole. Alex thought that in Susanna's position, she would have hidden herself rather than the dog, but there wasn't any time to regret that either. She thought of throwing the package of explosive into one of the firepots that lined the courtyard. That might kill enough of the hounds and give Robert's men a chance against the survivors. But she would have to throw it into a firepot nearby, and that might kill more than just the hounds.

"No." Victoria was on her knees too, but she spoke with all her usual authority. "We will not surrender. Sir Michael, prepare to destroy the machines and fight to the—"

"No!" Robert's voice was hoarse, but it stopped the knights in their tracks. "There's been enough blood shed on both sides here, General. I offer you a truce instead."

Nalle's fingers twitched and a thin red ribbon spilled down Susanna's throat. "A truce, when I could have a victory?"

"A poor victory," Robert said, "if we did as Lady Victoria says. We could destroy the Quorum weaponry and fight you to the death. We could spill more blood on this holy ground." Lightning flickered overhead, and when he paused, the thunder rolled out. "Or we could call a truce."

Nalle's lip curled. "And what would we gain from a truce?"

"More than you'd gain from following Garnath," Robert said. "He uses Iternan sorcery as well as your good steel. Perhaps there'll come a time soon when he favors the one over the other—especially if his sorcerer can reach into men's minds and force them to obey him."

Alex didn't dare turn her head, but she glanced at Nalle out of the corners of her eyes. The muscles of his face had stiffened. "And what would you offer me instead?"

The swivel of Alex's eyes hurt, as if the movement had pulled strings within her skull. She looked back down at the flagstones and the pain sharpened. Robert was saying something, but she couldn't hear him. There was only a foreignness in her head, something swelling like a tumor inside it, forcing her consciousness down. Her mouth opened of its own accord.

"She speaks with Ohallox's voice, Nalle," her voice said. "And the rebels have a sorcerer too, one who walks the Outward Way. How do you think they used those catapults against you, raised that banner over the city? His name is Mayerd, and—"

"Where is he?" Nalle snapped.

Alex's mouth felt as though it was filled with dry bread, and no words could emerge. *Get out of my head!* she thought but nothing happened.

"I said, where is he?" Nalle took a fistful of her hair, wrenching her to face him. "You don't know?"

"I was monitoring your progress."

Nalle looked ready to put a fist into her teeth. "You lost sight of

253

him, so find him. I can deal with the rebels."

He released her hair and Ohallox let go of her body in the same moment. Alex crumpled forward. From a distance, she heard Nalle refuse Robert's offer and promise him only that the lives of his captains and his soldiers would be spared if he surrendered. If he didn't, he could watch his women have their throats cut like chickens in the market. Susanna touched her elbow and asked quietly if she was hurt, but one of the hounds pulled her away.

"The women too," Robert said. "I want honorable treatment for them."

"You'll have it from me," Nalle said. "Provided you give us the Quorum weaponry."

"No!" Victoria tried to struggle up.

Nalle pushed her back down and Robert replied, "You agreed that I command this army, Lady Victoria. My command is that we surrender."

He tore at his sword-belt and it struck the flagstones on which blood was already drying. Slowly, his men obeyed, and the hounds moved forward to take their weapons.

"Your captains and soldiers, Lord Robert," Nalle said when the rest of his army had poured in through the front of the monastery. The courtyard was nowhere near large enough for them and all their prisoners, but they lined the walkways with drawn swords. "But that still leaves the Quorum knights...and a survivor of the Eighth Regiment told me what they did to Celia Trovart. Kill them."

Alex closed her eyes, but she heard it all. Victoria's scream was lost as Nalle's men surged forward. The knights were disarmed but they still wore their armor, and steel rang off steel, crunched through mail links, ripped into flesh. Through the slaughter in the courtyard, she heard Robert shout an order to his men to hold their positions. *If they kill him as well, if Nalle goes back on his word and strikes him down too...*

She heard the monks pleading and there was a scuffle nearby as one of them rushed forward. The sound ended in a wet gurgle. "We have enough prisoners," Nalle said. "I only need the Quorum engineers alive. Get rid of the rest of them."

The battle raged outside too, but within the courtyard the loudest sound now was someone weeping, and all Alex could feel was a dull relief that it was not her. Slowly, she opened her eyes.

The courtyard of the inner cloister was an abattoir. A few of the bodies wore hounds' helms—the knights had fought, despite being unarmed—but she couldn't even be glad about that. The monks were dead as well. She thought she recognized Father Julian's body, but without a head she couldn't be sure.

That will happen to us too, she knew as Nalle ordered his prisoners to be bound and taken outside. *He won't kill us now, not when he could give us alive to Stephen, but it'll happen.* All Nalle had promised them had been good treatment at his hands. Once he reached Radiath, he would surrender them all to Stephen's jailers and torturers, and he would have done his duty without breaking his word.

Nalle walked a circle around the bodies piled in the center of the courtyard, and approached her. "Lord Garnath's mare?" For a cold moment she thought he would drag her into an inner room. "Or Ohallox?"

"Yes. I mean...he's gone." Speaking was difficult, and she gestured at the corpses instead. "Are we leaving them unburied?"

That seemed to reassure him; he looked merely annoyed at her weakness. "We're not digging holes in the mud. Get up."

Alex obeyed, and Nalle ordered his men to regroup outside. The horns pealed out, the sound muffled under the thunder. *Still no rain, nothing to wash the courtyard clean.* Her face was just as dry, and she managed to walk out without faltering, past the bodies outside. One of them pleaded with her for water before falling silent.

Nalle's men stacked the cannon into a cart, harnessed horses to the single remaining steam carriage to pull it to Radiath and took the remaining mounts for themselves. Alex's gaze leaped through the line of prisoners until she found Robert. Just looking at him made her heart clench. If he had been cut down in the courtyard, if he had been the corpse who had asked her for water, that would have been more merciful than a forced march back to Radiath where he would suffer before he died. She couldn't bear the thought of that.

Nalle ordered her, Susanna and Victoria onto horses as well. She had expected that as prisoners, they would walk, because the general had never given women any better treatment than he gave men. But she understood why they would ride beside him. He wanted her close in case Ohallox spoke through her again, and with Susanna as a hostage, Robert wasn't likely to try anything.

The Word had a horse too, so he stayed close to Nalle and as far from the prisoners as possible. Hounds on foot formed up around the cart which held the cannon, while the mounted ones used spears to herd the prisoners into a column before the cart, behind Nalle and his hostages. One of them was riding White Wind, Alex saw before she looked away.

Something trickled down her cheek and she thought she was crying, before the next drop hit her hand. It was only the rain. Nalle gave an order and the march began to Radiath.

Chapter Eleven:
The Eye of the Storm

The rain soaked Alex's dress so that it clung to her like a weight. She knew she was shivering, but the knowledge came to her as if passed through a filter that kept any emotion out. Her hands held the horse's reins loosely and her back was straight as she sat in the saddle.

But at least she was riding. The rain turned the ground to a slurry and spears prodded the prisoners on as the army's pace slowed. There was no light except for white-hot flickers in the sky. Nalle had left Radiath in such haste that he hadn't brought a baggage train or even lanterns. They were so close to the city that he had probably thought it wasn't worth the effort.

So close. She felt sure they would be at Radiath within the hour. Not much time left, and yet she couldn't think of any way to even slow Nalle down. If she simply bolted, his men would catch up with her, and with no fires she couldn't set the package of explosive alight either.

Even if she did, what difference would that make? If she ignited it at that moment, she would kill Nalle and the Word and herself. Then Nalle's second or one of his captains would take command and march the surviving prisoners back to Stephen. They had lost. The knowledge did not fill her with despair, but that was because she felt nothing.

"Alice?" Nalle said. "Do you know where their sorcerer is?"

There was a pause while she wondered who Alice was. "No. Perhaps he's flown."

"Flown?"

"Well, I wouldn't expect a sorcerer to walk, General." Alex looked

Marian Perera

straight ahead. "Don't they fly instead?"

The men close enough to hear her looked up, and she hoped they got a face full of water, but Nalle only nodded. "That was how he got away. Ohallox had better deal with him, or I'll kill them both."

The army continued its march. One of the prisoners fell and was urged to his feet again, but when the thunder rolled out overhead a man screamed. Nalle wheeled around. Alex turned as well, and in the next flash of lightning she saw a horse rear.

White Wind, she thought. The horse looked like a pale statue, and the hound clinging to its back howled in fear. Then they were both down, thrown off-balance. She thought the horse might have landed on the hound and crushed him, but the man was up at once.

He snatched a flail from his belt. The prisoners backed away—all except Robert, who stood his ground. Run, Alex thought desperately as the flail's spiked head flew through the air. She never saw if it had struck, only that Robert lurched ahead and slammed into the hound.

Alex sat motionless as more hounds closed on the struggling men and hauled Robert away. The anger she had felt during their quarrel was nothing compared to the fury that rose in her at the sight of anyone laying their hands on him. White Wind rolled and scrambled up again.

"What happened?" Nalle shouted.

"This bastard did it, sir!" The hound kicked out, and Robert doubled up. The flail still swung, whistling in a circle, and Alex couldn't take her eyes off it; even in the near-darkness the swift motion was visible. "He made that horse drop me!"

"Well, don't kill him," Nalle said. *Do whatever else you like*, his tone said, and the hound didn't hesitate. His arm whipped out and the steel ball flew through the air.

It struck the side of White Wind's head and bone crunched under the impact. Knees buckling, the horse sank slowly to the ground. The hound gave Robert another kick for good measure and then went to take his place with the rest of the infantry around the cart of cannons. Robert staggered when they released him, but kept his feet as the column began its march again.

Alex turned. The rain trickling down her neck felt like cold fingers, but her mind was colder. If the hound was right—if Robert had made his horse rear and drop a man—then he had done it for a reason. And since Robert was nothing if not practical, he had done it to gain some

258

advantage, however small. Her hate of the hounds helped, sharpening her thoughts like a whetstone to a blade. If she could buy him time—

Hoofbeats sounded in the darkness ahead, and Nalle halted. His hand went to the hilt of his sword, but the man who galloped up to them wore no armor.

"Sir!" he shouted. "There's fighting in the city. More of the rebels—"

"How many?" Nalle said. "Are they inside?"

"It's a trick, Nalle." Alex spoke as if she was bored with his naivety. "One they've used before, or don't you remember?"

Nalle turned to her. "Ohallox?"

"Yes. They're trying to make you rush ahead. You know why."

His eyes narrowed. "They've trapped the ground ahead of us."

Thank you for doing my work for me. "Yes. I hear something from their minds." She spoke as if pronouncing foreign words. "Sub-terranean de-tonation devi-ces."

She had heard about that from the Quorum mechanics, and the Word had fallen back enough that he was not within earshot. Victoria was, and when Nalle used the back of his hand to question her, she said through swollen lips that the devices responded to fast movement. Alex held her breath, afraid Nalle would ask about the connection between speed and explosions, but he only ordered two dozen of the prisoners to go before them, to spare the horses the devices.

The army inched forward. The storm raged around them but she still heard the sounds of battle in the city ahead—distant cries and a crash that she hoped was another wall giving way. The horns from the city were no longer measured battle peals but long and frantic calls. "Auditory illusions," she said.

"Have you found their sorcerer?" Nalle asked her.

"I'm doing what I can."

"If we put a sword to his master's throat and ordered him to reveal himself..."

"If you could produce illusions that make men attack each other, would you have a master?" Alex said. "But I can—"

A light bobbed in the darkness ahead and she stopped. So did the army. The cordon of prisoners ahead looked like statues as the firefly glow grew larger, to a lantern. The man who held it came close but when his mouth moved, the sound was nearly inaudible.

Marian Perera

"General." He had been injured, and his other arm clutched a rent in the side of his militia uniform. "General. They came in by the river. They broke the chain—"

"He's lying," Alex said. "Anyone can put on a dead man's clothes and come here to lure us into a trap. I've looked into his mind."

One of Nalle's guards suggested questioning the militiaman further, but he refused. "We don't have the time." The militiaman looked from him to them, shaking his head in a spasm. "Take his lantern."

The guard spurred his horse forward, reaching down, and the militiaman didn't try to stop him. He kept speaking but the words were lost in a shout from behind. Another hound rode up, leaned close and spoke too softly for her to hear. Nalle frowned, then turned to Victoria.

"My men say there's a sound rising from the machines. The cannon. They're..." He paused. "They're hissing, like a nest of snakes. What do you know about that?"

Victoria's face went pale, and Alex was glad Nalle's attention was no longer on her. She knew about the cannons, how they needed both water and fire to be activated. And the rain had soaked through their coverings, trickling into them.

"I'll examine them." Victoria clambered down from her horse. "I'll need light."

Alex hoped that Nalle's guard would give her the lantern, but he dismounted and drew his sword. The lantern swung from his other hand as he gestured Victoria on. She sludged through the mud, on the outside of the column of prisoners, heading towards the cart.

Susanna gasped, the reins falling from her fingers. She doubled over as if someone had punched her and when she raised her head, her eyes were wide.

"We're under attack, General!" she said. "Have you gone deaf? What are you playing at out there?"

"Ohallox?" Nalle stared at her, then at Alex. "You told us it was a trick!"

From Susanna's expression, she might have been the general and he a junior officer who had not just tried to backstab her, but had done so ineptly. "Are you trying to blame your loss of nerve on me? Get back to Radiath *now*, before they reach the castle!"

Alex sighed. "They'll try anything, General. They're desperate—"

260

"What message did I send to Lord Garnath when we emerged from Galvede Forest?" Nalle snapped.

"A stag's head." Susanna's own head tilted to one side. "Oh. Who tried to convince you that I was speaking through them?"

Nalle drew his sword and turned to Alex. "No one."

Before he could strike there was a scuffle in the column of prisoners. The guard beside Victoria fell as someone slammed into him, and the lantern rolled away in the mud. Victoria was on it at once, staggering upright with it, and she tossed it to Robert. His hands were free somehow, Alex realized, and he caught the lantern, turned and flung it. The lantern's frame hit the covered masses of cannons in the cart and the glass shattered. Burning oil splashed out.

The cart exploded. The blast sent hounds, and pieces of hounds, through the air. The sound turned solid as it thumped into Alex's ears. Her horse bucked and the night roiled with movement but she couldn't hear anything. She threw herself forward, clinging to the horse's neck. There were bodies all over, sprawled in the mud, struggling up and running.

A sharp whistle cut through the numbness in her ears but it was too late. A hand snatched the reins from her and a man grabbed her riding-cloak, nearly dragging her off the horse's back as he threw himself into the saddle. The cloak tore away from her and fell.

Alex struggled for balance in the saddle, then thought, *What am I doing? Jump!* She felt the steel of a breastplate against her back and spikes pricking her skin. Before she could throw herself off, the man locked an arm around her waist.

"Break off!" he shouted. The horses, terrified by the blast, had scattered in all directions, and the ranks of Nalle's army were in disarray. More of the prisoners were free, and dogs barked wildly. Nalle raised his voice even further. "To the city!"

Alex didn't fight as her horse broke into a gallop. Nalle was too strong for her and if she tried to wrench his arm away, he could simply hit her senseless. Even if she somehow yanked the reins free, other riders flanked them as the tatters of the army came together.

Then they were at the open side gate of the city, and someone on the wall screamed a warning. Nalle reined in hard, just before the pit in the ground. One of the other hounds didn't stop fast enough and his horse plunged in. Alex heard the bones in its forelegs snap. Nalle's mount picked its way around the pit, then plunged ahead.

The city was in chaos. Streets away, swords clashed and people screamed, but Nalle took the Palace Road at a gallop that rode down anyone in his path—whether insurgents or cityfolk, Alex didn't have time to see. He stopped before the gates of the castle and shouted for passage.

Alex's mind raced as the gates began to open. There was the dagger against the small of her back, but she couldn't draw it without alerting Nalle. Was there anything she could offer him in exchange for his releasing her? She tried to speak and he took his arm from her waist, closing a hand lightly around her throat instead.

"One word out of you and I'll break your neck." He spurred his horse through the half-open gates, past the stables and storehouses to the inner ward. There were men on the wallwalks and dogs barking in the kennels, but Nalle ignored everything as he rode to the servants' entrance at the side of the castle. The guards shouted to someone inside as he dismounted, then grabbed her wrist to pull her after him.

Light streamed out of the servants' entrance, and when Alex pushed wet hair out of her face with her free hand she saw the Word dismount as well. Since his own guards hadn't been mounted, they had been left behind in the ride to the city. He looked composed but wary, like a man standing on a precipice and aware that he was safe as long as he didn't panic or move.

Someone pushed past the guards and stood just within the door. Alex recognized the red hair at once—it was Jack Iavas, Stephen's aide.

"Those are the only two prisoners?" he said.

Nalle nodded. "What news? How many of them?"

"They came in from the river on make-do rafts," Iavas said. "We'd raised a chain and they broke it somehow. Can't have been more than four, five hundred of them, but they've got an Iternan sorcerer."

"Who's leading them?" Nalle said.

"Nicholas Rauth, but he's dead." Alex still heard hoofbeats, the jingle of mail and the grumble of distant thunder, but there was a strange silence in her mind. She tried to remember if she had thanked Nicholas for the gold coin. "And they won't take orders from an Iternan, that's for sure. So you can deal with the rest of them. Take as many of the garrison—"

"No," Nalle said.

"What do you mean, no? These are Lord Garnath's orders, General." Iavas stressed the rank. "Doesn't matter who's with them, not when we outnumber them and we're fighting on familiar ground. Besides, they haven't got Quorum weaponry now. They must have used it up."

"It doesn't matter." Nalle released Alex and put a foot into a stirrup. "They still have the Bloody Baron. And they followed him even after I'd beaten him."

"Are you going over to their side?" There was an edge to Iavas's voice, and Alex hoped for a moment that the guards would attack Nalle and give her enough of a distraction to run.

"I'm no turncoat," Nalle said. *As if Robert would have you,* Alex thought. "But I won't risk my life for Lord Garnath any longer. I'll gather the soldiers who'll follow me, and we'll give our service to an honorable lord who doesn't use sorcery." He looked down at the guards, a long stare that evaluated them all. "Want to order anyone to stop me, Iavas?"

"Let the coward go," Iavas said, and Nalle turned the horse's head. "Bring them inside."

Into the castle where she had been a mare until Robert took her away, except there was no reason for Stephen to keep her alive now. From where Alex stood, the castle's walls were too tall for her to see Radiath and even if she could watch the city, she knew there was no escape in sight, no hope of help. She wondered if Robert was still alive.

Then Iavas dragged her inside and the door slammed shut behind them.

In the dark, Robert couldn't see the hounds. They couldn't see him either, but it hardly mattered when there were so many more of them. He had a sword again, taken from a man killed when the cannons exploded, but when the lightning flashed he saw three of the hounds close in on him. One of them swung a flail and when the light faded he heard the *hish-hish* of the spiked ball moving faster.

Susanna whistled again. Something leaped at one of the hounds, knocking the man over with its weight, and Robert struck out at another, then threw himself away from the flail's swing. He scrabbled up to a pile of debris that looked like half a cannon, still smoking and red-hot at its heart. The flail whipped out again, the chain coiling around his sword to yank it out of his hands, but for an instant that left the hound wide open.

Robert leaped off the cannon, the height adding to his momentum as he crashed into the hound. By the time he got up he was dizzy and bruised, blood and rain running down his cheek, but the hound lay face-down in the mud and didn't move. By then, he knew the battle was over.

He had managed to take a dagger off the man White Wind had thrown, cutting his bonds and then flinging the blade to Victoria just before the cannons exploded. He and the men had thrown themselves down to escape the worst of the blast, and Victoria had freed as many of them as she could before the hounds recovered. She was still doing that. *Almost as good as one of us. Pity she's a Quorumlord.*

Susanna's dog broke off and padded back to her, while Robert retrieved the sword he had found. His men were regrouping around them, so he didn't hug her, only asked if she was hurt. She shook her head and told him what had happened, ending with, "They have Alex."

Robert already knew that, and his heart sank as he formed up what was left of his army. "The city's under attack," he said to Lawrence. "That means Nicholas struck at it. I'd wager anything that Mayerd's with them—that's how they broke the chain across the river."

"Do we go on, then?" Lawrence said.

They hadn't much of a choice. Nalle would have reached Radiath by then, rallying the hounds and the militia with help from Garnath's sorcerer. He couldn't leave Nicholas and his half-an-army to face those alone. And Alex was in the city.

"We go on," he said. The steam carriage, the Javelin Fly, had escaped the explosion. It was all that remained of the Quorum weaponry now but it was out of coal. Still, since they were so few in number, there were enough horses for everyone to ride and to pull the carriage too.

He left a few of his men behind to help the wounded, telling them to fall back to the monastery. Despite the carnage there, it wasn't burned or ruined and might still have supplies and medicines. Then he wearily mounted a horse that might have been a bay, but which looked black in the rain and the darkness, and began his last ride to Radiath.

The city's falling, was his first thought. People fled through the shattered gates, screaming when they saw him and the rest of his men. He spurred the bay and it burst into a last flagging gallop that got it past the gates before any of the few defenders still on the walls could react. The air was thick with the stench of blood and burned wood.

No one tried to stop him until he reached the King's Bridge, where a handful of militiamen and two hounds barred the way. They all carried swords, and one crouched over a firepot as if ready to throw it.

"Get out of the way." Robert drew his sword and braced himself to take down the one with the firepot first. Even White Wind, steady as a stone pillar, might have shied at a face full of fire. "Or we'll run you—"

"Run," someone said, like an echo.

The hounds and militiamen turned. Mayerd stood at the other end of the bridge. He was alone, and hadn't even drawn his sword, but the ridges across his face were as evident as the flat lack of fear in his voice.

"Run." He began to walk forward as if they weren't there. "Run."

Iavas shoved Alex forward, and she sprawled on the ground. A guardsman carrying a hammer stepped over her prone body as if she were a rug and went to the door. She picked herself up, saw two servants hurrying down the narrow corridor with planks of wood in their arms, and quickly pushed herself against the wall as they passed.

"Make sure you seal that door up good," Iavas said before he turned to the Word. "Excuse us, your worship. I'll make sure the mare won't run off."

Alex's heart drummed, but her mind was coldly clear as he came to her. Could she kill him? She had her dagger, but the guards would cut her to pieces. She let her gaze slide away as if she was afraid, but it gave her a chance to see the barred door, flanked by alcoves in which guardsmen stood alert. Even if cannons bashed through the thick wood, the men would not be harmed, and the servants nailed planks over the door with feverish haste.

Iavas took her arm and spun her around, pushing her face against the wall. Alex thought of her one chance, the package of explosive still hidden against her belly. No point in wasting that—it was for Stephen. She felt Iavas pull her hands behind her back.

"What is the *meaning* of this?" the Word said.

"Just a small precaution, your holiness," Iavas said. Ropes went around her wrists and were drawn tight, knotted. Surely they weren't binding the Word of the High Quorum as well, she thought and dared to hope Iavas had been distracted by the Word, that he hadn't seen the dagger thrust down into her sash.

Black cloth went over her eyes and was tied behind her head. Now she knew what they had done to the Word.

"It's all right." Iavas took her arm again. "We won't let you fall. Let's move."

Alex's heart sank. She knew at once that Stephen would not be in his own rooms, with which she was familiar. Blindfolded, she had no idea of where Iavas led them, up stairs, floor after floor, through echoing passages, until the cloth was wrenched from her eyes and she saw a small room with only one guard outside. Of course. If the castle fell, Stephen wouldn't be caught in his own quarters, and he wouldn't even give the impression that he was in that particular room.

She turned to see the corridor and Iavas threw her into the room. She nearly fell, but caught herself just in time, and when she turned to face Stephen, her body was as numb as if she were encased in ice.

"What a pleasant homecoming, Alex!" Stephen's voice was cheerful, but his stare flicked to Iavas. "Where are the rest of them?"

Not as strong as you thought you were, Alex thought as Iavas replied, "Nalle dealt with them, but he heard of our friend and magic doesn't sit well in his belly. He says he's gone."

"Let him go," Stephen said. "He won't find too warm a welcome anywhere, and we'll hold them off for as long as it takes Ohallox to finish them." Alex turned so that she faced the three men, and her fingers brushed the outline of the dagger beneath her sash.

Candles burned on a table beside two silver goblets, and Stephen filled one with wine. "A drink?" he asked the Word.

"No, Lord Garnath," the Word said. Alex slipped her fingertips beneath her sash and grasped the dagger's hilt, pulling it free. Sweat trickled down her sides, and she hoped no one noticed the small careful movements of her arms. For the first time, the Word looked out of his depth. His smile had gone and his copper gaze was fixed on Stephen and full of wariness.

"What does a Quorumlord do here?" Stephen sipped the wine.

"The voice of the High Quorum," the Word said. "One who knows every detail of the rebels' new weaponry."

The ropes were so tight that Alex's fingers began to go numb. Never losing her calm expression, she worked the dagger's hilt into her grip and rotated her wrist until the blade rested against the ropes, as Stephen said, "Well, good for you. And no doubt you're the only person with such knowledge. My mare isn't privy to any details, is that right?"

The Word glared at her, his eyes filled with loathing. Alex ignored him and worked at the ropes, sawing them away strand by strand. *Don't rush. You have enough time if he's stalling.*

"You will find, Lord Garnath," the Word said, "that I alone am capable of negotiating with the High Quorum on your behalf. That isn't something my servants or yours can do."

Alex knew at once that he had said the wrong thing, and Stephen grinned. "I don't need to negotiate with anyone. What should we do with him, Jack?"

Iavas nodded towards the open window. "Have him *negotiate* his way across the roof, m'lord."

"Do you take advice from your underlings, Lord Garnath?" the Word said.

"When it comes to disposing of vermin, yes." Stephen folded his arms. "Have you anything else to say before you leave my presence—one way or another? Because I see no use for you."

There was growing fear in the Word's voice. "I have money."

"That's good. I like money." Stephen drew his sword, a jewel-hilted affair meant more for decoration than for fighting, but honed to an edge regardless. Alex felt the ropes give way, the tension easing as fibers snapped. "For the life of the voice of the High Quorum, I'd have to charge ten thousand gold. Nothing less would suffice." He looked around. "Where's the money, Your Grace? I don't see it."

The ropes parted. Alex clutched them before they could fall.

"Might be under his fancy dress, m'lord." Iavas leaned against the doorframe. "Maybe he should disrobe."

Sweat shone on the Word's forehead, but he seemed to gather some last strength. "You wish me to climb across your roof, Lord Garnath?" He looked at the window, at the darkness and lashing rain, and his mouth jerked. "I am willing to do that."

Stephen raised his eyebrows. "I'd like to see it. Go on."

Alex didn't dare turn around, because Stephen would see the dagger in her now-freed hands, but she watched the Word as he made his way to the window. His steps were halting, as if he hoped for a last-minute reprieve. He put a hand on the windowsill and leaned forward, into the storm.

Then he spun on his heel, white robes flaring, and a knife gleamed in his hand as he ran for the door. Stephen was a moment too slow to intercept him, and Iavas had not drawn his own sword. The Word stabbed down at him, a desperate lunge with no skill behind it.

Iavas caught his wrist, wrenching it, and the Word screamed as the knife hit the floor. *Not that he could have hurt Jack anyway,* Alex thought, *the man's wearing a breastplate.* Then Stephen reached them, and the point of his sword drove into the Word's spine. Alex thought the Quorumlord would scream, but he only gave a small choking sound as Stephen twisted the sword with vicious force. Tasting bile, she forced herself to look away as the Word crumpled.

Do something. Except she had no idea how to get the better of two armed men, and if she lit the package of explosive, where could she hide? She heard footfalls across the floor as Stephen came to her, and she raised her head to meet his eyes.

"You see what happens to my enemies, Alex?" He shook his head. "What a shame you threw your lot in with the wrong man. Did you think you could defeat me?"

Alex shrugged, knowing that she radiated cold indifference, the one reaction he hated the most. "I did once, didn't I?"

His face hardened, but she had already braced for the blow. His fist lashed out and she rolled her head as best she could, fighting the reflex to bring her hands up, to plunge her dagger into his chest. What if he wore chainmail under his tunic, as Susanna had done? She would have to stab him in the throat, but what if he was too quick for her and blocked the strike?

Steady. Wait for the right moment. She looked at the floor, always the best idea when Stephen was angry. The submissive stance tended to calm him down, and she waited for the pain to subside. The corner of her mouth was sore where he had hit her.

"Or is there something else?" Stephen took her chin and tilted her head up. "Did Nalle let him live? Yes, that's what makes you so confident. Is there some other trick he's got?"

Alex didn't think she was confident at all, and her skin crawled. "I wouldn't know," she said levelly. "Robert didn't confide in me."

"Oh, it's 'Robert', is it?" Stephen said in mock-surprise. "Tell me, sweetheart, did he fuck you?"

"Of course," Alex said, to take away any advantage he had. She sounded surprised that he had even asked, but she didn't expect the jeering look to be wiped off his face.

"Ohallox told me differently," he said.

"Then you don't know which of us to believe."

Stephen's gaze raked her from head to foot, and Alex knew what he saw, the dress that Robert had given her. Even stained after weeks' travel, it was obviously not the kind of garment a man flung at a whore simply to cover her, because the green linen suited her eyes and the black lace matched her hair, while the sash drew attention to her narrow waist. A muscle twitched at the side of Stephen's mouth.

"You." His voice was low and cold. "You're the kind of woman he would want. But he wouldn't trade victory for your life, so there's no point in keeping you. I'd like to tup you once more, for old times' sake, but this is the only upraised weapon you deserve."

He lifted the sword that still glistened with blood.

"Run."

Robert's skin crawled. A hound took a step forward, sword extended across his body, and a clot of earth flew up to slap him across the face. "Run," Mayerd said again. Furrows sprouted on the ground to either side of him, as if unseen fingers were drawing lines from him to the bridge's guardians, a path for him to walk and reach them.

Before he could do that, they ran. Robert's horse sidestepped and the rest of his men moved aside as well, though Susanna's dog took a snap at one of the militiamen. Mayerd held on to one of the struts of the bridge, and he only spoke when Robert reined in beside him.

"They're at the castle," he said without looking up. He seemed to be looking inside instead. "Eric Chyrefen, Lord Nicholas's second, he's leading them."

Why wasn't Nicholas...? Robert knew the answer at once. "Can you help?"

Mayerd tilted his head at the marks on the ground, as if gesturing at a shameful mistake of his. "That's the most I can do." He still wouldn't meet anyone's eyes. "I don't have the strength for anything else."

"It'll still help." Robert didn't know if that was any consolation, when a normal Iternan could have razed the walls, fired the buildings and probably boiled the river as well. "Let's go."

Lightning flickered down and struck a bell tower just ahead. Robert ignored the crash of broken stones and the sharp acrid smell in the air as they reached the castle gates. There were even fewer of the insurgents circling the castle walls than he expected, but Eric Chyrefen told him that they had swept the wallwalks clean of defenders. Robert could see that. The ground was littered with corpses, and the rain trickling down the walls was the color of rosewine.

"What about the gates?" he said. "Axes?"

Chyrefen shook his head. "I left our axemen at the Broken Bridge. Ordered them to bring it down, cut us off from the rest of the city."

No way to fire the gates when the rain streamed down and nothing to use as a battering ram...except for the last steam carriage. The men took hold of the spikes on either side of it and rolled it forward, picking up speed before the spikes at the front crashed into the gates, biting deep into the heavy wood. The carriage was so heavy and solidly built that it even remained on its wheels at the end.

Wrenching aside the remains of the gates, they poured into the castle's outer ward unopposed. No one was in the courtyard, and Robert guessed that Garnath had withdrawn his forces and sealed the castle up. He galloped into the inner ward and pulled his horse to a halt as the rest of his men drew level with him.

"What now?" Mayerd said.

He had clearly recovered somewhat, but if he was asking for orders, Robert knew they couldn't expect any spectacular displays of magic. Dismounting, he stepped back and looked up at the deserted balconies of the castle's towers. The doors were all barred, and he didn't have the numbers for a battle, much less a siege. He would have tried both, if he could have been sure they would save Alex.

That was his point of no return, his moment of lightning. He had had to lose her to see how much he needed her—barrenness be damned, he would take her blind and crippled if he could only have her back. And now it was too late.

No. It wasn't. And he knew what to do.

"They expect us to get through that door," he said to Mayerd. "So we'll make enough noise to satisfy them. Lawrence, can you supervise that?"

Lawrence nodded. "Where do you actually plan to enter?"

"A tower. Mayerd, lift me to the level of that lowest terrace."

"The Outward Way doesn't work on living creatures."

"Damn the Out..." Robert controlled himself and turned to the one person who was certain to be practically equipped under her frippery, even if they had been taken prisoner and had galloped through the dark and the storm. "Sus, a rope?"

She nodded. "But I don't have a grappling iron."

"We don't need one." Robert went to the base of a tower. "Lift the end of it up to a rail, Mayerd, and tie it there."

As the men started hacking at the door, the end of the rope rose into the air and he watched as it disappeared into the darkness. "Done," Mayerd said finally.

The rail was forty feet above their heads, and Robert drew his dagger, but Mayerd took the rope. "I'm the captain of your guard, and I go first. When I shake the cord three times, start climbing."

He took the rope and began to pull himself up. It was a slow process and Robert listened to the chop of steel against wood as his troops continued the distraction. He wondered how many of Garnath's remaining garrison had been drained away to watch this new threat, and how many defenders they would find in the towers of the castle.

The rope lashed repeatedly, but at the same time Robert heard steel clash high above his head. He put the hilt of his dagger between his teeth and hauled himself up, careless of the friction of the rope in his palms or against his knees. Again weapons rang against each other, and there was a choked cry.

"Robert, look out!" Mayerd shouted.

That could only mean someone was trying to cut the rope. Robert clenched his teeth so hard that he tasted bitter leather, but that gave him a last spurt of strength to overcome aching muscles and near-burned flesh. He couldn't see anything, and he heard little over the pounding of his own heart, but when he thrust one hand out, it closed over a rail of the balcony.

The rope snapped apart. Robert fought an urge to gasp—if he opened his mouth, he would drop his dagger—and grabbed another rail with his free hand, just in time. His body jerked from the sudden pull of forty feet, and he thought, this would be a good time for one of those bastards to start cutting through my fingers.

Which indeed the bastard tried to do. A sword blade made a harp of the railing, but the darkness worked to the guardsman's disadvantage, and a sword was not the best weapon to use against a small target behind closely spaced rails. Robert braced himself, hoping for one chance, and it came when something smashed into the balcony door. The guardsman jerked around, and Robert used the moment to hook his elbow around the rail, hanging from that arm.

He grabbed the dagger with his free hand and plunged it as deeply into the guardsman's leg as he could.

The man's scream was followed by the sound of a blade cutting through flesh and cartilage. Robert didn't know what had happened. All he knew was that he couldn't lift himself up any more, because his arms felt as if they had been soaked in oil and dipped in fire. Then Mayerd's hand closed around his wrist.

"Come on," he said, and for that, Robert managed a last effort that brought his foot up to the level of the railing. When he was finally over it, he leaned back against it, panting. Mayerd kicked the balcony doors open, and in the faint candlelight from the chamber inside, Robert saw what had smashed into the balcony doors first—a brick with a rope tied to it. Someone had tossed it up from below, and he was only grateful that hadn't struck Mayerd.

"How many of them?" he asked. The coils of rope vanished through the rails, pulled taut from below, and the brick jammed against two of the rails. Robert knew at once that Susanna was climbing. Anyone else would have waited for his orders, but it was too late to stop her now.

"Two. I took them by surprise—I was half over the rail before they knew what was happening."

Robert frowned. "Then how did you fight them?"

"With the Way, of course," Mayerd said. "It wielded my sword."

Robert rubbed his arms. "Couldn't you just pull their own swords away from them?"

"I tried. Ohallox sensed me—he must have been aware of my presence when I used the Way to tie that rope, and he extended his power over those men. The Inward and Outward Ways have peculiar effects on each other—sometimes they cancel each other out, but sometimes they have a synergistic—"

"Later. For now, make sure no one else is waiting to spring a trap."

Mayerd looked through the chamber as Susanna pulled herself up to the balcony. Robert frowned at her. "What are you doing here? It's too dangerous."

"Help me lift Bobby," Susanna said. "I tied the other end of the rope around his chest."

Ordinarily, his cousin's tendency to ignore pointed questions would have annoyed Robert, but he was too tired to argue. He sighed and helped her drag up the maddog's weight. Susanna untied the rope, which had been padded with a folded wad of cloth, while Mayerd came back to say that there was no one in sight.

"How badly are you hurt?" Robert said. Even by candlelight he saw a dark stain spreading over Mayerd's sleeve.

Mayerd didn't even bother to glance at the wound. "It's nothing compared to what Ohallox could do. That's why I'll take him alone. The two of you would only get in the way."

Robert nodded and they made their way through the chamber. "I'll find Alex. Somehow."

"Not somehow," Susanna said, catching up with them. "Bobby could find her. The cloak tied around him is hers. Why do you think I brought him up here?"

Robert hadn't thought he could smile again, but he did. "If he finds her, he can have chicken bones and fish heads any time he's in Fulmion. And pig's trotters!"

"Just buy me a new hat." Susanna stepped out into an empty passageway. She knelt and held the cloak before the dog's noses. "Come on, Bobby."

"Good luck," Mayerd said and walked away down the corridor.

Ohallox barred his door, but he knew that such things were only amusing diversions to the Outward Way. What he didn't know was how strong Mayerd's control of it was. Twelve years of inaction had slowed the man's responses, feebled his talent and reduced him to only the most basic actions, like propelling a sword—a sword! Who in Iternum would waste time with a sword?—to fight the fools on the balcony. On the other hand, Mayerd *had* surprised him before...

He gathered all his strength and channeled it into one aspect of the Inward Way—the creation of pain. Thought and emotion were honed to hurt and ravage. He unleashed it.

The mental blast shook him with its strength, and then it surged on to Mayerd, as unstoppable as a volcano. Ohallox knew what it would do—scramble thoughts, set senses to reeling, leave his enemy incapacitated or comatose.

Mayerd staggered from the battering-ram strike, lurching against the wall and grabbing a tapestry for support. Through the howl of unrestrained power in his own ears, Ohallox heard words repeated: "Keleit, Jeyarel, Shiren." The same names, over and over like a litany, in a voice hoarse with agony. Who were they? Ohallox halted the attack for a moment in fear that this was some trick of the Outward Way, but then he remembered. He had seen those names in Elinah's memory, preserved forever on the Inward Way. Those were her children.

"Keleit, Jeyarel, Shiren," Mayerd whispered, and Ohallox understood. Mayerd had never before allowed himself to think of the children he had left in Iternum. Now he did, and the remembered pain—mingled with love—overwhelmed even the effects of the Inward Way. Rather than trying to fight back on Ohallox's terms, Mayerd found something that held his thoughts too strongly for Ohallox to shatter them, something that absorbed his being too deeply for any power to touch it.

Grinding his teeth, Ohallox tried to reach into those memories, the names and faces of lost children, but all his training couldn't twist them. Configured to the Outward Way, Mayerd's mind didn't permit that kind of fundamental alteration. It was like trying to mix oil and water.

Ohallox broke the contact, fists clenching. *Very well, let's try something else.*

Coercion whipped out from him into one of the few remaining castle guards, and the man hastened down a flight of stairs, approaching Mayerd with sword drawn. But even as Ohallox watched dispassionately from the man's eyes, the tapestry wrenched itself from the wall and brought the guardsman to the ground beneath its weight. Mayerd was in too much pain for fancy swordplay, but he didn't need any to kick the prone man behind his ear. Without even pausing, he walked on slowly.

That was the Outward Way, if I had any doubts, Ohallox thought. Despite all his skill, he couldn't reach into Mayerd's mind the way he had twisted the mare's, couldn't search through Mayerd's memories, couldn't even lure him on to the winding crossroad path of the Inward Way.

Though Mayerd had touched the Inward Way once, when he had spoken to the mare. Ohallox wondered if the small drop of the Inward Way that Mayerd had once possessed—the wall—had enabled that. It would have made an interesting case study, not that he would ever be able to publish that in Iternum.

And if he didn't stop Mayerd, he might never have the chance to write it. Still, despite Mayerd's resistance, his own power was formidable and he prepared to use all of it. However, to be on the safe side, he opened a drawer in his desk and took out a dagger. Its hilt was inset with emeralds, and he pressed the largest jewel.

The hollowed emerald turned on a hinge. Fluid from a cavity inside ran down the length of the blade, and Ohallox smiled.

"Come on, then, Mayerd." He watched the door.

Alex felt as though she was caught on the Inward Way again, held mesmerized as Stephen raised the bloodied sword. Even when she had been beaten in the past, she had never seen a weapon drawn to kill her. It was as if she had been called for, one last time, because her body felt cool and numb, her mind detached from it.

No, she thought, and as the sword plunged forward, she flung herself aside, shoving the dagger into her sash as she did so. Drops of blood flecked her dress as the blade hissed past her, and she struck the ground, scrabbling to put some distance between her and Stephen. His eyes widened as he saw her hands were free, but before he could strike again she was on her feet, pulling the package of explosive out from beneath her sash.

"Stay back!" She tried not to look at the candles. If he or Iavas realized that the explosive needed to be lighted first, she would die. "This is one of the Quorum's weapons. If I drop it, it will tear this room apart."

Stephen hesitated, but Iavas said, "She's lying, my lord. That's some rations she was carrying."

"Alex?" Stephen still held the sword poised to strike. "You wouldn't kill yourself too, would you? Jack, open the door."

"No!" Alex said sharply. "Stay where you are."

"I said, open the door."

Alex felt herself trembling. She couldn't enforce the threat she had just made. "Do that, Jack." She forced a smile. "I'll want to leave fast when this alchemist's creation unleashes a force greater than an earthquake." She stepped towards the candles, trying to make it look as though she was angling for a glimpse of the door.

The door opened and the guard looked inside. "My lord?"

"I still say it's her rations," Iavas said. "Look, it's even got a cord to tie up the sacking."

Damn him to hell. Alex doubled the trailing cord at its base so that the fire would have less to burn.

"That's not a cord," Stephen said, a sudden insight in his voice. "It's a wick!"

He slashed at her, but Alex had a hand free and she grabbed the candelabra, dashing it in one desperate sweep to block the sword. Steel rang off silver, and the impact shivered down her arm painfully. Candles rolled in all directions, but she had deflected Stephen's blow, and in the moment it took him to recover she brought her foot up into his groin.

A gasp tore from his throat as he dropped the sword. Then an arm whipped around her chest, driving the air from her lungs, and the guard dragged her back. His other hand closed around her wrist, clenching so tightly that she nearly let go of the package of explosive.

"Kill her!" Stephen's voice was a harsh gasp.

Alex dropped the candelabra and snatched the dagger from her sash, careless of the blade slicing through her dress. She drove it into the guard's arm, and when his grip slackened she pulled herself free.

"Kill her, damn you!" Stephen said again.

Alex stumbled away from the guard as he drew his own sword, his face a mask of fury. She needed a fire, but she couldn't take her eyes off the man who advanced on her, Iavas hovering a safe distance behind him. Nearly tripping over something as she took a step back, she saw that it was Stephen's fallen sword. The guard was watching her so closely that she knew she could never dodge the strike.

She looked over his shoulder and her eyes widened with the start of a smile. "Robert!"

The guard whipped around, and in the moment when he realized he had been tricked, Alex caught up Stephen's sword and ran forward with it. Her weight drove it into the guard's neck. He took two shuddering steps forward, pulling the hilt from Alex's hand, and toppled to the bloody floor.

Fire, Alex thought again, struggling to control her gorge. She saw a candle alight and caught it up, pushing the wick into the flame. The linen cord was alight at once.

Before she could do anything else, Stephen grabbed her wrist, twisting so viciously that she screamed. Her fingers went numb and the package dropped. She lunged for it, and Stephen swung his arm against her. His face was taut and his movements crabbed, but he was still strong enough to knock her aside, throwing her against the table as he caught up the explosive.

Kill him. I don't care what happens to me, just kill him. The flame had eaten its way below the level of the sacking.

Stephen flung the package out of the open window. The sound of the explosion was a distant crash, and before Alex could look back from the window, he was on her. He pushed her back so hard that her head struck the wall, and revulsion drowned out even fear as she felt his body press closely against hers. She couldn't bring her knee up.

"Anything more you're hiding under there?" Stephen tore her sash away and Iavas came closer. He hadn't wanted to touch her when she had the explosive, but now that Stephen was in control again, he didn't mind joining in.

"What about here?" Stephen said. "What have you got here?"

He ripped open the front of her dress and Alex's body grew cold, her mind beginning to drift. Iavas was licking his lips.

"I think I do have time for one last tumble after all." Stephen ground his hips against hers, and the sudden unwanted contact snapped Alex's control. She spat in his face.

He hadn't expected that. She had not shown open contempt of him in years, and now he jerked back, incredulous. Alex threw her entire weight at him, pushing off from the wall, and it worked. Off-balance, Stephen staggered back and nearly crashed into Iavas.

They were between her and the door, so Alex picked up her skirts and fled to the window. Her heart pounded as she lifted one leg over the sill, then the other. Rain beat down on her, washing cold over her face.

"You filthy bitch!" Stephen shouted, and she knew he was coming after her.

She pushed off the sill and landed on the slated roof. It sloped down gently for about ten feet, then dropped off. Was there a raindrain she could use to climb down? Turning, she hurried to the edge of the roof and dropped to her knees by the gutter. She leaned over the edge.

She saw nothing but a smooth wall of stone slicked with rain, and the ground was so far below her that it looked black even when the lightning flickered. No drains, no pipes, nothing that she could use. Then leather rasped on stone behind her and she spun around to see Stephen climb out of the window. Rain trickled gleaming down the length of his drawn sword.

Alex got to her feet, eyes fixed on him. On either side of her, the roof ended in gables that rose at steep angles, but even if she could climb those, he would reach her the moment she bolted. Could she tip him off the roof somehow? She was so afraid she could barely think as he came towards her.

Talk. Her old training asserted itself at the last moment. "Do you want me to jump?"

Stephen stopped, his sword inches from her stomach, and Alex kept her voice as calm as she could. *Just keep talking, stall him.* "Do you want to watch me step off the roof?" *You won't get your nice clothes stained that way.* "Or would you rather run me through?"

"I'd crush you under those machines if I could. Slowly." Stephen raised his sword and touched the point of it to the hollow of her throat. She thought she heard dogs barking, but the sound was lost in a thunderclap. "But since you've given me a choice, throw yourself off."

It's quick enough, something whispered in the depths of her mind. Less pain that way. "Yes." She drew her foot back, and felt nothing beneath the heel of her boot.

She saw the shape in the lit window from the corner of her eye, and she looked back at Stephen at once. But he saw the flicker of her gaze and plunged the sword forward—just as Robert flung a silver goblet through the air. It smashed into Stephen's arm. The point of his blade drew a line fine as a wire across Alex's throat and she jerked back on to empty air.

Everything inside her body seemed to drop first, as if her guts were made of lead, but her arms flew out and caught the edge of the roof as she fell. The gutter dug into her flesh. Stephen whirled around to parry Robert's blade with his own, bringing his foot down in a backward stamp on her hand as he did so, but Alex was used to pain and her grip didn't loosen. The goblet rolled down the wet slates and fell from the roof, plummeting soundlessly to the ground eighty feet below.

Steel rang against steel so fast that the fresh blows sounded like echoes of the first ones. She realized Robert was trying to get to the edge of the roof. He sidestepped and cut and blocked, fighting to inch his way between her and Stephen. *If Stephen ever thinks hacking a blade into my head is worth dying for,* Alex thought, *it's over.*

But she knew in the next moment that Stephen was outmatched. He was good enough with a sword, but he had never had to buy his life with that skill. He held his own in the flurry of steel, trading blow for blow, but it made no difference. Robert backed him away from the roof's edge and Alex swung her leg up over the lip of the gutter, pulling herself back on to the roof.

"You can surrender, Lord Garnath." Robert was breathing hard, but his voice was still steady. "Or die."

"I don't surrender," Stephen said. "And as for dying—"

He feinted high, and as Robert's sword whipped up, he struck low in a powerful arc. Robert twisted, nearly slipping on the wet slates. The jewel-hilted blade ripped through the cloth at his knee and came away dripping, but it wasn't fast enough. Robert brought his sword down.

Stephen gasped and went to one knee, clutching his wrist where Robert's blade had opened leather and flesh alike. His own sword dropped with a clatter. Robert kicked it aside and Stephen's leg buckled, his body thudding against the slates. Sword at the ready, Robert stepped forward, but when Stephen flung up a hand as if to plead for his life, he paused.

No, Alex thought, but it was all over. Stephen's other hand was beneath him and when it came up, it held one of the loose tiles. Robert slashed out at him too late. The slate hit him on the side of his forehead and when he reeled, Stephen kicked out at his uninjured knee.

Off-balance, Robert stumbled back. Alex sprang forward as his foot struck the lip of the gutter, but he didn't have time to cry out, much less grab her hand, before he fell. The darkness swallowed him up.

Over the pounding of blood in her ears, over the hollow rasp of breath through the emptiness of her chest, Alex heard loose tiles shift behind her. Like a puppet pulled on strings, she turned. Stephen got to his feet, and a slow smile stretched the corners of his mouth.

"As for dying," he said softly, "you first."

Chapter Twelve : Rainfall

It took all Mayerd's training—his old training, learned in the Halls of the Heart and the house of the Waymistress—to overcome the shattering blow. His body felt as if a giant hand had picked him up and shaken him. When his stomach heaved, it brought up blood and bile. His lateral lines burned, and his mind teetered on a line strung over the abyss of the Inward Way.

Don't give in, he thought. *But don't even* try *to fight on the wrong battlefield.*

Years with Elinah, years during which Mayerd had learned every trick of the Inward Way, came into play. He tasted the fear that the Way's touch easily produced—who wouldn't be afraid when their sanity hung by a thread?—but he overrode it. He imagined his children waiting for him on the other side of the chasm.

For a moment reality intruded, reminding him that his children had been raised to hate him, but in the past, Mayerd had become adept at living in a fantasy world with a woman who cared for him and a family he could protect and love. It was that dream that he called on now, raising it from a grave of his own making, and it was the long-held and long-forgotten dream that guided him slowly back, prying Ohallox's power away from him. The pain eased and faded. His eyes closed, Mayerd felt consciousness slip away—which was when the guardsman ran up, the sound of his footfalls echoing down the corridor.

"Thanks," Mayerd said to no one in particular, and used what little of the Outward Way he could to defeat the man. His stomach jolted again, but he ignored it, turning his attention to the task of finding Ohallox.

He recalled what he knew of the Inward Way. Illusions were unavoidable, since they didn't directly interfere with a subject's mind, simply creating an alternate image for the eyes. Therefore, he was careful to navigate using the Outward Way, and even when archways switched places, he simply let the Outward Way's directional sense guide him. Never lost in mazes or puzzles, that was the Outward Way, and he was surprised to find how much he had missed it.

He found a passageway that led beneath the rooftop summit of the castle to the Spiral Tower. Buried under so many layers of stone that he could no longer hear the thunder, he was still aware of the storm, of each impact of wind on the castle. That, too, was part of the Outward Way, ranging from him to monitor everything physical. If he was stronger, he could have sensed individual drops of rain—and could have told the difference between them and falling tears.

The pain caused by the Inward Way had faded to raw exhaustion by the time he found the stairs to Ohallox's tower, a spiral-patterned rug at their base. He began to climb, forcing himself on with bitter determination. Ohallox's room was at the top of that staircase.

The children ran giggling down the stairs towards him, chasing each other—no, chasing an escaped frog—but they stopped abruptly when they saw him. The little girl had been in the lead and she nearly fell, but her brother grabbed her arm, his lateral lines sinking as his smile vanished. Hostility filled their eyes, and their lips drew back from their milk teeth. Mayerd felt loathing rise from the three children as they backed away from him.

"No." He hated the begging tone in his voice even as he thought, *It's an illusion. Don't be fooled by it.* And in the next moment, he wondered why Ohallox would bother with illusions now, when the game was almost over.

He knew the answer when the guardsman came at him from behind, running silently up the stairs. Caught off-guard, Mayerd raised his sword an instant before the guardsman's blade drove through his chest.

Alex couldn't move. She watched as Stephen pulled himself to his feet, but even fear was distant, unimportant. *Whether he kills me or not, it won't change what's happened.*

Run.

It came from the part of her mind forged by her training, cold and unyielding, and yet it sounded a little like Robert's voice. That was enough to break her paralysis. Within her chest something was slowly tearing apart, but she bolted to the left, towards the side of the gable far higher than her head. She didn't know how she could escape, but she no longer cared about that as she threw herself at the upward slope, scrabbling for handholds.

She climbed it, kicking and dislodging as many slates as she could to deter Stephen. It didn't work. He made no sound at all as he came after her, but she felt his fingers grasp her foot. The wet boot slipped from his grasp. Alex would have liked to stamp on his face, but she couldn't see anything through the rain in her eyes, not even the spine of the roof.

Emptiness on her right, and a smooth stone wall rising to the sky on the left. Through each separate pain in her body as the slates rasped her bare skin, she tried to remember where she was, what the structure to her left could be. Of course, the Ivory Tower, which had no windows that she could open from outside.

Climb. The slates scraped her fingers. She heard Stephen behind her as if they were tied together. And then her outstretched hand found the roof's top.

It was flat for a few feet, enough space for servants to stand on as they cleaned the sides of the Tower. Every muscle in her arms had turned to hot jelly, but Alex hauled herself up over it, the edges of slates scraping her belly. She sank down, then forced herself up on her elbows just as Stephen's hands closed on the edge of the roof. Before she could kick them away, he pulled himself up. Alex took one look at the roof's end, at the rainwater dripping from it to fall into the nothingness beyond.

No. Make him pay for...for what he did. Push him off.

Even as she got to her knees, so exhausted that she felt she was moving through treacle, Stephen jerked away, putting as much distance between them as he could. His back was to the Tower, and Alex's fists clenched in frustration. If anyone was going to be knocked off now—

In the darkness, she listened for the sound of a sword being drawn. Instead, she heard a squealing wrench—it sounded like rusted metal tearing apart. What was he doing?

The lightning flickered and she saw his weapon—an old drainpipe.

The pipe was more than half her height, and thicker than her forearm.

"Even if anyone finds your body," Stephen shouted, "they won't recognize it!"

Terror gave Alex a last spurt of strength and she scrambled to the roof's edge. Before she could reach the downward slope, Stephen was on her, the pipe whistling through the air. Alex flung an arm up. The pipe smashed into her, and the world vanished in a haze of white agony as her arm broke.

Mayerd slumped against the wall. The images of his children disappeared and all he saw was the blade that had pierced his chest, pulling back in a spurt of blood. He felt nothing, only a great numbness that constricted his throat. *I'm bleeding to death.* His own blood should have smelled coppery, felt hot, but he registered neither—

Cold clarity speared through his mind harder than the impact of the sword, and he brought his hand up. The guardsman jerked away, but it was too late, and Mayerd's fingers passed through the sword. Another illusion, a masterful one that time—he had come close to simply passing out from the shock.

Then he heard a footfall on the twisted stairs above him, and he knew Ohallox had sent that illusion to distract him. If he had not staggered back against the wall, if he had been standing in the middle of the steps, the guardsmen creeping down might have killed him before he could recover. Swiftly, the sweat cold on his skin, he lunged out to the center of the stairs and slashed at the first man, who parried just in time.

Mayerd knew that he was not as strong or as fast as he had been. Pain and shock and exhaustion had taken their toll, and he barely blocked the return blow. The next slash opened his shoulder. Luckily the narrow stairwell provided room for only one guardsman at a time to confront him. Gritting his teeth, he drew on the Outward Way, forcing it through him. It should have leaped to his sword like an undammed river, but instead it trickled from him like drops of water wrung from a damp rag. Still, the blade jerked into the air, drawing the guardsman's attention for the moment Mayerd needed to step up and drive a fist into his belly, and then his sword flew back to him and he thrust it forward into the guardsman's chest.

The second guardsman shoved the crumpling body forward and the dead weight slammed into Mayerd. He fell, and thought of the stone steps and their base far beneath, where the rug—

The Outward Way took the spiral rug to him a heartbeat before he could strike the steps, and even then the impact almost broke his concentration. The rug shivered under him, and he felt the nothingness of air beneath as his sword leaped into his hand again. The second guardsman seemed ready to run. Mayerd hoped he would but his lateral lines tingled again, and as the guardsman's face grew blank, he knew the man had been taken over by Ohallox.

For an instant, the rug hovered in the stairwell, the spiral on it seeming to turn in a circle. Then it flew forward, and Mayerd threw himself off it at the guardsman, diving below the man's drawn sword. The momentum took the man down and Mayerd twisted aside, grabbing both hands full of the guardsman's uniform. The muscles in his arms and shoulders wrenched from the weight, but he hardly noticed as he tipped the dazed man down the stairs.

Many thuds and crunches later, there was no sound but Mayerd's own breathing. Reeling as he got to his feet, he forced himself up the last few steps and he saw what waited at the end of the stairs. A door marked with the dual arrows of the Outward and Inward Ways—the symbol of Iternum.

Ohallox was there. And few Dagrans would willingly stay in a magician's workroom, so he was alone. Except Mayerd wasn't sure he could deal with Ohallox. He was too tired, he was losing blood, and all Ohallox needed to kill him was a moment of distraction. Mayerd sank to his knees, fingers gripping his bleeding shoulder. *Then I need a distraction too, and I know where I can find one.*

The bottle of ink tipped over and a red pool spread across the table. Ohallox jolted away, but he had already registered the tingling of his lateral lines. The Outward Way was in effect, but Mayerd had barely used the Way for years…

A quill dipped itself in the ink and drifted to a sheet of paper, slashing the white surface in jerky tired movements. Ink sputtered and smeared, but the Iternan words were legible.

Ohallox. Death is coming for you.

Ohallox swallowed, tightening his grip on the dagger. *We'll see. You might have killed my guards, but I have wounded you beyond the point of weakness. Come on.*

He fixed his gaze on the barred door. Nothing happened. The

284

candles burned lower.

The windows swung open with a crash and rain poured in, a shower of stinging needles. Ohallox flinched, half-expecting to see Mayerd hurtling in through the windows. He told himself not to be a fool and hurried to close them. When he had done that, he whipped around, thinking Mayerd might have used the distraction to enter. But the door was still shut.

Perhaps he'd opened it, sneaked in and rebarred the door. Ohallox made a quick search of the room, glancing every few seconds at the door. The room was empty.

His nerves were raw, his breathing labored. He stumbled to his worktable and sank into his favorite chair—except the chair pulled back and he collapsed on the floor. Snarling, he grabbed the edge of the table and hauled himself up just as all the candles flickered out.

He's toying with me. Any controller of the Inward Way needed malleable minds to affect—and Mayerd's was not especially malleable, Ohallox saw that now. Mayerd had survived Elinah's worst, and if the Waymistress herself hadn't broken his sanity—

His hands shaking, Ohallox relit the candles and sat down, looking at the door. Mayerd was close enough to be within shouting distance, close enough for a steady tickle of sensation along his lateral lines, but not doing anything...much.

Melted wax dripped to the table's surface as the candles burned far faster than ever before.

The sand in the hourglass began to trickle upward, to fill the upper half of the glass.

A leather-bound volume toppled from the bookcase, falling open, pages riffling although there was no wind.

"I can't bear this," Ohallox said aloud. The hilt of the dagger was slick with sweat. He usually monitored events in the castle, but now his world had shrunk to a single room in which the Outward Way played. He felt like a fly in a spider's web.

"I can't bear this. I have to kill him."

He leaned back in his chair and took the Inward Way.

The full power of the Inward Way could only be harnessed by a practitioner who stood on it. When Ohallox was grounded in reality, he could use aspects of the Way, but he could not ride its deepest strength. Now he detached from reality. His workroom faded into mist, and the haze grew to grey clouds as he looked down at the crossroads of the Way.

Feeling more confident already, he dismissed Elinah's failure. At some level, she had cared for Mayerd and had wanted him in her life. Ohallox wasn't encumbered by emotion and he could teach Mayerd a trick or two that might be new even to Elinah's out-of-favor consort.

He prepared his last strike. He had tried to affect Mayerd with his own skill and failed, but there was another source of strength he hadn't tapped yet—the deep hungry potential of the Inward Way. Ohallox knew he could never lure Mayerd on to the web of crossroads by himself, but the Inward Way was powerful enough to drag anyone into its coils, provided Ohallox let it act through him instead of controlling it. And now he was willing, even glad to be its stepping stone if it destroyed Mayerd. He didn't quite know how he would get the Way back under his grasp, but he would worry about that later. He prepared to relinquish his control.

"It's something of a waste, don't you think?"

The words drifted up from far below him. Frowning, Ohallox glanced down, and the sight chilled him to his bone marrow. He saw the crossroads with the snake on one white path and the tree growing in the other, but this time the woman who stood at the junction was Elinah, not Alex. She smiled at him.

"*Listen*," she said. Her voice had a tone of authority, but her eyes were a woman's eyes, warm on him. "Why waste a good mind? Turn it to your own use. The battle is lost, but you could flee this rat trap if both the Inward and the Outward Ways were yours to command."

Ohallox went still. It had never occurred to him that it might be possible to hold both the Ways in one hand. The first thing each Iternan learned about magic was that he or she walked either the Inward or the Outward Way, not both.

"Control him?" he whispered.

"Yes. As I did once."

"How?" It wasn't possible...but if anyone knew, she did.

"Like this," Elinah said, and a wedge of hot agony drove through Ohallox's neck.

He choked, and there was a bubbling sound as blood spilled into his lungs. Elinah scattered into a shower of stars that wheeled up to the sky, and Ohallox saw what had happened. As if looking into a mirror, in the last moments of clarity, he saw.

He saw his own body leaning back in his chair, and a deep wound bisected his throat. He saw Mayerd take the dagger from that wound and he understood. Mayerd had guessed that he would seek the Inward Way—he had sensed it with his lateral lines and used that moment to enter the room. The Way had recreated Elinah from Mayerd's memories of her, and the words she had spoken had come from Mayerd. Now that he was no longer trapped behind a wall, Mayerd didn't need to shout to reach someone on the Inward Way—he could whisper instead, and he had whispered something Ohallox wanted to hear, distracting him long enough to use the dagger.

Ohallox felt the poison stop his lungs and wrap itself around his heart. Caught on the Inward Way, he watched it happen with the calmness of utter disbelief, and then the numbness gave way to terror. He was dead. But he was still *there*. Where? On the Way.

He looked down to see the familiar pattern of crossroads, but it had vanished. Everything was grey, not even shifting, no patterns, nothing, because physical bodies grounded people on the Way and acted as anchors. How could he ever get off the Way now? He had nothing to return to, no reference point.

"No!" he screamed, but the sound was swallowed up in the vacuum. Ohallox knew then that he could wander forever in the emptiness—no sensation, no thought, only a downward spiral of madness. He lunged for the looking glass, the only discrete object in the grey expanse.

Mayerd looked at him from the other side of the mirror, and Ohallox stopped, afraid to touch the glass. If he sprang at it, would he pass through it, into reality? Or would it break? Could Mayerd even hear him? He tried to speak, but no words came.

"With the compliments of Mayerd," Mayerd said indifferently, and broke the glass. Fragments rained down and vanished, leaving Ohallox alone in the void.

Alex cried out, but the thunder drowned her voice. She thought she would faint as the world wheeled around her and the pain spread like a fang-filled mouth to swallow her up. She bit down on her tongue until she tasted blood, thinking, *Stephen. I won't let him do this to me.*

He swung the pipe again, whacking her on the side of her other arm so that she was knocked flat to the slates, pushed away from the edge of the roof. Through a grinding haze she realized that now he didn't want her to throw herself off—a quick and easy death.

"Bastard," she tried to say. The rain ran into her open mouth.

Lightning picked Stephen out as he stood over her, and copper gleamed on the broken end of the pipe. A memory flickered through her mind like a falling bird, and she struggled up on her good arm. She couldn't push him over the roof's edge—she wasn't strong enough—but there was one final thing she could try. With the last of her strength, she drew in a breath.

"Do it!" she shouted. "I'm not afraid of you—I never will be, and there's nothing you can do to change that."

That was the response Stephen had always hated from her, and he raised the pipe again. He did it slowly, prolonging the anticipation, each moment stretching longer than the last, while Alex's heart beat so painfully that she thought she might die before he hit her. But her eyes never wavered, watching the line of the copper pipe as it rose high over her, over Stephen's head—and the lightning struck.

A flicker of white heat cut through the sky. Alex flung herself back, careless of her broken arm, but she did not cover her eyes. She saw the tip of the lightning bolt touch the pipe and disappear into it. Metal glowed red, and Stephen's eyes went wide. His body jittered wildly and the return stroke leaped from the pipe in blinding heat. Instantly the second bolt of lightning sprang down. Alex threw an arm over her face as Stephen's body was ripped apart, flesh burnt black. She heard nothing over the earsplitting crack of thunder, but clumps of ash settled on her.

Choking on the sharp odor, she lay on the spine of the roof. Her broken arm throbbed, so that even the slates beneath her felt like a bed of nails. She looked up at the night, and the rain poured over her to wash the last remains of Stephen Garnath away.

Even when she began to shiver, her skin pebbled with gooseflesh, she didn't want to move. She concentrated on not thinking—especially not thinking of Robert. *No one can survive such a fall, so face it and bear it.* That didn't fill the emptiness, or reassure her that she wouldn't miss him for the rest of her life.

Move, her training ordered, and Alex wearily pulled herself to her feet. She had to climb down the slope of the roof from which she had come, because the other side of the roof slanted towards the guardsmen's quarters.

She worked her way down, a difficult task as she held her broken arm at her side. The roof was speckled with gaps where she had kicked away the slates. It took a long time before she finally reached the nearly flat part of the roof, and by then, she was drained. Even the ends of snapped bone in her arm felt far away.

She would have to tell Mayerd or Lawrence, if they were still alive. Swaying, she put her good hand on the slope of the roof just behind her and got to her feet. *And I'm going to find his body.* She remembered what Stephen had said—that no one would recognize her once he had finished. *Well, that won't happen with Robert. I'll find him. I'll find all that's left of him. I'll recognize.*

Something scraped on the roof to her left and Alex turned. She saw only the roof and the sheer drop, but a slate fell and she heard a muffled curse which seemed to come from midair.

Magic, she thought. *Ohallox? Doesn't matter, just get a weapon.* In the light from the open window, she saw the gleam of Stephen's sword and she knelt beside it. Her fingers brushed the cabochons in the hilt...and something beneath them, a thick coarse line stretched taut.

Rope. She looked at the length which extended to the roof's edge and below—

Fingers caught the edges of overhanging slates, scrabbling on the wet surfaces. Alex's throat tightened and her mouth was dry as cotton, but she managed to speak. "Robert?"

"Here." Tired though he sounded, his voice brought her to her feet. "Don't come too close, Alex. I don't want you falling."

"I thought you were dead!"

"I wouldn't be so impractical as to run about on a wet roof without a rope around me, for all our sakes. Can you go for help? Susanna's guarding a prisoner—that aide of Garnath's."

"I could test the roof," Alex said. The rain was a drizzle now, and she could see more clearly. "Robert, to your left there's a raindrain. It hugs the side of the building, and the roof is flatter there. You could pull yourself over the edge."

She kept her eyes on the sky as he did so, prepared to push him off again at the first sign of lightning, but the storm was over and the rain stopped as Robert climbed over the edge of the roof. He went to his knees and when she slipped her good arm around him, he drew her close in a hard protective embrace. Alex felt a flare of pain from her broken arm, but it was nothing compared to the warmth that filled her when she rested her cheek on his shoulder.

Whatever else had happened between them, he was safe, and she let her eyes close. For a few minutes longer she could lean against him, because a man wasn't likely to spurn a woman who had done away with his greatest enemy. Robert put his hand on the back of her head, stroking her wet hair, and his other arm around her waist held her so tightly that she felt each beat of his heart.

"How badly are you hurt?" he asked.

"Just my arm. What about you?"

"My head feels like a drum." His lips brushed her temple, her eyelid, the corner of her mouth. "What happened to your arm?"

"Broken," Alex said, without thinking.

"Broken? Bloody hell, why didn't you tell me before?" He started to slip his arm beneath her knees, then paused. "Where's Garnath?"

"Dead."

It was not in Robert to rejoice at anyone's death, so he only nodded before he lifted her carefully and took her inside.

Alex woke in darkness, to the softness of sheets beneath her and the weight of a splinted arm across her chest. She remembered accepting a posset that had sent her to sleep so a physician could set her arm, and now she wondered how the battle had ended. Both she and Robert had been too tired to talk earlier. It had been enough to simply touch.

I'm not in my old room. This doesn't feel like my bed. She stretched out her good arm and touched warm, solid flesh. Her fingers stilled for a moment before trailing over a chest matted with soft hair, over a nipple—

"Talk about forward and indelicate," Robert said, amusement filling his voice. His hand closed over hers and he kissed her fingers. "Well, I can tell you're feeling better."

"Mmm," Alex agreed. It didn't matter where she was as long as Robert was nearby. "The battle's over?"

He settled his body comfortably against hers. "More or less. That rooftop duel secured the castle, and now we'll bring the city under order. It won't be easy after all our losses. But Garnath's dead and Nalle's vanished and our own standard is flying over the castle. Oh, and Mayerd did something to that Iternan."

"Killed him?"

"Yes and no. I don't understand Iternan magic."

As long as he can't harm us again, Alex thought, *but we have losses too.* "Nicholas is dead, isn't he?"

"Yes." Robert spoke more quietly. "I'm sending him...his remains back to the White Horn with an escort guard. He would have wanted to be laid to rest there."

So you won't return home for now. "Can we hold the castle?"

"I think so. It's still relatively intact—we couldn't use the cannon on it—so the surviving hounds would have to besiege us. They can try. This place is built for defense, and I'd like to see them take on both us and Mayerd's magic. And I've offered amnesty to whoever lays down their arms and swears loyalty to us."

Relief filled Alex, but it quickly gave way to the question of what she was doing in a darkened room alone with Robert, in his bed. Did nearly dying mean she could sleep there without his moral standards shouldering their way into the bed as well, or was she so ill he had to watch over her? "Will I recover soon?"

"I should think so," Robert said. Alex was mildly disappointed; people with grave injuries always got more attention. "You don't crumble at the first tap, even one from Garnath."

"But how long will we stay here?" Damn, she should have said "you" instead. "Even if you restore order in Radiath, some other usurper might seize power after you leave the city."

"That's another concern. I'd like nothing better than to leave for Fulmion, but we can't risk anyone taking advantage of the chaos— especially now that people are aware of the Quorum's weapons. I'll wager anything Victoria's sent word to her superiors about this too."

"I wouldn't want the Quorum taking the position of a dictator either."

"Exactly. So while my influence still persists here, I'll create a council to govern Dagre."

"Like—" Alex cut herself off, but not in time.

"Like Garnath once did? Yes, but for different reasons. Besides, I haven't any wish to reign over Dagre."

"What if another man on your council does?"

She felt the muscles shift in his body as he shrugged. "I'll have to set up the council so that no one person has too much power—that's how Lunacy is ruled. I wouldn't have thought anything good might come out of that land, but the more I think about it, the better it sounds. Still, all this will take time. And I'm going to need your help, Alex."

"My help? Why?"

"Because I don't know whom to trust," Robert said simply. "Once they realize what's happening, the dukes and prelates and merchant princes will gather in Radiath like crows to a calling. I won't know if they sympathized with Garnath in the past."

"But I'll tell you whatever I know about them." It was one more reason to be with Robert, and she could use the time to decide what to do when he left for Fulmion.

"Yes. And I'll try not to be jealous again."

Jealous? Again? Two puzzle pieces clicked together in her mind. "You mean, you were jealous when I mentioned De—the Duke of Goldwood?"

"When you mentioned him in my bedroom. I could stand to hear about other men anywhere else." In the dark she couldn't see Robert's face, but his voice grew softer, more teasing. "I told you you didn't understand everything about men."

"Well, insulting me about something else is hardly going to help me know if you're jealous." Alex didn't feel in a mood to be jollied, and whatever the drug she had taken, it was starting to wear off. There was a dull throb from her splinted arm.

"I know." Robert turned her hand over, pressing his lips to her palm, and a slow surge of heat flowed through her. "I'm sorry. I just don't want to think of any other man touching you."

They only touched the surface. None of them could go beyond that, as deep as you do without even thinking about it. She didn't say that, because with Robert it was difficult enough to keep her defenses in place when she was healthy, fully clothed and upright, let alone under those circumstances. She felt like a turtle with its shell off, and those were usually not long for the soup.

"We both made mistakes." She hesitated. "Let's put them behind us." If she left it all in the past, the memories as distant as Fulmion was, then her future would be bearable. It wouldn't be happy, without Robert, but she could and would endure it.

Two days later, the castle physician pronounced Alex well enough to rise for short periods, so she thanked him, not wanting to say that she already had. She had spent hours at the window, looking out over the castle grounds as the work of rebuilding the fortifications went on, but she was still unused to her new freedom in the castle. Robert hired people from Radiath to replace servants who had fled, placing them alongside his men-at-arms, and none of them seemed to recognize her as the Black Mare when she went out, but she was glad to reach the privacy of her room.

Not my room any longer. She found her books propping up a broken table leg and her locket tossed in a drawer, but even that didn't make her feel much better.

"Alex?" Victoria called from outside. When Alex asked her to come in, Victoria shut the door behind her, which was normal, and leaned against it, which was not. "I'm glad to see you. I need your help."

"What's wrong?" Alex said, surprised.

"Do you know what happened on the night the battle was won? We used our last steam carriage, the Javelin Fly, to smash the castle gates, and it's not to be found anywhere now."

"Could it have been destroyed?"

Victoria blew out her cheeks. "Philip was rendered insensible during the fighting and did not notice. I asked Chalcas, who was responsible for protecting the Quorum's property, but he is evasive when he is not outright insulting. I shall have the Quorum investigate his activities."

Alex raised her eyebrows. "What would you like me to do?"

"Talk to him," Victoria said. "Find out what happened to our property. If it is in his possession, convince him that it will be in his best interests to hand it over."

Alex doubted that anyone could do that. "Lady Victoria, may I ask you a question?"

"Certainly."

"Once you find the machine, what will you do with it?"

"Take it back to the Mistmarch," Victoria said. "I am now the Word of the High Quorum in all but name, and I have requested that more Knights of Katash be sent to protect the Quorum's interests in Radiath. Some of them will guard the carriage on the journey home."

"Yes, and then?"

Victoria looked puzzled. "Then? Then we'll keep the carriage in case it's ever again required."

"I see," Alex said. "Would you like me to speak with Lawrence immediately?"

Victoria smiled at her.

"Alex! How are you?" Lawrence's servants brought tea while he helped her to a chair. "It's good to see you recovering."

"I'm sure," Alex said with a smile. "Could we talk alone?"

"Of course." He waved all the servants out, found Susanna's dog eating chicken legs behind a couch and chased it out too. "May I pour you some tea?"

"Thank you. Where's the carriage hidden?"

Lawrence's hand jerked, but he filled a cup for her. "How did you know?"

"Who else would have done it? Nicholas is dead, Mayerd doesn't care about technology and Robert wouldn't take a button which didn't belong to him."

Lawrence sighed. His movements were stiff and careful, favoring his own injuries. "Are you going to tell Victoria?"

Alex wasn't sure, so she evaded the question. "What will you do with the carriage?"

"Take it apart," Lawrence replied. "I have sympathizers in the city, so I barracked a few of my men with them and hid the vehicle there. I'll have its construction studied in such detail that Chalcas Heights will be able to build its own machines before the year's out."

"Are they that important to you?"

"Hell, yes! Alex..." He was almost stammering. "Do you know how much a steam engine can do? We don't even need to fit them with wheels—simply to drain mines, they're perfect. And when they have wheels, why, with a few improvements we could make them faster than the Quorum ever dreamed."

"And that's all you're going to do?" Alex looked at him over the rim of her cup.

"Of course not. And I can't do it alone. I'm going to begin a school—a place where people can combine their skills and ideas. The Quorum makes little progress because they're hidebound, but in my school, engineers and alchemists can congregate from everywhere. And they'll build better and better machines."

"It'll be dangerous," Alex said. "The Quorum—"

"To hell with the Quorum. After facing down Garnath's hounds, I'll take the Quorum any day. Besides, my family has plenty of money, and that usually smoothes over rough spots."

Alex nodded. "And once you start making these machines, you'll have power."

"Don't try to scare me." Lawrence smiled. "I don't intend to hoard secrets. Besides, I plan to sell a lot of these engines and cannons myself, once I learn how to build them. Susanna can handle that, since she knows about trade. I'd be a fool to make war on anyone who has the same weapons as I do."

He had said everything she expected to hear. Alex put her cup down.

"Well?" Lawrence's voice was tense. "Are you going to tell Victoria?"

"No." She met his eyes and saw the relief in them. "You can keep the steam carriage. I may even...have some more information to pass on to you, about its internal workings. I don't want you to kill yourself experimenting with them."

Lawrence's smile flashed out again. "The Chalcas family pays its debts. You'll be compensated for anything you do to help my school. The Chalcas School of Engineering Sciences." He gazed off into the distance, then looked back at her with an apologetic grin. "I've been planning this for a while."

"I'm sure you have." Alex tried for an admonishing tone, but she didn't succeed. "Now, if you'll excuse me, I must think of a convincing story for Victoria."

"There you are, Alex," Robert called from the other side of the summit hall. "Dinner is being served downstairs."

Alex turned, suppressing her pleasure that he had searched for her. He must have looked a long time before he found his way to the summit. Other than the towers, it was the highest part of the castle, built above the roofs and left open to the winds. The two longest walls were parallel rows of white columns, so that the summit gave a commanding view of Radiath. Seated at the base of a column, leaning against the stone, Alex had been watching for the sun.

"I'm not hungry, Robert," she said, rising as he walked up to her.

"Thank you, though."

"What's wrong?"

"Nothing. I just don't want to go down to dinner."

"Would you rather leave?" Robert said abruptly.

Alex's spine stiffened, like a wave of liquid iron traveling upward so that her head straightened. "Do you want me to leave?" She couldn't believe that after nights in his bed, even if she had done nothing more than sleep in his arms, he would dismiss her so summarily.

Robert looked startled. "Do I... Alex, if I want you to do anything, whether it's pour me a glass of water or share my bed, I'll do my best to tell you. I may find it easier in the former situation than the latter, but no doubt that'll change with time." He pushed a hand through his hair. "I asked you that because I didn't know whether you wanted to stay with me now that the battle's over."

I don't know either. Alex could endure a great deal, but the one thing she couldn't do was watch as Robert pledged his life and love in marriage—which he would have to do if he wanted an heir. "I'm not sure. What would I be doing if I stayed with you?"

"Exasperating me, I imagine," Robert said. "But I'll put up with that if you marry me."

A ringing sound filled Alex's head, like an after-effect of being smacked lightly on the ears. The most she had expected him to say was that he was fond of her.

Robert looked at her closely. "Are you all right?"

"No." Alex found herself able to speak again. "Marry you?"

"I know I could have picked a better time, Alex, but rather late than never." He took her hand. "Will you?"

Thinking clearly was always difficult when Robert touched her, and one of them needed to keep a straight head. *Don't answer right away.* "Marry you." She tried to smile. "Well, at least you came out and said it, instead of trying to push me into proposing instead."

"Don't remind me. That wasn't one of my proudest..." Robert paused. "Oh, would you have proposed to me if I'd just waited a little longer? Damn, that would have made it so easy." Alex pulled her hand back, but that didn't seem to deter him. "I'd have accepted too, instead of leaving you in doubt."

"If you're trying to make me feel guilty, you're shaking the wrong tree." Alex braced herself for another battle, because while he could be downright indulgent with her, Robert didn't quite seem like the kind of man who could be henpecked either. "There are good reasons I can't accept your proposal."

Robert sighed. "I miss the old Alex. She would have said 'if it pleases you, my lord' and done exactly as I wanted." He seated himself on the ledge beside a column and patted his knee.

"Robert, please. We can hardly talk seriously if I'm sitting on your lap."

"I beg your pardon. What are these reasons?"

Alex sat down on what she immediately knew was a puddle. She ignored it. "You need an heir."

"I already have one," Robert said. "My brother. Oh, don't give me that look. I want you, not a broody hen."

I never thought any man would look beyond that, but... Alex marshaled her self-control, because inexperienced though she was when it came to marriage proposals, she knew how to ride out her emotions. She wanted Robert's position to be secure, and allowing him to marry a barren woman wouldn't help in that regard, but she could imagine his reaction to the idea that she was either protecting him or permitting him to do anything.

Instead she said, "A broody hen would be more acceptable than a black mare. Defending your cousin's reputation was one thing—she has one to defend. Defending me..." She tried not to think of him becoming a laughingstock.

Robert shrugged. "If we're talking about reputations, mine isn't exactly pristine either. And I would want you if all of Eden stood in my way. Besides, I like the idea of taming a mare who was too fast to be caught and too proud to be broken."

Alex had always hated being called a mare, but for the first time, the word made her think of something swift and graceful. "I don't want you fighting any duels on my behalf."

"My dear Alex, you do realize what the rumors will say about me, don't you? There's the Bloody Baron who coerced the Quorum into handing over their machines, and his friend *was* a sorcerer after all, but the gods still favor him, because they struck a mighty blow for him when he fought Lord Garnath. I don't think too many people will be half-witted enough to insult you in my presence." When she didn't reply, he frowned. "I don't understand. I thought you'd want to marry me. I mean, isn't this what I should have said before we even started out for Radiath?"

"No," Alex said slowly. His honesty could always do that—disarm her, strip her of artifice and make her tell the simple truth as well. "No, because if you'd proposed to me then, I'd have accepted. Without thinking twice, because I didn't have any other choices, and that wouldn't have been best for either of us. We need to—"

"Do you love me?" Robert said.

Stopped in midspeech, Alex set her teeth and tried to steel herself against the vulnerable, questioning look in his eyes. She did love him, but how could she just come out and say that? She had never before told any man that she loved him.

But she couldn't *not* answer. Coward, she thought and straightened her back.

"Yes," she said, in the hard direct tone with which she would have confessed to a crime. "But that has nothing to do with—"

Robert held up a hand. "Well, that's one thing we have in common."

"Really? You love yourself too?"

She had a moment to see his eyes narrow, and then his hands closed on her shoulders as he pulled her close. When she tried to tell him that she hadn't meant it, the words became a whimper muffled by his mouth, and his tongue took anything else she might have said. His arms slid around her in an embrace, and his mouth was hard on hers at first, slowly melting to a tenderness that made the world turn around her as she kissed him back.

Robert lifted his head, and Alex shivered as he ran the tip of his tongue over her lower lip. He kissed her cheek, then her ear, nuzzling it so that his beard softly rasped her skin. She gasped when he breathed out into her ear. Her good arm went around his neck, but when she pressed closer he drew back, glancing down at the sling that held her other arm.

"You didn't hurt me," she said.

"Good." He tugged her hand down, then kissed the inside of her wrist. "Though there are times when you deserve a bloody good spanking, and this is one of them." Slowly, his tongue traced a pattern on her skin.

Alex had never known her wrist was so sensitive. His touch was light, a feathery trace that left the slightest trail of warm wetness, and yet her body tightened inwardly with need. When he released her, she dropped her hand into her lap, pressing her fingers into her palm.

Robert's smile was the barest upturn of one corner of his mouth. "Say yes, Alex. We suit each other. And you know how much I care about you."

Alex closed her eyes. There was that damned honesty again, and what was worse, she knew he wouldn't remind her of everything he had done for her. He had comforted her, made her laugh, brought her body to trembling fulfillment under his. And he had nearly died defending her. Any other woman would jump at this, so why couldn't she say yes? Maybe she *was* abnormal.

Swallowing hard, she opened her eyes again. "I know. But if it's taken me this long to be able to admit that...that I love you, then it'll also take me some time to agree to your proposal."

"But you will agree, eventually?"

Alex wished she was anywhere else in the world. No, if she could tell him she loved him, then she could tell him the truth about this as well. "I don't know."

Robert looked up and addressed the ceiling. "Benevolent Ones, give me the patience to deal with this woman."

"A heretic like you praying? No wonder they don't listen."

"Worse than that." Robert's gaze dropped to his hands. "They've cursed me to fall in love with someone who doesn't think I'll be a good husband."

"I *never* thought you..." Alex caught his quick upward glance and stopped, wishing she could shake him. "Don't do that again."

"I'll do whatever it takes to make you say yes."

"Then will you give me some time? Please, Robert. Most women take it for granted that they'll be married, so when they're proposed to, they have an idea what to say. I don't."

There was a long pause. Her heart thudded as Robert got to his feet, but when he extended a hand to help her rise, she took it reflexively.

"All right," he said, to her relief. "The sky always takes hours to build up to the moment of lightning." Alex wondered what he was talking about, but before she could ask, he continued. "I'm a traditional man, though. I want us to be affianced and then properly married."

Affianced? Alex thought. For how long were people normally "affianced"? And however long that was, at the end of that time would be a wedding. She tried to picture herself in a long formal gown undergoing a long formal ceremony, but how could she wear the crown of white roses that her bridegroom had to replace with the crown of red ones? She couldn't promise fruitfulness either.

And that was just what she would go through if she married an ordinary man, which Robert wasn't. He was a lord of the land. If he wedded some duke's daughter, she would slide like buttered bacon into her place as his baroness, but that was one role Alex had no experience at playing.

"I don't know whether I want to marry anyone," she said, "but if I did, it would be you."

"That's good to know." Robert sounded so relieved that Alex looked at him in surprise. What she felt for him was so obvious to her that she had thought it was clear to him as well.

"I couldn't stop loving you even if you married someone else and sent me away, Robert." She spoke quietly—not because she was embarrassed or shy, but because the vision of him with another woman was painful. "You mean more to me than anyone in the world. I just can't...say it very often, that's all." She nearly said, *But I'll show it in any way I can* before she realized that she wasn't showing it in the one way Robert wanted most—marrying him.

"Your wife needs to suit your people," she said slowly, thinking aloud. "I can tell you this, Robert—it'll be difficult enough giving them a mare as their lady, but a mare who doesn't know anything about their lives or the land will be a disaster. Up here, it's just the two of us. Once we leave, we have to deal with everyone else."

"Would you do that?" Robert said, and from the softness in his eyes, she knew he was pleased that she valued his estate. "Learn about the townsfolk and the farm and the land?"

Alex considered, then nodded. Even if his people never welcomed her, she would be with him that much longer. "It might not be so difficult. My parents had a farm once."

"I suppose I don't mind waiting, then."

"You'll have to, if you care about your household and your townsfolk accepting me." Alex could have manipulated them into fearing or avoiding her, but she didn't want that. She wanted to belong there...which would take more than just a wedding ceremony.

But if I don't have what it requires? For a moment all her old uncertainties crept like a coolness into her blood, before she realized that three months ago, she would never have loved a man enough to even consider marrying him. With time, things changed.

"And what happens then?" Robert said. "Once the people are satisfied I've chosen well for a baroness?"

"Once *I'm* satisfied you've chosen well for a baroness, if I can tear you away from the lambing or the harvest, we'll sit down in the window seat and...discuss it again." Alex took his hand, feeling the calluses and the ridge of a scar, feeling his fingers close on hers in a clasp that could not be broken. "Would you take me back to my room before dinner? My old dresses are still in the wardrobe."

"Certainly, but that one looks very well to me."

"It's a little damp." She knew at once that she should have said it was torn, too tight, not as attractive as a black sheer. Robert looked her over from the front. Then he glanced at the back.

"I see." His smile was distinctly satisfied. "Quite the compliment to me."

"I sat on a puddle. From the rain." She rolled her eyes when he bent to inspect the marble ledge. "Obviously it's dry *now*."

"Oh, obviously." Robert straightened up. "Strange that *I* didn't sit on any puddles, but perhaps the Benevolent Ones have that much pity on me. I'll take you back to your room to change, and after that, we'll go down to dinner."

"If it pleases you, my lord," Alex said, and went with him.

About the Author

Marian Perera was born in Sri Lanka, grew up in the United Arab Emirates, studied in the United States and lives in Canada—for the time being. She can be found in a laboratory during the day and in a fantasy world otherwise, though the two frequently converge when science enters a medieval world in her stories. *Before the Storm* is her first novel.

To learn more about Marian Perera, please visit www.marianperera.com. Send her an email at mdperera@hotmail.com or check out her blog at http://marianperera.blogspot.com

LaVergne, TN USA
21 January 2011
213400LV00001B/51/P